Delirious

Delirious

DANIEL
PALMER

KENSINGTON BOOKS
http://www.kensingtonbooks.com

KENSINGTON BOOKS are published by

Kensington Publishing Corp.
119 West 40th St.
New York, NY 10018

Library of Congress Control Number: 2010938699
ISBN-13: 978-0-7582-4664-6
ISBN-10: 0-7582-4664-1

First Hardcover Printing: February 2011
10 9 8 7 6 5 4 3 2 1

Printed in the United States of America

To my wife, Jessica,
thank you for making our life the perfect place to be.

Delirious

Prologue

Eddie rode the 28-19th Avenue bus to the bridge. He carried with him enough change for a one-way fare. He had no identification. It wouldn't matter if his death was properly recorded. Nobody would care about it, anyway. Through the wispy morning fog he strolled upon the walkway that linked San Francisco with Marin County. The bridge had opened to foot traffic two hours prior, and few pedestrians were out. The thruway, however, was a logjam of cars. He spent a few minutes watching the commuters as they went about their morning rituals—sipping coffee, talking on their cell phones, or fiddling with their radios. He burned their images into his mind and savored the voyeurism with the passion a dying man gives his last meal.

He walked to his spot. He knew it well. It was at the 109th light pole. He would face east, toward the city. Few jumped west, as most everyone wanted their final view to be something beautiful, like the elegant curves and hilly rise of the San Francisco skyline.

The fall, he knew, would last no more than four seconds. It was 265 feet down from where he would jump, gravity pulling him down at over seventy-five miles per hour. The water below would be as forgiving as cement. Perhaps a nanosecond of pain, then nothing. He always found it calming to know details. He was all about facts and logic. It was what made him a world-class software engineer. In preparation for the jump he had studied the stories of many of those who had gone before him. He had hundreds of sad tales to choose from. The stories were now his own. He would soon be part of the legacy of death that had been the Golden Gate Bridge since 1937, when WWI vet Harold Wobber said to a stranger, "This is as far as I go"—and then jumped.

At his mark, Eddie hoisted himself over the four-foot security barrier and lowered his body onto a wide beam he knew from research was called "the chord." There he paused and stared out at the seabirds catching drafts of warming air off the cool, choppy waters below and took stock of what little life he had left. Lifting his feet ever so slightly, until he was standing on his toes, Eddie began to push against the rail to hoist himself up and over the chord.

He closed his eyes tightly. Thirty-two years of his life darted past his mind's eye, so vivid that they felt real—vignettes played in rapid succession.

The pony ride at his fifth birthday party. Weeping beside the graves of his parents. Seven years old, still in shock, sitting at the trial next to the sheriff who had apprehended the drunk driver. The orphanage, then the endless chain of foster homes. Studying, alone in his room, so much reading. Then college. His graduation. How he wished his parents had been there to see him. The business. A startup. The energy and hours. The first sale. The euphoria was fleeting; the sting from his partner's betrayal would never subside.

He took a deep breath and lifted himself even higher. A part of him, the most secret and hidden part, was awash in a terrible, heavy sadness. It was overwhelmingly disappointing to him that he hadn't had the courage to do what needed to be done. It would be his dying regret.

With an assuredness that seemed born of much practice, he pushed himself up and over the thin railing that ran the length of the chord. The moment his feet left the bridge, Eddie regretted the jump. He hovered for an instant in midair, as though he were suspended above the water by strings. The depth seemed infinite. Sun glinted off the rippling water, shining like thousands of tiny daggers. His eyes widened in horror. Was there still time to turn around and grab hold? He twisted his body hard to the right. And then he fell.

The acceleration took Eddie's breath away. The pit of his stomach knotted with a sickening combination of gravity and fear. His light wind jacket flapped with the whipping sound of a sail catching a new breeze. The instinct for self-preservation was as powerful as it was futile. His eyes closed, unwilling to bear witness to his death.

Pitching forward, his arms flailed above his head, clawing for something to grab. His legs pumped against the air. Two seconds into the fall. Two more to go. He could no longer see color, shapes, light, or shadow. *Mother, please forgive me,* he thought. A barge he had seen in the distance before the jump faded from view. The sun vanished, casting everything around him into blackness. He could hear his own terrified scream, and nothing else. Time passed.

Two . . . then . . . one . . .

His body tensed as he hit, his feet connecting first, then his backside, and last his head. The agony was greater than he had imagined it could be. The sounds of his bones cracking reverberated in his ears. He felt his organs loosen and shift about as though they had been ripped from the cartilage that held them in place. Pain exploded through him.

For a moment he had never felt more alive.

Water shot up his nose, cold and numbing. He gagged on it as it filled his throat. A violent cough to expel the seawater set off more jolts of agony from his broken ribs.

Facedown, he lay motionless as he began to sink. From the blackness below something glowed brightly, shimmering in the abyss. He couldn't see it clearly but wanted to swim to it. It rose to meet him.

It was his parents. They smiled up at him, beaming with ghostly white eyes and beckoning for him to join them.

Chapter 1

Monte eased himself out of his cozy bed, stretched while yawning, then crawled from underneath the expansive oak desk and lazily made his way over to Charlie. Charlie, leash in hand, looked down at his tricolored beagle and couldn't resist a smile.

"Who heard me getting his leash, huh?" Charlie asked, scratching Monte in his favorite place behind his ears.

With his tail wagging full speed, Monte looked longingly up at Charlie, his inky eyes pleading for a quick start to their morning walk. Charlie, who didn't even own a plant before he brought Monte home from the breeder, now couldn't imagine life without his faithful friend. Named after jazz guitar great Wes Montgomery, and in honor of his lifelong passion for the art form, Monte wouldn't have come to be had Charlie not been such a lousy boyfriend. It was Gwen, his last in a string of short-lived relationships, who suggested that Charlie's rigid routines and dislike of, as she put it, "messy emotions" made him a better candidate for a dog than a girlfriend. She packed up what few things she kept at his loft apartment, and on one rainy Saturday morning she was gone.

Charlie, who had left as many girlfriends as had left him, wasn't one to dwell on the past or wallow in self-pity. Instead, intrigued by her suggestion, Charlie spent the next several hours researching dog breeds on the Web, until he finally settled on the beagle. It was a good-size dog for an apartment, he reasoned. Short hair meant less shedding, tipping the scale away from the Labrador breed. He briefly contemplated a poodle, with its hair coat and cunning intellect, but couldn't get the image of the groomed poodle pouf out of his mind.

He found a breeder only a few miles down the road, made a quick call, and minutes later was surrounded by a litter of feisty beagle puppies, each yipping for his attention.

Monte was an older dog and seemed to be above the attention-getting tactics of the young pups. He sat quietly in a corner of the breeder's living room while Charlie picked up and put down puppy after puppy.

"What about that one?" Charlie asked, pointing to the quiet dog in the corner.

"Him?" the breeder replied, somewhat incredulous. "I rescued that little one from the pound. They warned me he liked to chew on things, but I never figured he'd gnaw enough of my shoes to fill up a Dumpster. Still, he's been a good dog. You can tell by the eyes sometimes. The good ones, that is. We always hoped somebody would want to give him a home, but most of our clients are interested in the pups. Then again . . ." Her voice trailed off.

"What?" Charlie asked.

"Well, I'm guessing that you're single, or you'd be here with somebody making this decision. And if you're single, you're probably working, maybe a lot. And I can see that you keep in shape, so I'm guessing you take good care of yourself and that takes time. Perhaps you're not really a puppy guy, after all. I mean, they are loads of extra work."

Charlie nodded as he took it all in. He wore his sandy brown hair in nearly a military crop, and his ice blue eyes were framed by oval, matte silver wire-rimmed glasses. Nothing about Charlie's appearance suggested he had the easygoing personality of a puppy man.

"Perhaps," was all he said.

"And if you're single and busy," the breeder continued, "an older dog might actually be best. He's only three, but that's a good age for a beagle, long past pup. Look, if you want that dog, he's yours. In fact, you'd be doing me a favor. He's a good boy, just a bit unruly is all."

Charlie glanced over at Monte, who, as if knowing their destinies were somehow linked, rose, walked over to him, and lay quietly at Charlie's feet. Charlie bent down to pet his new dog.

"Seems gentle enough to me," Charlie offered. Fifteen minutes, a modest fee, and a few signed papers later, Charlie and the soon-to-be-named Monte went outside for their first walk as guy and dog. Gwen would have been proud, impressed even, at Charlie's capacity to love and care for something other than Charlie. Monte's shedding turned out to be more endearing than it was annoying. It was a gentle reminder that he was sharing his life with another living being.

If anything, Monte taught Charlie that his capacity to love was far deeper than he had known, and if Gwen were at all interested in trying again, she might find a very different and a far more fulfilling relationship. But she had moved on, and Charlie had yet to find another woman who compared.

In the three years since adopting him, the only consistent part of Charlie's life had been Monte. His start-up electronics company had continued to grow at a frenetic pace until, after much courting, it was finally acquired by electronics giant SoluCent. As part of the acquisition deal, Charlie became a senior director at SoluCent and was then forced to shutter his office and move all operations east.

Both Charlie and Monte had grown accustomed to spending the workday together. As a result, Charlie was the only employee at SoluCent allowed to bring a dog to the office. As pets, per company policy, were prohibited on campus, those who had been vocal to HR about Charlie's special treatment had been told only that it was part of the acquisition deal and that a special provision had been worked into Charlie's employment contract, approved by SoluCent CEO Leon Yardley himself.

Since it was a widely held belief that Charlie's product and new department would be a significant boon to SoluCent's bottom line, and would fatten an already healthy stock price, that explanation proved satisfactory for most. Charlie, who stood six foot two, and Monte, who was all of fourteen inches high, were now as much a part of SoluCent as the carpeting upon which they walked. But as familiar a pair as they were, Monte was also a symbol to others that Charlie was not really one of them. He was special. And he was treated that way.

Eager for his morning walk, Monte let out a quiet, but excited yip a mere ten seconds before Charlie's Tag Heuer watch alarm and meeting reminder sounded. Apparently Monte's internal clock, Charlie marveled, had the same precision as a high-end timepiece. Charlie fixed the leash to Monte's collar and made his way along the carpeted corridors through a maze of quiet cubicles, on his way to the front entrance of the SoluCent Omni 2 building. His team would be waiting for him there, on time as always—just as he insisted.

Charlie had once prided himself on the anxiety and dread his Monday morning meetings inspired, mistaking fear for efficiency. Now there was not a member of his team who would deny that bringing Monte into the picture had lessened the intensity and anxiety of the Monday meetings. Lessened, though not eliminated. Not in the least. "What's good for the heart is good for the mind and that means good for business," Charlie had often explained to those curious about his team's ritual Monday morning group walk. But today business wasn't so good. No, it wasn't good at all.

Chapter 2

The morning sun was high and bright in the cloudless sky. Monte made his trademark lunge for the bushes lining the front entrance walkway the moment they stepped outside. Charlie said a quick hello to his five senior managers waiting for him there. Before they were acquired, they were all VPs. But that was a smaller company. In the bloated corporate structure of SoluCent, Charlie was a director and they were senior managers. Sal, Barbara, and Tom were checking e-mail on their mobiles; Harry Wessner and Steve Campbell were stretching in the front parking lot. Everybody wore sneakers; they had grown accustomed to Charlie's athletic pace. Charlie's executive assistant, Nancy Lord, was there, too, giving Monte some much appreciated petting.

There had been doubt at first, at least from some, that combining the Monday executive team meeting with Monte's walk would be an effective use of time. To that Charlie had replied that a clear head from a brisk walk improved not only morale but decision making, too. Soon as Monte's business in the bushes was done, the five members of Charlie's Magellan Team set off at what Charlie believed to be about a fifteen-minute-mile pace. He'd keep accelerating that along the way. By the end of the walk they'd be closer to twelve-minute miles and they wouldn't even know it.

As was routine, Charlie waited until they were on the bike path, which bordered the campus, before starting the agenda. Here they were far enough from the main road to speak at a normal volume without being drowned out by the incessant traffic flow.

"Good morning, team," Charlie said. "I trust you all had a restful weekend and are ready for the week ahead."

Nancy Lord was the only one to nod. The rest were bleary-eyed and sweating out their stress. Working for Charlie meant that weekends were nothing more than days of the week. To keep pace with Charlie's demands and lofty expectations required sacrifices many would not be able to make—time being the most precious of all. The reward for those sacrifices, however, in bonuses alone, not counting stock, put all on the Magellan Team within an eyelash distance of what most would consider to be obscenely rich.

Monte kept the pace and walked a few yards ahead of the "pack."

"So," Charlie began. "Why don't you tell me about the Arthur Bean situation, Harry?"

Harry quickened his stride until he was walking alongside Charlie. The others fell behind but remained within earshot. They knew what was coming and that it wasn't going to be good for Harry. After all, Arthur Bean was his guy. He was a senior quality assurance engineer who posted source code on his blog as an invitation to his hacker friends to try and hack the InVision operating system, or OS—the "code" that made everything work. Bean remained convinced that several generations of the InVision product line had serious security loopholes that made the product susceptible to hackers. He had raised the issue to Harry, and Harry had brought it to Charlie's attention.

Charlie felt confident that the code was up to standard. Bean wasn't as convinced. When his pleas for greater attention had gone unanswered, he'd taken matters into his own hands. Charlie wasn't against Bean's commitment to quality. It was his methods he questioned. Authority on major rewrites of the OS was Charlie's alone. The InVision source code was as precious to Charlie as the eleven secret herbs and spices recipe was to KFC. You just didn't mess with it, no matter how good your intentions. Bean had done just that and, what was worse, had undermined Charlie's chain of command in the process. Not acceptable at all.

"Charlie, I know you're upset about what Bean did," Harry began.

"Upset doesn't really begin to cover it, Harry," Charlie said.

Harry nodded. "I understand," he said. "I'm just pointing out that Arthur Bean's friends . . ."

"You mean his hacker buddies," Charlie corrected.

The pace of their walk left Harry struggling for breath. The escalating tension only made it worse. "You could say that," he managed to say.

Monte stopped to relieve himself. Charlie's team stopped as well, forming a ragged semicircle behind Harry. Charlie's face, they could now see, was red, and they knew it was from anger, not exertion.

"That's what they are. They're nothing more than a bunch of renegade hackers given access by our employee to parts of our source code by your man," replied Charlie.

Monte started to trot along the bike path again; Charlie followed and the others fell into step behind him.

"Only after Arthur felt he had exhausted all available channels," Harry offered, again having to quicken his step to keep pace.

"And what did Bean's collective uncover?" Charlie asked, though he knew the answer.

"A major flaw that we've corrected in rev six-point-one."

"Major flaw? As I understand it, that flaw at most could be used to change InVision's outside temperature reading," said Charlie. "Not really what I'd consider a serious shortcoming. Wouldn't you agree?"

Harry nodded. "I realize that," he said. "We made a change to the application code on account of Bean's report. And I did talk with Arthur about his approach."

"Perhaps talking isn't enough," Charlie said.

Harry fell behind Charlie at that one. The blog in itself had done little damage, and in fact a couple PR reports had highlighted the blog as an innovative user-community approach to coding. Charlie could have let it stand. But it meant allowing the Magellan Team's authority to be undermined. That was something he couldn't stand for. Process and authority had to be respected. If they weren't, future digressions were almost certain. It set an unacceptable precedent.

"I'm taking appropriate action," Harry said.

"Okay. Action, I like action. What kind of action are we talking about here?" Charlie asked.

"I've asked HR to reprimand him, and we've put him on program. That's how we're handling it."

"Doesn't feel like we're really 'handling it,' Harry," Charlie replied. "I agreed to sell our company to SoluCent so we could be better. A start-up company might let that incident go. We're the real deal now. And I'm sure Leon Yardley would back up that statement."

"Yes, I understand," Harry said. "But HR agreed it was negligent on Arthur's part to use his blog and connections in such a way. They're the ones who suggested I issue Mr. Bean a formal reprimand and put him on program."

"A formal reprimand and program doesn't send much of a message, does it? Every division of SoluCent needs to know how important our product is to the bottom line," Charlie said. "If that means we take swift and immediate action to correct a problem, then that's what it means."

"It's not that simple. There are some extenuating circumstances." Charlie gritted his teeth.

Harry continued, "He and his wife have been, how do I say it . . ."

"With words, Harry. Use words."

"They've been having marital troubles. Financial stress, mostly, from some bad investments. At least that's how he explained it to me."

"And that's my problem how?"

Charlie felt his stomach churn. How many times had people used family and personal issues as an excuse to overlook ineptitude and poor judgment? If he had used his schizophrenic brother and father and his absentee mother as crutches to justify his mistakes, he never would have graduated from high school, let alone earned an academic scholarship to MIT.

"Harry, I don't care if the bank is ready to take his house tomorrow. He crossed the line, and once is more than enough. His job is to manage software quality. Period. If he felt the only way to do that job effectively was to use our software as a playground for his devious crew of computer hacks, so be it. He can do that for another company. Does that make sense?"

"Yes, Charlie, but I'm sure he thought—"

"I don't care what he thought. I care what he did. He screwed up. As far as SoluCent is concerned, our product is basically out in the market, even though we're still in the pilot phase. Does that register with anyone? Pilot means test. They're testing production, testing distribution, testing select retail channels, testing consumer response. If this fails, if our resellers believe the product is severely deficient—which it isn't—SoluCent may lose some enthusiasm to bring InVision to market. Do you know what that means?"

Most now had drifted well behind Charlie and Harry and had to scamper to catch up. Charlie knew that his team respected him and hated to disappoint. Not to mention, they feared his wrath. But fear, Charlie had learned, also meant focus. Fear could be good. A tool even. And if Charlie sometimes had to use fear to inspire action, and that action brought them results, then so be it.

"It means InVision will be shelved. It means most of you will probably be let go. It means that if you want to go back to Silicon Valley, you'll have to pay your own way to relocate," he warned. "I was the one who convinced SoluCent that you were the key members of the Magellan Team, and if I was being relocated here, you'd have to come with me. If I'm gone, you're gone. Who do you care more about, Harry? You and your family, or Mr. Bean and his bad debt?"

Charlie stopped walking. Sal and Harry had to put their hands on their knees to catch their breath. Monte absently poked his nose into the grass and walked behind a tree. No matter how much he paid these executives, Charlie knew they could never emulate the pride and passion he felt for InVision. After all, could a neighbor love a child as much as its parent did? And InVision was no ordinary child. It was his child—his golden child. It was the 4.0 student, varsity in three sports, with a long-ball arm capable of bringing college recruiters tears of joy. It was a prodigy violinist, the dazzling head cheerleader. Charlie was aware of the subtle jabs at his devotion from colleague and competitor alike, and he welcomed them. He knew the whispers were no different than those of envious parents, jealous of the accomplishments of the child next door.

For him, InVision represented far more than the major advance in the multibillion-dollar consumer electronics industry that the Magellan Team took it to be. It was his legacy—his offspring shaped not by blood and bone, but by wires, circuits, and plastic. Most new car stereos had the ability to play digital music files that consumers downloaded off the Web. Many automobiles even came standard with built-in DVD players, so the kids had something to do other than fight during those long car trips to Grandma's house. And some cars, typically the higher-end luxury lines, came equipped with built-in voice-guided GPS systems. But for the average consumer, getting movies to play in the car meant DVDs scattered about the floor or unreachable between the seats, CDs clattering down from above the visor or wedged in overstuffed storage compartments. Favorite TV shows weren't even accessible, unless recorded to a DVD. Helping average consumers consolidate their digital entertainment into a single device, making it portable and available in their cars, while expanding in-car entertainment options to include TV shows stored on home digital recorders, was the driving force behind InVision.

And InVision could store more digital content than any product on the market—thousands of hours of DVD movies, digital music, and TV shows, all in a device so compact, technical wizards from Silicon Valley to Beijing couldn't figure out how it was done. Battle testing the little wonder during countless focus groups with soccer moms and technophobic dads ensured everyone could use it. Unquestionably they would. Simply put, InVision was a cell phone, satellite radio, an iPod, TiVo, a Web browser, and voice-guided GPS all rolled into a package not much bigger than a deck of playing cards. Head cheerleader, hell! This was the whole squad.

Auto manufacturers from around the globe were lining up to private label the technology and install it as standard-issue equipment in their vehicles. One whiff of InVision's intoxicating possibilities at the International CES, the largest consumer electronics trade show in the world, was enough to drive the buyers from Best Buy and Wal-Mart into a near frenzy. Guarding the secrets of InVision was job one. He had been betrayed once before. It wouldn't happen again. Everything Charlie had worked fifteen years to create hinged on a successful production launch. Arthur Bean and his quality standards weren't going to get in his way. Nobody was.

"Let me put it another way, Harry," Charlie said.

"Yes?" Harry said.

"If Arthur Bean does something like this again, but this time it blows up big, hurts SoluCent in ways you can't imagine, are you willing to stake your career and reputation on your decision to keep him around?"

"Charlie, I really don't think—"

"No, Harry. Clearly you don't, or you would have done something about it already. I'm not joking, people. This is the real deal. Do or die. If you want to make this happen, the way I want to make this happen, then you'll do the right thing. Agreed?"

Everyone was silent.

"Agreed?" Charlie said again.

Charlie looked around and made sure each Magellan Team member had reaffirmed their commitment to the mission. He kept his gaze focused on Harry the longest, requiring that he make eye contact.

"I'm glad we understand each other," Charlie said. "Now, let's move on, shall we?"

Charlie checked his watch. They would have to get to a twelve-minute-mile pace to complete the loop. One by one, the Magellan Team executives gave Charlie their status. Already, the Arthur Bean incident was a thing of the past. Bean had made his own bed. It was his problem now, not theirs. Charlie already knew the status of every project. He kept close watch on all the moving parts of his division. The good news, aside from some minor production issues and Bean's contempt for authority, was that everything seemed to be on track.

They finished their walk three minutes ahead of schedule. Most left feeling refreshed from the exercise, walking taller and with a renewed sense of purpose, not to mention, from Charlie's perspective, a healthy dose of fear. Charlie gently caught Harry by the arm as the others made their way to the locker room to change.

"I understand your motives, Harry. Sometimes it's not easy to do the right thing," Charlie said.

"Sometimes it's not. You're right. Why don't we just transfer him to another department in SoluCent?"

"You realize I can't personally endorse a department transfer for him, don't you? I'm careful about who I give a reference to, Harry. My reputation is very important to me, and I'm not going to tarnish it with Arthur Bean, but he's more than welcome to try on his own. He can't stay with us, however. We'll give him two weeks to try and find another home within SoluCent. Sound good?"

Harry nodded.

"Tell you what else. I'll personally put Bean in touch with my financial advisor. If anybody could get him out of debt, it's my man Stanley."

"Thank you, Charlie. Folks know that you're demanding, but it's nice to know that you aren't cruel."

Charlie laughed. "Well, Bean messed up bad. I'm sure he'll land on his feet. Software types tend to do just that."

Harry thanked him again, and they went inside. As he and Monte made their way back to his office, Charlie thought about something troubling him more than Arthur Bean's extracurricular activities. It was an e-mail he'd received from a woman named Anne Pedersen the night before. He didn't know who Anne was. They had never spoken before, never exchanged e-mail, and never been in a meeting together. He'd looked her up in the Outlook directory and seen only that she worked in the consumer electronics marketing division. Although they were strangers, she had e-mailed him, urgently requesting that they meet for lunch. She'd refused to say what it was about, only that the fate of InVision was at stake. Whoever this Anne Pedersen was, she sure knew how to get his attention.

With a few minutes to spare before his next meeting, Charlie decided to clean up some documents that had been on his To Do list a day longer than the date he had given himself to complete the work. Charlie opened a desk drawer and took out an old shoe he kept there. He put it on and immediately felt Monte go to work on it. Charlie smiled. He loved having Monte in the office with him, but his beagle's chewing habits hadn't changed much since he first brought him home. Anytime Charlie sat down, he put on the old shoe to keep his new ones from being ravaged.

Charlie opened his laptop and was greeted by a bright yellow sticky note on the dark monitor screen. The penmanship, near perfect script, was clearly his own. Perhaps it was just the pressures from the upcoming product launch testing his nerves, or some late-night misguided attempt at crafting inspirational, team-building messages, but he couldn't recall when he'd written it, or the reason for jotting down the cryptic affirmation. The note read simply:

If not yourself, then who can you believe?

Chapter 3

If not yourself, then who can you believe?

On a normal day Charlie could make more decisions and progress in three hours than most directors at his level could make in a week. Those decisions came to him naturally; if Charlie believed in anything, it was himself. He spent a minute trying to remember when and where he'd written that note, came up blank, then transferred it to the inside flap of his BlackBerry holder.

Recall was his strength, a gift for names, faces, and events that had served him well as his product's ambassador. But with all that was going on at SoluCent, he wasn't overly concerned. His meeting with Anne Pedersen was nearing, and he had little time or patience to think of much else.

Monte eventually stopped gnawing on his shoe. Charlie listened a moment, until he heard quiet snoring coming from underneath the desk. He found it comforting. Charlie made sure to change his footwear, having once forgotten to take off Monte's chew shoe before a meeting with Yardley. He rarely made such thoughtless errors, and certainly never the same one twice. Next, he made a halfhearted attempt to answer e-mail. Most of it was a waste of time to begin with, but today was especially bleak. He shut down Outlook, grabbed a container of Lysol disinfectant wipes, and began to clean around his desk.

Charlie's office was noticeably sparse. Some had commented that they thought it was empty or occupied by a contractor. Those who found Charlie's militant commitment to office cleanliness excessive did not know how he had grown up, otherwise, they would have understood.

His childhood had been chaotic, unpredictable, and far from perfect. Charlie was determined that his future would not compare to the past. As part of that commitment, everything in his life had to have order. For Charlie, order equaled control and control was his secret ingredient for success. But he knew his methods came at a price—the most obvious being his failed relationship with Gwen. Thinking back on how much more relaxed he'd become since bringing Monte home, it was hard to believe Gwen and he lasted as long as they did.

If one thing hadn't changed, though, it was his opinion of people who were out of control; those who could not place their hands on a file within seconds of a request were no closer to ascending the tops of the professional ranks than the interns still in college. As a result, he kept his office clean and tidy with religious dedication—there were no manila file folders tossed about, no pens, coffee cups, or desk toys of any kind.

While most professionals at SoluCent reminded themselves that real life existed outside the cubicle or office walls by adorning their desks with framed pictures of family, Charlie had none. He had dated a few times since moving back east, but instead of a blossoming romance, he'd found distraction and drama. A relationship wasn't out of the question, but it wasn't a priority, either. InVision was. Still, it wasn't all work. His life had been here before moving to California. There were friends he saw on occasion, though less frequently as product development heated up. He made a much more conscious effort to stay in touch with his mother, who lived a few towns away from his Boston apartment. She was delighted to finally have "her boy" and "granddog" back from the West Coast, and they made it a point to have dinner together at least twice a month. He preferred they go out, as visits to her house were purposefully short and always tense. Monte, however, greatly enjoyed going there, but more to harass the neighbor's poodle than for the change of scenery.

His mother still lived in the same forsaken multifamily house where Charlie grew up, in a not-so-nice section of Waltham. Charlie wasn't one for grandiose gestures, nor did he easily part with his hard-earned money, but the sight of that house on that decrepit, drug-trafficked street was stomach churning. No matter how much he'd insisted, though, Charlie's mother would not accept his offer to buy her a new house. For the past several years his brother, Joe, had been immersed in an experimental, intensive cognitive therapy program at Walderman Hospital in Belmont. Charlie's mother had voiced concern that moving to a new house would upset Joe's treatment and result in a setback, thus prompting her to decline the generous offer. That didn't surprise Charlie in the least. His mother's life had for years revolved around Joe.

Despite the five-year gap in age, Charlie had once felt close to his older brother. Joe's adolescence had arrived the same year their father left and things changed for the worse. He'd often been moody and quick to anger. Joe would spend hours listening to their father's favorite jazz albums in what Charlie described to friends as a deep trance. Sometimes Joe would disappear for days on end, with no memory of being gone, and while at home, his severe temper flareups worsened, prompting their mother to seek medical help. Months later doctors had diagnosed Joe with and treated him for a rare epileptic condition. A boy in Charlie's school had had a seizure once, and so Charlie had asked his mother about it.

"Why doesn't Joe shake?"

"There are different types of seizures," his mother had explained.

"Is Joe going to die?"

"No."

That had been good enough for Charlie. He'd been eight years old at the time.

For a while life in the Giles household returned to normal, albeit without their father around. Then Joe turned eighteen, and that year he was diagnosed with an entirely different ailment—the same one their father also suffered from—schizophrenia. Turmoil and heartache became the norm for the Giles family once again. It stayed that way even after Charlie left home to attend college, even during his years out West. It was a blessing the day Joe found the Walderman program. At last life in that beat-up old house in Waltham started to get better.

Since joining Walderman, Joe had shown remarkable progress. When Charlie first moved back to Boston, Joe couldn't even organize his day, let alone hold down a job. Two years later and after countless hours at Walderman, Joe was working a night security detail for a downtown office high-rise. Those evening hours passed so slowly, Joe complained, but it was—as he put it—a paying gig.

From the day Joe was diagnosed, Charlie's mother had dedicated her every waking minute to his care and well-being. Charlie had been too young to understand exactly what was happening, but in looking back, he understood that her passion had turned into an obsession. There was no blame or anger, but the family lacked closeness. It was simply how he grew up—his mother so deeply involved with his brother's care that she had nothing left to give to anybody else. Instead of lamenting a past he could not change, Charlie put all his attention on what mattered most—how not to become like them.

Sometimes Charlie wondered what would have happened if his brother hadn't gotten sick. Perhaps he, Charlie, never would have been as driven and successful. Perhaps he owed his brother a debt of gratitude. As for brotherly love, however, those years had proved deeply scarring and had left an indelible chasm between them.

Growing up, neither brother knew their father was schizophrenic until after he left them. His mother justified the deceit by explaining it was at their father's insistence—he believed the less the children knew about his disease, the better.

After Joe was diagnosed, Charlie was understandably interested in the role genetics played in schizophrenia. Much that he found on that subject was unnervingly speculative. One disturbing fact Alison Giles shared was that Charlie's father had stopped taking his medicine. It was probably the reason he'd abandoned the family without warning one rainy October so many years ago. No one had heard from him since.

Charlie sat back down after giving his desk a thorough wipe-down and tried to guess what Anne Pedersen had to say that could possibly jeopardize InVision. The thought that something threatened InVision was both troublesome and puzzling. It angered him that he couldn't come up with an answer, and pride begged him to believe she was mistaken without even knowing what she had to say.

InVision, Charlie had been led to believe, was essential to SoluCent's growth strategy and a key factor in sales forecasts and revenue projections. It was why the A-team from the strategic acquisition committee had been so relentless in their pursuit of Charlie's start-up, and had paid handsomely for it, too. There was no possible explanation for why these senior executives would have misled him.

Charlie had made almost fifteen million in cash from the transaction and stood to make millions more in stock and incentive bonuses, based on performance and product success. The decision to sell his company had been a no-brainer. It had been the fastest way to go from good money to the big leagues. Yet here he was, wondering if his dream was now being second-guessed by the very people who had convinced him to sell. He silently berated himself. When would the fear that everything would vanish go away? he wondered. When women like Anne Pedersen stopped insinuating that it might.

Charlie reached for his BlackBerry to check his calendar, not waiting for Outlook to restart. There he saw the note again.

If not yourself, then who can you believe?

A mentor from his MIT days had warned him that when you reached the top, plenty of people were always waiting below to pull you back down. He'd brushed it off as a cliché. It now seemed prophetic.

People were always hungry to pull him down. He wasn't there to win any popularity contests. He was there to make it happen, and that meant having a work ethic that few could stand. He had no patience or interest in anything that wasn't going to advance his cause.

Since coming to SoluCent over two years ago, Charlie had never set foot in any of the five campus cafeterias. Lunchtime was reserved for Monte's afternoon walk, not eating. With his fourteen-hour workday, he needed those walks to help keep the pounds off in an industry notorious for overweight, sedentary workers.

Today would be an exception. Today he would meet Anne Pedersen at 12:00 p.m. in the Omni Way cafeteria. Only then would he find out what was so important that it had to be confided in person.

Charlie brought Monte over to Nancy, whose cubicle was just outside his office. She agreed, and would agree to do so every day if he asked, to take Monte for his afternoon walk. He couldn't tell who was more excited to see the other.

"He's still your dog, Charlie," Nancy said as Monte rolled onto his back to expose her hands to his warm belly.

"But with you in the picture, I don't think it would take long for him to get over me," Charlie offered.

Charlie went back inside his office and locked his computer using the Task Manager. He changed his log-on password weekly, months before corporate IT demanded it be changed. It was his private defense against hackers and unauthorized access. Nobody ever touched his files. He made sure of it. He closed and locked his office door and kept his head down as he walked the carpeted corridor toward the stairwell. He wanted to seem preoccupied and unavailable for a quick sidebar chat on some problem that wasn't his in the first place.

He said a brief hello to Tom Connors, who was senior VP and division head for the electronic solutions consulting group, but ignored the rest of the rank and file. Tom expected Charlie to address him. Charlie didn't much care what the others thought.

Chapter 4

Charlie glanced at his watch just as he arrived at the cafeteria. It was 11:55 a.m., and the cafeteria was already nearly full. This wasn't his campus building, so Charlie wasn't surprised not to recognize a single person seated at the rows of cafeteria tables, nor did anyone in the lunch line recognize him.

He was a bit surprised that Anne Pedersen came right up to meet him, hand extended. Her badge was turned around, so he couldn't see her photo ID. The IDs had employee numbers, which would have helped Charlie gauge how long she'd been working there. She was a slender, attractive woman in her early forties, with shoulder-length dark brown hair and playful dark eyes. She wore a formfitting blue blouse and a knee-length black skirt that accentuated what he assumed were runner's legs.

Charlie made sure to look directly in Anne's eyes as he gave her a firm handshake. It was one of the few lessons his father had taught him before he disappeared: never look away when you shake somebody's hand. "It's a sign of weakness," he'd always say. Anne seemed tense, her gaze shifting and avoiding Charlie's eyes.

"I'm glad you could come," she said. Her voice was deeper than Charlie had expected. He liked it. It made her sound assertive, which he found attractive.

"How could I pass it up?" Charlie said. "You made it sound like it wasn't really an option."

"It wasn't," Anne said. "Let's get our food before I fill you in."

Anne ordered a Buffalo chicken wrap and got the chips instead of fries. Her fit figure was apparently the result of exercise and good genes, not a rigid diet. Charlie went with a small salad, vinaigrette dressing, a whole wheat roll, and a bottle of Poland Spring lemon-flavored water. Since he seldom ate lunch, he wasn't sure how a hearty meal in the middle of the day would impede progress on the list of things he still had to do.

They found a circular, raised table with three stools toward the back, away from the crowds at the long tables.

"Your product is in real trouble," she began.

Charlie looked up from his food. "How do you know?"

"Listen, Charlie, I'll be candid with you. I know you don't know me, but I used to work here years ago and came back to SoluCent only because I had to. I just got divorced."

"I'm sorry to hear that," Charlie said.

"It doesn't matter," Anne said. "Anyway, I just got divorced, and I have two kids at home and an ex-husband who doesn't understand that working means getting off your butt and doing something for money."

Charlie leaned back on his stool, surprised by her hostility but attracted by her candor. "We all do what we have to do." It was the only thing he could think to say, but it felt awkward.

"Well, if I'm here for the long haul, which it looks like I am, I don't want to be stuck under Jerry Schmidt one day longer than I have to be."

"Oh. Jerry mentioned there was some dissension in his ranks," Charlie said. "I suppose he was referring to you." Charlie grimaced inwardly at the white lie, but it accomplished two things. First, it made Anne believe Charlie was a person with insider knowledge. It also made a point of not corroborating her opinions of Jerry. It was common knowledge that Jerry Schmidt was an incompetent baboon, whose math and science prowess had stopped developing somewhere around the eighth grade. But he was still two levels higher than Charlie and in tight with Leon Yardley, the company's CEO. Jerry Schmidt was not somebody he wanted to upset.

"Interesting that Jerry's caught on," Anne said with a smile. "To be honest, your product was my way out of Jerry's group. Caroline Ramsey is positioned to be the head of InVision marketing. She loves me, and I want nothing more than to work for her. We know each other from a past life at TechTime. Anyway, I see InVision as being a major force for SoluCent in the coming years."

"Tell me something I don't know," Charlie said. "SoluCent tracked my company for a while before they swooped in and made their offer. I know it's a significant part of their growth strategy."

"Well, Jerry thinks it's garbage, and he's preparing some presentation to the executive steering committee to try and convince them to back away from the GM deal. He's certain we will lose our shirt on this one because of contingencies they've put in the contract specific to our InVision product."

"GM is a terrific deal for everyone!" Charlie snapped. "What we have is light-years ahead of their current in-car entertainment and navigation system."

"Well, I'm sure Jerry's just concerned about what InVision will do to his Ultima digital music and DVD players."

"Ultima is a fucking dinosaur!" Charlie reddened and looked around for anyone important who might have overheard. Assured of their privacy, he whispered it again, this time leaving out the expletive. "Why are you telling me this?" he asked.

"Because," Anne said, "I want out of Jerry's group more than you know. He's oppressive, arrogant, and most of the time flat out wrong. But for some reason Yardley loves the guy. If Jerry gets his way, I'll be working on Ultima until my kids go to college."

"What's his argument? Why is he so against InVision?" Charlie couldn't help but think of the Magellan Team and what shutting down InVision would do to them. Many had uprooted their families to be part of Charlie's executive management team at SoluCent. Losing InVision would be a crushing defeat for all involved.

"First of all, he doesn't understand the technology. No matter how many times I've tried to explain it, he just doesn't get it. I'm sure that his PowerPoint attacking InVision is riddled with flaws. He's just playing the fear factor, capitalizing on all the unknowns to keep InVision stuck in R & D and to continue marketing and selling Ultima. That's his bread and butter. It's how he's made his millions."

Charlie grimaced. "What are you suggesting?" he asked.

"I'm not technical enough to understand all the data in his presentation. I'm sure he doesn't understand it, either, but if I were to give it to you without anybody's knowledge—and if I were to forward you an invite to the meeting where Jerry is presenting his plan to Yardley—would you be interested?"

Charlie bit his lower lip. Going against Jerry meant risking every-thing the two-year-old acquisition had bought him. If he won, he'd advance the cause of InVision and the patents that SoluCent had paid a princely sum to acquire. If he lost, it would tarnish his credi-bility and potentially doom him to middle management.

"I want out of Jerry's group," Anne said. "The only way I see that happening is through InVision. I need your help and you need mine. We both know what's at stake."

"You want me to crash the meeting," Charlie said. Anne nodded as he continued. "And you want me to bring data that counters the arguments Jerry's concocted in his PowerPoint."

Again Anne nodded.

"And you want me to risk my neck and career that what you're telling me is true."

At this Anne stayed motionless. "We all come to crossroads, Char-lie." She slid her hand across the table and lifted it to reveal a USB storage key.

Charlie assumed Jerry's presentation was on it.

"You let me know what you want to do. The meeting with Yardley is this Tuesday," Anne told him.

"Not much time to prepare for battle," Charlie said.

"This isn't a battle, Charlie," Anne said. "This is a war."

Chapter 5

Charlie wore a blue pin-striped Brooks Brothers suit with a solid red tie and carried his black leather Tumi briefcase in his right hand. His eyes were sunken and hollow from a stint of sleepless nights, but they showed no fear.

He moved confidently down the long carpeted hallway, passing the offices of several colleagues he knew without so much as a wave hello. Focus was everything. If it wasn't related to the meeting—if it wasn't reflecting on how he would enter, what he would say, every detail of his presentation—it wasn't worth consideration. He needed complete and total control if he was to deliver what he believed would be a professional dismantling of Jerry Schmidt. It would be piece by piece. And it would be merciless.

The days leading up to the meeting had been a blur. They'd been a dim passage of what Charlie called blackout time, hours spent working so hard, he didn't remember living them. He'd kept Monte at home and hired a service to come four times each day and into the night to take him for his walks. He had briefly thought about a kennel, but the idea of his dog being in lockdown had proved too unnerving.

During the exhausting days spent staring into the soft glow of his LCD monitor, sifting through mountains of raw data, Charlie had sunk his teeth deep into the problem, tearing it apart and rebuilding each argument until he was certain it was bulletproof, only to reassess every assertion at microscopic levels again. His appointments had been canceled, and he'd spoken to the Magellan Team only when absolutely critical.

Steady as a dull headache, persistent but not overpowering, Anne Pedersen had been the only distraction that seeped into his thoughts. The urge to seek her out and thank her for risking so much on his behalf had been compelling, but he'd managed to resist. E-mail and voice mail were risky, and he had good reason to be cautious about leaving an electronic paper trail. If everything played out the way he expected, Jerry Schmidt would be caught in a shit storm. Under no circumstances would Charlie supply ammunition that Jerry might use to take Anne Pedersen down with him. When InVision grew to greater prominence at SoluCent, Charlie would find a way to repay her kindness.

He arrived at the closed double doors, made from heavy, dark wood. He read the marble plaque on the adjacent wall: THE FALCON ROOM. He paused, let out a deep breath, reached forward, and grabbed the brass handle, pulling the door open and stepping inside.

Leon Yardley sat at the long conference table. He was hunched over, scanning through a shuffled mass of papers. He looked up and gave Charlie a queer, confused stare.

"Hi, Leon," Charlie said. "Having a good day, I hope?"

Leon Yardley was a pale, thin man near seventy with a horseshoe head of silver hair. His forehead was sun-spotted from too many winters golfing in Boca. His neck was wiry with age and seemed physically incapable of holding up his head. Although Yardley lacked the physique to fill out his tailored suits, Charlie felt intimidated. He prickled at the notion of participating in one of Yardley's meetings.

A shadow of the man whose pictures lined the hallways and conference rooms of SoluCent, Leon Yardley still spoke in a booming voice that belied his withering frame.

"Charlie," Yardley said. "I didn't realize you were attending." His voice was husky and warm. Charlie observed Yardley fiddle with his Harvard class ring. He would twist the thick gold band back and forth around his spiny finger intermittently. Either it was an unconscious nervous habit, or the man wanted to reinforce his belief that Harvard outshined all other universities.

"I've had this meeting on my calendar for a week now," Charlie said.

He had practiced the lie in his apartment several times that morning, even using Monte as a test audience. He had no margin for error. He had to be accepted and welcomed into the meeting as if he had belonged there all along. To do that required confidence and attitude, qualities Charlie possessed in abundance. If it played out the way he expected, Yardley and the others would assume that Charlie was supposed to be there and that someone had simply forgotten to update the agenda. In a company of twenty thousand employees, those mistakes happened.

Jerry Schmidt was in the room as well. He looked up at Charlie and then over to Yardley but didn't say anything. He didn't even acknowledge that Charlie was there.

"Well, it's always good to have you," Yardley said with polite sincerity. "Todd, you compiled the agenda. What is Mr. Giles here to discuss?"

Todd Cumberland, a junior vice president in marketing, stared at Charlie.

"InVision," Charlie said. "I'm here to discuss InVision. What else?"

Jerry Schmidt perked up. Jerry had a round, expressive face, bushy brown hair, and squinting oval eyes that shifted and blinked constantly, as though he had just awoken and was adjusting his sight. Stuffed into a brown suit that had been in vogue years ago and wearing tan shoes in desperate need of a good polish, Jerry was at least fifteen pounds overweight. From what Charlie could tell, that didn't bother him in the least. Charlie knew his type well—not an appearance guy, but an old-fashioned workhorse, who had built a sizable fortune through marketing savvy and diligent follow-through, not engineering brilliance, qualities that greatly contributed to the company's bottom line and Yardley's steadfast loyalty. Convincing Yardley to turn on Jerry was going to be an uphill climb.

"Don't trust marketing to represent you, Charlie? Or did Mac tell you to come here and cover?" Jerry asked.

"I'm here on my own," Charlie said. "Mac is out of town, so we didn't have time to connect on my topic."

Charlie's boss, Simon "Mac" Mackenzie, was on vacation and wouldn't be back for another few days. The timing, from Charlie's perspective, could not have been better. He hadn't worked for Mac long, but Charlie knew him well enough to know he would never have condoned such aggressive tactics. Fortunately, Mac had one quality that served Charlie's mission well: the discipline to stay out of office affairs while on vacation.

Charlie settled into a vacant seat next to Todd and soaked up his surroundings. It took everything he had to suppress a childlike wonderment. It was a privilege to be invited to a meeting in the Falcon Room, and unheard of for new directors, such as Charlie, to be included in steering committee sessions. No doubt there had never been a gate-crasher before.

The Falcon Room was the epicenter of the most high-powered, important meetings at SoluCent. It was a museum of sorts, with floor-to-ceiling glass shelves that displayed the company's distinguished history of product successes with a peacock's flair. Charlie couldn't help but notice that the wall behind Yardley's seat was devoted exclusively to the VidOX gaming system, one of SoluCent's flagship products. He knew that it wouldn't be long before InVision eclipsed VidOX in product importance and secured its rightful place of prominence on the wall behind the company's CEO and chairman of the board.

On the rare occasion when one of SoluCent's major investors grew skeptical of the company's direction or industry relevance, they had only to enter the Falcon Room for their opinions to change. The sea of blinking lights and illuminating glow from the two dozen brightly lit monitors dazzled away the doubts of even the harshest critic.

Over the next several minutes other executives shuffled into the meeting, some staring at their BlackBerrys, thumbs firing off e-mails, others chattering on cell phones, finishing conversations. Charlie noticed how none of them spoke to each other. It amused him how out of touch people became the higher they climbed. Charlie vowed never to lose touch with his employees when he made vice president.

As more executives entered the room and the seats around the conference table began to fill, Charlie's confidence weakened, while his pulse quickened. He hadn't realized the size of this meeting. The invite Anne Pedersen had forwarded didn't contain the complete attendee list. As it turned out, everyone who was anyone at SoluCent was present.

Charlie cast aside his anxiety with the thought of what was at stake. He had no choice but to counterstrike before Jerry Schmidt could poison his future.

It was true that the move risked alienating him from the power source. If Leon Yardley disagreed with Charlie's claims about how In-Vision would revolutionize SoluCent's business, if he was dismayed by Charlie's aggressive tactics, everything Charlie had worked so hard to achieve would be lost.

Charlie took a breath and reassured himself. He had no choice.

When everyone was seated, Leon Yardley spoke. "Ladies and gentlemen," he began, "we have a full agenda, so I want to get started on time. For those of you who have not met Mr. Charlie Giles before, he is the wunderkind behind InVision. I'm sure you've heard me speak fondly of him."

Charlie felt twenty pairs of eyes boring into him. His heart still raced. He kept rubbing his hands against the cool leather chair to wipe away the sweat from his palms.

"Hello, everyone," Charlie said, greeting the room, hoping nobody noticed the slight waver in his voice.

"Naturally, Charlie is here to speak about InVision," Yardley said. "But I must admit that I'm not entirely sure what topic he is here to cover."

Megan Sullivan, vice president of North American sales, let out an audible sigh and asked, "Doesn't Jerry have InVision on his agenda?"

"I do," Jerry said. "But apparently Charlie has something he wants to say as well."

Megan made it a point to look at her watch before responding. "Leon, I want to make sure we have time to discuss the MicroComp issue."

"Of course, Megan," Yardley said. "It's foremost on my mind. Charlie, if it wouldn't trouble you, since we have a full agenda and you're somewhat of a surprise guest, we'll give you five minutes or so to discuss your topic. Can you cover what you need to in that time?"

For a moment Charlie couldn't look up. *Is this how Harry Wessner felt when I confronted him about Arthur Bean? Trapped and terrified?* Charlie hated feeling this out of control. The room seemed to dim, although nobody had adjusted the lights. Blood from his pumping heart pounded in his ears. Who was Charlie Giles to attack Jerry Schmidt in this way? Granted he was climbing the ladder, but he wasn't on Jerry's rung, at least not yet. And this was going to be a humiliating experience for Jerry. For a moment, Charlie almost felt sorry for the man.

Then he remembered what Jerry was here to do. He was here to shut down InVision.

You brought this fight to your door, Jerry, he thought.

Charlie pushed his chair away from the table and stood up. He made brief eye contact with each of the powerhouse attendees. He stayed quiet for a second, collected his nerves, then spoke with authority.

"Leon, I'll be glad to take the floor for five minutes," Charlie said.

"And what exactly are you talking about, Charlie?" Jerry asked.

"Well, Jerry," Charlie said, "if you must know, my topic is you."

That caused some commotion, a few laughs, and some sidebar conversations. Jerry Schmidt smiled, but it was nervous and forced.

"I'm confused," Jerry said. "What do you mean, me?"

"Better to show you than to tell you," Charlie said.

Inwardly Charlie smiled. The moment was his to control.

Chapter 6

The room grew silent, and all eyes rested on Charlie. Moments later Charlie plugged his USB key into the computer and projected his PowerPoint presentation onto the large, retractable white screen at the front of the conference room.

"I don't want to say how I know, Jerry, because that wouldn't be fair to my source," Charlie began. "But I know what you're here to present today, and I respectfully must disagree with it."

"I'm sorry. What did you say? You disagree with me? I find that a bit strange, Charlie," Jerry returned.

"Well, it's the reason I'm here today. I'm here to implore this executive team to consider all sides and to not make any hasty decisions about InVision's future based on a single perspective. Based on *your* perspective, Jerry." Charlie made sure to face his adversary when he spoke his name.

"I'm still confused, Charlie," Jerry said. "How is it you came to know about my presentation?"

"That doesn't matter right now," Charlie said. "I thought the best way for you to understand how and why InVision will help to shape SoluCent's future is with facts and data. For some of you seated here, I'm sure this will just be a refresher course."

Charlie's PowerPoint deck was only six slides in all, but each helped tell a carefully crafted story: healthy consumer interest in InVision, lower than projected production costs, a multipronged sales strategy that included a comprehensive advertising plan and details of the partnerships with some of the world's most prominent automotive manufacturers. The business case was as airtight as a killing jar.

Charlie's presentation style, forceful but not overly animated, was no less convincing than the content. His word choice had been carefully crafted and memorized. His timing ensured the presentation took less than five minutes, without him seeming rushed or vague. Having run his own executive-level meetings, Charlie had anticipated a tight agenda and limited floor time.

The final slide was a direct comparison of Jerry's assertions, taken from the PowerPoint Anne Pedersen had provided, with Charlie's data in larger, bold type. Several sub-bullets backed up his claims and illustrated just how wrong Jerry's assertions were.

"These numbers are irrefutable," Charlie concluded. "I welcome an audit, and I promise you, the Magellan Team uses GAAP for all our figures. There is no fudge factor here."

Everyone in the room sat quietly after Charlie finished. There was some shuffling of papers, the soft creaking of chairs.

"Any questions or comments?" Charlie asked.

Charlie stood awkwardly at the front of the room. He faced the silence and rocked back and forth on his heels, praying that someone would speak up.

Jerry Schmidt put his elbows on the table and rested his chin on his hands. He took in an audible deep breath and let it out slowly. In the quiet of the room, it was as loud as a scream. He looked puzzled and concerned. *Good,* Charlie thought. *You wanted to play hardball, Jerry. How does it feel to be on the losing side?*

"Charlie," Jerry began slowly. He spoke in a very authoritative tone, as though he were confronting a child who had just done something against the rules. "How is it again that you came across my *presentation* you're attacking?"

Charlie couldn't help but let out a little smirk. *Gotcha, you jackass.*

"That's not important, Jerry," Charlie said. "The bottom line is that I knew what you were presenting and I felt it was my obligation as a shareholder in SoluCent to present the counterargument. You now have the facts as I see them. You have both sides. We'll each have a chance to have our say. I'm comfortable leaving it up to the executive team to make any final decisions."

"I'm glad you feel that way, Charlie," Jerry said. "Really glad. It's just . . . well, it's just strange that you thought I was here to *attack* In-Vision."

The comment stunned Charlie. He took a step for balance and wound up standing in front of the projection screen, casting warped numbers from his slide across his body and lighting up his reddening face with the white-hot light from the projection bulb.

"I'm sorry, Jerry. What are you saying? I don't think I follow you."

"What I'm saying Charlie, is you should have looked at my presentation before you got up here." Jerry leaned back in his chair. "*My presentation*," Jerry added for emphasis. "The one *I* planned on giving today. The one I've always planned to show."

Jerry stood up; the room remained silent. He went over to the computer, opened his PowerPoint presentation from the network, and projected it on the large white screen. Charlie had moved back so he could read the title slide. A sinking, sickening feeling of horror washed over him.

The Future is here and now! Winning big with InVision
By Jerry Schmidt, Vice President, Channel Marketing, the Americas

"I'm confused," Charlie said.

"Well, darn it," Jerry said in a mocking singsong voice. "So am I, Charlie! Confused and bewildered at that. Do you want me to go through my deck? I mean, you covered most of it already."

"I . . . I . . . don't understand." Charlie felt flushed, blood racing through him, his heart beating mercilessly in his chest. For a moment he thought he might be sick.

"Leon, you can scratch me from the agenda, okay?" said Jerry. "Charlie covered all my slides. Growth, new market position, new consumer demand, cross-selling opportunities, and projected increase to net revenue of one hundred forty million year one—and that's a low estimate."

"Charlie! Jerry!" Yardley said. "What the hell is going on here?"

"I'm asking the same question, Leon. I think only Charlie knows the answer," replied Jerry.

All eyes turned to Charlie.

"I was told by a very reliable source that Jerry was here to try and shut down InVision, to push it into R & D. This person gave me Jerry's presentation," Charlie explained. "I don't know what is going on, but I'm guessing Jerry caught wind of it and changed his deck to make me look bad."

"Well, you look bad," Yardley said. "Jerry, is this true?"

"Absolutely not!" Jerry snapped. "That is completely absurd. I have one position on InVision. Sell the shit out of it. That's all! The product is great, and it is going to make SoluCent better. End of story."

"Charlie?" said Yardley.

"I have his deck, Leon! I don't know who he thinks he's fooling," said Charlie.

"Who I'm fooling? Who are you fooling, Charlie?" Jerry asked. "Tell me, who gave you this alleged PowerPoint of mine?"

He had no choice. The situation had changed. "Anne Pedersen," Charlie said after a pause. "I got the deck from Anne Pedersen. She gave it to me a few days ago at lunch."

Charlie didn't have time to think of the consequences, but the moment he spoke her name, he was awash with guilt. He remembered what she had told him. That she had just gotten divorced. He thought she had mentioned children to support. Surely she'd be fired after this came out in the open. But he wouldn't let her down completely. He knew people. He could get her another job in another company if he had to.

Charlie could see Jerry processing, thinking intently.

Jerry spoke in a calm, dispassionate voice. "I don't know who that is," he said.

Charlie glared at him. "You . . . you . . . don't know who that is?" He was enraged at the audacity, Jerry's ruthlessness. It was bad enough that Jerry had somehow switched presentations to cover his tracks and humiliate Charlie in the process, but to lie flat out was inconceivable.

Charlie looked around the room for signs of support, anyone who was willing to speak on his behalf, at least acknowledge that they knew, worked with, or ate lunch with Anne Pedersen. But it was clear that nobody wanted any part of this. They stayed quiet.

"Watch out, Charlie," Yardley interrupted. "You're getting a bit out of hand."

"I'm out of hand? I'm out of hand?" Charlie said, the second time much louder. "Jerry here is playing games, and I don't know what this is all about. A woman named Anne Pedersen contacted me. She gave me this file," he said, holding up his USB key. "I looked her up in the corporate directory. She works for you, Jerry! For you! And you don't know a thing about this? Come on!" Charlie slammed his open palm against the polished mahogany table with a resounding thud that shot through the silent room like a clap of thunder.

"That's enough! Enough!" Leon Yardley stood. He pointed to Charlie's empty chair. "Mr. Giles, it is in your best interest to take a seat now."

Charlie did as instructed as Yardley turned to speak to Jerry.

"Jerry, you stand behind your claims? You never intended to discredit InVision today. And Anne Pedersen is not your employee."

"I do," Jerry said.

"Let's get to the bottom of this, then." Yardley grabbed the conference room Polycom and dialed the operator. He asked for Gail Lyndon in Human Resources. The moment she answered, he asked that she look up Anne Pedersen's employment history.

"We don't have any employee named Anne Pedersen," came her reply over the speakerphone.

Yardley spelled the name, looked to Charlie for confirmation. Charlie nodded. For a moment, the only sound was that of a keyboard typing on the other end of the phone.

"I'm sorry," Gail said. "But we don't have any employee with the last name Pedersen."

Yardley clasped his hands tightly together and looked over at Charlie. "I'm listening," he said.

Charlie stammered, "I told you what I know. A woman named Anne Pedersen, who claimed to work for Jerry, gave me the file. She was an employee. She had a badge. Leon, she gave me the file!" He sounded desperate. Of course it happened, Charlie thought. It was as real as this nightmare was now.

"How do you account for her not existing, Charlie?" Jerry said.

Charlie thought for a moment. "I'll show you how."

He stood and walked to the computer and opened the Power-Point presentation that Anne Pedersen had given him. The title slide was projected on the screen.

"Each PowerPoint file has associated properties. These properties tell when a file was created, modified, and who made it. Any file created by a person on the SoluCent network will list that person's name as the author. This is your file, Jerry, so I'm guessing your name is the listed author."

Charlie clicked the file menu in PowerPoint, moused down to the properties entry, and opened the pop-up window. He clicked on the summary tab in the pop-up.

Charlie stared at the screen but couldn't register what it said. Several attendees coughed, and at least one person let out a gasp of surprise. It wasn't Jerry's name that was listed as the author, or even Anne Pedersen's. And the file hadn't been created days ago, as Charlie had claimed. According to the file's date and time stamp, it had been created just yesterday morning. And the name in the author field was Charlie Giles.

Chapter 7

Charlie's walk from the main entrance to his BMW, parked in an early bird front lot space, felt interminable—as though he were stepping through molasses along an ever-expanding horizon of asphalt. The once energizing campus had morphed into something ominous and foreboding. Glancing behind him, at the tall brick-and-glass buildings of SoluCent, Charlie's mind flooded with questions.

Rising above that noise, the most consistent and resounding of these jumbled thoughts was the need to get away as fast as he could.

Once inside his car he felt safer, cocooned in the familiar. He stared forward, through the spotless windshield, and reconstructed her face from memory. As her image came into sharper focus, he felt a calming sureness that Anne Pedersen was real, even though all logic seemed to lead to the conclusion he refused to believe. Anne Pedersen did not exist.

The image faded. He thought of Leon Yardley. The CEO had been kinder than Charlie had expected, or deserved. His only insistence was that Charlie leave for the day as he and other managers tried to get some clarity and perspective on the situation.

A little distance might be the only way to figure out what was going on and how he could clear his name. As Charlie turned the ignition, the BMW fired up with a quiet hum. Monte's pillow in the backseat was empty, and Charlie had never felt more alone. The InVision system spoke in soothing tones from his newly installed Polk speaker system.

Each of the early prototype models of InVision had been code-named after famous explorers. This dovetailed with the Magellan code name of his executive team, while exploring new territory was a running operational theme throughout his organization. The system in his car was the Columbus prototype—a top-of-the-line model and only two generations removed from what he believed would be the first mass-produced line.

"Hello, Charlie. I hope you're having a great day," it said.

"I'm having a fucking fantastic day," Charlie said. "Jim Hall, 'Alone Together,' please."

Soft chords from Hall's guitar spilled out from the speakers, rounded out by Ron Carter's mesmerizing, but wandering bass line. Charlie sat motionless and waited for the distinctive melody of Jim Hall's guitar solo to follow. He focused on Hall's playing in particular, picturing each note in his mind, while his fingers danced against an imaginary fret board. The stress of the SoluCent acquisition had inspired him to pick up his guitar again. Thanks to muscle memory, it had taken months, not years, to return to his past fluency. And because his fingertips had quickly callused over, practicing had stopped hurting after a few days of regular playing.

Of all the jazz guitar greats whose style and compositions he had mastered, Hall was an elusive favorite. "An undiscovered gem," his father once called him, Hall had a gift for improvisation, which Charlie himself was unable to exemplify in his own playing. Imitation, it turned out, was Charlie's musical specialty, while spontaneous creative expression was not. His lack of looseness had kept him out of the recording studio and away from live gigs. Technical precision was fine for the living-room player, but on a CD or when playing live, it was all about feeling and improvisational ability. Someday he would become that player, Charlie promised himself—free and unencumbered by his overthinking each measure and demanding perfection. All he needed to do was to keep listening to Hall.

Charlie pulled out of the driveway and onto the main thoroughfare that would lead him to Route 128 and eventually onto Route 2 toward Boston. In his head he replayed events from the last several days, hoping that something would jar a memory or give him some direction.

The small green car icon displayed on the InVision street map screen—the color indicating that he was "on course"—should be red, Charlie thought. If InVision were a mind reader, it would be red.

"I met Anne Pedersen last Thursday. It was twelve thirty. We were in the Omni Way cafeteria," he muttered. With little effort he could see her face; her fine porcelain features; the lean, long legs; dark brown, shoulder-length hair; smile warm and embracing; teeth white and straight. "Anne Pedersen gave me this file, dammit!"

Charlie squeezed the USB key with white-knuckling force, imagining for a moment that he crushed it under the pressure and somehow, with its destruction, ended the nightmare.

"She forwarded me the invite to the meeting. . . ." Charlie's voice trailed off. "She forwarded me the invite," he said again. "Of course. I have her e-mail!"

Charlie's eyes lit up as he reached in the pocket of his blazer and extracted his BlackBerry. Practiced at driving without giving it his undivided attention, Charlie turned on the device and accessed his e-mail over the network. He switched to calendar view and noticed, with a growing sense of dread, that the invitation he had in Outlook for the executive steering committee meeting was gone.

Blood pressure rising, Charlie fumbled with the device, nearly rear-ending a car as he inadvertently changed lanes. He scanned through several days' worth of e-mail, looking for Anne Pedersen's first e-mail message to him, the one where she requested they meet face-to-face. That e-mail wasn't there. It wasn't in his deleted folder, either.

He thought about his next move. He saw no point in contacting Caroline Ramsey, even though Anne Pedersen had claimed she was positioning herself for a job in Caroline's group and had given that as her reason for warning Charlie about Jerry's power play. If the company had no record of Anne Pedersen's existence, it was certain that Caroline Ramsey would have no knowledge of her, either.

Charlie knew it was counterproductive to keep asserting that Anne Pedersen was a SoluCent employee. Leon Yardley had already taken Charlie aside to ask if pressure from the pending product launch was impacting his mental health. It was obvious what the CEO had been implying—that Charlie had invented Anne Pedersen as a way of self-sabotaging his career. Of course, Charlie had denied that was true. To clear his name, however, Charlie needed to find out who Anne Pedersen really was, without further raising Yardley's suspicions.

Before departing SoluCent, Charlie had returned to the Omni Way cafeteria but had left frustrated that not a single employee remembered serving him or his lunch companion. He wasn't a regular at the cafeteria, a cashier had explained, otherwise he would have chatted with Charlie and perhaps remembered him coming through. There was no point in trying to find out if an Anne Pedersen had swiped her security badge at the Omni Way cafeteria, either. As far as corporate was concerned, Anne Pedersen did not exist. But perhaps someone had lost a badge or had had theirs stolen? It was worth checking into. In addition, Charlie wanted a log of his Outlook access. Someone might have been messing around with his system. Perhaps they'd changed property files on the PowerPoint document or sent and deleted his e-mails.

One thing he knew for certain was that he had read Anne's message. It had stood out from the others, for the simple reason that he hadn't known who she was. Besides, he reasoned, without that e-mail, how would he have known to meet her at the cafeteria? To accept any other explanation would be to embrace the possibility that they had never met. That Anne Pedersen, as Yardley had implied, was his invention.

Charlie switched the BlackBerry to phone mode and dialed SoluCent. He asked to be connected with Lawrence Washington in IT.

"Lawrence here," a husky voice growled into the phone.

"Lawrence, Charlie Giles. How are you?"

"What do you want?"

Charlie found it ironic that those in IT who manned the help desk were often the least friendly and helpful people in the company. Lawrence was no exception. Even though he liked Charlie and respected his level of technical acumen, years on the job had made Lawrence a hard man.

"I need a favor, Lawrence."

"Don't we all."

"This is serious," Charlie said.

"Okay, I'm listening."

"I need to know if my e-mail has been compromised."

"Why do you think it has?"

"Doesn't matter. Trust me. I just need to know all the times I've logged into my e-mail. I need to know the exact date and time."

"Might take me a little while. When do you need it?"

"Yesterday."

"Big surprise. That it?" Lawrence asked.

"No," Charlie said. "I need to know if anyone has reported a stolen or lost employee ID. I need it over the last few months."

"Can't give that out, Charlie."

"Lawrence . . . I . . . need to know." Desperation had replaced the confidence in Charlie's voice.

"Sorry," Lawrence said. "But that ain't your business."

"Are the Red Sox yours?"

Lawrence paused.

"This Saturday. Green Monster, against the Jays," Charlie said.

"That's bribery, Giles."

"It's the Red Sox," Charlie said.

"No e-mail. I'll drop by with a disc. You can see the names."

"And I'll drop by with the tickets tomorrow." *They'll cost only a hundred and fifty dollars each from Corner Ticket.*

Charlie slid the BlackBerry back into its holder and caught the yellow flash from the sticky note he'd found days earlier and taped to the inside flap. He read it again.

If not yourself, then who can you believe?

The words had taken on an almost prophetic significance. What was happening to him? First a note that he didn't recall writing, then a woman who didn't exist, then a presentation he apparently authored without any recollection.

A sickening thought swept through him, like a wave of grief. Could Yardley be right? Perhaps the pressure was more than he could handle, and now his subconscious mind wanted a way out.

Charlie shook his head side to side.

"No. It can't be," he said aloud. "I know what I saw . . . don't I?"

He looked back down at the sticky note on the inside flap of his BlackBerry holder, resting open on the passenger seat. His handwriting looked both familiar and alien.

"When did I write this?" he asked. "And why?"

He pulled the Post-it note from his BlackBerry holder and stuck it to the inside cover of a notebook he kept in the glove compartment. He didn't want to give the note any more thought, but he wasn't prepared to crumple it up and toss it away, either. At least not until a few other mysteries were solved.

Charlie drove as if on autopilot into a hazy midafternoon sun as he replayed the events of the day. Assuming Anne Pedersen did exist, it still did not explain his authoring the PowerPoint presentation, the missing e-mails, or unfamiliar notes in his handwriting.

Is it the pressure, Charlie?

Yardley's biting words came to him again.

It had been obvious from the man's eyes that he had already embraced that conclusion. If Yardley was thinking that way, Charlie lamented, the others would soon follow.

I'm going to be branded a nutcase.

Step one, Charlie decided, was to prove that wasn't even a possibility. It seemed inconceivable that work pressures could trigger his creating an elaborate fantasy world—the sort of altered reality he associated with Joe or his father. If it wasn't the pressure, could it be some sort of mental illness? Charlie was knowledgeable enough about his brother's disease to know that symptoms manifested themselves in the late teens, midtwenties on the outside, but almost never in someone as old as he was. But was it possible?

Jerking the steering wheel hard right, Charlie swerved the BMW in front of a fast-traveling Toyota 4Runner. The driver reciprocated with a customary Bostonian salute of his middle finger. Hitting the exit ramp at forty mph, the wheels of the BMW hugged the road with the advertised precision and control. Charlie shot over the overpass, got into the left lane, downshifted into second, then turned onto the entrance ramp heading in the opposite direction on Route 128, back toward Waltham.

If he could medically disprove the possibility of work pressures or some late-blooming brain disease as the cause, it would go a long way toward reestablishing trust within SoluCent's leadership team. That would give Charlie access to the necessary corporate resources to find the real culprits.

"Please dial Mother," Charlie said aloud.

"Dialing Mother," responded InVision.

The phone rang six times before someone finally answered.

"Hello." The voice on the other end was heavy, as though the person to whom it belonged had been roused from a deep slumber.

"Joe."

"Charlie? That you?"

"I need a favor. I need you to look up a number for me."

Joe said nothing for a moment. "You need a number?"

It seemed to Charlie an exceptionally long time to process information, only to repeat the request. "Yes. That's what I said," he said.

"What number do you want, Charlie?"

"Rachel Evans," Charlie said.

Charlie could hear the surprise in Joe's voice. "What? Why do you want to talk with Dr. Evans?"

"Why do you care?" Charlie said.

"She's my psychologist, Charlie. There's a reason to care."

"It's research, Joe. Nothing more."

Charlie had heard Rachel's name mentioned dozens of times over the years. Joe was besotted with her. He praised her with a sense of wonderment typically reserved for the divine. And admittedly, since joining her experimental cognitive therapy program, Joe had made remarkable progress.

All Charlie wanted was an expert ear. Hers was the only name he had.

Joe gave him the number and Charlie thanked him.

"Are you going to come visit Mom?" Joe asked. "I'm sure she would appreciate it."

"I can't today, Joe," Charlie said, hanging up without another word.

Research, Charlie thought. *Yeah. That's what it is. Research.*

He shifted the car over into the fast lane and dialed Rachel's number. The receptionist patched him through.

"Dr. Evans," a friendly voice said.

"Dr. Evans, this is Charlie Giles, Joe's brother. There's something I need to talk to you about."

Chapter 8

The redbrick edifice of Walderman Mental Health rose from its perch atop a grassy knoll and cast an eerie, elongated shadow as the late-day sun settled in the west. Charlie drove his black BMW up the winding driveway. He noticed xenon headlights automatically turned on, as onboard sensors determined dusk was approaching. Charlie downshifted into first and glided his car to a gentle stop in the farthest corner space in a parking lot void of other vehicles.

He had been to this place only once before. It had been a few months after moving back east; Charlie had asked his mother if he could attend a group therapy session at Walderman Hospital. This had brought a look of surprise to her face, since she'd been asking him to participate in Joe's therapy for years. In her mind, for Charlie to spring this on her out of the blue had been nothing short of a miracle. He had never admitted that the request was more selfish than selfless. He had found it embarrassing to live so close to Joe and still have the same uneasiness he remembered feeling as a boy.

Doctors had diagnosed Joe as epileptic just after Charlie's eighth birthday. That disease hadn't disturbed Charlie in the least. Perhaps because his brother's seizures were internal events, more like an altered mental state. Joe didn't convulse when he seized, the way a boy in Charlie's school had who was also epileptic. Unlike that boy's, Joe's eyes didn't roll back in his head; nobody had to stick something into his mouth to keep him from swallowing his tongue. The only clue Joe was even having a seizure was his trance-like detachment.

The schizophrenia, diagnosed years later, however, was far less discreet and had permeated every facet of Charlie's relationship with Joe. Joe would hear voices, complain of strangers reading his thoughts, or express fear that he was being followed. Sometimes his brother would spontaneously burst out into song or converse bizarrely with a stranger, which always embarrassed Charlie. For a fifteen-year-old boy, Joe's breakdown had been at first haunting, soon scary, and had ultimately driven a wedge between the once close siblings.

It had angered Charlie to feel so apprehensive, scared even, around Joe. He had interpreted those feelings as a sign of weakness in himself. He'd known his fear was irrational, but rather than try to overcome it, Charlie had taken another approach—avoidance. It was a passive solution, but an effective one as well.

Charlie had attended a group therapy session at Walderman Hospital in an effort to substitute his long-standing apathy with empathy. It was then that Charlie had found himself in a small, windowless basement room with about eight patients, two doctors, and a half dozen or so relatives.

Claustrophobia had overwhelmed him. Trying to rein in his anxiety, Charlie had stood while the others took their seats. He'd gone over to a small kitchenette and poured himself a cup of lukewarm coffee in a Styrofoam cup, added some Coffee-mate, and, when glances from the staff made it clear that his standing was a distraction, found a seat closest to the door.

Throughout the hour-and-a-half-long session, he hadn't listened to a word. For the life of him, he wouldn't be able to recall one story of hope, sadness, or survival. Instead he'd focused on how some of the patients fidgeted in their seats, and how one man stood up on his chair and shouted out his name to get everyone's attention. Another just kept muttering to himself. They'd all looked so helpless, unclean, and lost.

And Joe, who would slap the back of the folding chair in front of him as if it were a drum, his way of applauding for each person after they spoke, had evoked a familiar sense of shame.

The experiment had failed miserably, and Charlie had taken nothing away from the session, except the decision that he'd never set foot in Walderman again.

That had been almost two years ago. It felt like a lifetime.

The crisp fall air caressed Charlie's face as he stepped from the car. The leaves had just begun their retreat from green to orange and red. It was nature's normal course of life, and he noticed the change with some sadness. Normality was something Charlie could no longer take for granted. He appreciated the simple beauty in a way he hadn't since he was a boy.

An empty pit formed in his stomach as he started toward the entrance. Charlie breathed in a deep sigh and looked around the minimally landscaped grounds, wary of others who might be observing his approach. For many, the short walk across the parking lot and along the slate-and-gravel path to the large wooden double door entrance was a bridge back to a life lost, a way to recapture the essence of being alive, to learn to embrace the simple joys of living again. But for Charlie, it was a journey into the blackest unknown, a retreat from the reality he had once thought unshakable.

Charlie passed through the entrance into a large foyer identified by a black-and-gold-leaf plaque as Saunders Hall. Nothing about the main foyer was clinical. The regality of it made it difficult for Charlie to believe he was even inside a mental health hospital. He had never been to this building before. The group therapy session he'd attended a few years back had been held in a much smaller campus building, about a quarter mile away. This was a mansion. It had been donated to the state by a successful psychologist and his wife, under the condition that it be used solely for the purpose of mental health treatment. The interior of Walderman Mental Health echoed a bygone era of civility and grace, and Charlie could imagine that it had once been the epicenter for the social elite. It would have made an elegant home to entertain and showcase jewelry, evening gowns, and culinary extravaganzas.

He marched along the checkered marble floor, past leather sitting chairs and mahogany tables that seemed swallowed by the cavernous, high ceilings. On the far right wall, directly across from a wide winding staircase leading to the second floor, was a mahogany reception desk. Charlie crossed toward it, his footsteps echoing loudly as he approached. The receptionist kept a firm gaze on him as he neared. What he would normally construe as flattery here seemed tainted with judgment. It would be better, he thought, if the place were bustling with patients and physicians. At least it would provide him some cover. He wouldn't have to be the center of her attention.

She probably thinks I'm crazy, Charlie thought.

The receptionist was a cheery-faced woman, no more than twenty-five. Her brown hair was pulled back in a tight ponytail. Charlie found her large, expressive eyes to be unnecessarily sympathetic. She greeted him with a toothy smile and a slight conciliatory cocking of her head to the side.

"Hello. Can I help you?" she asked.

Charlie stammered for a moment, then pushed aside the unease. "I'm here to see Rachel. Rachel Evans."

"You have an appointment?"

"I . . . I . . . I do. Yes."

Charlie sensed movement behind him, turned, and saw a woman descending the staircase with quick steps and sharp clicks from her high-heeled shoes.

"Mr. Giles?" she said, hurrying down the stairs.

Charlie followed her approach as she reached the bottom step and moved to the reception desk to greet him.

"Yes," Charlie said.

"I'm Rachel Evans," she said, extending a hand. "It's very nice to meet you. Joe has told me a lot about you."

The first thing Charlie noticed was her eyes: warm, inviting green ovals that projected sensitivity without judgment. They helped to put him a bit more at ease. His hands, clenched in tight balls in his pockets, unfolded.

He shook her hand. Her grip was firm. Her eyes never looked away from his. She wore her auburn hair long, draped down her slender back. The smoothness of her skin suggested an age far younger than he assumed her to be, and he could not help but take in her willowy figure. For all her delicacy there was something rugged about her, even with her fine features and graceful manner. She exuded a quiet confidence that, he suspected, made her equally comfortable camping in the mountains and dining in the city's best restaurants.

"It's nice to meet you, Dr. Evans. I appreciate you taking the time to see me on such short notice."

"It's Rachel, and it's not a problem. Why don't we go upstairs to my office to talk?"

Charlie signed in with the receptionist, anxious about leaving a permanent record of his visit. He followed Rachel upstairs, through a set of swinging double doors—these with red vinyl padding—and down a long corridor with what appeared to be offices on either side, spaced evenly about every fifteen feet.

"Not exactly what I expected from a mental hospital," Charlie said, quickening his pace to walk beside Rachel.

"It surprises a lot of people," Rachel said. "But this is just one of three buildings, and it's mostly administrative and physician offices. Some research labs. Our other buildings may be a bit more what you'd expect."

"What is it that I'd expect?" Charlie asked.

Rachel turned to him, letting out a slight knowing smile. Charlie put his hands in his pockets and retreated from her gaze. He ran his left thumb over the tops of his fingertips, feeling the calluses. At that moment he wanted nothing more than to lose himself in guitar, practicing the Jim Hall melodies still fresh in his mind.

"We both know exactly what you'd expect," she replied, her tone insinuating that she and Joe had devoted several sessions to Charlie. "Anyway, we are a fully functioning mental health institution. State-sanctioned, partially funded. Patients at Walderman come for all different reasons. Some are inpatient, some outpatient, and some are on our secured floors."

"Secured?"

"Yes, Mr. Giles. Secured. We have facilities to address all our patients' needs, thanks to the generosity of George Walderman." As they walked past it, Rachel pointed to a large oil portrait of the late Dr. George Walderman, the only picture in the otherwise antiseptic corridor.

They reached Rachel's office at the end of the long corridor.

There she fumbled with her keys and unlocked her office door. Entering the dark, windowless room ahead of Charlie, Rachel reached to her left and flicked on the light switch, filling the space with a dense, sickly white light from two exposed fluorescent bulbs. She crossed over a deep red oriental rug, which, along with the black bookcases filled with medical and psychological texts, provided the only warmth to an otherwise claustrophobically small office.

Charlie took quick note of how she kept her office and appreciated her sense of order—the noticeable lack of decorations; paperwork filed, not messily left about; a single bamboo plant in a bubbling water fountain on a small wooden pedestal near her rectangular oak desk, nothing like the forest of plants some of his coworkers at SoluCent voluntarily maintained.

"Please take a seat, Mr. Giles," Rachel said, pointing to a small cloth-covered armchair nestled in a corner diagonally from her desk.

"Charlie, please," Charlie said as he took a seat.

"Yes, of course, Charlie. So now, you sounded very urgent on the phone. I should be up front in saying this is not an official visit. I'm not going to give you clinical advice."

"No. No. Of course not," Charlie said. "I'm just looking for some information and didn't know where else to go."

"Have you tried the Internet?"

Charlie laughed, quick and unsettled, more like a cough. In his panic, it hadn't even occurred to him to research this on his own. Now, seated in front of Rachel, he was glad of the oversight. Reading faces was one of the attributes that made him such a successful negotiator. A few minutes with Rachel, discussing his situation, monitoring her reaction closely, would give him enough information to tell if there was real cause for alarm.

"I'm not sure I trust it entirely. I felt a more professional opinion was in order. In light of what's been happening."

Rachel reached for her notebook and opened up to a blank page. Charlie could see a small frown escape her. After uncapping her pen, she sat still for a moment. Charlie found the pause and the profound silence of the office unsettling.

"I'm not sure how I feel about this," Rachel said. "If you need professional help, you should seek proper medical attention."

Charlie tried to recover his already shaky poise.

"I'm not sure there is a problem that I need to address," Charlie began. "The situation . . . my situation, well, it's a bit complicated."

"They're all complicated in their own way. The mind is the most personal and private thing we have. When we're questioning it, we are questioning our very selves. That's almost always complicated, Mr. Giles."

"Charlie," he said again. "I'd prefer if we could keep this informal. I promise I won't take up much of your time."

Charlie could see Rachel processing her next move. She was calculating. A thinker. He liked that. If they had met under different circumstances, Charlie was certain he would have been interested in getting to know her personally. Perhaps that would still be a possibility, he thought. *Assuming she doesn't think I'm a nut job.*

"Listen, Charlie," Rachel said, her green eyes fixed on him. "Your brother, Joe, is a patient of mine. That automatically disqualifies us from having any professional relationship. You can ask me your questions, but if I feel a line is being crossed, I'm going to stop the conversation short. Is that all right with you?"

Charlie nodded his head. "Yes, of course," he said. "I understand."

"Good. Then talk. What is it that you want to know about?"

"Well . . . I'm not sure where to begin."

"The beginning is often a good place to start," Rachel said.

"Of course. The beginning. Well, you know my family history. Both my father and brother have mental illness."

Rachel leaned forward, interlocking the fingers of her hands. It was a gesture of apprehension. Had she already suspected this conversation would head out-of-bounds?

Charlie shifted slightly in his chair and crossed his legs. It was a defensive posture, but he was unable to resist the urge to protect himself. To hide his vulnerabilities.

"I'm aware of your family history, Charlie. And, I'm also aware that any discussion of that on my part would be completely inappropriate."

Charlie sat back in his chair, uncrossed his legs, and tried his best to assume a more carefree, less concerned manner. He needed her perspective. The last thing he wanted was to scare her off with his own alarm.

"Understood. Well, lately I've been interested in learning more about my family genetics. I won't trouble you with all the specifics, but suffice it to say, it's extremely important to me."

"All right," Rachel said. "I'll see what I can do. What do you want to know?"

"I'm wondering how you come to the diagnosis that you do. I mean, what are the symptoms that might make you think somebody needs treatment?"

"What treatment are you referring to, Charlie?"

Charlie looked at his shoes. They were polished to a mirror finish, the way he was accustomed to maintaining things—perfectly. "I'm referring to the diagnosis and treatment for schizophrenia," he said. There was nothing liberating about asking the question. It embarrassed him to ask, and the flushness of his cheeks suggested Rachel knew that as well. He had contemplated avoiding the term altogether by asking if work pressures could cause someone to lose their memory or concoct elaborate fantasies, but he wasn't ready to be specific with her.

Rachel stayed seated and made no gesture to end the conversation. From her pursed lips and narrowed eyes Charlie could sense she was being cautious with her word choice, a sign he interpreted as a willingness to walk a very thin line.

"I find it interesting that you've taken such a sudden interest," Rachel said.

Charlie thought about that for a moment. "Are you implying something?"

"I know about you through your family, Charlie," Rachel said. "You realize we encourage family to participate in a patient's treatment. Studies have shown that strong support from immediate family has tremendous benefit for the patient."

Charlie avoided her gaze. "No, I hadn't realized that," he said.

"You've never come around, even though Joe has invited you to several of his milestone events. So I'm just curious. Why the sudden interest?"

"I've had some experiences over the past few days," Charlie said. "Let's just say that they've heightened my curiosity."

"Why don't we do this?" Rachel said. "Tell me about those experiences. What it is that made you feel you needed to speak with me so urgently. We'll put that story into context. I could run through a series of questions that a psychiatrist or someone in a position to form a diagnosis might ask. Take notes if you want. It's more of an exercise, you see, not really a formal assessment. Think of it as a case study. Just an information session. Got it?"

Charlie nodded. He didn't ask why but accepted that Rachel was willing to extend herself beyond the boundaries of what she knew was ethically and perhaps even legally correct. He decided, fighting back his initial hesitation, to open up to her. Charlie went through the events of the last several days, careful to mention details he hoped would convince Rachel, and even himself, that Anne Pedersen was real, that their meeting had taken place, and that he wasn't the author of the PowerPoint discrediting his InVision product.

Rachel listened intently and gave no indication of her verdict. "Charlie, now I understand your reluctance to be honest about the situation."

"You do?"

"Yes. But if I had known beforehand, I wouldn't have agreed to meet with you."

Charlie looked down. "I understand," he said.

"But I do want to help."

"Could it be related to work? The pressure I'm under, I mean."

"I don't know the answer to that. You would need to be properly evaluated."

"Listen, I don't think I'm crazy. I really don't. I mean, what if I'm being framed? Set up by someone jealous of my success?"

Rachel pursed her lips. "Charlie, suspecting that people may be planning to hurt you is actually a symptom of schizophrenia."

Charlie laughed. "Now that's a catch-twenty-two. Somebody may be messing with me to make me think I'm going insane, but to suspect that means I'm insane?"

"It's not that simple, but I agree, it complicates matters," Rachel said. She stood up, moving away from behind her desk so that she was now closest to the door.

Charlie shrank at the implication. *Perhaps,* he thought, *she feels threatened.* Since they were together alone in her small office, she must have sensed danger.

Maybe she's smart to be afraid.

Chapter 9

Monte pressed his cold nose against the stubble of Charlie's cheek and licked at his face. The affection was enough to wake Charlie from a night of disjoined dreams and fitful sleep. Sun splashed through the large bay windows in Charlie's bedroom. The warm light, normally welcomed, was a painful reminder that on any other Thursday he'd be at work at this hour. Charlie ran his fingers through his short hair and then gave Monte some requested attention. The dog walkers would be here around noon. Charlie wasn't certain if it was close to that hour or not.

The calluses on his fingertips were raw and peeling from his marathon practice session, which had lasted well past midnight. He rarely played his prized Gibson ES-175, preferring to treat it more like a showpiece than an instrument. It had been outdoors only for transport from the music store to his apartment in California and briefly again for the move to Boston. It would be the guitar he'd use if he could ever get loose enough to feel inspired to play a live gig. Last night he'd uncorked the Gibson, expecting from it some magic, but ultimately he'd been disappointed at his perpetual inability to improvise. At least for now, the Gibson would stay indoors.

Dressed in a white T-shirt and a pair of green hospital scrubs, Charlie made his way to the kitchen, and Monte followed. There he made coffee from his French press and, once brewed, took his cup into the living room, again followed by Monte, and gazed out the window at the traffic bustling below. It was earlier than he thought, 8:30 a.m., but still much later than he and Monte were accustomed to starting their day.

Charlie's apartment in Boston's Beacon Hill was the entire third floor of a brownstone on the south side of a steeply sloping hill. The apartment was barely furnished, but the cost of what little he owned could buy enough furniture to fill homes three times the size. Monte rubbed against his legs and gave a soft bark, fair warning that he needed to be walked soon, or else. Charlie didn't react; his mind, already racing, even with what little caffeine he'd had, was replaying his meeting with Rachel. She hadn't administered any mock tests or tried to delve deeper into his unexplained experiences. Instead she had suggested a medical MRI. Perhaps a brain lesion or even a tumor—uncommon, but known to cause hallucinations similar to schizophrenia—was to blame. Rachel hadn't ruled out work pressures as being a cause, but she hadn't jumped on the theory, either. There were other possibilities she'd suggested, infection being one, though she'd thought that unlikely given his lack of other symptoms. A comprehensive psychological evaluation and further medical testing, she'd insisted, were the only legitimate path to a diagnosis.

She had also provided the names of several doctors at Walderman who were accepting new patients. That had stung. He had crumpled the paper with the phone numbers on it and thrown it in the trash as he left. He was desperate to find any reason to discredit her professional assessment that he should seek psychiatric help. The MRI was at least medical—hopeful, so long as the cause was curable.

The stress of the last several days had left Charlie with dark circles under his eyes and an ashen complexion. The idea that his mind was a ticking bomb, perhaps ready to detonate, perhaps destined to send him to the same fate as his father and brother before him, went far beyond any corporate stress he'd ever faced. He knew he needed to find the real Anne Pedersen, but he had no idea where to start. He jotted himself a note to call Corner Ticket and get the Sox tickets he'd promised Lawrence. Right now Lawrence was his only hope of tracking her down.

Crossing his sparsely furnished living room, Charlie went to his computer, which stood on a drafting table he'd bought at a Scandinavian design center. Monte continued to shadow him and barked louder this time to get his attention. Charlie bent down and petted him gently on the head.

"I hear you, Monte. Just need to check one thing and we'll go for a long walk today. Sound good?"

As if Monte understood, he barked again, turned, and trotted off into the kitchen. Charlie heard him lapping at his water bowl. His computer powered on, Charlie inwardly breathed a sigh of relief that he could still access the SoluCent corporate network, through the secure VPN connection. Not that he had expected otherwise, just that with the Anne Pedersen situation escalating the way that it was, he could no longer take anything for granted. He opened Outlook and scanned his in-box. Charlie prided himself on never having taken a sick day in his more than two years at SoluCent—the Cal Ripken of software engineering, someone once had dubbed him. Charlie was about to break that streak with a quick e-mail to his boss, Mac.

Unfortunately, Mac had contacted him first. Even worse, it was his first day back from vacation. His message was characteristically short, but from the scathing tone it was evident that both Leon Yardley and Jerry Schmidt had given Mac earfuls.

Mac had meetings until 11:00 a.m. and expected Charlie to contact his assistant Jean for an appointment with him in the afternoon. Typical Mac, not a "manage by walking around" guy. You had to make an appointment if you wanted to see him. Seldom did anyone want to.

His promised long walk with Monte finished and shortened considerably, Charlie dressed in gray slacks, a blue oxford, and a gray sports jacket. He studied his sunken face in the mirror and decided against shaving. There was no reason to pretend this was just another day at the office.

"Be good, boy, okay?" Charlie said, hand-feeding Monte his favorite beef-flavored treat. "Brenda will be here in a few hours. I'll see if she can take you for another walk before I get home. Okay?"

Monte gulped down the treat in one bite and looked longingly up at Charlie.

Guilt washed through him. Monte was accustomed to spending his days with Charlie. This home-alone trend wasn't sitting well with him in the least, Charlie could tell.

"How about I give you a new shoe?" Charlie suggested.

At that Monte perked up. Charlie went into the bedroom closet and there fished out a brown shoe from a pair he had bought months ago but had never worn.

"Will this do?" Charlie asked, bending down to hold the shoe up to Monte's nose.

Monte let out a delighted little yip and trotted over to his bed, shoe in mouth. Sun pouring in from the living-room bay windows washed over his tiny body and warmed his fur. He seemed so at peace, and Charlie felt foolish for feeling jealous.

The traffic along Storrow Drive to Route 2 and eventually 128 was stop-and-go, reminding Charlie why he normally left for work before seven. On the radio, Dennis and Callahan prattled on about the up-coming Sox series in New York and the blessed arrival of the Patriots season. Every part of the commute offered signs of normalcy, includ-ing the SoluCent parking lot, with nearly every space taken by work-ers already well into their workday.

Climbing out of his BMW, Charlie spotted Harry Wessner coming down the stairs of the terraced parking lot. It looked as though he was coming from the Omni Way building, where Charlie and Anne Pedersen had supposedly had lunch just days before. Charlie had hoped to avoid the Magellan Team altogether, at least today, until after this mess could be sorted out. But Harry saw Charlie and waved hello, then quickened his pace to catch up with him. Harry's heavy frame was not built for bursts of speed, and he was breathless by the time he reached Charlie.

"Hi there," he said, still working to catch his breath.

"Hi, Harry," Charlie said.

They walked together in silence toward the front entrance. Harry seemed distracted, his gaze averted. Charlie could feel his awkward-ness and hated the uncomfortable tension. Harry was senior man-ager, quality assurance, for the InVision division within SoluCent, and his governance extended well beyond software, into manufac-turing production as well. It was unlikely that Harry's apprehension was due to the Albuquerque production problems that had been a hot button topic of late. Charlie figured the rumor mill about his flameout at the steering committee meeting had been running over-time for the better part of a day.

"I spoke with Arthur Bean," Harry said. "He decided not to even bother trying to change departments. He's leaving SoluCent. But he did want to thank you for putting him in touch with your financial advisor."

"That's good news," Charlie said.

The look in Harry's eyes suggested that Bean still harbored a good deal of resentment over his dismissal. Charlie caught something else in Harry's eyes, too, a look implying a link between his current crisis and karma.

"Also, I got a good report out of our Albuquerque production plant. The plant manager promises that defect counts are down and within projections. Assembly issues seem to be slowing down, too. I also made an impassioned plea on all our behalves to our silicone provider for them to rush that shipment, with which they complied."

Charlie nodded. "Great job, Harry. I'm glad you're on top of it."

Charlie tried to muster some of his characteristic passion for anyone who found solutions to complex problems, but it felt forced. Everything seemed unimportant and permanently tarnished. The idea of punishing Arthur Bean for ineptitude seemed almost comical now.

"I don't think you'll need to go on-site and personally bail out the plant manager anymore. Although I told him that you were planning a trip," Charlie said, with a slight sadness in his voice that he hadn't intended.

"Well . . . right . . . I . . ."

Harry paused, and the two stopped outside the glass double doors to the office building entrance.

"What is it, Harry?" Charlie asked.

"Nothing. Just . . . Is everything all right, Charlie? We heard things. About yesterday. Mac called us into a meeting."

Charlie's pulse quickened and his face flushed.

"What did Mac tell you?" Charlie couldn't hide a quivering undertone of rage. The situation was bad enough, but Magellan was Charlie's team. They were his leadership council, a select group he trusted with every aspect of the InVision business. Mac had no right interjecting anything into Charlie's organization without speaking directly to Charlie first. No matter how much trouble Charlie was in, Magellan was still his team to run.

"Well," Harry said, "he said there was a bit of a mix-up. Between you and Jerry Schmidt, and that he was going to speak with you about it today."

"That's true," Charlie said, feeling somewhat relieved. A mix-up was playing the situation down to the point of nonexistence.

"But he made it sound like we might be working for someone else."

Charlie's hands clenched into fists. He felt his muscles tightening and breathed deep to regain his composure. "He did? What made you think that?"

Harry looked down at his feet. Charlie appreciated his loyalty and chided himself for the times he'd treated Harry unfairly. It was more times than he cared to remember.

"He said you might not be well enough to lead the team. He made it sound like you might be really sick, Charlie. We're all pretty concerned—Nancy, Tom, all of us. What's going on? Is what Mac said true? Are you sick, Charlie?"

"I don't know, Harry," Charlie said after a moment's pause. "I guess I just don't know."

Charlie opened the door for Harry and was about to follow him inside when his BlackBerry whistled from within his jacket pocket. Charlie extracted the device and saw an urgent message from Mac. It was a simple line, but it sent a shiver down Charlie's spine.

CANCELED MY 10. COME TO MY OFFICE IMMEDIATELY.

Charlie read the line several times and wondered what had caused the change in plans. In Mac's previous message, he had said to schedule a meeting through his assistant for sometime after lunch.

"I need to go see Mac now," Charlie said to Harry. "Would you do me a favor and tell the others that I'm fine? We'll work this out. Okay?"

"Sure, Charlie. Whatever you need," Harry said.

Charlie turned and headed across the parking lot toward Mac's office, located in the same executive building as the Falcon conference room.

In some respects Mac's urgent request was a blessing. The last thing Charlie wanted was to be confronted by other Magellan team-mates. But it was odd that Mac would cancel a meeting to address the Jerry Schmidt debacle. That damage had already been done. A meeting hours earlier wasn't about to fix anything. To access the executive floor, Charlie needed to use his security badge. For the first time since becoming a SoluCent employee, he appreciated that access, as though it somehow assured him, for the moment at least, that he still had the life of a privileged corporate executive.

He exited the elevator on the fourth floor of the four-story building and turned right down a corridor that was home to most of the executive marketing team, including Jerry Schmidt. Thankfully, Jerry wasn't in his office when Charlie passed. He had enough on his plate without adding another confrontation with Jerry into the mix.

As in most companies SoluCent's size, the office buildings were under constant renovation and repair—new carpeting in the Jensen building, air-duct work outside Charlie's office. It had become so constant that maintenance costs were factored into the company's 10-Q SEC filings. It was not surprising, then, for Charlie to see much of the corridor leading to Mac's office draped in green painting drop cloths from the floor almost to the ceiling. The painter, working on his hands and knees, was dabbing his white-tipped paintbrush at a spot near the baseboard and did not look up as Charlie passed. Charlie followed the drop cloths right into Mac's office, where the same green cloths covered most of the walls.

"Love what you've done to the place," Charlie said as he crossed the threshold. He took a few steps forward and then went numb. Seated inside Mac's spacious corner office, around a conference table in the center of the room, were Rudy Gomes, the senior security officer; Leon Yardley; and Mac.

Charlie knew Gomes from a company user conference he'd attended in Phoenix a year back. An ex-rugby player, sizable but not outwardly intimidating, Gomes had a shock of red hair and a boyish face that often put his targets at ill-advised ease. He had his PI license and was essentially an investigator. He was tasked with rooting out internal corruption, such as expense-account violations, corporate spying, or the more benign but equally career-ending hobby of surfing the Web for adult content on company time.

Seeing Yardley and Mac together was bad enough. Having Gomes involved escalated the situation way outside Charlie's comfort zone. Each wore a grave expression.

"Take a seat, Charlie," Mac said.

Simon Mackenzie was a ruggedly handsome man in his early fifties. The worry lines etched in Mac's face had grown deeper since Charlie had seen him last; the gray in his hair more pronounced. Even seated, Mac's six-two frame seemed smaller, sunken by whatever burden he carried. Mac had been one of Charlie's strongest advocates since the acquisition. He believed in Charlie's business acumen and had said on several occasions that he was starting to put the full-court press on Yardley to get Charlie promoted to a more senior role at SoluCent. The success of InVision would play a major part in any future advancement decisions.

"What's this about, Mac? I thought we were meeting sometime after lunch," Charlie said.

"Sit down, son," Yardley said. As in the steering committee meeting, the softness of his voice suggested a father on the verge of sharing terrible news with a child.

Charlie took the only available seat at the round table. Mac reached underneath and pulled out a large manila folder, which he dropped on the table with a resounding thud.

"We have a serious situation, Charlie," Mac began.

"Mac, I know that. This whole Anne Pedersen thing is totally out of hand. I promise you, I am trying to figure out what's going on. I even contacted Lawrence in IT to see about a possible security breach." Charlie paused. "Was there a security breach?" he asked. "Is that why Rudy is here?" Charlie gestured to Rudy Gomes, who stayed stoic and unresponsive.

"Charlie, this is very awkward for me," Mac said. He was choosing his words carefully. "You've been a shining star at SoluCent, and we truly value your abilities and what you've brought to the company."

"Cut the bull, Mac, and tell me what's going on." Charlie's voice was quivering. He despised his own lack of self-control. Whatever pills Gomes was taking to keep so dispassionate, Charlie wanted some for himself.

Yardley took over.

"Your involvement in yesterday's executive meeting was most unprofessional," Yardley began. "I respect your passion, but not necessarily your methods."

"I understand. I was doing what I thought was right," said Charlie.

"Yes, well, after your judgment . . . shall we say . . . came into question," Yardley continued, "we felt it was in our best interest to evaluate you, Charlie. In the only way we could."

Charlie shook his head in disbelief. "You audited me?" He turned and faced Mac, who looked away.

Yardley went on. "We are a publicly traded company, Charlie, with strict guidelines and operating principles. We expect our employees to follow them, and our senior directors, like yourself, to abide by even higher standards."

"I don't care," Charlie muttered. "I have nothing to hide."

"According to this, you do," Gomes said at last, tapping his hand on the manila folder stuffed with papers.

"What's in there?" Charlie asked.

"We were hoping you could tell us that," Gomes said.

"The hell if I know. Stop toying with me and get to the point," replied Charlie.

"The point, Charlie," Mac said, "is that according to this Internet audit, you've been spending your time looking at things you shouldn't have been looking at."

"You even stayed late to surf porn, Charlie," Gomes said with a widening smirk. "What's wrong? Home ain't good enough for you? No time for girlfriends?"

"What are you talking about?" Charlie stammered. "Mac, you know me! You know I'm not into that crap. I just work."

"We double-checked the logs, Charlie," said Mac. "These http requests clearly originated from your computer. The time stamps match your badge usage and your network access time. We have e-mail records sent from your computer to adult sites."

"Mywhore.com, hotsex.com, bigjuggs.com—real classy stuff, Giles." Rudy Gomes was almost laughing.

It took everything Charlie had, including clutching the side of the table, to keep from leaping up and pummeling Gomes with his fists.

"That's insane! Are you kidding me? I never visited those sites!"

Charlie stood and paced about the room. His arms were raised in the air in defiance.

"Sit down, Charlie," Yardley said.

"No! No! I won't sit down. This is crazy!" Charlie exclaimed. "Did you check my PC for spyware? A rogue engine installed on my PC could auto-send http requests without my knowledge."

"We did, and it's as clean as a whistle," Gomes said. "But if porn were your only problem, Giles—"

"What? What are you insinuating?" Charlie sputtered.

"Sit down, Charlie," Yardley said again.

Charlie obliged, his hands still shaking with rage and fear.

"We checked your e-mail, Charlie," Mac began. "It was a precaution, given your erratic behavior of late. We saw some exchanges that we're not at all comfortable with."

Charlie could only look down at the floor. It was all spinning out of control too fast. Everything was going so terribly wrong.

"What are you talking about?" Charlie said.

"You e-mailed InVision product plans to a product development manager at Sony," Gomes said. "Unbelievable."

"I . . . didn't . . . I didn't do anything like that." Charlie's voice sounded weak and defeated, even to himself.

"Our lawyers contacted Sony. Best we could get was a promise that the e-mail was destroyed and that the document was not printed. We are not going to press them any harder," Mac added. "We really don't have a legal case to audit their records for proof."

"You're not going to be so lucky, Giles," Gomes said.

Charlie looked over at Yardley, his eyes making a plea for mercy.

"It doesn't look good, Charlie," Yardley said. "None of this looks good for you."

"Anne Pedersen, the PowerPoint file, your browsing habits—and now this Sony e-mail incident. What are we supposed to do, Charlie?" Mac asked.

Charlie walked to the wall and pounded his fist against the green painter's drop cloth until his knuckles turned red. "Are you guys setting me up?" Charlie turned around and shouted, his fingers pointing at Yardley and Mac. "Is that what this is all about? You don't want me to have a big payday for InVision, so you're setting me up to cut me out of what's mine! Is it a money thing with you, Leon?"

Rudy Gomes was on his feet in seconds, putting his body between Charlie and the others. Charlie took one step toward Yardley, and Gomes lunged, connecting with Charlie's sternum with a lowered shoulder, expelling all the air from Charlie's lungs in a violent burst. The force of the blow was enough to send Charlie crashing into the wall. Stunned, he slumped to the floor and tried to catch his breath.

"Security! Security!" Gomes called into his radio. "Situation urgent. Send two teams. I repeat, send two teams."

Charlie stood as Gomes was putting the radio back. He took a wild swing with a right hook, which Gomes easily dodged. Stepping behind Charlie with a quick feint to the left, Gomes grabbed his elbow and wrist and forced him to the floor. Gomes put his knees on Charlie's back, while continuing to hold on to his wrist. He kept applying pressure to keep him motionless on the floor.

"Mac! Mac! This is crazy. Why are you doing this to me? Why! Whatever you get from InVision is mine! To cut me out like this is stealing, Mac! Do you hear me? Stealing!" Charlie cried out in pain as Gomes pressed his knees deeper into Charlie's spine and gave a slight twist to his wrist.

"Shut your trap!" Gomes said.

Leon Yardley was out of his seat and standing in the corner farthest from Charlie.

"You're out, Charlie. We're letting you go, effective immediately," Mac said.

"Fuck you, Mac," Charlie spit.

"You're lucky it isn't worse, Charlie," Yardley said as the two security teams arrived, four stern-looking men in total. They weren't armed, but Charlie knew they had permits to carry Mace.

Gomes let Charlie up.

Charlie stood, shaky on his feet. The security teams surrounded him and began to escort him out of the office. Charlie swung around, the security teams now pushing him backward out the door.

"I'm not going to let this go, Mac. You, too, Leon," Charlie stormed. "I'm not going to quit. I'm going to figure out why you're setting me up. I'm going to figure it out! Do you hear me?"

Moments later Charlie was outside. A police cruiser was parked out front, lights flashing, presumably to escort Charlie out of Solu-Cent forever. The police officer and Gomes talked a moment.

The officer approached Charlie. They exchanged a few words. Charlie showed his ID, and after several embarrassing moments crowds began to gather. Eventually, the officer let Charlie go. Charlie felt the stares burning into his back as he walked away. He walked to his BMW and climbed inside. The police car stayed a good distance away. Gomes could have pressed assault charges if he wanted. *He still might,* Charlie thought.

The sun was low in the midmorning sky, making it difficult to see as Charlie drove out of the parking lot. Instead of grabbing for his sunglasses, which were in his bag in the backseat, he pulled down the sun visor. When he did, a shiver of fear shot through him. A yellow sticky note was taped to the inside flap. As with the other note, the one line was written in his handwriting. He had no memory of writing it, but there it was in black ballpoint pen. The sentence was a part of one of his favorites. It was from a Kurt Vonnegut novel, *Mother Night,* a book he'd discovered in college while putting off studying for a chemistry test.

It read: *We are what we pretend to be!*

Chapter 10

Joe had never missed a therapy session before, and Rachel was growing worried. She took another sip of coffee, filed some papers, and waited for the wall-mounted clock to read 8:15 a.m. before calling Joe's house again. Still no answer. If Joe was scheduled to work the overnight, his shift would have ended hours earlier, leaving him plenty of time to make their weekly one-on-one session. Rachel wondered if Charlie's stunning visit yesterday, his disturbing revelations, and Joe's unprecedented absence were connected. Her skin prickled at the thought.

If her meeting with Charlie had in any way derailed Joe's therapy, it would be an unforgivable breach of trust. Rachel understood the ethical boundary she had tiptoed across by helping Charlie out, yet at the time, she believed her actions to be harmless. Now Joe was a no-show, and her belief was fast giving way to fear.

Could Charlie have hurt Joe? Could she have unwittingly pushed Charlie over the edge?

The mystery of the mind meant that anything was possible—from the benign to the unfathomable. The more Rachel dwelled on it, the more she regretted ever meeting Charlie Giles.

At quarter to the hour Rachel gave up waiting for Joe and began readying herself for the scheduled staff meeting. Lately, it seemed as though meetings and administrative make-work were consuming more of her time than patient care. It was a disturbing trend that showed no signs of reversing. On her way to the conference room, Rachel spotted Dr. Alan Shapiro, one of several staff psychiatrists on the Walderman payroll, making his way to the same meeting.

Perhaps, Rachel thought, if Shapiro agreed she'd done nothing wrong, it would lessen her mounting anxiety. Shapiro was a bit irritating at times, with his know-it-all smirk and fondness for rubbing elbows with anybody on the Walderman board of directors, but she respected his abilities and opinions equally. All Rachel wanted was a simple affirmation—along the lines of "I would have done the same." Hopefully, that would be enough to set her mind at ease.

Rachel quickened her step to catch up with the slight-framed, short-legged psychiatrist, who favored obnoxious-colored ties and rainbow-hued shirts. After exchanging perfunctory hellos, Rachel kept pace alongside Shapiro as they made their way toward the conference room.

"Did you get the budget numbers straightened out?" Shapiro asked.

"Mostly. Well, close enough at least. Budgeting is part art, part pseudoscience, if you ask me."

Shapiro laughed warmly. Immediately, Rachel felt more comfortable and approached him about Charlie.

"Alan, can I ask you something?"

"Anything," Shapiro replied.

"If a relative of a patient of yours came to your office for psychiatric advice, would you give him any?"

"Treatment?" Shapiro said with noticeable concern.

"No, just information. Something you could get off the Web if you were researching a topic."

"Maybe. I don't know. You said this person is somehow connected to a patient I'm treating?"

Rachel felt a knot form in her stomach. "Yes. A relative."

"What's the motivation? Is it really research, or is it a personal inquiry?"

Rachel hesitated a beat. She wanted to lie and say it was for research, knowing Shapiro would take no exception to that.

"More personal."

Shapiro shook his head. "Slippery slope," he said. "I mean, you don't really know what they're after. What if they take whatever information you share as actual medical advice? Not saying it could happen, but suppose something were to happen—a car crash, whatever. A shady malpractice attorney might try to use a meeting in a professional setting without a professional relationship against you. These days I'm a big fan of caution."

Rachel nodded her head slowly. Her lingering doubt about inviting Charlie into her office had just mushroomed into full-blown anger at herself for allowing it to happen.

What was her motivation?

Did she find him attractive?

Perhaps, but that was not a conscious factor in her deciding to let the interview continue. More likely, curiosity had got the better of her. There was something about Charlie Giles she found irresistibly intriguing. According to Joe, Charlie was awash with confidence, but to Rachel, he appeared adrift, scared even.

There was no doubt in her mind that something chemical was happening to Charlie. She was convinced he was in mental distress, perhaps even suffering the onset of some sort of psychotic breakdown. Without thorough testing and a complete medical workup, forming an uneducated diagnosis was not only unprofessional, but it could be dangerous. All she did, she reassured herself, was to give him the names of some doctors to call, including a neurologist. That seemed a harmless outcome.

Or was it?

Shapiro now had her thinking about malpractice, which only made her concern over Joe's whereabouts all the more grave. Clearly Alan Shapiro would have taken a different approach when it came to Charlie's information gathering. If only Joe had shown up for his therapy session, she might not be so troubled.

Rachel waited outside the conference room and used her mobile to try Joe's home number again. She hung up after seven rings.

Where was he? she wondered.

Chapter 11

Wearing a scowl, Charlie walked into Chaps Sports Bar in Kenmore Square. The room was smoke-free, and Charlie, who wasn't much for frequenting bars—he worked most nights well past last call—wondered how much more time he'd be spending in them since losing his job.

He spotted Randal Egan slouched over the bar, clutching a half-drunk pint glass of Guinness stout. Randal and Charlie had been friends since high school. A soccer teammate who'd grown up in Waltham, Randal was the better of the two at staying in touch and regularly sent Charlie e-mail, even while buried in law books. After a few years in private practice, he'd ended up taking a job with the FBI in the Boston field office for less than half his pay, saying he felt a need to do something more tangible to help people. He'd been there ever since. "A lifer," he often joked. Charlie agreed—Randal was a lifer when it came to helping people.

Charlie had few people left to turn to. He had called Lawrence in IT from the car. As expected, Lawrence had reneged on Charlie's search request, passing up the Sox tickets in exchange for keeping his job. Charlie assumed that as word got out, more and more people would turn their backs on him. Randal wasn't like that.

Charlie approached the bar. He was still grappling with how he would explain to Randal what had happened to him without seeming totally insane. He felt he could trust Randal, but he wasn't sure what benefit a full disclosure would bring, other than release.

The bottom line was, he had to talk to somebody or he'd explode.

"Hey, stranger," Charlie said, placing a firm hand on Randal's broad shoulder.

"Giles! Giles! Holy shit. What's up, amigo!" Randal stood and gave Charlie a warm embrace. He called to the bartender, who was washing glasses at the other end of the bar. "A Guinness for my friend here, when you have a minute," he said.

"And a shot of Jack," Charlie added

"Whoa. Okay. I got it, fella. And a shot of Jack," Randal called out.

The bartender grunted and began pouring the Guinness from the tap. He reached for the Jack on the top shelf.

"Thanks for coming to meet me," Charlie said. "Sorry I'm a bit late. Parking in Kenmore isn't easy."

"Tell me about it," Randal said. "I'm way down Beacon."

"You look great, man. How have you been? It's been a while."

"Yeah. It's been a while. Too long," Randal said, poking Charlie's shoulder with his finger. "Everything is good with me. Jenny and the kids are fine. But it's you I'm worried about. Midafternoon cocktails aren't exactly your MO, if you know what I mean."

Charlie nodded. "I just needed to talk to somebody, Randal. I didn't know where else to turn."

The boy who'd played varsity striker three years at Waltham and fullback for BC was still present in Randal's dark Italian eyes and smooth olive complexion. The familiarity comforted Charlie, especially in a world where nothing seemed familiar anymore. The bartender dropped two shots in front of Randal and went to finish the Guinness pour.

"Talk," said Randal, pushing a shot toward Charlie, who picked up the fingerprint-stained tumbler and downed it with a single gulp. Without being prompted, Randal ordered another.

"I've been fired," Charlie said.

"What? What for?"

"Let's see . . . surfing porn and corporate espionage," Charlie said.

"Oh, is that all?" Randal laughed as though that were the punch line.

Charlie didn't flinch.

"No, really. What for?" Randal asked.

"I told you," Charlie said.

Two more shots came along with the Guinness round Randal had ordered. This time Randal downed one before Charlie even lifted his off the bar.

"Are you serious?"

Charlie nodded.

"What were you thinking?" Randal asked.

"I'm thinking I don't remember any of it. I'm thinking that fucked-up things are happening to me."

"Like what?" Randal asked.

Charlie told him about the e-mail exchange and subsequent meeting with Anne Pedersen. Then about the PowerPoint presentation that supposedly Jerry Schmidt had authored but that somehow it had his name and not Jerry's in the document's "created by" property, and how Anne Pedersen apparently didn't even work at Solu-Cent to begin with. He confided about the strange cryptic notes he'd been leaving himself, about his meeting with Dr. Rachel Evans at Wal-derman, and lastly about the morning's confrontation in Mac's office.

"I'm screwed," Charlie said. "Totally screwed."

Randal let out a sigh. "Your family history isn't good, Giles. Tell me again what that doctor said."

"She's not an M.D., but she's an expert on mental health, especially schizophrenia," Charlie said. He couldn't believe the words coming out of his mouth. How could he, an MIT graduate, a successful entrepreneur, be schizophrenic? It wasn't fathomable. And yet there was his family history to account for. A father and brother both afflicted with the illness. It was an inescapable truth.

Randal took a healthy sip of his beer and thought a moment.

"At the Bureau I have my fair share of cases involving that disease, Charlie," he began. "I have to say, I'm no expert, but you're a bit late in life to be developing symptoms. Mostly it happens in teenagers and young adults."

Charlie nodded. "I know. That's what Rachel said as well. She suggested I have an MRI. Maybe there's some sort of lesion, a tumor, or something on my brain. It could cause similar symptoms. It's a theory, at least."

"Any other theories?" Randal asked.

"Sure. Somebody is out to get me," Charlie said.

"Makes sense," Randal said.

"It would if paranoia wasn't a symptom of schizophrenia," Charlie said.

"Do you think somebody is setting you up?"

"Of course," Charlie said, almost letting out a smile. "That's why I'm crazy."

"Seriously?" Randal asked. His expression was both grave and concerned.

"I don't know, Randal," Charlie said. "I wish it was that. I really do. A few days ago I would have said yes, but now I'm not sure. Nothing is adding up. Mac and Leon deny they had anything to do with it. Not that they'd just go and confess. And I don't know anybody else who would have such a vendetta. And how does it explain everything—Anne Pedersen, the PowerPoint, the e-mail, the notes? It's too much for even me to believe somebody could pull that off."

"I don't know," was all Randal could think of to say.

"Believe it or not, the espionage is what's really getting me. I mean, it's all so unbelievable and out of character for me. You know how strongly I feel about protecting company secrets. You know what I had to do when that trust was broken before."

"Have you forgiven yourself for that?" Randal asked. "Do you think it's catching up with you? Maybe this has all been triggered by some suppressed guilt."

"It wasn't my fault," Charlie said. "He made his choices. I didn't make them for him." Charlie looked away. He had enough on his plate without reliving that nightmare.

"So where does this leave you?" Randal asked. He nursed the few remaining sips of his beer.

"Nowhere, I guess," Charlie said. "Unemployed. Unemployable. Crazy."

"Charlie, you know I'm here for you," Randal said. "Are you telling me everything? I mean, are you in any legal trouble?"

"Not yet. But Mac and Yardley have a case against me for the e-mail to Sony. They may come after me. But they said they wouldn't. Like I said, I don't know who to trust anymore." Charlie picked up his Guinness and downed most of it in one long gulp. His hands shook, while his throat closed and his eyes moistened. He hadn't felt that empty pit feeling since he was a kid, but it was a precursor to tears. Charlie looked away, staring out the window.

"Brother, you know I'm here for you. Honest," Randal said after a moment's silence. He extended a hand to Charlie, who took it, gave him a firm shake. It was the best he'd felt in days.

Maybe all he needed from Randal was an affirmation of their friendship. For the first time in as long a time as he could remember, Charlie needed to feel close to somebody. He needed someone he could trust.

"I'll call when I get the MRI results. Okay?"

"I'm expecting to hear from you sooner."

"Thanks, Randal. I really appreciate it."

"It's the least I could do. Have you talked to Joe or your mother about any of this? I'd think if anyone would know something about what might be happening to you, it would be them."

Charlie shook his head. "I can't talk to Joe, and I wouldn't want to worry Mom," he said. "You know that. You know the history."

"Yeah. Just a suggestion. Family is always there for you, even when you don't think they'd be much of a support."

"I'll keep that in mind."

Charlie and Randal stayed in the bar for an hour before Randal looked down at his watch.

"Gotta run, pal," Randal explained. "I'm dangerously close to a night of warm beer and a cold shoulder."

Charlie thanked his friend, and the two exchanged a quick hug good-bye. One of the best traits about Monte was that he wouldn't care when Charlie got home, just that he did. Besides his furry little friend, the only thing waiting for Charlie back home had a thin neck, six strings, and spoke only when his fingers did the talking. At that moment a warm body would have felt a lot better than another drink. He thought about Gwen. That she came to mind, given that they hadn't spoken since he left California, was more than a little surprising. Briefly, Charlie flirted with the idea of calling her but resisted the impulse. Gwen's number in his BlackBerry might have changed, and he wasn't in the mood to explain the real reason behind the call if it hadn't.

Charlie opted to stay in the bar. He'd parked in a garage. He already had too much of a buzz to drive home. He'd rather pay Brenda double her standard rate to take Monte for an evening walk than go home to his empty apartment. He pulled out his cell phone to call his dog walker—making another resolve that he wouldn't break down and dial Gwen, anyway.

He noticed that he had missed a call and saw that he had a voice mail waiting for him. The number from the missed caller came up as restricted. Charlie dialed his voice mail and then entered his code. The message was marked urgent, and voice mail said it had arrived this morning. Charlie didn't know how he'd missed the call. His blood turned icy cold when the caller's message played.

"Charlie, it's me, Joe," his brother said, speaking with quick, breathless urgency. "You have to come to Mount Auburn soon as you get this. Mom's had a stroke, and I don't know how long she can hold on."

Chapter 12

Joe Giles sat by his mother's bedside. His eyes were fixed to the floor; his chin was resting on the knuckles of his hands. To the nurse standing behind him, he appeared merely deep in thought, but his insides were roiling from the private war he waged. Though Joe could not see his enemy, he could readily sense its dark presence. His adversary was as merciless as it was shapeless, relentless as it was cunning. Blessedly, years of treatment had made it possible to detect his foe's advancement. Early detection—that was the preferred weapon Joe had learned to wield; it was the key to defeating this scourge before it could consume him.

Inside his mother's equipment-jammed hospital room, Joe felt the enemy creeping steadily forward, searching for holes in his defenses to exploit. Stress and fear were fuel for this adversary. With his mother comatose, both emotions were in ready supply. If he was less vigilant, cracks in his barricade would widen, allowing the enemy to push deeper within. He had to stay mindful of its presence. For his mother's sake, he had to stay sane.

Joe looked to fortify his defenses with a sound—some specific noise in the room that he could focus on. It would help, he knew, to ground him in the reality of his mother's condition, painful as that reality was to face. In the early years after the onset of his disorder, Joe's hallucinations were a constant threat. To combat them required not only increasingly high doses of antipsychotic drugs but also constant engagement and stimulation. An idle mind was an invitation for his adversary to enter his house and tear apart reality with the thoroughness of a demolition team. Thanks to Walderman, Joe was learning new ways to stay episode free. Right now he needed every trick in the book.

It took a moment for Joe to lock onto a useful sound, but it was there, a soft, rhythmic rise and fall of a machine breathing steadily in the stillness of the room like a sleeping animal. The ventilator that kept his mother alive could help keep Joe present with her as well. He concentrated on each mechanical breath as though it were his own.

The nurse tending to his mother's needs touched Joe's broad, muscled shoulders with a practiced tenderness. Her touch surprised Joe, and for a moment he let his concentration wane. Joe clenched his eyes tighter, demanding more of himself in the process.

Focus!

Focus! he commanded himself again.

It was too late. Soon as he unclenched his eyes, he saw that his mother had miraculously shifted position. It was a startling sight, because he knew it was an impossible one as well. She had turned her head and was now facing him. Her eyes, shuttered before, were open wide and golden yellow, like those of a wolf. He could smell her, too, a sharp and pungent odor, as though she had been bathed in some medicinal antiseptic. The stench filled his nostrils and made him gag. The noise of her ventilator rose, too, in a crescendo so deafening Joe had to cover his ears.

His mother's mouth, framed by thin lips that were cracked and raw, somehow had been freed from the repressive oxygen mask. As she began to speak, all color in the room faded to shades of gray, except for her eyes, which stayed that disturbing yellow.

"Help me," his mother wheezed in a breathy whisper. "Pleeaassse, Joe. Help me."

His mother's bony, veined hand reached out from her hospital bed and touched Joe on the leg. He leapt to his feet, startling the nurse standing behind him, who in turn cried out in fright. With a shake of his head, Joe made a furtive glance about the room, relieved but also saddened to see his mother's gaze as it had been before, fixed to the ceiling, her eyes again closed, the oxygen mask back in place.

It was a dream perhaps, he thought. Maybe he had fallen asleep and had a dream, nothing more. But it could be more. It could be the enemy, the schizophrenia that had plagued his adult years creeping up on him, craftily beating back the drugs, which formed only part of his defenses.

Schizophrenia.

Joe settled himself back onto the vinyl-covered armchair. His breathing grew shallower and more rapid. The nurse came around to face him. She kneeled low, perhaps to make her presence less threatening.

"Are you okay?" she asked.

She touched him on his knee, and this time Joe did not flinch. He nodded that he was fine, but did not feel ready to speak.

"You gave me quite a fright," the nurse said.

Joe knew better than to ask if she had seen his mother open her eyes or heard her speak to him. Whether it was a dream or a waking nightmare, the moment was his alone to experience. If it was the schizophrenia baring its teeth, Joe reminded himself that it was simply a chemical reaction in his brain, something to do with too much dopamine in the nerve cell synapses and D2 receptors, or so he'd been told.

Despite the nurse's continued attempts to reassure him, Joe still felt ill at ease. He wasn't sure if he had been dreaming or not, and decided the experience might make for an interesting post on his blog, the aptly titled Divided Mind, taken from the Greek roots of *schizophrenia.* Comparing dreams to a schizophrenic episode would get his readers chatting, Joe suspected.

Over the years Joe's blog had garnered a loyal readership, and its popularity had been growing steadily among mental health patients and professionals alike. There was a powerful sense of community that Joe had unwittingly tapped into with his entertaining, often self-deprecating prose. Heartrending comments from readers claiming their lives had been changed in positive ways because of Joe's informal community motivated him to keep updating the blog regularly. It was as healing for Joe to write and interact with his virtual friends as it was for them to read and interact with each other. He felt he needed them now more than ever.

"When will she wake up?" Joe asked the nurse.

"I don't know," the nurse replied. "You must be tired."

"A little. I'm more afraid of what will happen to Mom."

"Of course you are. I understand."

No, you don't understand, Joe wanted to say. *I need her more than you can imagine.* Instead, he kept silent.

"Would you like me to get you a drink of water?"

"That would be nice," Joe said.

After she left the room, Joe reached out to take hold of his mother's limp hand. Intellectually, he knew her hand was cold and clammy to the touch, but at that moment it felt as warm as an August sun.

Chapter 13

The automatic doors to the main lobby of Mount Auburn Hospital opened the moment Charlie stepped in front of the sensor.

Inside, he took one short breath of the antiseptic hospital smell and shuddered. He found it strange that a smell, so innocuous at that, could trigger such powerful memories. But hard as he tried, those times were not easily forgotten. When he was a boy, just turned seven, his father had driven the family station wagon through the storefront window of a popular boutique clothing store in downtown Belmont. Charlie didn't know it at the time, but the explanation he gave to the arresting officer was that the mannequins were looking at him funny. From that moment on hospitals became Charlie's second home—a blur of lockdown floors in the mental health ward, inpatient treatment centers, and emergency rooms. He'd first visited his father, then soon after his brother, too. He'd spent so many hours breathing in the ammonium vapors of hospital antiseptic that the smell alone was like a return trip into a nightmare.

Awash in the sickly glow of the overhead fluorescents, Charlie walked down the long corridors to the elevators that would take him to Ellison 5, the hospital's critical care floor.

Inside the crowded elevator, Charlie waited with the others. He positioned himself in a spot toward the back right corner. He found the cramped quarters of an elevator bad enough under normal circumstances, but in a hospital, jammed together with the sick, it was almost unbearably claustrophobic. Doctors and nurses were mixed in with patients and visitors. Charlie wondered if any of them were tending to his mother.

The reality of her stroke was just beginning to set in. He wanted to ask a doctor standing beside him how a woman in such excellent health could have suffered a stroke, but he refrained. He didn't know exactly what caused a stroke. What he did know was that his mother was the least likely candidate for one. Her refrigerator was a *Prevention* magazine poster child for wholesomeness. If food at the grocery store was stocked on a shelf even near a trans fat, she'd think twice before buying it. She walked five miles a day, in part because walking was less stressful on the joints than running. She, like Charlie, shared a constitution that most Americans would buy on eBay for a good part of their 401(k) if they could.

The years hadn't been easy for his mother. As the elevator ascended, he took some comfort in that fact. If anything, she was stronger than most women half her age. She would pull through this just fine, he assured himself. After all, she had survived a philandering, mentally ill husband who'd snuck out of the house with only a note good-bye, then single-handedly raised both her sons to be independent and self-reliant. That was, at least, until Joe got sick. If anything, the years spent caring for Joe had made her stronger, not weaker.

The doors opened on seven, and Charlie exited alone. Two large glass doors secured access to the ICU. Through the glass Charlie could see inside. The floor was bright blue linoleum. Nurses and doctors raced about, but none took notice of him. Charlie buzzed the intercom outside and waited.

A few seconds later a nurse answered. "Can I help you?"

"Alison Giles?" he asked.

"She's here," the nurse said. "Are you family?"

"I'm her son," he said.

There was a brief pause and then a buzz. Charlie opened the door and stepped inside. The lights in the ICU were less diffused than in any other part of the hospital. In the center of the floor was the nurses' station. It was a large open space cluttered with monitors and an array of computers, separated from the main floor by a wide hexagonal counter. Charlie couldn't help but take notice of the ICU's technical sophistication. From that observation alone, he was certain his mother was in the best possible hands.

Along the perimeter wall were the patient rooms. They were spacious cubicles with sliding glass doors for privacy, a dozen or so. He was prepared to check them all when a nurse approached him.

"Who are you looking for?" she asked.

"Alison Giles," Charlie said. "Someone buzzed me in and—"

She held up her hand to stop him. She pointed to a corner room. "She's in seven-oh-six A." She turned and left without another word.

Charlie quickened his pace as he drew closer. Through the glass doors of 706A he could see that his brother, Joe, was inside. Joe was seated by his mother's bedside.

It wasn't until he stepped into the room and saw his mother for the first time that the gravity of the situation became real. A large mask covered her mouth. He assumed it was delivering oxygen. His mother's normally porcelain skin was ashen and sagging. There was a red mark on her cheek. Had she fallen when she had her stroke?

Her eyes were closed and surrounded by dark, haunting circles. It was difficult to reconcile the woman lying on the bed with the vivacious and spirited woman he knew. But it was her. She was still his mother.

The mark on her cheek was the only indication that she was gravely ill. Her gray hair, which she refused to dye, was tousled. Charlie's first instinct was to straighten it out. The appearance of control and put-togetherness would be something she would want for herself, no matter her condition. She always kept the house immaculate, her clothes perfectly wrinkle free. She never let anyone know how hard life had become for her. Not in words or in appearance. It was her way, Charlie assumed, of confronting and controlling circumstances that were beyond her control.

He walked around the bed and stood on the other side, facing his brother. He used his hand to straighten his mother's hair. There was no television set in her room. Only monitors, IV drips, and several machines that dispensed medicine.

"Joe, what's going on?" Charlie asked.

Joe didn't bother to look up. He hadn't acknowledged that Charlie had even entered the room. Joe kept his gaze fixed to the floor while he held his mother's hand. He kept muttering, "I'm holding Mom's hand. I'm stroking her hand. I'm holding her hand. Now I'm stroking it."

"Joe, what is going on?" Charlie asked again. He could hear the patience in his voice fast fading.

At last Joe looked up at Charlie. Joe's eyes were red from crying, his plump cheeks streaked and splotched. He was dressed in a short-sleeved white button-down shirt that was sprinkled with food stains. He barely fit into the small green vinyl armchair by the side of the bed. With his free hand he ran his fingers through his bushy, curly hair, brushing it away from his reddened eyes. Then he wiped at his running nose with the back of his hand.

"Joe!" Charlie shouted. "What's going on with Mom? What have the doctors told you?"

His brother stopped muttering and let go of their mother's hand. He gave Charlie a doleful, bewildered stare.

"What is going on with Mom?" Charlie asked again. He made no effort to hide his irritation. "Where is the doctor?"

"Hi to you, too," Joe said. "And no, I'm not having a good day. Thanks for asking." Joe went back to holding his mother's hand and talking to himself.

Charlie took a deep breath. This was familiar. *You know how to handle this. It's the stress, that's all.* There were plenty of nurses around for Charlie to speak with. He could easily leave to find somebody capable of giving him the answers, but he felt obligated to hear the news from family first.

"Joe, I'm sorry," Charlie said, softening his tone. "I know this is difficult for you. It's hard for me, too. But I'm in the dark here. Please. Tell me what's going on with Mom."

Joe looked up at his brother. His expression changed, as though Charlie's arrival was a blessing and source of strength.

"Mom's not lost to us, Charlie," Joe said. "She suffered a massive stroke. She can't talk. She can't move. The doctors don't know when or if she'll come to. I've just been sitting here holding her hand. It was awful. I came downstairs for breakfast, and she was passed out on the kitchen floor." Joe breathed in deeply, trying his best to hold his composure. He took a few shorter breaths, but there was no way he could stifle his tears. "I didn't know what to do," Joe blurted out between sobs. "I called nine-one-one, and then I called you."

"It's going to be all right, Joe," Charlie said. "Mom's going to pull through this fine."

"And what if she's not fine?" Joe shouted as he stood up. His fierceness made Charlie extremely uncomfortable. At six foot four, 245 pounds, Joe could destroy the room in seconds if he went into a rage.

"I know you need her, Joe. I know that this is very hard for you," Charlie said.

"You don't know that!" Joe cried. "You don't know anything! I can't make it without her, Charlie. I'll die without her! I don't know what I'll do. She's all I have."

Charlie stepped around behind Joe. He rested both hands on his brother's massive shoulders. Everything Charlie did next was pure instinct. First was getting Joe to sit down; then it was having him focus on a sound—a machine beeping in the room. After a few minutes Joe started to calm down.

It was all ingrained in Charlie from years of living with him. He never forgot the lessons his mother had reinforced. *Help him to find a reality he can relate to. Remind him of his routines. Help him get grounded again.*

"Listen, Joe. Mom's going to pull through, and you're going to help her. And when she comes through, everything will return to the way it was. What was she doing for you before all this happened? You said she was making you breakfast? What were you going to have?"

"Eggs and bacon," Joe said, taking deep breaths.

It was working, Charlie thought.

Joe began to regain his composure. "Mom always makes me eggs and bacon on Tuesday."

Charlie shook his head as if he'd been slapped. *Tuesday? It can't be.* He braced himself against the back of the armchair. Given everything that had already happened today, Charlie wasn't certain he'd be able to remain calm. He had to remember that this wasn't entirely Joe's fault. His brother had a disease.

"Joe," Charlie said, doing his best to disguise his rising anger, "you said Mom had a stroke after breakfast. That you came down, saw her on the floor, and then you called nine-one-one."

"Yeah."

"And then you said that Mom makes you eggs and bacon on Tuesday. Right? Tuesday. But it's not Tuesday today, Joe. Today is Thursday."

"Yeah. That's right. It's Thursday. I was supposed to meet with Rachel this morning. I knew that. But I was here with Mom instead."

"But I talked to you on Tuesday, Joe. You didn't say anything about Mom."

Charlie felt a chill rip through him as his chest began tightening. He recalled with clarity his last phone conversation with Joe, hours before he met Rachel Evans at Walderman. At the end of their conversation Joe had asked, "Are you going to come visit Mom?" At the time Charlie had assumed Joe meant a visit to the Waltham house. Now he feared he understood the real significance of Joe's question. Charlie could only pray his suspicions weren't true.

"Joe, listen to me carefully," Charlie continued. "I need to understand something."

"Okay."

"Did Mom make you eggs and bacon today, Joe? Please, please tell me that she did."

"No," Joe said.

Charlie's knuckles whitened as he clenched the back of the armchair. "Joe, please tell me, how long has Mom been in the hospital?"

"Two days now," Joe said without emotion. Then Joe took his mother's hand back in his.

"Why didn't you call me!" Charlie said.

"I did call, Charlie. I'm not sure exactly when, but I think I called you right away. We talked a while about it. But when you didn't show up for a few days, I called you again and left you a message. I'm glad you're here, Charlie. Mom is, too. I can tell."

Had Joe called him? Charlie asked himself. Given that he had no memory of writing those notes to himself, was it possible he had forgot Joe's call as well? Possible, but unlikely, he decided.

Charlie closed his eyes to block out all distraction. He kept pushing deeper into the recesses of his mind, searching for any memory of that call. None came. Losing focus, defeated, Charlie listened to his brother as he comforted their mother, softly muttering, "I'm holding Mom's hand. I'm stroking her hand. I'm holding her hand. Now I'm stroking it."

Chapter 14

There was constant foot traffic in and out of Alison Giles's hospital cubicle. Until now Charlie had seen only one shift change, but that was enough proof for him—his brother, Joe, was on a first-name basis with every nurse on the floor. Without fail, every time a nurse came in to check on Alison's condition, they would first go over to Joe. With sympathy in their eyes, they would ask how he was holding up and if he needed anything. He'd always say fine and no, but Charlie could see the delight in Joe's face when they asked.

Charlie wished that a nurse were in the room with them now. It was also clear to him that the doctor in with them now wasn't going to be able to talk any sense into Joe.

"You've been here two days already and home only once," Charlie said. "You need some rest, too, you know." He took off his glasses and rubbed at his eyes.

"I'm not going anywhere if she might wake up," Joe said. "Is she going to wake up?"

Charlie sighed. He looked to the doctor, who offered only a slight shrug. It was as if he were saying, "He's your brother. You deal with it."

"Joe, nobody knows for sure. You've been told that a hundred times," Charlie said. "You can't go on living in the waiting room until she does. You need to get some real rest."

"And someone needs to be here for Mom when she wakes up," Joe said.

Charlie turned back to the doctor. "Tell him again," he said. "Is she going to wake up tonight?"

Dr. Stan Abrahams looked down at his pager while he spoke. His long, slender fingers worked his keypad as he typed his message. This was Joe's third go-around with the same exact questions. By the impatient look on Abrahams's face, Charlie suspected the doctor wouldn't be sticking around for a fourth.

"It's unlikely that she will wake," Abrahams said. "As I've said, your mother experienced something called hypertensive encephalopathy with brain swelling and, as a consequence, suffered multiple is-chemic strokes. I'm sorry to say that she is in a near-vegetative state."

The rhythmic drone of Alison Giles's ventilator seemed suddenly louder to Charlie. Maybe it did to Joe as well, because he looked over at her ventilator, too. Several bags of IV fluids circled her bed, and tubes seemed to flow from her in every direction. Charlie touched his mother's arm. Then he reached across her lap and took her thin, frail hand in his. Her skin felt cold, clammy to the touch—perhaps without the constant rhythm of the ventilator he might even think lifeless. How many times had she bandaged his skinned knee or cheered for him from the sidelines of his soccer games? All the grati-tude, love, and admiration he felt for her at that moment was soured by the specter of regret that she might never hear him say "I love you" again.

"Is there anything we can do to help her?" Charlie asked.

"Just being with her. Talk to her, though research on that is incon-clusive. The good news is we didn't see any other life-threatening processes, such as a hematoma or abscess," said Abrahams. "Though she had extensive hemorrhaging, which isn't common in patients with kidney failure, and which we believe contributed to her hyper-tensive encephalopathy. We're treating that with platelets and vita-min K IV drips. It seems to be helping to stop the bleeding and protect other organs from failing. We are looking into what's causing the hemorrhaging, but I do have to remind you, we believe chances for her recovery are very slim. She may partially come out of the coma, but she will be severely injured. Do you understand?"

Abrahams seemed cold and detached. Normally Charlie would be able to relate to his demeanor. He often acted the same way at work—a pragmatist, his workplace mantra was to hold back your tears and piss them out later. But this was his mother, and Abra-hams's icy professionalism, though tactical, was borderline offensive.

"How did it happen? Is she going to be paralyzed?" Joe asked.

Abrahams looked back down at his pager and took in a deep breath.

"You need to be patient with my brother, Doctor," Charlie explained, his voice firm, but calm. "He's under a great deal of stress, as am I. But Joe handles stress differently than you and I. So I appreciate your explaining things to him again, even though you feel they've already been explained."

He watched as Abrahams hesitated for a second. Charlie was glad to see him put his pager away. This time Abrahams kept eye contact with Joe while he spoke. Charlie could see that it helped Joe to relax.

"We're not sure exactly what caused the stroke. My first suspicion, and I told you this earlier, was confirmed by lab tests. It was her high blood pressure."

Charlie snapped his head toward the doctor. "What did you say?" he asked.

"I said we're suspicious that her high blood pressure might be a factor."

"I heard you, but that's impossible," said Charlie.

"I'm sorry, Mr. Giles. One of the first things we did when your mother was brought to the ICU was to perform an ophthalmoscopy, an examination of the blood vessels in the eyes. They showed clear signs of hypertension. That is a leading cause of stroke and would explain her kidney failure."

"I don't care what you did. Have you contacted her primary care physician?" Charlie asked.

Abrahams nodded. "We have left messages. Apparently she's on vacation."

"Great. That's just great. Well, listen, Doctor," Charlie said, staring Abrahams down, "if you do talk to her, then you'll know my mother doesn't have high blood pressure."

"The evidence seems to be contrary," Abrahams said.

"What about waking up?" Joe asked. "When will she wake up?"

"We're still running tests," said Abrahams. "We can't predict when a patient will come out of a coma or if. Okay? The best thing you can do is get some rest. We promise she's in the best possible care, and that you'll be notified immediately if her condition changes." Abrahams turned to leave.

"What about operating?" Joe yelled to his back.

Abrahams turned. "Surgery isn't really an option," he said. "I believe I told you that already. Several times. Listen, I have other patients I have to attend to. The nurses are here. I promise they're taking excellent care of your mother." Abrahams glanced over at the nurses' station. "I'll be back to see her in the morning. Dr. Saunders is working the overnight. I'm sure she'll be happy to answer any other questions you have."

Then he was gone. A few seconds later a young nurse came into the room. Joe recognized her, and he said a warm hello. Charlie figured she had overheard the conversation and could see that Joe was upset. Without hesitating, she put her arm around Joe's shoulders, having to stand on her tiptoes to reach. She patted him on his back.

"If they could operate, they would," she said.

Charlie blessed her arrival. He had been keeping Joe calm for the last several hours and was beginning to run out of steam. He looked at the white board hanging beside his mother's bed. If she was the on-duty nurse, then her name was June. *Saint June is more like it,* Charlie thought.

"What if she's paralyzed? I hear strokes can make you paralyzed," Joe said.

June guided Joe into the small green vinyl armchair by the side of the hospital bed. "Dr. Abrahams said only time will tell. So that's what we're going to do. We're going to wait. And I'll wait with you. How does that sound?"

"Thanks. You're really kind," Joe said. "Do you want to get married?"

June didn't skip a beat and played along, laughing. Charlie didn't even break a smile. To him Joe's impromptu proposal was like nails on a chalkboard. Vintage Joe—out of the blue and socially bizarre.

"I already am, sweetie," she said. "You're just a few years too late for me."

"Well, just so you know, I'd marry you. And then if we had a son, you know what we'd have?" Joe smiled his signature Cheshire smile.

"What?" June said, grinning in return.

"June's son and Joe's son. Get it. Johnson and Johnson, just like the baby shampoo," Joe said.

Charlie grimaced, but June laughed.

"I get it. Like the baby shampoo. That's funny, Joe. Really funny," June said.

"Do you think they can operate?" Joe asked.

"I don't know, Joe. Only time will tell. Remember?" June replied.

"Yeah, I remember," Joe said, taking hold of his mother's still hand.

Charlie decided that if Joe was going to stay the night, he wasn't going to do it in his white, food-stained shirt. It was just a few minutes past midnight. He had already arranged for Brenda to take Monte home with her. Given the circumstances, there hadn't been a moment's hesitation on her part. Another saint in a long line of saints he suspected he'd be needing.

He decided to take a cab to Waltham to pick up some clothes. Joe would never agree to wear any of Charlie's clothes. It had to be his own stuff, or he'd rather go naked. That was part of the disease. Then he'd come back and crash at his own apartment, which was only a ten-minute walk from the hospital. He wanted to stay close. There was something else he wanted, too. He caught up with June, who was filling out a chart at the nurses' station.

"Is there any way I could get some flowers for my mother's room?" Charlie asked. "She loves sunflowers the most."

"Florist is closed now," June said. "But I do have some flowers at my desk. I can put them in her room for you if you like. You can get new ones in the morning."

Charlie nodded in appreciation. She reached for him and touched his hand. The moment she did, a lump formed in his throat. The adrenaline of the crisis had long worn off, leaving in its wake the raw emotions of fear, regret, and hope.

"Thank you," was all he could manage to say.

Bleary-eyed and wobbly, Charlie stepped out into the cool night air for the first time since arriving at the hospital that afternoon. He slumped across Beacon Street and began searching the deserted road for a cab. The third one to pass saw him and stopped. Charlie slept for a minute or two en route but kept waking as the cab jostled him from side to side. Normally he'd pass the time fretting over work, firing off e-mails from his BlackBerry, but that had all been taken away.

In his gut, Charlie believed he would come out of this on top. He trusted his instincts. That perseverance was a trait for which he could thank his mother. Running from adversity would be his father's genetics, he supposed.

Arriving at Cleveland Street in Waltham, Charlie stood outside the two-family home where he grew up. He paused before climbing the paint-chipped wooden stairs to the front landing. There were memories of this home he longed to forget. He went in through the back door, entering into the kitchen, using the key his mother hid under the flowerpot.

The house, as always, was impeccably clean. For Charlie, it was like stepping back in time. Nothing had changed since he had lived there. Same yellowish linoleum floor, same brown electric stove, same flimsy round kitchen table. But the chairs weren't pushed under the table as he would have expected. And a cupboard had been left open. There were still dirty dishes in the sink. Charlie reconstructed the moment his mother had collapsed by examining the mementos left behind.

Leaving the kitchen, he took the narrow staircase to the upstairs floor. The stairwell still had the same claustrophobic feel he remembered from his childhood. The drop ceilings on the second floor were so low, he had to stoop a bit when he walked. The place always made him feel the same—anxious to leave.

Charlie went into the guest room first. It had been his room before he moved. He remembered his mother saying something about it being converted into Joe's practice studio since he had started playing the drums. Charlie knew Joe enjoyed listening to music, but had never thought he had the inclination or interest to actually play it. His mother had explained that playing an instrument helped him to stay focused, improved concentration and communication. It was suggested therapy, a part of the new treatment program Joe was involved with at Walderman Hospital. The program headed up by Dr. Rachel Evans.

Charlie figured Joe's choice to play drums had something to do with his brother's borderline obsession with the rock band Rush and their undeniably talented drummer, Neil Peart. He was somewhat impressed to see that it was a real kit, not some cheap knockoff set. Charlie ran his hand across the smooth pearl white base drum and banged his knuckles against one of the three Zildjian cymbals. The kit itself rested on a nappy carpet that Charlie thought used to be in the basement. Flakes of paint from the peeling walls littered the floor, probably shaken off the walls by a vicious snare snap.

He wondered what sort of player Joe was—if his skill was commensurate with the quality kit he owned. Charlie had begun playing music when he was seven years old, after his mother bought him a guitar for a Christmas present. That winter their father had been well into his losing battle with reality, though Charlie hadn't known it at the time. His mother later admitted to buying the guitar with the hope that Charlie would learn to play and reach his fast-fading father through his one remaining love—jazz music. Charlie understood now that his quick-to-develop devotion to guitar study had been largely fueled by his own desire for the same thing.

After Joe's diagnosis of the rare condition musicogenic epilepsy, and the stunning revelation that Joe's listening to their father's favorite Miles Davis song, "So What," was triggering his brother's trance-like seizures, Charlie had put the guitar down and boxed the turntable. Jazz music had been as much a part of the Giles household as their father had been, and like him, it was gone.

Joe didn't turn his back on music entirely. It was only the song "So What" that doctors proved was dangerous for him to hear, but as a precaution not a single note of jazz music was played in their house again. In place of jazz, Joe became somewhat of a devotee of rock music—the classics mostly and, of course, Rush. Charlie wasn't surprised to see Joe's makeshift studio walls decorated with some of the same rock posters he recognized from when they were kids. The Bowie, Beatles, Dylan, and Hendrix posters were less faded, and Charlie assumed them to be new. There was a small turntable on a paint-chipped white table next to the kit, with about a dozen classic rock albums scattered about on the floor beneath. Keeping music in his life, Charlie figured, was Joe's way of keeping their father in it as well.

Charlie closed the door to Joe's studio and went across the hall to Joe's bedroom, the same room he'd had as a kid. The wallpaper had been changed—cowboys and horses replaced with adult-appropriate wide stripes of alternating brown, white, and yellow. Curious, Charlie moved the bureau away from the wall, until he could see the long, thin groove he had made in the wood with his penknife. That had been more than twenty-five years ago.

Most of the furniture he recognized from when they were kids. He had offered his mother so much: money for new furniture, even to buy a new house. But the familiarity of his belongings was comforting to Joe. Their mother had been fine with things just the way they were. So he'd let it rest. Still, coming here made him feel guilty about the luxuries of his modern apartment, knowing that his mother's furniture and appliances put together wouldn't add up to the price of his living-room set.

By Charlie's standards, Joe's room looked as if it had been ransacked by thieves. Charlie couldn't tell the clean clothes from the dirty ones, so he just grabbed a handful of whatever he could find on the floor. Perhaps he could convince Joe to stay with him for a day or two, but he knew it was unlikely. He and Joe weren't close, but that didn't mean he'd want him sleeping at the hospital every night.

There was a time Charlie had felt privileged just to be granted entry into his big brother's bedroom. The two had had an undeniable closeness once. Even now, when Charlie noticed the time was 7:57, be it morning or night, he thought about how they had pretended to be airplanes for precisely sixty seconds, flying up and down the narrow staircase, fingertips scratching the walls as mock wingtips. But the time for brotherly play was now long past.

On occasion, whenever a movie or commercial depicted two brothers with a close bond, Charlie would find himself playing a what-if game. What if my brother didn't accuse me of stealing from him things he had never even owned? What if he wasn't calm one minute, yelling at me the next, accusing me of the most absurd, fantastical offenses against his make-believe world? What if his schizophrenia didn't terrify me? To have stayed in a close relationship with Joe would have required sacrifices beyond Charlie's emotional capacity to make.

There were two options going forward as Charlie now saw it. Either Joe would have to move in with him until their mother recovered (and she would recover, Charlie assured himself), or he would hire somebody to look after Joe. At least Joe owned his own car and could drive himself to and from work, which was good for all involved. Charlie ran his fingers across the windowsill in Joe's room and then blew away the dust he had picked up in the process. One thing was for certain: there was no way Charlie was moving back home to live with Joe and look after him.

On his way out, Charlie noticed the small silver-framed picture of sunflowers hanging on the wall by the front door. Joe took the picture years ago, while apple picking in the quintessential New England town of Hollis, New Hampshire. The trip was one of several Walderman-sponsored outings, intended to foster a greater sense of community and camaraderie among patients and staff. Joe thought the picture magnificent and enlisted Charlie's help in getting it printed and framed. It had been hanging in the same spot ever since. Charlie took it off the wall. Their mother would like it with her, he thought.

The cabdriver was waiting outside, just as instructed. Charlie's cell phone rang minutes after they pulled away. He didn't recognize the number. *Might be the hospital.*

"Charlie Giles?" a woman asked.

"Yes?"

"Charlie, this is Rebecca Harris. I'm your mother's attorney. I'm sorry to call so late."

"That's not a problem, Rebecca. What can I do for you?"

"I just found out about Alison. She and I had an appointment this evening. When she didn't show, I called the house. Nobody answered, so I got worried. It's not like her to miss an appointment," she said.

"That's true," Charlie said.

"Normally Joe would answer the phone if she was out. Anyway, I couldn't stop worrying, so I started calling area hospitals to check and see if anything had happened."

"You found her," said Charlie.

"I had no idea she'd been there so long. It's just terrible."

"I know how you feel," Charlie said.

"The reason I'm calling is to check up on your mother, because the hospital wouldn't give me any information. Also, I needed to talk with you."

"With me?"

"Yes. There are reasons. How is she doing?"

"I don't know, Rebecca. She's in a coma. The doctors have no idea how long it could last. The only good news I've heard is that she doesn't have any other life-threatening conditions. At least, not that they're aware of."

She let out a loud sigh. "Okay . . . God, that's such good news. Is it all right if I visit tomorrow?"

"Of course. That would be fine. Was there something else? You said you wanted to speak with me specifically."

Charlie found Rebecca's pause uncomfortable.

"Your mother is a very thorough and well-planned person," she began.

"I know. She raised me."

"Of course. Well, she left instructions regarding Joe should she ever become . . ." She paused again. "Incapacitated. It's her living will, Charlie."

Charlie's heart dropped. *Instructions regarding Joe?*

"Go on."

"Joe's schizophrenia is severe," she said.

"You're telling me things I already know."

"He's in a specialized treatment program at Walderman Hospital. He's been making wonderful progress. Your mother was so encouraged with the neurophysiologist he's been working with. The difference has been tremendous."

"It's possible," Charlie said, though after what he'd seen that day, he wasn't convinced. He softened. "I'm not with him as much as my mother."

"I see," Rebecca said. "To get to my point . . ."

"Please." Charlie could not disguise the anxiousness in his voice. He wasn't at all sure where this was going.

"Your mother felt it was imperative that Joe continue with his treatment at Walderman. That his home life not be disrupted in the event something was to happen to her. She knew that Joe wouldn't trust anyone to live with him—unless, that is, it was someone he knew intimately. She was worried that without the care he needed, he might be remanded to a state institution. That would be devastating to her. Joe can lead a normal, healthy life. He's getting closer every day. To go into state care . . . Well, that would just destroy all the progress they've made together."

"What is it that my mother wanted?" Charlie asked.

"She wanted you to become Joe's legal guardian."

Charlie hands trembled.

"And she wants you to move into the Waltham house. To live with Joe until she recovers."

"And if she dies? Does she want me to live with Joe in Waltham forever?"

Rebecca stayed professional. "You would be the only family Joe has left, Charlie. I suppose your mother trusted you to do what's right."

The cab sped past the neighborhoods and memories Charlie had struggled long and hard to leave behind. Now he was being asked to return. Moving back into that house would be no different than being handed a prison sentence. Charlie held the phone to his ear but did not say anything to Rebecca. For the first time, he could empathize with his father.

Sometimes running away makes the most sense of all.

Chapter 15

Charlie sat in the dining room of his childhood home. Instead of warm nostalgia, staring at the furniture, drapes, and dishes he recalled from his childhood brought him only a sense of shame. He marveled at how far he had traveled, only to have arrived back to where it all began. Home.

His résumé flickered on the screen of his laptop computer. It was opened as a Microsoft Word document. He had converted the dining-room table into a makeshift desk; the dining room itself was now a temporary office, complete with newly installed wireless Internet access. Unable to concentrate on work, or the lack thereof, he opened a Web browser and resumed his online research of hypertensive encephalopathy, brain swelling, and comas. As usual, much of what he read was discouraging. He knew better than to share his grim findings with Joe. His brother seemed to power through each day, fueled only by the fumes of hope.

A few hours ago Charlie had been by his mother's bedside. The regret he felt for having let their monthly dinner dates lapse as his work obligations took more time had been palpable.

"I'm sorry, Mom," he'd whispered to no one as he held her hand. "I promise I'll make more of an effort when you wake up, okay?"

Only the ventilator had replied, its ceaseless, rhythmic drone not only her breath but also her voice.

Charlie visited his mother every day, at least for an hour, sometimes more, and kept her room freshly stocked with flowers. He brought her sunflowers mostly, and when he could, peonies since they were another of her favorites, though harder to come by in the off-season. He bought her a Bose SoundDock and an iPod, which he refreshed with new songs on each visit. There was some research he'd come across suggesting improved outcomes for coma patients who listened to music. Though the results from the study, the authors repeatedly pointed out, weren't conclusive.

As for her treasured sunflower picture, Charlie had hung it on the wall across from her bed, hoping it would be the first thing she saw when she opened her eyes. *If* she opened her eyes, he remembered thinking while hanging it.

On the end table adjacent to her bed he'd placed a picture of the three of them, their mother sandwiched between her two smiling sons. It was one of the few photographs he could find where they were together and smiling. Knowing Joe would want the picture, too, he had scanned a copy and hung it on the refrigerator door with the help of a pineapple fridge magnet. He'd also given his mother a framed picture of Monte, her beloved *granddog,* resting on his belly on the green grass of the Boston Commons, facing the camera, with his paws extended. Alison's friends visited often and were sometimes there when Charlie arrived. They would exchange strained pleasantries and share what little information they each had learned. Charlie preferred to visit alone. To grieve for his mother privately. As he did most things.

It had been nearly five days since he'd last set foot in his own apartment. His clothes were still packed in a large suitcase resting on top of the living-room sofa, which, unfortunately for his back, also doubled as his bed. Bone-weary from the awkward living arrangements and with no change in his mother's condition, the coma still deep, Charlie contemplated the possibility that this could morph into something more permanent. The thought was worrisome.

Monte was apparently adjusting to his new life on Cleveland Street in Waltham far better than Charlie. He had Maxine to thank for that. Monte's interest in Mrs. Cummings's poodle, Maxine, was bordering, he feared, on obsession. Despite having been neutered before Charlie brought him home, some part of his little doggie libido had clearly been left unfazed. When he wasn't hovering by the window, paws resting on the sill, trying to sneak a peek at his beloved Maxine, he was whimpering by the door, begging to go out for an illicit rendezvous. In a way, though, Charlie was proud of his furry little friend's undaunted resolve. Mrs. Cummings, however, was far less enthralled.

"If I catch him humping my Maxine again," she had scolded on the day they moved in, "there will be consequences."

"I'll make certain he's aware of your feelings on the matter," Charlie had replied.

Monte dropped from his windowsill perch and trotted under the dining-room table to rest at Charlie's feet. Charlie felt him start to gnaw at his right shoe but made no attempt to stop him. With his reputation severely tarnished and his mental health questionable, he doubted he'd have much use for a good pair of work shoes for a while. Letting Monte nibble away at the leather in a way helped him to accept the situation for what it was. Still, what it was wasn't an all that easy thing to accept.

Making matters worse, Charlie's one attempt to contact Mac at SoluCent had been met with a terse reply from the company's legal department. As much as Charlie hated it, he was an outcast, both with the company and himself. If working on his résumé could provide even a brief respite from the fear about his own mental health, he'd go at it all night long.

Discouraged by his medical research, Charlie thought he might make some headway on the career front and opened his résumé again. But he could only stare at the jumble of words for a minute or two before the anger took hold and he lost concentration. The frustration and hurt that his days at SoluCent were over, that he had lost his brainchild to a multinational conglomerate, were still too raw. He couldn't plan his next move when he couldn't yet accept his fate.

He replayed his conversation with Randal at Chaps a dozen times, haunted by the catch-22. The only explanation for his crazy behavior was that people were out to get him, but just thinking that was true would be enough to make someone think he was crazy.

He had made a call to a neurologist, wondering if Rachel's theory about a brain lesion might be worth investigating. The office was booked solid. Since it wasn't a medical emergency, it would be at least three weeks before anyone could see him. That left him alone with his résumé and his thoughts, living back home with his brother, Joe, as if he were once again a twelve-year-old boy with dreams of a better life.

He pushed through his malaise and continued tweaking his résumé. Ten minutes had passed when he heard a drumroll from upstairs. As he typed, he read over each sentence for clarity and structure. But the drumroll morphed into a steady beat, and Charlie's concentration waned again. Between Joe's playing and Monte's chewing, progress was simply unattainable.

He saved and closed his résumé, quit Word, pushed the chair away from his makeshift desk, and marched upstairs. Monte, of course, followed close behind. By the time he reached the practice studio, Joe was in the middle of an inspired solo. That Joe could practice his drums freely, while Charlie couldn't even hint at playing jazz guitar while living under his roof, only aggravated him more. Charlie banged on the closed door as loud as he could.

"Joe! Joe! I'm trying to work downstairs. Could this wait until, oh, I don't know . . . sometime when I'm not here?"

No answer. Charlie tried the doorknob, but the door was locked. He banged again with his open palm. Monte barked in solidarity.

"Joe! Please stop playing for a moment!" He kicked at the door. Charlie had played drums in the high school marching band; he was kicking a counter-rhythm to Joe's bass drum beat.

After several seconds of both Charlie and Joe banging away, the drumming stopped. Joe opened the door.

"Hey!" he said, smiling. "Is it nine fifty-five already?"

Joe had left Charlie with explicit instructions to come get him five minutes before 10:00 p.m. There was some show Joe watched religiously, and their mother had served as the alarm clock. Charlie wasn't sure what would happen if Joe missed that show, but he suspected it wouldn't be good.

"No. You still have an hour," Charlie said.

"Okay, then," Joe said with a grin. "More time for me to rock!" He turned away from Charlie and went back to his drums.

Charlie kept the door open and stared at his brother in disbelief. His brother's mass overflowed down the sides of the small drum stool. He wore a grimy white undershirt and his boxers. It looked as if he hadn't bathed in days, even though Charlie had heard him singing in the shower a few hours ago.

Charlie sighed deeply. He wasn't certain he could survive living here until his mother recovered, even if he had a moral and arguably legal obligation to fulfill. If it came down to it, Charlie had already earmarked Randal to get him off the hook.

"Joe!" Charlie yelled over the rhythmic pounding of the tom-toms.

Joe stopped a moment. "Yeah?"

"Why do you think I'm at your door?" Charlie asked.

Monte, sensing an opportunity to explore, darted into the cramped practice studio and proceeded to smell a pile of clothes heaped on the floor in front of the kit.

Joe looked puzzled. "I don't know. You want something?"

"Yes. Yes, Joe. That's an accurate statement. I do want something. I want some freaking quiet around here so I can work."

"Ohhh . . . you want quiet," Joe said. He reached behind himself and pulled a pair of brushes out of a small box. "Is this quiet enough for you?"

Joe proceeded to play a soft rhythm, the brushes making a smooth washing noise as he glided them over the snare drum.

Charlie nodded. "Yes. That is quieter."

Joe nodded in return. "Good. Because after I finish practicing with the sticks, I switch to the brushes." Joe dropped the brushes and picked up the sticks. He hit the snare with a quick roll, landed a hard snap on the tom, and drifted into a steady four-four groove.

"So you're going to keep playing?" Charlie shouted over the beat.

Joe stopped and stared back at his brother. "No, Charlie. I'm not going to just keep playing," Joe said in a teacherlike tone. "I'm going to keep out of my head and keep my reality in check. And if this is what I need to do that, then I guess that's what I'm going to do." He did a few more quick pelts on the snare for emphasis.

Joe continued talking as he drummed. "The noise helps me to stay present and focused," he yelled over his own playing. "Dr. Evans suggested we each take on an activity that creates some noise— singing, woodworking, anything that has focused action and noise. If you don't like it, you can go work lots of other places. Starbucks or, I don't know, some coffeehouse somewhere. But in the meantime, I need this, okay? I'm in a heightened stress phase with Mom being in the hospital, and I appreciate your being so understanding."

For an instant Charlie was the younger brother again. Joe wasn't sick at all. They were back in high school. Charlie wanted something from Joe, and Joe had a reason why Charlie couldn't have it. It was as simple as that. *Score one for the big brother,* Charlie thought.

"Sure, Joe. I understand. Listen, I'm going to go out for a while. Get some air. I'll be back a little after midnight. You're an adult. Do what you want. Play as loud as you want. Go to bed when you want. I'll see you in the morning."

Joe gave him a mock salute good-bye. Charlie left the room. Monte stayed behind.

"Come on, boy," Charlie said.

Monte looked up, cocked his head slightly, and went back to sniffing around the room.

"He can stay," Joe said.

"Suit yourself," Charlie replied, more to Monte than to Joe. He closed the door behind him and never felt more alone.

Two brothers, Charlie thought. *Both desperate to stay out of our own heads because of the stress. Both afraid of what we might do if we can't.* In that instant Charlie understood his brother better than he ever had. And that scared him the most.

The day had caught up with Charlie. He felt exhausted and drained of life. With Joe's playing and what soon would be some obnoxious TV show blaring in the living room, the house could offer him no solace. Maybe he'd get a beer at Chaps. Perhaps even call Randal, see if he'd want to meet up. Heading to the bathroom in his mother's room on the second floor, Charlie turned on the shower and let the warm water wash over his body. For a few blessed moments Charlie found some peace. The rushing water drowned out all sound, including Joe.

He dressed quickly. Charlie descended the stairs to get his jacket without saying a word to Joe, whom he once again heard banging away on his drums. Passing the closet at the foot of the stairwell, he grabbed his jacket and slipped it on. He jiggled the jacket, hearing the familiar rattle of keys in the front right pocket.

Walking past the archway opening to the dining room, Charlie peered to his right and froze. His laptop shone in the darkened room. The white page of a Word document glowing like the beacon of a lighthouse.

"Hadn't I closed my résumé?" Charlie said it aloud as he walked into the dining room. He stared at his computer, confused that some document other than his résumé was open. It was a single line of text that read: *Don't forget to check under the sofa.*

Charlie's pulse quickened. He scanned the room, looking for any signs of an intruder, someone who might have entered the house while he was upstairs. Except for Joe's drumming, the house was silent. Charlie darted in and out of the lower-level rooms, his heart pounding in his chest, his eyes wide with adrenaline. He was satisfied no one else was in the house only after several minutes of exhaustive searching. He'd even checked the closets.

Walking back into the living room, Charlie stared at the sofa, which had somehow turned menacing, even with its faded floral pattern. His suitcase was where he had left it. Nothing seemed disturbed or out of place. He slowly knelt to his knees, then lowered himself flat onto his torso. He lifted the upholstered fabric covering the front rail and peered into the dark underside of the sofa. He hesitated before reaching his hand into the blackness. His eyes, adjusting to the dark, made out a rectangular shape on the floor. It was flat and clearly distinguishable from the floor itself. Charlie's outstretched fingers felt for the edges of what he presumed to be an envelope of some sort.

It made a scratching sound as he pulled it across the wood floor with the tips of his fingers. His mother would have vacuumed under the sofa, but dust had gathered in her absence and some particle remnants escaped in a loose cloud as he slid out the manila-colored clasp envelope from underneath. Standing up, Charlie stared at it, the clasp still closed, the envelope free of dust, as though it had been placed there recently.

Charlie unhinged the flimsy metal clasp and opened the envelope. Half-expecting some powder to come shooting out at him, Charlie was momentarily relieved to see only a single sheet of paper within. Peering inside, aided by the dim light from the living-room lamp, Charlie could see something written on the paper.

He took out the document and held it up toward the light. His stomach lurched and he nearly lost his balance as he read. Steadying himself against the arm of the sofa, Charlie read it again, several times, but still couldn't believe it.

My Kill List

The following people are to blame. Now they'll die.
  1. *Rudy Gomes*
  2. *Simon "Mac" Mackenzie*
  3. *Leon Yardley*
  4. *It's a surprise. . . .*

"It's impossible," Charlie said aloud, slipping the paper back into the envelope. "I didn't write this. I couldn't have."

But a seed of doubt planted days earlier was growing into a forest. These were the people who'd thrown him out of SoluCent. Charlie was the only one who knew their names. He hadn't even shared that information with Randal. Perhaps a former coworker had put the envelope there as a joke—guessing that Mac and Yardley would have been involved in his firing. He checked to make certain the front and back doors were locked. They were, and he saw nothing to suggest a forced entry. Someone had put the envelope under the sofa recently, and the Word document telling him where to look hadn't been there when he went up to berate Joe for his playing.

"Nothing makes sense. It doesn't make sense," Charlie said. "I wouldn't kill anybody. No matter what they did to me. These people don't deserve to die. I wouldn't do that." He closed his eyes and took a deep breath.

Then it came to him. He reddened with anger. There was only one possible explanation. Clutching the envelope in his hands, Charlie bounded up the stairs two steps at a time and came to a stop outside Joe's closed practice studio door.

"I was in the shower," Charlie muttered, breathless. "This envelope was put under the sofa not long ago. There wasn't any dust on it. That can only mean one thing."

Charlie recalled the e-mail he'd written to Mac earlier that evening. In it he'd mentioned both Yardley and Gomes. Joe could have easily checked the sent mail in his Gmail account. The Web browser with his e-mail account had still been open when Charlie went into dining room, and the computer had been connected to the Internet. Joe knew that something was wrong at work. But all Charlie had told him was that he was taking some time off—nothing more. Joe could have been snooping around in his e-mail. He must have seen the message I sent to Mac, Charlie thought. Then he wrote this kill list, put it in an envelope, and slipped it under the sofa. Charlie didn't understand why Joe would do it. But he was about to find out.

Chapter 16

Charlie opened the door to Joe's practice studio with enough force to leave a black mark where the knob connected with the wall. The noise startled Joe, who was seated on his drum stool, putting his drumsticks back in the box on the floor. Monte jumped, too, and then barked.

"Is it nine fifty-five yet?" Joe asked with a wide grin.

"Why, Joe? Why did you do this?" Charlie shouted.

The anger and force of his voice was enough to startle Monte and send him bounding down the stairs, probably back to the window to pine for his beloved Maxine. The color drained completely from Joe's face. His was the look of a child, scolded but unaware of the offense.

"I don't understand," Joe said. "You seem angry."

"That's because I am angry, Joe. This is really sick and twisted, you know that?" Charlie waved the envelope in front of him like a flag.

"I don't know what that is," Joe said.

"Don't play me like that, Joe," Charlie countered. "I'm in the shower, and you decide to play a little joke on me. Why? Was it because of Rachel? Because I went to see her?"

"You actually went to see Dr. Evans?" Joe asked. "Why?"

"Why do you think? Because I don't want to be a nut job like you or Dad. So tell me, is that what this is all about? Are you trying to make me into one?"

"I don't know what you're talking about!" Joe screamed the words with shocking intensity. His voice echoed throughout the room and seemed to hang in the air with the foreboding of a storm cloud.

Charlie could now see that Joe was being pushed beyond his ability to control the stress.

"I'm talking about opening up a Word document on my laptop, printing out a list of names, and then slipping this envelope under the sofa. That's what I'm talking about."

Joe shouted even louder. "I don't know what that is! I don't know what you're talking about!"

"That's a lie, Joe, and you know it. Just admit what you've done and apologize."

"I didn't do anything," Joe said, softly this time.

Charlie's mind flashed with images of Anne Pedersen and Jerry Schmidt. Of Gomes, Yardley, and Mac, seated around Mac's table, accusing him. He pictured Harry Wessner and the rest of the Magellan Team. Everything flooded him at once. But the most upsetting thought of all, though, a thought to which he couldn't bear to give credence, was that Joe was actually telling the truth. He couldn't—no, wouldn't—allow it to be.

"Admit it now!" Charlie demanded.

Joe shook his head in denial. Charlie knew of only one way to get him to confess, and it sickened him to use it.

"Oh, just you wait until I tell Mom what you did. She's going to be very upset and disappointed with you."

"Stop it," Joe demanded.

"Maybe she won't even wake up unless you tell the truth, Joe. Tell me the truth, dammit! You put this envelope under the sofa."

Joe's face turned crimson. "Don't you say that. I didn't do it. I didn't do anything. I didn't do *anything*!"

Click.

Charlie saw something shift in Joe's eyes, as though an imaginary sequence of switches were being turned on. The result, he knew, had the potential to be disastrous. He knew he needed to stop pushing, to keep those switches in their safe "off" position, but he couldn't.

"Forget about me. Don't lie to Mom, Joe."

Click. Click. Click.

The switches of Joe's mind were dusty and cobwebbed from having been unused for so long. Joe's treatment at Walderman had implanted some sort of mental lockbox over them, one of the many tools he'd been given that helped to keep his emotions balanced and his anger in check. Now Charlie was picking at the lock. Prying open the rusty door to that lockbox. Flicking his switches on, one by one, mindless of the consequences.

"Keep her out of this," Joe growled.

"She'd want you to admit you're lying. . . ."

C-l-i-c-k.

Joe sprang. He leapt over the drum set and bounded for Charlie with outstretched arms.

"Give me that! I'll rip it up! I'll tear it apart! Give it to me now!"

Charging at him like a crazed rhino, Joe rammed full force into Charlie, pushing his brother backward. Charlie, stunned by the impact, landed painfully against the doorjamb, letting out a cry of equal parts surprise and pain. The envelope dropped from Charlie's hand and floated silently to the floor.

Trying to counter, Charlie pressed his heels into the floorboards and drove the weight of his body into Joe. The move left Charlie off balance, though still standing. Sensing the advantage, Joe threw his massive weight hard left this time, keeping a firm grasp on Charlie's jacket collar, and in one motion tossed Charlie sideways, as though he were throwing a pillow across the room. Legs and arms flailing, Charlie landed hard into a standing cymbal, knocking it over with a loud crash. The impact expunged all air from Charlie's lungs, as though sucking it out with a vacuum, leaving him gasping madly for breath. Startled by the noise, Monte raced up the stairs and stood in the doorway, barking loudly but not daring to step inside.

Charlie had done it. All switches were on. Joe was no longer home, and he was the last person anyone wanted to fight when he was out of control. History had proved that. Joe couldn't and wouldn't stop. With Charlie winded, Joe climbed on top of his brother, pressing both knees mercilessly against his sternum. What little air Charlie could take in was now constricted by his brother's weight.

"I didn't do anything. Take back what you said about Mom!" Joe shouted, covering Charlie's face with spit. He slapped at Charlie's cheeks with alternating blows, each time demanding a retraction.

"Joe . . . please . . ." Charlie could barely speak the words. His vision began to go dark. "I'm sorry . . . I believe you. . . ."

The first time Charlie experienced one of Joe's rages, he was eight and his brother thirteen. It was the year Joe was diagnosed with epilepsy, and his doctors linked his hulklike tantrums to the condition. Treating the seizures put a stop to Joe's dangerous and terrifying rages.

When fate dealt Joe another blow years later, and he was diagnosed this time with schizophrenia shortly after his twentieth birthday, Charlie thought his rages would return. But they didn't. Joe had some lingering anger management issues, compounded by his paranoia, but it was nothing close to the brutal ferocity displayed when Joe angered during one of his seizures. Joe hadn't had a seizure since his seventeenth birthday, and Charlie prayed he wasn't having one right now. If he was, Charlie had every reason to believe his life was in danger.

"I believe you, Joe," Charlie said again. "I'm sorry for accusing you."

The pressure on Charlie's arms lessened. Joe stopped swinging his fists and peered down at Charlie's bloodied and already swelling face. Tears flooded Joe's eyes. He stood up, then bent over to extend a hand to Charlie.

Click.

Something in Joe's eyes changed. Realization? Switches were turning off in his mind.

"I believe you . . . please . . ."

Joe got off of him. "I'm sorry, Charlie. I'm so sorry," Joe cried.

Charlie rubbed at his neck and shook his head from side to side, hoping to clear his vision. He was battered and bruised, but he'd live.

"It's okay. It's all right, Joe," Charlie said. "It was my fault. I asked for it. I came after you."

"Why?" Joe asked again.

"Because I thought you wrote this." Charlie retrieved the envelope from the floor. He handed it to Joe. "Please tell me you did. I won't be mad. I promise."

Joe took the envelope, opened it, and read the list. Then he looked up at Charlie. The concern and worry showed on his face. "You said you went to see Dr. Evans, right?"

"Yes," Charlie said.

"Why?" Joe asked.

"I thought she might have some answers."

"Are you afraid?" Joe asked.

"Yes," Charlie said.

"Of what?"

"Of being like you," Charlie said.

"I didn't write this, Charlie," Joe said. "You have to believe me."

Charlie closed his eyes and paused. "I know you didn't," he said.

The two embraced. Charlie felt the thin trail of a single tear as it stretched down his cheek. He couldn't remember when last he'd cried.

Chapter 17

A post from Joe Giles's blog, Divided Mind:
It's late, but I can't sleep. I had a really hard night, and I'm still freaking out about what just happened. I lost my temper and got into a fight with my brother, Charlie. I haven't lost my temper like that in years.

So why did I fly off the handle, you ask? Charlie accused me of doing something I did not do, that's why. It's too disturbing to tell you what he accused me of, but suffice it to say, it was an appalling accusation. I think I now understand why he blamed me, though. He's scared something is happening to him, but that's his business and not mine to share. What I want to write about tonight is how I reacted. Like I said, I haven't lost my temper like that in years. Tonight I did.

Here's my fear, irrational as it may seem, but perhaps Mom's sudden illness (you have to read my last post for more about that) is affecting my schizophrenia. Perhaps there's a chemical change taking place in my brain, altering my behavior in ways I can't yet predict. I've always wondered if my childhood epilepsy, seizures triggered by music (click here for my ancient blog post about that) was some sort of precursor or warning that schizophrenia was heading my way, still a few years out, but planning on staying forever. Doctors found my hypothesis interesting, but since my type of epilepsy was rare and my schizophrenia is a more common form, nobody ever explored the link. They just said it was an unfortunate double whammy, so to speak. Maybe there is a link, but it's been dormant in my brain all these years. Now something has changed in my brain chemistry, and the same anger—that uncontrollable violence—is back, but without the seizures this time.

I know all too well the stigma and misconception linking schizophrenia to violent behavior. I also know there are those with the illness who do behave belligerently and sometimes violently. There are "sane" people who do the same.

My illness, however, has never manifested itself in a violent way. It's more like a warping of reality for me. I see things that are not there. I hear things that are not said. The illness has touched every facet of my life. My behavior may be unpredictable, but it hasn't been dangerously violent before. My disorder makes it hard to organize my day, not to mention hold down a decent job, which I now can do (thank you, Walderman). My disorder doesn't demand that I harm others. If anything, the person I've wanted to hurt most is myself (click here to read about my one and only suicide attempt).

So here's the question you can help me answer. Am I being paranoid (ha, ha, ha, ha)? Could my fight with Charlie tonight be linked to chemical changes of schizophrenia? Don't people get into fights all the time who aren't schizophrenic?

I know it's not easy for my brother to live with me. I know I'm not always easy to live with. But our mom wanted us to be together in case she ever got sick. She didn't want just anybody looking after me; she wanted it to be family. And let's face it, I sometimes need looking after. It's a big deal for me to admit that, but Walderman has made it possible for me to do so. I love my brother and I always will. For the sake of both of us, I hope there won't be a repeat of tonight's events.

Writing this out is cathartic for me. Normally, I'm not all woe is me in these posts, but tonight I needed it to be this way. Tomorrow it will be better. I'll remind myself to take it one day at a time. I'll take my meds and endure the side effects same as I've always done. I'll go see Rachel. And in the morning maybe my brother will forgive me. More important, maybe I'll forgive myself. I'm still pretty angry at Charlie right now, though, so I don't know if either is going to happen. I could use some thoughts and comments. I guess I'm feeling a little lonely right now. Thanks for reading, as always.

Chapter 18

Rudy Gomes was going to die. Charlie felt it in his gut. It was the only thing in his upside-down life that Charlie was certain about. He'd spent a sleepless night after fighting with Joe and most of the following day trying to figure out his next move. This was it.

The mysterious kill list, with Gomes identified as the first target, rested on the passenger seat of Charlie's BMW. He was parked outside Gomes's home and had been there for the past three hours. The only things he had to pass the time were his thoughts, which he no longer trusted, and the list.

For Charlie, the list was an undisputable artifact of what he had been denying ever since the incident with Jerry Schmidt at the steering committee meeting. He might be losing control over his mind. As much as he feared the list, he couldn't stop looking at it or bring himself to destroy it. He picked up the list at least a dozen times, rereading it, searching the darkest recesses of his mind for any recollection of being its author. Nothing came to him. And yet no other explanation worked.

Sitting alone in the car gave Charlie time to contemplate his situation and try to piece it together. Joe hadn't written the note. Of this Charlie was certain. Joe's reaction to Charlie's accusation was enough proof. If anything, Joe lacked guile. And from his careful inspection of the house, it was clear nobody else had been inside. For that matter, nobody except for Randal even knew about his being fired from SoluCent, let alone the names of those who had taken part. That left only one person responsible for the kill list. For Charlie, it meant looking square in the mirror.

He gripped the steering wheel hard. Admitting he wrote the kill list was tantamount to admitting he was crazy. That he had created Anne Pedersen, sent e-mail to Sony with the InVision product plans, written cryptic notes to himself, and surfed the Internet, looking for porn, while at work. None of it made sense. Charlie couldn't bring himself to accept that he could have written such a list, let alone carry out its horrific promise. It simply wasn't possible. He had proved time and time again, through all his achievements, that fate hadn't dealt him the same lonesome hand that it had to Joe or his father.

What was it that hurt the most? Charlie wondered, scanning the dark street for any sign of Gomes. The windows of his car were rolled down slightly, and a cool breeze washed over him from the outside. It was invigorating and, for the briefest moment, dealt Charlie the illusion that he was closing in on the answer.

The feeling faded with the breeze. Everything that had defined him and proved to others that he was as successful as he was brilliant had over the course of a few short weeks been rendered meaningless. For all his hard work and achievement, he might end up no better off than his brother, Joe. Two lost minds. Two lost souls.

"It doesn't matter what you did yesterday," Charlie muttered, "when all you have is today."

His only hope was to find something redeeming in this. Some small salvation he could steal from this nightmare.

Doing that meant keeping a watchful eye out for Gomes. If this threat was real, as he suspected it was, then Gomes's life was in grave danger. If Charlie was the threat, then at least Gomes would see Charlie out in the open and would have a fighting chance to defend himself.

"I'm here to save Rudy either from myself or from someone I don't know," Charlie said aloud, laughing.

Using an address that he had swiped off Yahoo! People, Charlie had played out a couple of scenarios on the drive over to Gomes's house. His favorite plan involved somehow convincing Gomes to work together and trap whoever was planning to hurt him. But Charlie wasn't certain Gomes would even believe the threat was real, let alone that he would cooperate with Charlie to set up a trap. As far as

Gomes was concerned, Charlie was crazy, and handing him a typed-out *kill list* wasn't going to do anything to change his opinion.

By the time nine o'clock approached, Charlie was thinking about packing it in and trying again the next day. Just then Gomes came lumbering down the street, his massive frame casting a long shadow down the cracked sidewalk as he passed beneath the yellow glow of a streetlamp.

Now that Gomes was here, Charlie realized he had no idea what he was going to do or say.

Gomes was talking on his cell phone. There were a couple bars and restaurants near the center of Arlington, where Gomes lived. Perhaps he had been out to dinner nearby. Charlie had already suspected that Gomes was on foot. He'd seen two cars parked tandem in Gomes's driveway and recognized Gomes's hot-rod Mustang from the SoluCent parking lot.

Gomes was just starting up the steps to his apartment in a two-family Victorian home when Charlie emerged from his car. A lifetime working in security had trained Gomes to be on alert. He caught the movement and swung his head in Charlie's direction. Gomes stopped dead in his tracks. His expression was one of stunned disbelief.

"What the fuck are you doing here?" Gomes snarled.

Gomes was wearing a blue blazer and tan khakis. Charlie saw his hand reaching inside the blazer. Was he carrying a weapon? Charlie couldn't believe his own stupidity. He had been so concerned about how he'd convince Gomes that the threat against him was real, he had completely overlooked the possibility that Gomes would view his presence as a hostile act. Perhaps think it was a revenge attack for his being fired from SoluCent. Ironically, just like the kill list said.

"Rudy, don't do anything stupid," Charlie said from across the street, still watching Gomes's hidden hand. "I'm not here for that."

Gomes gave Charlie a long, cold stare. Through the ghostly glow of the streetlamp, Gomes looked even more terrifying.

"What are you doing here, Giles? I will fuck you up bad. I mean it," Gomes growled.

"I need to talk to you," Charlie said, trying his best to keep his voice down, not wanting to attract attention. "Let me just cross the street so we can talk."

Charlie felt blood race to his head and his heart jump in his chest. It was fear. It had seemed so easy to get Gomes to listen to him when Charlie had practiced what he would say alone, in the safety of his car. Now, face-to-face with the hulking Gomes, Charlie knew that whatever he had to say wasn't going to be well received.

"I have reason to believe your life might be in danger," Charlie said.

Gomes took his hand out of his blazer pocket. The hand was empty: no gun. He then started across the street; after a few long strides he accelerated, running full out toward Charlie.

"Oh yeah? From who, jackass? You?" Gomes yelled it like a battle cry as he sprinted across the street. When he was in range, Gomes lowered his shoulder and drove it hard into Charlie's sternum.

The force of the blow sent Charlie sprawling backward into his car. He was still sore from the fight with Joe the night before. The pain in his chest was staggering. Winded, Charlie slouched down on the street. Then he felt two hands grab him by the shirt collar and lift him up until both his feet were several inches off the ground.

Gomes let go with one hand and took a large windup to throw a punch with his right. Charlie timed it perfectly and ducked his head quick to the left. The blow glanced off his ear but was much less damaging than it could have been had he not moved in time. The body weight shift was enough to force Gomes to let go of Charlie's shirt and drop him to the ground.

Charlie hit the asphalt, landing hard on his hands and knees. Adrenaline coursed through him as instinct instructed him to flatten himself on the pavement and slide underneath his car. His arms were tight against his sides, palms flat against the ground, forearms extended over his head, as though he were about to try and do a push-up. He could see Gomes's massive feet pacing back and forth by the side of the car. Then he noticed Gomes's right foot disappear from his sight as his left foot pivoted. Next he heard an explosive crash and saw falling glass pepper the ground.

"Want me to shatter all the windows in your Beamer, you sick prick?"

"Rudy, please!" Charlie said from underneath the car. "You're not listening to me. I'm here to warn you about something important."

"How about this for important?" Rudy snapped. "A guy I helped to fire comes stalking me at my house, talking nonsense, acting threatening, and I put him in the hospital. Do you think any judge is going to hold that against me?"

"I'm not here to hurt you, Rudy. But if you have your mind set on hurting me, you're going to have to come and pull me out from under here yourself," Charlie replied.

"You know what, Giles? That's not a bad idea. I've been looking to blow off some steam. You're giving me the perfect outlet, and I have the perfect defense. I think you'd rather take a couple shots from me than a night in the slammer. Wouldn't you agree?"

He knew he had to act quickly if he wanted to avoid being Gomes's punching bag. Charlie breathed a little easier as he recalled the keys still being in the ignition. That bit of good fortune might just be enough to save him.

Gomes crouched down to look under the car in response to the challenge. Charlie slid his body to the opposite side of the car, opened the passenger-side door, and jumped inside the instant he saw Gomes going into his crouch. By the time Gomes realized what had happened, Charlie was already in the driver's seat. He slammed the driver's side door shut and hit the automatic locks.

Gomes's thick arms and strong hands reached through the broken glass of the driver's side door and clawed at Charlie's face, leaving large red streaks that burned down one side of his cheek. Charlie cut the wheel hard the other way and jammed the car into drive, reaching across the seat to close the passenger door as well. The car jumped off the curb, rolled back onto the street, sending Gomes sprawling backward, away from the vehicle as it took off.

From the rearview mirror Charlie could see Gomes getting to his feet. His head was thrown back, as if he were having the biggest laugh of his life. Hopefully it wouldn't be his last, Charlie thought as he slipped out of sight. Although if Gomes were to meet an untimely end, Charlie wasn't sure he'd care much anymore.

Soon after he pulled away, the BMW's InVision system came to life. The sweet, calming voice of the computer wafted through the speakers. It settled Charlie's jostled nerves.

"Hello, Charlie," InVision said. "Where would you like to go?"

"Home," Charlie said. "I just want to go home."

"To home," InVision repeated.

"No," Charlie said. "Waltham. Home in Waltham."

"Home in Waltham. Enjoy the trip."

Compared to that experience, he thought, *anything would be enjoyable.*

Chapter 19

Monte must have heard keys rattling and let out a delighted yip the moment Charlie entered through the back door. He saw Joe standing in front of the hall mirror, buttoning the last button on his blue-collared security guard work shirt. Joe waved at Charlie's reflection as he approached.

"What happened to you?" Joe asked. He pointed to the large red scrapes running nearly the full length of Charlie's cheek.

"Cat attack," Charlie said, scooping Monte up in his arms and carrying him past Joe and into the living room. He fell onto the sofa, letting out a grunt. Monte rolled onto his back, legs pawing at the air, hoping to entice Charlie into a little roughhouse, or at least a good tummy rub.

Joe clasped his Hanover Security badge around his neck and made no further attempt to speak with Charlie. Charlie knew his brother. If Joe was being quiet, it was because he was still raw about their fight last night. Otherwise, he'd be talking up a storm. As drained as he was, Charlie was thankful for the moment's peace.

"I'll be home after nine," Joe said. "Shift ends at seven, and I want to go back to the hospital and sit with Mom. I'll try to stay quiet," he added.

"That's fine. Do what you have to. Don't worry about me."

"Don't worry. I won't," Joe said under his breath.

The brothers had worked out a schedule so that their mother was rarely without company. Joe had been with her most of the morning, and it didn't surprise Charlie that he was going back for a couple hours after his shift. Charlie had even set up a wireless hub in her private hospital room but still couldn't muster the focus and energy needed to start the job search in earnest. What he liked best, despite his loathing for hospitals, was to sit by her bedside and read aloud to her. His mother had once lamented not having time to go back and read the classics she loved as a young girl—Jane Austen and Dickens especially. He was about midway through *A Christmas Carol* and thoroughly enjoying it. Perhaps she was, too, but he couldn't tell. Her face was still and without expression; her body a statue. He wanted to believe that reading to her helped, but even if it didn't, at least it made him feel useful. And that was a rare feeling of late.

"So, you're coming Saturday, right?"

"Excuse me?" Charlie said.

"To Walderman. You're coming, right? Mom always comes. You know this is a pretty significant checkpoint for me. I'm getting my three-year progress report and feedback on how I've been doing with my work assignment."

Charlie wasn't thinking about Walderman or Joe's checkpoint. His mind was on Rudy Gomes and the kill list.

"I don't know. Why do you need me there?"

"Gee, I don't know. Let me think. . . ." Joe let his voice trail off. He began rubbing at his chin as if deep in thought. It was a precursor to a particular brand of sarcasm that Charlie knew all too well, for he used it himself.

Brothers will be brothers.

Joe's fingers kept rubbing at his chin as he spoke. "Let's see . . . Well, you are family. The only family I have right now. And I guess support is a good thing. Yeah, I think it is. And you know, you could be . . . I don't know . . . supportive, and be there for me when Mom can't. Doesn't that seem like a good use of your time?"

Charlie scratched at the scruff of his beard. Every joint in his body ached. It was still amazing to him how quickly he had let himself go. He was no longer the lean, fit corporate executive he had been just weeks before. He was now nothing more than a vagabond; an unshaven, out-of-shape, jobless wretch who thoroughly disgusted himself.

"I don't know, Joe," was all he could manage to say.

"Thanks, Charlie. That really means a lot to me. I'll make sure to slam the door hard when I get home."

Charlie lay on the sofa but was unable to sleep. Monte curled himself into a tight ball against Charlie's side. Minutes later, after Monte stopped squirming and found his spot, he began to snore.

What if it is me? Charlie thought. *Like a night stalker, a sleepwalker.* Charlie remembered a movie he'd seen back in his MIT days. It was a German expressionist film titled *The Cabinet of Dr. Caligari.* Cesare, the somnambulist, was compelled by the evil Dr. Caligari to commit murder without any self-awareness. Charlie's mind traveled down that winding road, in search of possibilities, explanations, anything. He headed deeper and deeper into that abyss, until finally, somewhere lost in that darkness, he found sleep.

Charlie didn't wake until nearly ten o'clock the next morning. Light flooded the living room, rousing him from a night filled with horrifying dreams. Only flashes of those nightmares remained. Rubbing his temples, he tried to force himself awake, then rose slowly and creakily from the lumpy sofa. His cheek was throbbing and raw from where it had been scratched the night before. He groaned.

"You finally up?"

Charlie heard Joe call to him from the kitchen. It was then he noticed the warming aroma of bacon and the earthy, aromatic smell of fresh brewed coffee. Charlie entered the kitchen and saw eggs were scrambled in the pan.

"You're making breakfast?" Charlie said.

Joe looked back at his sleep-eyed brother equally quizzically.

"Of course I am," Joe said. "You asked me to."

"I did?" Charlie asked.

"Sure. You left me a note," Joe said, waving a piece of paper in front of his face.

Charlie's eyes widened, and he lunged for the paper, ripping it out of Joe's hand, tearing one of the corners in the process.

"Hey! Easy does it," Joe said. "Breakfast will be ready in a minute."

Charlie read the note. It was definitely his handwriting. Pen written on lined paper.

Joe,
I'm sorry about our fight. Let's start again. How about you make breakfast, eggs, bacon, and coffee, and I'll buy lunch? Deal? Count on me for Saturday at Walderman, too. I'm really proud of you, Joe.
Charlie

Charlie gasped, then covered his mouth with his hand. "Where did you find this?" he asked.

"It was on the kitchen table," Joe said.

Charlie's heart began to race. Same as it had when he'd found the kill list and all the other notes he had no memory of writing. A terrifying thought occurred to him.

"Joe, were there any other notes?" Charlie asked. His voice was low, as if he were asking his brother to reveal a secret.

"Yeah. One. But I didn't know what to make of it."

"Give it to me," Charlie said.

Joe slid another piece of paper on the kitchen counter over to Charlie. Charlie could tell without even reading it that the note was scribbled in his handwriting. He read the single line, and his blood turned ice cold.

One down. Three to go.

"God help me," Charlie said.

Chapter 20

Charlie swerved his BMW in and out of traffic down Massachusetts Avenue. Wind and cold air blew in through the broken driver's side window and whipped at his face. It was a stinging reminder of the unraveling of his life. He nearly ran a stoplight at the intersection of Mass Ave and Route 16, his concentration less on driving and more on what might have happened to Rudy Gomes.

Joe had been upset at Charlie's departure. Charlie felt guilty about leaving him in such a rush. But how could he have made Joe understand why he had asked him to cook breakfast but wasn't going to stay to eat it? It was a no-win situation. Charlie didn't have the time or the answers.

"Turn right in two hundred feet," InVision said.

Charlie waited for InVision's navigation cues as a matter of habit, even though he could have driven the route unassisted. He pulled in front of Gomes's house, in the exact spot where he had parked the night before. As Charlie exited the car, his feet crunched on shards of broken glass, which he assumed were remnants of his shattered window. The house was peaceful. The street was quiet. Charlie's heart sank when he looked in the driveway and saw only one car parked. It was Gomes's.

He walked up the wooden stairs to the front entrance and peered into the only window that was not obscured by a curtain. He couldn't see anything inside. Knowing Rudy lived on the first floor, Charlie walked over to the left-most door of the two-family home and reached for the doorknob.

Then he froze. Pulling down the sleeve of his jacket, Charlie created a crude, makeshift glove, surprising himself. He was already assuming guilt for something that he wasn't even sure had happened. *It's just a precaution.*

The doorknob turned with ease, and the latch clicked open. *Unlocked,* Charlie thought. He slipped off his shoes.

"Rudy?" Charlie called. "Are you here?"

There was no response.

The apartment was dark and drab, similar in layout to an apartment he had lived in with his mother and father in Belmont. To his right was an archway leading into the living room. Peeking inside, Charlie saw no signs of Gomes. Only a brown leather chair, a ratty yellow sofa, and a forty-five-inch plasma TV. In front of him was a short hallway leading to the master bedroom. There was a door halfway down, which Charlie assumed opened to a bathroom. He stood outside the door and heard the rushing of water from what sounded like the shower.

Using his jacket sleeve to conceal his fingerprints again, Charlie slowly turned the bathroom doorknob. The moment the door opened a crack, steam spilled out into the hallway. Charlie stood in the doorway and waited for the steam to dissipate. As the air cleared, he could see hot water spewing from the silver showerhead above a leopard-patterned shower curtain, which was pulled closed around a claw-foot tub. Water vapor that had condensed on the tile floor soaked the bottom of Charlie's feet. Since he'd left his shoes outside, only his socks shielded him from the dampness.

"Rudy?" Charlie called out. "Are you in here?"

Instinct told Charlie that the only surprise would be if Rudy responded. Inching forward, Charlie reached for the shower curtain, ignoring the precautions he had taken earlier about his fingerprints. Pulling the curtain toward the wall, Charlie let out a loud gasp as he staggered backward.

Rudy Gomes lay dead in a pool of water. The water from the showerhead cascaded downward and pelted Gomes, turning the clear liquid into crimson drops as it mixed with his brownish blood. Gomes's throat had been cut. Fatty tissue and frayed ligaments exploded outward from the dark, crescent-shaped gash. Had it been any deeper, Gomes would have been decapitated. Charlie quickly pulled the shower curtain closed.

As the blood rushed from Charlie's head, his stomach churned and roiled inside. Falling to his knees, Charlie slid across the damp floor and vomited into the toilet, his body shuddering and convulsing with each gag and expulsion. The shower curtain covered most of Gomes's corpse, but from his kneeling position on the bathroom floor Charlie could still see his legs and those cobalt blue feet sticking out at the end of the tub. He spent the better part of a minute on his knees, listening to the dreadful sound of water as it fell on a dead man.

After regaining enough strength, Charlie stood and stared down at Gomes's lifeless body. The gaping wound was no less repulsive than when he'd first laid eyes upon it.

Backing out of the bathroom, Charlie was again mindful to keep his hands from touching any objects or walls. It was bad enough that he had grabbed the shower curtain with his bare hands. He hoped that the steam would act as some sort of a masking agent. A sickening thought then occurred to him. *What if I did kill him? Who knows what other evidence I might have left behind?* The idea that evidence pointing to him could be anywhere in the house was no less terrifying than the body in the tub.

Putting the thought aside, Charlie left the apartment and walked toward his car. His hands were shaking as he put the key in the ignition. His stomach hadn't yet settled.

He took his time leaving, the cliché of trying to behave inconspicuously not lost on him. He searched for signs that somebody might have witnessed him entering Gomes's apartment. A front door ajar. A light or TV on in a living room. The street was thankfully deserted. Every window he looked at was either dark or had the shades drawn. There were no pedestrians in sight or cars coming down the narrow street.

As he settled in his car, terrifying thoughts took hold and would not let go.

"I killed him. I must have killed him. But I don't remember anything. Oh, God, please help me. Please . . ." Charlie muttered the words as if in a trance. The mantra lasted minutes before he realized he had to drive away from there as fast as he could. Nobody had seen him come out of Gomes's apartment. It wouldn't help if someone saw him loitering in his car outside the home of a murder victim. He didn't know where to go. He knew only that he had to distance him-self from the crime scene.

"Pull it together, Giles," Charlie muttered. "Whatever crazy thoughts you have, you better pull it together now."

Charlie drove five miles down Route 2 and took the 95 North exit toward Burlington. There was a Barnes & Noble at the Burlington Mall. Without any protection from the driver's side window, the car was frigid in the midmorning sun. He blasted the heat to help warm his hands. He pulled into the parking lot of Barnes & Noble and shut off the engine.

They'll find the glass on the sidewalk, Charlie thought. *I need to get this window fixed. I'll pay cash. I can't leave a trace that I had any work done.*

He kept vacillating between covering his tracks for a murder he had no memory of committing and refusing to accept the possibility that he had.

If I did kill him, why wasn't there any blood on my clothes? I woke up in the same clothes I went to sleep in. Did I wake up in the mid-dle of the night, change, drive over to his house, kill him, and then drive home? If so, what did I do with the weapon?

None of it seemed possible to Charlie, but he could think of no other explanation. He had left the notes for Joe and himself. *One down. Three to go.*

Frozen with fear and anxiety, he felt lost, displaced, and without any idea of what to do next. It was inconceivable. The perfect, orga-nized, meticulously planned Charlie Giles might be the most out-of-control beast imaginable.

The one gnawing need was the desire to know the truth. Even if it proved what he feared most, he had to know if it was even within the realm of scientific possibility.

Charlie picked up his cell phone. He scanned through his con-tacts. Then he dialed Rachel Evans. She answered on the fifth ring.

Chapter 21

"This is Rachel."

Charlie's spirits lifted at the sound of Rachel's voice. It was angelic, like a heavenly gift. Charlie couldn't even speak. He just kept the phone pressed tight against his ear.

"Hello? Is anyone there?" Rachel asked.

"Rachel," Charlie managed to say. "It's . . . it's Charlie Giles, Joe's brother."

Rachel gave a laugh. "I know you now, Charlie. You don't have to qualify yourself as Joe's brother anymore."

"Yeah. Yeah. Okay." Charlie felt rushed. His thoughts came in disjointed spurts. He still had flashes of Gomes lying dead in the tub, the grotesqueness of his gaping wound. His agitation must have come through over the phone.

"Charlie, you sound distressed," Rachel said. "Is everything okay?"

Breathing deeply, Charlie tried to collect himself. "I need to ask you something, Rachel."

"Professional or personal?"

He wished it *was* personal. If only this were just a friendly, flirtatious call. He traced her image in his mind—first those green oval eyes, then her willowy frame, her gentle, feminine allure combined with an inner strength and aura of ruggedness. So much of his life he had devoted to his ambition. It had cost him Gwen. And might very well have pushed him into madness.

"It's professional," Charlie said. He thought he heard a sigh of disappointment but couldn't be sure.

"I don't think that's such a good idea."

"Please, it's important. I need to know something. Something very important."

Another sigh. "What is it?"

Her icy tone did nothing to deter him.

"Could a person . . ." Charlie paused. "Could a person do something, something horrible, and have no memory of committing that act?"

"Why are you asking?"

"I just need to know," Charlie said.

Rachel hesitated. "It's possible," she said. "It's certainly not common. In cases of amnesia a person could suffer from transient global amnesia, which is a temporary loss of all memory. But this is rare, and mainly seen in older people. It generally dissipates within forty-eight hours."

"But what about specific events? Not all memory."

Charlie heard Rachel take a deep breath.

"Then we're talking about some sort of dissociative identity disorder."

"What's that?" Charlie asked.

"At least two personalities are at work, and the subject often has a sense of lost memory that goes far beyond normal forgetfulness. But missing time is still a controversial theory in DID cases. It's been linked to UFO and abduction phenomena—not exactly hard science. There are certainly clinical cases of this sort of missing time in patients with DID, though."

Charlie didn't speak. All he needed to hear was that it was possible. He caught a glimpse of himself in the rearview mirror and recoiled at what he saw: his dark haunted eyes, bordered by deep gray circles. Raccoon eyes—eyes of death. *How could something like this have stayed hidden for so long? Why is it happening to me now?*

"Joe's condition, my father's . . . could . . . they . . . Is it possible that they have multiple personalities?"

"Charlie, you know I can't speak to you about your brother's condition. And I never worked with your father. I've only seen his file, which is confidential information as well. Why don't you tell me what this is all about?"

Charlie didn't know how much to tell. If he told her about Gomes, he might be the instant target of a manhunt. But he also wanted her to confirm that he could have committed the crime. Whether his behavior was a result of multiple personality disorder or schizophrenia or both, he had to dig for the truth. The fact that memory loss and dissociative identity disorder were linked wasn't enough proof for him.

Charlie decided to test the waters. "What if I told you I wrote a list of names of people who I thought needed to die. And then I slipped that note into an envelope, put it under the sofa, and left another note for myself to go look under the sofa to find it—"

"Did you do that?" Rachel asked.

"—because I had no memory of writing the kill list in the first place."

"Were there specific names? Did you put down names of real people you wanted to harm, Charlie?"

Charlie disliked her tone. It was disconcerting how quickly she could turn from friendly to clinical; she was on the job now, doing what she did best.

"Yes," Charlie said. "There were specific names."

"Who, Charlie? I need to know the names."

"There was only one name," Charlie said, feigning confidence in the lie.

"Can you tell me the person's name?"

Charlie hesitated. "Simon Mackenzie. He was my boss at Solu-Cent."

Through the receiver, he could hear Rachel scratching something down on a piece of paper.

"Where are you, Charlie?" Rachel asked.

He hesitated. "I'd rather not say. Rachel, I don't know what's happening to me."

A silence followed. Charlie could hear the softness of her breathing through the receiver. It was calming to know that she was still on the line with him—that she hadn't hung up, or the call hadn't been dropped. He needed her to stay with him right now. He found her silence to be unsettling. He figured she was deciding how best to proceed. He knew it was her professional training at work, but the sound of her words alone was enough to slow his racing heart a few beats. He was ready to listen and act upon whatever she had to say.

"Charlie, I believe that to answer your questions and continue this conversation would be medically and ethically irresponsible."

He tried to hide his disappointment. "I understand," Charlie said. "I never meant to bring you into this, Rachel. I just didn't know where else to turn."

"Listen to me, Charlie. You need to go to a hospital," Rachel said. "It is my strong professional opinion that you require immediate medical attention. I cannot diagnose what may be happening to you over the phone. When you get to an ER, you can have me paged. My number is on my card. Do you still have my card?"

Charlie fumbled through his wallet.

"I have it," he said.

"Good. I'll get one of my colleagues, someone who doesn't have a conflict of interest, to come down and see you. Where are you now? Which hospital can you get to?"

Charlie thought a moment. "I'm not sure I can do that, Rachel."

If Rachel was thrown off by his defensiveness, it did not show.

"Charlie, the kill list you said you wrote . . . Tell me, do you want to hurt anybody right now?"

In answering this question, Charlie didn't hesitate at all. "No." It was affirming to feel confident in his response and in control of his emotions. He had no desire to hurt anyone. He couldn't remember a moment when he had. If a monster was lurking inside him, it remained well hidden.

"Charlie, do you own a gun?" Rachel asked.

Charlie didn't, but his father did. If he knew his mother, his father's .38 Special would still be in a shoe box in the attic, behind a floor fan. Dust-covered, for sure, but still there.

"I don't personally own a gun," Charlie said.

"Do you want to hurt yourself, Charlie? Are you thinking about that? You can be honest with me right now. It's extremely important that you are."

Did he want to hurt himself?

How could he live with himself if he were some sort of monster capable of that brutal murder? But to take his own life would mean accepting responsibility for acts that he had no memory of committing. In his heart and soul he did not believe he was a murderer. Until proven otherwise, he would never consider violence against himself.

"No," Charlie said. "I'm not going to do that. But I am lost, Rachel. I'm so totally lost right now." For the second time in a week, tears welled in his eyes. A sob caught him by surprise, as if it had come from someone else.

"I gave you my opinion, Charlie."

"I understand," was all he could manage.

"I need to tell you something else, Charlie."

"Yes?"

"The law requires that I contact Simon Mackenzie. That I warn him of the threat you've made against him."

Charlie's blood went cold. "You have to what?"

"I have a legal obligation to contact Simon Mackenzie and inform him of your written intentions. That you have made a threat against his life."

"But I didn't threaten Mac directly," Charlie said.

"You wrote his name on a list with the intention that those named should die by your hand. Under Massachusetts General Laws, Chapter One-twenty three, Section Thirty-six B, I have to take reasonable precautions."

"What precautions?"

"I'm legally obligated to warn any person who you might harm of the threat against them."

"But I'm not going to hurt Mac," Charlie said. "I told you that already."

"It's an obligation of every mental health professional, the duty to warn if a patient presents a physical danger to a named individual."

"But you said yourself that I'm not a patient. You can't be my provider, because of your professional relationship with Joe."

"That's a semantic I'm not entirely certain is worth my risk taking, or that would even withstand legal scrutiny."

Charlie's heart rate jumped, and he felt light-headed. He knew exactly how the scenario would play out. First, Mac would be alerted to the threat Charlie had allegedly made against him. The police would go looking for Gomes, too. The kill list would be evidence tying him to Gomes's murder. He had a motive and no alibi. Worse still, he couldn't be certain he had left the crime scene completely clean of his DNA. With the technology available today, it was impossible to be that careful. It wasn't a big leap to predict a grand jury verdict against him. And that would be only the start.

At all costs, he couldn't let that happen.

"I'll go to a hospital, but under one condition," he said. His mind worked quickly to find some negotiating position with Rachel. It was how his business background had trained him to think—analyze the situation with computer-like speed, determine all possible outcomes, and make a move.

"What's the condition?" Rachel asked.

Charlie assumed she was accustomed to thwarting all types of stall tactics. The next moment was crucial. If Rachel didn't believe in his sincerity, he was doomed.

"I go to the hospital right now, on the condition that you don't call Mac."

"I can't make that deal, Charlie. I wouldn't if I could."

"Listen, Rachel," Charlie said. "I honestly don't know what is happening to me. I admit some extraordinary behavior, but I have no anger or hostility toward Mac or anyone else. I swear to you this is the truth. If you go to Mac now, it will destroy my reputation forever. Any chance I have of rebuilding my life since all this insanity began will be gone. You have to give me the opportunity to prove one way or another who or what is behind all this—even if the ultimate answer lies within me. Please, Rachel. Give me that chance. Let me go to the hospital. Let me get evaluated before you sound the alarms."

"The law, Charlie . . . how can I . . ."

"Rachel, listen to me, please," Charlie said. His mind kept working in hyperdrive.

"I don't see how . . ."

"That law!" Charlie shouted the words loud enough for shoppers entering Barnes & Noble to turn and stare his way. He imagined he had startled Rachel as well. "Can you read it to me?"

Rachel cleared her throat. It was an unconscious response that Charlie interpreted as a willingness to compromise. A good sign. He listened as Rachel typed something on her keyboard—a Google search to retrieve the exact text of the law, he hoped.

Rachel read Section 36B into the phone. When she got through sub-point A, Charlie smiled. He listened carefully as she reread the passage at his request.

"The patient has communicated to the licensed mental health professional an explicit threat to kill or inflict serious bodily injury upon a reasonably identified victim or victims and the patient has the apparent intent and ability to carry out the threat, and the licensed mental health professional fails to take reasonable precautions as that term is defined in section one."

"And the patient has the apparent *intent and ability* to carry out the threat," Charlie repeated, emphasizing that the law required a showing of ability along with the threat.

"Yes. That is what it says."

"Well, I don't have that ability, Rachel," Charlie said.

"How can you prove that to me, Charlie?"

"I can prove it by going to the hospital, as you suggested. I can get evaluated. They can make a diagnosis. Perhaps offer some recommendation or treatment. The proof is when I call you from the ER."

This time Rachel's lengthy silence was not punctuated by her quiet breathing. She was deep in thought, perhaps even holding her breath. Charlie did the same. He knew her answer meant everything.

"Which hospital?"

He could have used InVision to locate the nearest emergency room, but it wasn't necessary. He knew exactly where the closest ER was to him. How could he not? His mother was a patient there.

"Mount Auburn Hospital. Fifteen minutes away."

"I'm calling the ER in twenty. If they don't know who you are, the next call I'm going to make is to Simon Mackenzie."

Charlie tried to thank her, but the line was already dead.

Chapter 22

Rachel Evans stared at the phone on her desk but could not bring herself to reach for the receiver. When she finally did, she made a surprise move and pulled her hand away before picking it up. She knew she had to make the call to Mackenzie's office; it had been her intention to do so all along. At least by offering Charlie the impression of a deal, she felt confident he would heed her advice and go to the nearest hospital. It wasn't a technique scripted out of any training manual she had studied, but Rachel wasn't a rising star at Walderman for her linear thinking, either.

Charlie was a good talker; she had to give him credit for that. Without missing a beat, he had capitalized on a potentially viable loophole in the law with decisive precision. Intellectually, she understood why Charlie opposed her contacting Mackenzie, but instinct made Rachel suspicious more was at stake than his sterling corporate reputation. Even so, she still felt guilty for deceiving him and wondered if more harm than good would come from her contacting his former boss. The law, however, demanded she take action, but that didn't make it any easier.

Rachel distracted herself from making the call by examining Joe's extensive case file. Perhaps something in it would help to shed light on Charlie's erratic behavior. She would feel better making the call if armed with even a cursory hypothesis to work from. Yet everything about Charlie's situation presented her with a truly unique conundrum. What she gleamed from Joe's file suggested only that the dice of DNA had come up lucky seven when Charlie was born.

The only references pertaining to Charlie that Joe had made in therapy had to do with his understandable frustration at his brother's ongoing apathy. Perhaps Alison Giles's sudden illness was a factor, or maybe the stress of moving in with Joe had extracted too great an emotional toll on Charlie. The timing wasn't quite right, though, she concluded. Charlie had come to see her before he knew about his mother being hospitalized. Nothing in Rachel's notes from her last session with Joe, the make-up appointment for the one he'd missed, hinted at Charlie's stunning decline. In fact, she had noted that Joe seemed to be enjoying having his brother around.

Indeed, the lack of any warning signs troubled her greatly. Charlie was fine one minute and falling apart the next. Not unheard of, Rachel reminded herself, but certainly unusual. Either his case would prove to be a rare anomaly or perhaps, she excitedly considered, the spark of some startling new discovery in neuroscience. Whatever the outcome, Charlie was in desperate need of help, and Rachel's trickery, though ethically suspect, should ensure just that.

No sooner had Rachel closed Joe's folder than her hand grasped the phone's receiver. It took a moment to route her call through SoluCent's main reception, but eventually she was put through. A cheery, mature-sounding woman answered on the first ring.

"Simon Mackenzie's office, may I help you?"

Rachel felt her throat tighten. It wasn't until she actually made the call that she fully understood Charlie's vocal opposition to the idea. If the industry was as gossipy and close-knit as he had implied, her call was tantamount to a lynching.

"Yes, I was wondering if I could speak with Mr. Mackenzie," Rachel said.

"I'm afraid Mr. Mackenize is out of the country on business and won't be returning until sometime next week. May I take a message?"

Rachel thought a moment, and a thin smile escaped her lips. Technically, her responsibility was to avert any immediate threat to persons named. Mackenzie was in no immediate danger, as he was traveling on business. What harm could come from her giving Charlie a chance for a proper medical evaluation? Perhaps she could spare him from the indignity he justly feared. Rachel decided to phone

Mount Auburn Hospital in ten minutes to check in on Charlie and take it from there.

"No message," Rachel said. "I'll just try back later if needed."

"Thank you for calling. Have a pleasant afternoon."

Rachel hung up the phone, feeling quite good about herself. Yes, she was feeling quite good indeed.

Chapter 23

The automatic doors of Mount Auburn Hospital opened as Charlie approached. It was midafternoon on a Thursday, and on any other day he'd turn right and walk the all too familiar fluorescent-lit linoleum hallway toward Ellison 5 and his mother's ICU bedside. This time he had to pause to scan a wall placard in front of him, looking for the directional arrow that would point him toward the ER. The ER was in the opposite direction of Ellison 5, and while walking along that corridor, he bumped into June Hollie, the nurse in charge of the ICU and one of Joe's favorites.

"Are you lost, Charlie?" June asked with a warm smile.

Charlie froze and stared blankly back at June. "Yes . . . I guess I'm just wandering the halls, thinking," he managed to say.

She squeezed his arm gently; her eyes felt kind and practiced.

"Of course," she said. "I just took a bit of a walk myself."

"Actually, I'm glad I bumped into you," Charlie said. "I was wondering if you got my message."

"About your mother's responsiveness?" June asked.

"Yes," Charlie replied. "It's just that I thought the last time I was here, she was moving her arm. And it seemed voluntarily to me, at least whenever I touched her. I pinched her even and was certain there was movement after that, too. Did you notice the same?"

June kept her eyes locked on his. Her compassion and empathy were visible, as though she were a part of the family and not a paid professional.

"We've kept a close watch. And we've tried the same things you reported," June replied. "I'm sorry, Charlie. But we didn't notice any movement at all."

Charlie nodded. "Perhaps, it's just that I wanted there to be," he offered.

"That can certainly happen. Will we be seeing you soon? I'll tell Judy and Samantha to be on the lookout."

He nodded again, more eagerly than he had intended. A lengthy visit to the ICU felt like a blessing compared to what he was about to go through.

"I'll be up soon," he said.

June squeezed his arm again, smiled politely, and walked past him, on her way to Ellison 5, the ICU, and Alison Giles's bedside. With a deep, anxious sigh, Charlie turned and made his way for the emergency room.

The waiting room of the Mount Auburn ER was mostly empty. A boy sat with his arm encased in ice, tears welling in his eyes, while his worried mother sat stoic by his side. On another chair a man in his late fifties watched a soap opera airing on the wall-mounted TV. He wore a tattered olive green army jacket that seemed to come straight out of the "to be tossed" bin at an Army-Navy store. Whatever his ailment, it wasn't visible to Charlie, and he showed no eagerness to be seen by hospital staff.

Charlie announced himself to the intake nurse. Mindful that Rachel might follow through on her threat to call, he made certain she wrote down his name before taking the forms and clipboard she handed him to the waiting area as instructed. Even without a heavy influx of patients, the wait lasted past the end of the soap opera and a good fifteen minutes into the start of another. The man in the olive green army jacket hadn't moved and didn't seem the least bothered by his wait. A nurse had called the boy into the ER, his mother in tow. A few others arrived, none seriously injured, and took their seats with the requisite forms to complete. Nobody sat near Charlie or the olive green army jacket man. They were the poisonous ones, Charlie thought. The men without cuts or visible trauma, loners in the ER, who seemed to be viewed by the other patients with a caution one might reserve for a wild animal.

Thirty minutes had passed before a nurse emerged from the waiting room and called his name.

"Charlie Giles?"

He needed a moment for his name to register. The idea that he was actually going to be a patient in the hospital had yet to sink in.

"That's me," Charlie said, standing.

"Follow me," the nurse said.

Charlie walked a few paces behind. She pulled back a thin white sheet hanging from a semicircular rod, like that in a hotel shower, and directed him to take a seat on the empty bed.

"How are you feeling today?" she asked. "Your chart indicates you were referred to us by your psychiatrist. You didn't list your physician's contact name. Can you tell me your psychiatrist's name?"

"She's not really my psychiatrist," Charlie said. "She's more of a friend, I guess you could say, who also happens to be a mental health professional."

"Okay," said the nurse, her tone warning him not to try additional avoidance tactics. "Then can you tell me why your *friend* suggested you come in today?"

He hated how she emphasized the word *friend*. Charlie took a deep breath and gathered his thoughts, hoping that she would nod her head, as if what he would say was commonplace.

"I've been experiencing lost time," Charlie said.

She looked at him. "Lost time?"

"I may have done things that I can't remember doing," Charlie explained.

"I see," she said. "That can be very scary."

Though her body language didn't offer any solace that a quick diagnosis was to come, Charlie was grateful that she didn't seem judgmental, or worse, act afraid of him. The willingness to listen to a total stranger who made outlandish, perhaps committable statements was beyond his comprehension. If the roles had been reversed, he would have dismissed the person as crazy. But her compassionate attitude suggested she was willing to listen and, above all, to believe.

She asked a few more questions and jotted down additional information on a PC tablet. Charlie was uncomfortable that his personal information was now the official property of the Mount Auburn patient database. If Rachel had not threatened to contact Mackenzie, Charlie would never have come.

The vital tests were quick. She checked his blood pressure, heart rate, and gave him a brief eye exam, presumably looking for drug use. In minutes she had completed her checklist.

"I'll tell the doctor to hurry. I can see you're anxious to get this over with."

They made eye contact. It was as though she could look right through his armor and tell that he was truly scared.

"I appreciate that," Charlie said.

"It won't be long. I promise."

The nurse slipped outside the curtained enclosure with a quick wave good-bye.

Charlie looked down at his watch. He wondered if Rachel had kept her promise to call. Perhaps, he thought, it was all a bluff to get him to seek the help she thought he needed. For the first time since this nightmare had started, he began to believe that she was right.

The curtain was pushed aside, and an Indian woman entered.

"I'm Dr. Asha John," she said, extending a hand to Charlie. Dr. John's handshake was strong, the nails on her hand cut short. She had wavy dark hair past her shoulders and wore a white coat over a pair of green hospital scrubs and white tennis sneakers. A pair of tortoiseshell glasses hung around her neck from a gold chain lanyard. Charlie stared at her name tag longer than he had intended.

"My husband is an American. I took his name," she preemptively explained.

Charlie reddened, then nodded.

"So tell me, Mr. Giles. What is troubling you today?"

Charlie repeated what he had told the RN.

"And these episodes . . . How many do you think have occurred?" Dr. John asked.

"If I could answer that, I wouldn't have lost that time, would I?"

Her expression revealed nothing. "Have you had any severe headaches since this began?"

"No."

"What about fevers? Vomiting? Drowsiness?"

"No to all," Charlie said.

She placed her long, delicate fingers along the sides of Charlie's neck and began pressing them against his skin, as though playing keys on a piano.

"My throat feels fine," Charlie said.

"Yes. I'm sure it does," Dr. John said. Then she moved her fingers higher and felt up by his ears and across his cheeks with the same pressing motion.

"Can I ask what you're looking for?"

"Well, Mr. Giles, normally I would have to phone the psychiatrist on call, seeing as I'm not trained in that specialty. However, patient volume is light today. I'd like to rule out some other possibilities if I could before making that call."

"Such as?"

"Encephalitis, for one."

"Encephalitis?" Charlie had heard of the condition before but wouldn't have been able to identify the symptoms.

"It's an inflammation of the brain," she said. "It's brought on by a viral infection. It has been documented to change behavior in some patients, alter personalities. It could explain your lost time. Do you have any viruses you know about? Herpes, for instance?"

"No," Charlie said.

She continued to feel around his cheeks. "I'm checking your parotid glands for any sign of the mumps. It's rare for mumps to cause encephalitis, but less so than mosquitoes. At least around these parts."

"Why do you think it might be encephalitis?" Charlie asked.

That stopped her examination. "Right now, Mr. Giles, my job is not to figure out what might be causing this," she said. "My job is to figure out what isn't. I'd like to rule out several possibilities. It's going to take some blood work. I'd like for you to stay here. At least until the blood work is done and I've had a chance to contact our staff psychiatrist if needed."

"How long will that take?" Charlie asked.

"A few hours," she said. "No more than three."

Charlie thought. It was strange that something as dire-sounding as encephalitis would seem like a blessing. It felt curable, at least. Even though he hadn't been entirely truthful about all his symptoms, he'd been honest about his lost time. Perhaps Rachel's first suggestion was correct: something was physically wrong with his brain. Waiting a few hours for an explanation for the madness of the past several weeks was a small price to pay. He couldn't do anything for Gomes now. The police would find him soon enough. But perhaps something could still be done to save himself.

"Do you want me to wait right here?"

"That'll be fine. I'll get one of the nurses to draw your blood."

"Bring it on," Charlie said. For the first time in days he felt a small glimmer of hope. A swelling brain felt a lot less scary than a mind he couldn't control.

Chapter 24

It took a few minutes of gnawing before Charlie realized that he was biting down on his knuckle. It was a habit he'd developed as a kid, around the same time his father had stopped taking medication for psychosis and started behaving erratically. Few in his class had teased him about it. Without peer pressure to stop it, the habit had become part of Charlie's makeup. His classmates had seen it as a sign of his competitive nature, a visible barometer of the intensity that propelled Charlie to excel in all facets of school life—academics, athletics, and popularity.

It wasn't until after a particularly stressful exam in college that he stopped. In study group, he had actually broken skin and begun sucking out his blood. A woman had noticed a thin line of red dripping down his chin and had screamed loudly. The embarrassment had brought the habit to an immediate and long overdue end—until now.

Charlie rose and paced around the small enclosed examination area. The equipment was for the most part familiar: a blood pressure machine, bins of sterile instruments, bandages, a small oxygen tank, and several intercoms and buttons for alerting staffers to emergent situations. He sat down on a swivel stool that he'd pulled out from underneath a desk fastened to the wall. The bed was making him uncomfortable. It felt more appropriate for the truly infirm. He kept the curtain drawn and listened to the sounds of patients crying out in pain, of doctors and nurses consoling and healing. Charlie pictured each measure from the first Charlie Christian tune that he'd memorized. The mental exercise was at least helping him to relax. Perhaps, he thought, when he held a piece of paper in his hands, something that had been generated from lab tests, produced by computers, validated by technology, he would embrace the idea that he could be seriously ill. Until then, this whole experience served one important purpose—to keep Mackenzie in the dark about the kill list.

Charlie began to think about what would happen if he was truly sick. With his mother in a coma and his brother incapable of help, what would he do? Who would take care of Monte? *Randal,* Charlie thought. If needed, he could call Randal.

Gomes's dead corpse came to him. *Would I be putting Randal's life in danger? Could I hurt him as well?* Charlie couldn't fathom the idea. It churned his stomach. If Charlie had a Dr. Jekyll living inside him, he remained elusive. That was the most frustrating thing of all. As much as he tried, Charlie could not recall any memory from the night Gomes was killed. Not a single one.

More time passed. Dr. John had yet to return. Despite the sounds and commotion taking place behind the thin white sheet, Charlie assumed that no major traumas had delayed her. He began to wonder what was keeping her and was growing increasingly anxious at the prospect of waiting longer than she'd estimated. He looked down at his watch and checked the time. Nearly two hours had passed since he first set foot in the hospital.

He thought about checking in with reception to see if Rachel had called. If she had, he might opt to leave. They could phone him with the lab results if necessary. Nothing about how he felt physically—no headaches, nausea, or other symptoms—made him concerned he might drop dead if he left.

He was just about to rise from his stool when he saw a woman's legs through a gap in the curtain. It wasn't Dr. John, for this woman's legs were white, not brown like the skin of an Indian woman. Charlie sat back down on his stool and waited for the woman to pull the curtain open. Her feet did not move. She just stood outside his examination area, her shoes pointing in toward him, as though she were about to step inside at any moment. *Perhaps she's just reviewing the results,* Charlie thought.

After what felt like an eternity, the woman turned away, her feet disappearing from sight. Charlie rose and pulled the curtain aside.

He peered out into the busy foyer. From the PA system he heard Dr. Asha John's name being paged.

From the bustle of patients and staffers milling about, he could not identify who had been standing behind the curtain. A movement to his right caught his eye. He turned his head just in time to see a figure disappearing down the corridor that led out of the ER. The figure paused, as if choreographed. She turned and looked directly at him.

He recognized her. She was real enough for his heart to beat madly in his chest.

Anne Pedersen waved her fingers in the air, as if taunting him, and then, baring her teeth in a grin, she laughed. With a tilt of her head, a silent call for him to pursue her, she slipped behind the wall and disappeared around the corner. Charlie shouted her name and took off running.

Chapter 25

Rachel Evans had lost track of the hour. Three emergencies had come up between the time she'd hung up on Charlie and the twenty minutes she had allotted herself before phoning Mount Auburn for the promised follow-up. Three hours had passed by the time Rachel finally picked up the phone to call Mount Auburn. It was a forgivable lapse given that Mackenzie was far from harm's way.

Admissions patched Rachel through to the ER. An RN named Jessica answered the call. Rachel listened to the garbled sound of Dr. Asha John's name being called out over the hospital PA.

"Yes? This is Dr. Asha John. How may I help you?"

"Dr. John, my name is Rachel Evans. I'm following up on a patient referral I sent to your hospital earlier this afternoon. Charlie Giles."

"Ah. You must be the friend who happens to be a mental health professional."

Their unofficial relationship meant added ambiguity when it came to discussing patient status. It might have complicated Rachel's ability to assess Charlie's threat level, were she not practiced at dealing with patients who gave only half-truths and misleading information. Dr. John needed to say very little for Rachel to know a lot.

"I realize I have no official relationship with the patient. His brother is a patient of mine. I offered to refer Charlie to a psychiatrist from our office. But I wanted to first get a sense of his state of mind and your initial perceptions if possible."

"There are no outward signs of infection or any other ailment that would suggest the need for anything other than psychiatric care, if that's what you're looking for."

"Yes. It's certainly a start. Did he seem agitated to you?"

"Nervous is more like it. We are running blood work on him. Just to double-check for infection."

"Sure, that makes sense."

"I can give you a call when we have those results if you'd like."

"That would be helpful. In the meantime, I'll put the word out to our staff to find some names for doctors he might be interested in working with. But again, he doesn't seem overly agitated or potentially hostile to you?"

"Not at all," Dr. John said.

Over the phone Rachel heard a scream. It followed the loud crash of a bunch of items hitting the floor.

"Anne Pedersen! Anne Pedersen!"

The cry was loud enough for Rachel to hear it clearly through the phone receiver. She knew the voice. Rachel listened as best she could as the commotion and chaos escalated. She heard somebody shout, "Charlie Giles in three. He's running down the hall, yelling after somebody. He just knocked Jessica over! You have to get security on this right away."

Rachel started to say something, but just as she had done to Charlie hours earlier, Dr. Asha John hung up the phone without saying good-bye.

Chapter 26

Charlie Giles sprinted after Anne Pedersen. She was no more than fifteen to twenty feet ahead of him.

Charlie turned the corner, but instead of gaining ground on Anne, he crashed into a nurse who carried a tray of supplies, sending them both falling to the floor. In the low-ceilinged corridor, the din from the clattering of instruments and her metal tray crashing onto the tiled floor echoed with the intensity of a car accident.

Charlie stumbled to his feet. He scanned the long corridor that connected the ER to other parts of the hospital. The nurse he knocked over stayed on the floor and made no attempt to rise. She looked up at Charlie, expecting an apology and a hand up.

"Anne Pedersen! Anne!" Charlie called. Charlie could see a fire door a third of the way down the corridor and ran toward it full sprint. He didn't open it at first. Signs posted on the door warned of alarms sounding if it was opened. He looked out the window, cocking his head to both sides, and saw nothing.

"He just knocked me over," the nurse said as an orderly helped her to her feet.

"You! You! Stop right there!" yelled the orderly.

The orderly was easily six foot five, at least 220 pounds. He wore light green hospital scrubs and carried a Nextel mobile phone.

"Did you see that woman?" Charlie screamed to the nurse, who was picking herself up off the floor. "Did you see her?"

She didn't say a word. Her knees were shaking as she got to her feet.

"You stay right there," the orderly said. He put the Nextel to his mouth. "Security! Security! Send a team to the ER right away."

"You don't understand," Charlie began. "That woman who was just here, she's the key to everything."

"I don't know what you're talking about, mister, but you better not try anything funny," warned the orderly. "Just stay right there until security comes."

Charlie saw Dr. Asha John appear from around the corner. She entered the corridor through the ER, her eyes wide with concern. Charlie figured he had thirty feet between him and the orderly. It would be enough of a head start.

"There was a woman. Please tell her that you saw a woman!" Charlie pointed toward the nurse he had knocked over, but she was gone. She must have slipped away when Dr. John entered the scene.

"Just stay where you are," the orderly said. "Security is on its way."

He pointed his Nextel mobile phone as though it were some sort of weapon. Past the orderly, down at the end of the corridor nearest the hospital entrance, Charlie saw two security guards approaching. They were armed. Both had hands on their belts, presumably readying to draw a real weapon. This time Charlie didn't hesitate at all. He took off running.

"Freeze!" one of the security guards shouted. "Get down on the floor with your hands behind your head!"

Charlie turned but kept running. He was stunned at the ground they had already gained.

Panic gripped him. Sprinting through a set of double doors, Charlie stumbled into a large industrial laundry facility. Large rolling bins piled high with towels and sheets were everywhere. Bags of laundry hung from heavy chains, attached to a matrix of ceiling-mounted guide tracks. Sounds from the loud washers and dryers bounced off the concrete walls and floors.

He pushed one of the bins aside and jumped another with a hurdler's stride. He reached the back of the room, flipped himself over another bin, this time tipping it over and spilling stained, filthy sheets and towels onto himself as he crashed hard into the floor. Charlie stayed buried under a mountain of fetid laundry. He began to gag and bit down hard on his tongue to keep the bile rising up his throat from spilling out.

He was at least fifty feet from the entrance now. He was shielded from the security guards' line of sight, low to the floor, with the pile of laundry on top and the felled bin in front. Unfortunately, that meant he couldn't see them, either. His only cue that they were in the room was the shadow cast on the ceiling from the swinging double doors as they swayed open and shut.

A minute passed before he heard them.

"Do not move!" one of the security guards ordered. "Do you understand? We know you are in here. There is no exit from this room. Stay where you are!"

They fell silent. Charlie's heart raced in his chest with a rhythmic pounding that mirrored the tumbling sound of the dryers. Charlie stayed pressed low to the floor. He kept the laundry piled on top of him. There wasn't much distance between him and the security guards now, he figured. If he stood to run while they were in front of him, he'd be an easy target. His only hope was to wait for them to pass and then try to slip out the door he'd come through.

"We won't hurt you. Stand and reveal yourself," said one of the security guards.

By the sound of their footsteps he knew they were flanking him and closing in fast. The guards kept shouting for him to stand up. Their voices echoed off the walls, making it difficult to discern just how close they were. Charlie's eyes caught the reflection of movement in the glass on one of the washers. He could see at least one of them! As long as he stayed on that trajectory, he could watch his progress in the reflection of the washing-machine glass. He watched the distorted reflection come and go between washing machines. They kept calling his name.

"Mr. Giles. We're not going to hurt you. We are here to help you," said one of the guards.

Keep on coming, he thought. The guard in his line of sight was closing in fast, no more than ten feet from him now. His distorted image disappeared from the bubbled washing-machine glass. The next time Charlie saw it, the guard would be standing right on top of him. Charlie took in a breath, held it. Then he sprang.

Grasping the underside of the laundry bin, Charlie leapt forward, using his momentum to force the empty bin knee level into the surprised security guard. The guard let out a cry as he went down, and Charlie thought he heard the electric buzz of a Taser gun.

"I see him! I see him!" the other guard shouted. Charlie had the edge he needed to scamper out of the room. He'd make a quick exit through the fire door. After that, he didn't have much of a plan. From his peripheral vision Charlie could see the guard he'd knocked over pushing the bin aside and getting back on his feet. The other guard kept shouting at him to freeze.

"I've got him in my sight, Dave!" his partner called out. "I'm taking the shot."

Charlie sprinted down the corridor. He didn't know the range of a Taser gun. He prayed it was less than thirty feet, because that was about the distance he had on the security guards. Racing down the hall, Charlie saw Dr. Asha John emerge from the ER and stand in the corridor, right between him and the fire exit door that was his escape. He looked past Dr. John and saw Anne Pedersen standing behind her, waving to him.

"Turn around! Turn around!" Charlie screamed. "She's right behind you! Turn around now!"

Anne Pedersen kept waving to Charlie from the end of the corridor. Dr. John kept her eyes fixed on Charlie. Charlie took one glance behind him. The guards had closed in. They were no more than twenty feet behind. When he looked past Dr. John again, Anne Pedersen was gone.

Charlie held up his hands. Dr. John did the same. But her intention was to stop the security guards from shooting Charlie in the back with a Taser.

"She's here! She's here!" Charlie said, panting to catch his breath.

"Yes, I'm sure she is." Dr. Asha John took a step toward Charlie.

"I can explain everything. Everything," Charlie said. He was surprised at how hard it was to catch his breath. The adrenaline from the chase and seeing Anne Pedersen again made it nearly impossible to slow his heart rate down.

Dr. John approached him. She kept her hands up, indicating to

Charlie that she was unarmed. "You need to calm down, Charlie. It's important that you calm down."

"I'm calm. I'm calm. I need to get that woman. I need to find Anne," Charlie said.

"Yes," Dr. John said. "We'll find her together. I just need to make sure you're okay. May I do that?"

Charlie felt his heart continue pounding in his chest. Anne Pedersen was still in the hospital. He could wait a moment. Calm himself, then find her with the doctor's help.

"Yes," Charlie said. "I'll catch my breath. Then we'll find her."

"Yes, catch your breath, Charlie. Then we'll find her together."

The security guards stayed back as instructed. Crowds were now in the corridor, watching everything unfold. Dr. Asha John moved in next to Charlie. She kept her eyes fixed on his.

"We have to go find her. She is the key to all of this," Charlie said.

"Of course she is."

Dr. Asha John moved with the speed of a mongoose making a kill. Charlie felt a sharp jab in his left leg.

"What have you done to me?" Charlie shouted.

"I've injected you with a sedative to help calm you down. If you try to run, they will shoot."

"You have to listen to me. There is a woman. She is here in the hospital. I have to find her."

The security guards moved closer. They held their weapons pointed at Charlie's back. From the end of the corridor Charlie saw a woman's figure emerge again. She was silhouetted by shadows from the light streaming into the corridor from two large bay windows nearest the emergency entrance.

The drug hadn't taken hold. He felt completely in control of his faculties. As she approached, he compared her figure to Anne Pedersen's—same long hair, willowy frame, familiar gait.

"Behind you," Charlie said to Dr. John in a near whisper. "Doctor, please turn around and look behind you. I'm trapped. There is no place for me to go. Look. That's all I ask."

Dr. Asha John turned her head to look behind her. "Do you know who that is?" she asked.

"It's Anne Pedersen," Charlie said, his voice shallow, his breathing still erratic. "That's what I've been trying to tell you."

The woman from the end of the corridor continued her approach. Her features came into focus.

"It's . . . it's . . ." Charlie's eyes widened as the realization set in.

"It's going to be all right, Charlie," Rachel Evans said.

Those were the last words Charlie heard before the corridor went dark.

Chapter 27

"Do you know where you are?"

Charlie blinked his eyes, trying to focus on the person seated across from him. His vision stayed blurred; the only way Charlie knew she was a woman was by the tenor of her voice.

"Do you know where you are?" the woman asked again.

For the first time in what felt like days, but was probably no more than hours, Charlie tried to speak. His mouth was parched and his throat dry. His jaw felt tight, as though it had been wired shut. Charlie wanted to scream, to beg her for something to drink, but his thoughts were too cloudy and confused. All he could manage was to stare at her. Any signals his brain was sending to the rest of his body—speech, movement—were either cut off or delayed. Panic started to take hold. *Could this condition be permanent?* He shook his head from side to side but couldn't clear the fog.

"Are you okay?" she asked. "You may be feeling groggy from the drugs we gave you. It's normal. There is nothing to worry about."

Charlie's vision began to return. A filmy cloud shrouded the scattering of familiar objects in the room: a chair, a desk, and a lamp. To his left were three small hopper windows. Through them he could make out the top of an adjacent building. Wherever he was, he wasn't on the ground floor. The warming colors of the setting sun contrasted with the starkness of the room's fluorescent lights and their unforgiving glow cast off a white tile floor.

Charlie tried to speak again. He could move his jaw this time but struggled with speech. At least he could move his mouth. That small victory was enough for him to let out a sigh of relief. The lethargy

was beginning to subside. He hoped that his vision would soon return to normal.

"Water. I need water." Charlie croaked out the words.

"Of course. Here you go. Drink slow," said the woman.

She handed him a paper cup. He put the drink to his lips and
swallowed the entire contents in a gulp. The water felt blissful against
Charlie's chapped, dry lips. He closed his eyes again and rubbed
them with his hands. Removing his hands from his face, Charlie
squinted into the light and tried once again to focus on the woman.
This time he could see her face more clearly. She had brown hair and
wore glasses. She also had on a white coat and looked to be some
sort of doctor. She held a clipboard in her hands and was writing
something down. He noticed other voices in the room besides hers.
He looked up and saw a man standing behind her. No. There were
two.

Charlie crushed the paper cup in his hands. It was an unconscious
release of nervous energy.

"I can take that from you if you'd like." She reached forward as
Charlie handed her the crushed cup.

"Thank you." Charlie's voice sounded weak and hoarse.

"Do you know where you are?" she asked again.

"No."

"Do you know what day it is?"

Charlie thought a moment. *What day it is?* His brain was starting
to come back to life. For a person accustomed to making million-
dollar decisions on a weekly basis, sometimes after only a fifteen-
minute meeting, being asked to confirm the day of the week felt
belittling at best. He didn't respond.

"Do you know what day it is today?" she asked again.

Uneasy at the prospect of some sort of penalty for not answering,
Charlie decided it was in his best interest to respond.

"Thursday," he said.

"The month?"

"Nineteen thirteen," he said. He remained expressionless.

"Was that a joke?" she asked.

"Did you think it was funny?"

"Was that your intention?"

Charlie sighed. "September. It's September," he said.

Nothing in her mannerisms indicated pleasure or displeasure at his attempt at humor. "You are in a hospital, Charlie. You're at Walderman Hospital. Do you know why you are here?"

Anne Pedersen's face flashed into his thoughts. Then he pictured Rachel Evans. He could see her walking toward him down the long corridor at Mount Auburn. He searched his mind for other memories, but there were none.

"I saw a woman in the ER at Mount Auburn," Charlie said. "I needed to talk to her. She ran away from me. I chased after her. Then I woke up here."

"Where is here? Do you know where you are now?"

"You said a hospital. You said that I'm at Walderman."

"Yes. That's right. That's what I said. I'm going to tell you three words, Charlie. I'd like for you to remember them. Okay?"

"Okay."

"The words are *piano, magazine,* and *wheel.* Can you remember those words?"

"I think so."

"I'd like you to close your eyes now. Can you repeat the words I just told you?"

"Piano, magazine, and wheel," Charlie said.

"Very good. Can you tell me what floor you are on?"

"You didn't tell me that," Charlie snapped.

"Please just answer the question. Can you tell me what floor you are on?"

"I don't know. How should I know that if you didn't tell me?"

Charlie watched as she wrote something on her paper.

"What? Is that bad? Is it?" He heard his voice rising and regretted the weakness.

"It's not bad, Charlie," she said. "I'm just making a note, that's all. I'm just trying to assess your condition, Charlie. It will help us with your treatment. I can tell you find these questions frustrating. Please trust me when I say that they are extremely beneficial in helping us assess your current state of mind. Can we continue?"

"Do I have a choice?"

She paused. "Not really."

"Then please, by all means." Charlie waved at her with open palms. He hoped she knew he intended it to be mocking.

"Do you know what country you live in?"

"America." Charlie felt anger rising again but managed to suppress it. Hostility would do him no good.

"And the state?" she asked. "Do you know what state you are in?"

"A state of confusion?" Charlie smiled when he said it.

Again she gave no indication whatsoever that his answers were appropriate or expected. It bothered him that he had no idea what it was she was looking for, the purpose of these questions. She offered no clues, in body language or otherwise.

"Do you know what state you are in?" she asked again.

Charlie looked at the two men looming behind her. Both were young. One was dark-skinned; the other fair. Both stared at him, with arms folded tightly across their chests. They regarded him as visitors to a zoo might look at a caged animal.

"I am in Massachusetts. If I'm at Walderman Hospital, then I'm in the town of Belmont," Charlie said.

"Thank you," she said.

"There are approximately twenty-five thousand residents in Belmont," he added.

"Are there?"

"And about four point six square miles of total area."

"I see."

She continued to write as Charlie spoke. He knew those statistics from the research he did years ago while selecting a town to move to for his relocation back east. He seldom forgot information that he'd read—especially if it was a meaningless data point. Perhaps, subconsciously even, he hoped reciting obscure facts would inspire her to judge him competent and send him on his way. Instead, she remained stoic, turned to the two men standing behind her, and held up her clipboard for them to see.

"Is that a twenty-seven or twenty-eight?" the fair-skinned man asked.

"Twenty-seven," she said. She made a subtle nod toward Charlie.

The fair-skinned man's face reddened. He scribbled something on his notepad and looked down at the floor.

She turned to face Charlie again. "Do you know why you're here?"

Charlie let out another exasperated sigh. "Do you mind telling me what the fuck this is all about?" He didn't mean to use profanity, but his frustration got the better of him.

The men standing behind her moved in response, positioning themselves on either side of Charlie. The fair-skinned man got as far as reaching under Charlie's armpit to pull him out of the chair. But the woman stopped him by holding up her hand.

"It's okay. Let him go." She spoke calmly.

The man lowered Charlie gently back onto his metal folding chair. Charlie straightened his clothes and rubbed under his arm where his skin had been pinched.

"Thank you," Charlie said. "I'm sorry. But I don't understand any of this."

"That's not uncommon. Can you answer my question, though? Do you know why you are here?" said the woman.

"Because somebody thought I was crazy."

"Do you think that you're having difficulties?"

Charlie hesitated before answering. "No . . . yes . . . I . . . I don't know anymore."

"Do you think that you need to be here right now?"

Charlie gave a long, hard stare into her cold eyes. She was no more than thirty. Unlike Rachel, she seemed more practiced at this than natural. For someone so accustomed to always having the upper hand, Charlie found her control over him extremely unnerving. He felt that she was purposefully shaping him with her questions, forming quick conclusions, but he was powerless to do anything about it.

"I'm not going to hurt anybody, if that's what you're asking me."

"Do you think it's a good idea if you stay here?"

"Clearly, you think it's a good idea," Charlie said. "What does that say about me if I say no?"

"What do you think it says?"

"That I have poor judgment."

"Do you?"

"And if I say yes . . . well, doesn't that mean that my bed is waiting for me? So you tell me. What choice do I really have here?"

She scratched more notes on her clipboard while he spoke. All he wanted to do was rip it out of her hands and toss it out the window.

"I need to ask you some personal questions now," she said.

"Oh? What were those? Just a warm-up?"

"Are you married?"

"Not yet," he said, grinning at her. "But I am available."

She didn't smile. Her questions continued for thirty minutes more. For each reply he gave only the facts as he felt she deserved to hear them—unembellished and unrevealing. *Yes, my family has a history of mental illness. Yes, my brother is a patient here. No, I've never been depressed. No, I have never had episodes of anxiety. No, I don't hear voices or see things that aren't really there.*

"Tell me about Anne. That's her name, right? Anne?"

"Yes."

"Do you think that she's out to get you?"

"Yes," Charlie said.

"Do you believe that she is real?"

"Yes." Charlie enjoyed his one-word answers. It was childish, but he could do little else to protest. The less he gave, the more he felt he was talking back for himself.

"Do you believe that you're here at Walderman now?"

Charlie looked at her. She shifted in her chair.

"You know," he said, "you've been poking at my brain for a while now. But I just realized something."

"Oh? What's that?" she asked.

"I just realized that I don't know your name."

"Okay. I can tell you that. My name is Susan. Susan Bishop."

"And are you a doctor, Susan Bishop?"

"I'm a PhD. A doctor of psychology."

"Well, then, doctor of psychology," Charlie said, "I'm getting a little tired of this, so let's just breeze through the rest, if you don't mind. Let me start. I'm not suicidal. I don't own a gun. I have no interest in hurting anybody, and I want to leave now. Right now!"

Charlie stood, knocking his chair over backward with a crash. He turned and walked toward the only door he saw in the room, a few feet behind from where he'd sat. Nobody moved in pursuit. *A bad sign,* he thought. He reached for the handle of the door and pulled. *Locked.* He pulled again, knowing that it was a futile act but unable to resist the urge. He scanned the rest of the room for any other possible exits. The hopper windows were too small to fit through and were probably locked as well. If they weren't, they were most likely too high up for him to make a safe exit.

Charlie eyed his metal folding chair, considering its value as a weapon. The darker-skinned man shook his head. Charlie looked away. Overpowering those two lumberjacks in his weakened condition would be impossible.

"Okay. Okay. You got me," Charlie said, walking back toward Dr. Bishop, with his hands held up in a show of surrender. He righted his chair and sat down again. "Listen to me, please. Listen. I'm fine. Trust me. I'm completely fine. You guys are the ones making me nuts. But I want to leave now."

"Yes. I understand that, Charlie," Dr. Bishop said. "But we don't think that's in your best interest at this time. A medical doctor is going to come by in a bit to talk with you."

"Medical doctor?"

"A psychiatrist."

"I see."

"He'd like to speak with you about medications. Are you allergic to any medications?" Dr. Bishop asked.

"How long?" Charlie eyes flashed.

"Pardon me?"

"How long do you intend to keep me here against my will?"

"Oh, I see." She averted her eyes.

"How long?" he asked again.

"Well, that depends, Charlie."

"Depends? Depends on what?"

"Well, on you, naturally. It all depends on you."

Chapter 28

A nurse approached Charlie from behind, tapping him on the shoulder. He spun around, startling her more than she had him. Her hand went to her chest. She was a black woman, late twenties, tall, with an athletic build and close-cropped hair. She reminded Charlie of Halle Berry. She was stunning, but never in his life had he felt so unattractive to the opposite sex. She just saw him as a patient in need, and it felt dehumanizing. No wonder Joe had become a hermit after his diagnosis.

For the first few years after his schizophrenic diagnosis, Joe had spent more days in the mental hospital than out. His mother rightfully had feared not only for Joe's safety but for Charlie's as well. The paranoia, hallucinations, and total lack of inhibition—which had often exploded into a fierce verbal assault directed at anyone Joe felt was deserving—had left his mother no choice. When at home, Joe had acted embarrassed about the disorder, as though he, and not the disease, were to blame for his behavior. He tried to keep to himself, but that had only made his hallucinations worse. Constant stimulation, Charlie's mother had explained, was the best way to keep his hallucinations at bay, and so she'd encouraged the younger brother to engage the older more regularly. Charlie had pretended Joe's behavior didn't frighten him, but it had been a difficult charade to keep up. So began the role of Alison Giles as savior and her seemingly 24/7 relationship with her ill son. In spite of the unsettling circumstances, Charlie had felt abandoned by his mother and envious of the attention Joe received. Intellectually, Charlie had understood why it was so; emotionally, however, he'd still been a fifteen-year-old boy without a father and now a mother, too.

Laughter had been a prized commodity back then. Charlie remembered Joe once saying, "Epilepsy is easy, but schizophrenia is hard," parodying the famous quote about dying and comedy. If what Charlie was feeling right now even hinted at the pain of Joe's near twenty-year relationship with schizophrenia, his brother deserved far more respect than he had got. Charlie wanted nothing more but to disappear. Being viewed by others as weak was almost worse than his confinement.

The nurse held in one hand a Dixie cup with two green pills and in the other a cup of water, half spilt from his having startled her.

"Dr. Raymond suggested you take these," she said.

"Doctor who?" Charlie asked.

"Dr. Raymond."

"I don't know anybody named Dr. Raymond," he said. "In fact, with the exception of Dr. Bishop, I don't know anybody here by name at all."

"Well," she said, with a slight laugh, "he knows about you, and he wanted you to take these."

Charlie grunted as she pushed the cups toward him. "You people are a revolving door of clinicians," he said. "One minute someone is checking me out, and the next minute somebody else is checking me out and asking me the same dumb questions. Now you're telling me that somebody I've never met is trying to push these pills on me? You guys could take a few lessons on streamlining and efficiencies."

"I know exactly how you feel," she said. "I mean, with all our rotations it's hard even for us to know whose staff and"—she paused—"who isn't."

"I don't find that surprising," Charlie said.

"Well, perhaps it was one of our residents who spoke with you. They're definitely green and, I hate to admit it, sometimes lacking in the facts."

She smiled at him, and Charlie smiled back but then caught himself. He knew better than to think their brief exchange was an invitation to flirt. It was a manipulation tactic he had often used himself. Get your adversary to trust you by offering information they didn't have but that wasn't important. He knew exactly what she was trying to do. Opening up about some of the inner workings of the floor might help lower his guard, make him see her as his ally. It would be that much easier than to goad him into swallowing whatever it was that she was peddling. Charlie had too many business deals under his belt to be that easily fooled.

"I'm not taking anything," he said. "I don't need anything. I don't want anything. So don't ask."

"Well, we can't make you take it," she said.

"No. Not without a Rogers guardianship, you can't."

"That's right," she said, pursing her lips and shaking her head at him to acknowledge that he "got her."

Charlie could see now that she was working even harder to keep the encounter between them conflict-free. She was trained, he assumed, in this exact sort of standoff. He might well be a time bomb just waiting for the right reason to explode.

"Do you want to make any phone calls?" the woman asked. "The doctor said you haven't notified anyone that you are here."

"There is nobody I want to call," Charlie said. "But thank you."

That, of course, was a lie. Joe was probably frantic. But until he had time to let everything sink in, it would be best to not call his schizophrenic brother to tell him that he'd been committed to Walderman.

Charlie stood alone in a corner of the common area on the psychiatric floor. He was still wearing his street clothes: Levi jeans, a black crewneck sweater, and a gray T-shirt underneath. His other possessions—wallet, watch, and keys—had been confiscated, probably while he was under sedation. He had never thought of his car keys as a weapon, but three hours on the psych ward at Walderman and he was able to ponder uses for them that he had never before imagined. The floor in the common area was linoleum, with flecks of color speckled throughout the floor tiles to help give a little life to the numbing gray slate. The furniture was sparse and made up entirely of mismatched, tattered cloth chairs and stained couches that would have seemed ordinary items at a swap shop or in a town dump. Scattered about were scuffed pine tables used for board games—backgammon, chess, and checkers. No women were on this floor, but Charlie had overhead a conversation between two nurses and knew there were female patients somewhere in the building.

In the hour he'd spent standing against the wall, staring out into nothing, Charlie had observed that the nurses' station, where medications were dispensed, was the epicenter of floor activity. Patients and nurses made frequent visits, most leaving with Dixie cups of drugs. There were no clocks or calendars hanging on the walls in the common area. That irony wasn't lost on Charlie. Apparently, at Walderman, both he and time were lost.

An orderly approached to announce that dinner was ending soon, to which Charlie replied that his appetite had taken a leave of absence and would return when he was around sane people again. The orderly didn't smile. A man approached him from behind. Charlie didn't see him coming and jumped reflexively when he spoke.

"The queen has no oven," the man said.

Since his arrival, Charlie had been mindful to speak only with the Walderman staff. He had yet to have a single conversation with any of the fellow patients, or *inmates,* as Charlie liked to call himself. The less he was involved with them, the less it felt real. For someone who prided themselves on fastidious dress and grooming, Charlie found the man's appearance frightening.

"I beg your pardon?" Charlie said.

"There are no more pancakes in Denmark. The queen has no oven."

The man was an imposing figure, standing nearly six-five and a good hundred pounds heavier than Charlie. He had a rugged face with a strong, pronounced brow and fierce brown eyes that had the wild look of a lost hiker. His brown-and-gray hair was thick and mangy and curled wildly just below his shoulders. Masking his face was a tangle of unkempt beard, twisted into knots by his fingers, which tugged nervously at the hairs. His skin was pockmarked and dotted with spiderlike red splotches, which Charlie recognized as symptomatic of alcohol abuse. But the fingernails were the most distressing feature of all. They were long daggers, with crusted bands of thick bluish dirt caked under them. He carried with him the unmistakable odor of dirty socks and sweaty running clothes.

"What are you talking about?" Charlie regretted the question the moment he asked it. He would have preferred to give the man no openings. The last thing he wanted was for this encounter to become an open invitation for all the patients to engage him on a regular basis. A low profile was the only way he could survive.

"I'm talking about the queen," the man said, more agitated. "And how we're just going to have to make do with something else to eat."

"That's great. Really, great."

Charlie had no idea what to say or how to react. He turned and walked toward his room. If it weren't for having to share sleeping quarters with a four-hundred-pound narcoleptic who snored at the decibel level of a jet engine, Charlie would have opted to spend his Walderman time locked in that room. Better still, if he had his guitar with him, he could stay in there without ever coming out, not even to eat. Now it appeared that he'd have to endure the displeasure of his roommate's company if he wanted to escape from Grizzly Adams's crazy brother.

Charlie marched down the corridor, glancing over his shoulder to confirm that he was being followed. Reaching the door to his room, Charlie marveled at how a cell could become a sanctuary. Grabbing the handle, he pulled to open the door but was distressed to find it locked. He pulled again. He started banging his fist hard against the door.

"You in there? Open up if you are!"

Charlie didn't announce himself by name. To his knowledge nobody on the floor but the staff knew it, and he wanted to keep it that way. In his mind, giving out his name somehow legitimized his residency. The only person he was fooling into thinking that he wasn't a patient here was himself, but that didn't bother him much.

Charlie saw a man approaching him from the other end of the corridor.

"That door's locked," the man said.

"That's why I'm trying to get the person inside to open it," Charlie said through gritted teeth.

"Well, that will be tough, because there is nobody inside. The door is locked from the outside. It's intentional."

"You locked the door to my room?" Charlie asked. "What am I? Twelve?"

The man laughed. "We do it to encourage patients to integrate.

We lock the doors while meals are being served downstairs. Otherwise, many would spend their time here barricaded in their rooms. It's important that you meet some of the other people here. It has a powerful and often underestimated healing effect. It's Charlie, right?" The man reached out a hand. "I'm Dr. Alan Shapiro."

Dr. Shapiro was several years Charlie's junior. He wore a blue oxford shirt, red tie, and tweed sports coat. Charlie had never seen him before. Yet somehow this doctor, like most of the staff, knew his name.

"Well, that just might be the dumbest thing I've heard yet," Charlie muttered.

"It's not healthy to spend too much time by yourself on the floor," Dr. Shapiro said.

Charlie let out a loud laugh. "And you think getting jumped by this psychopath is healthy?"

Charlie turned and pointed down the other end of the corridor, but the grizzled old man who had shadowed him moments before had vanished.

"Yes, I see," Dr. Shapiro said.

"Great," Charlie sighed. "Now you think I'm seeing things."

"Actually, believe it or not, I was coming to find you, but it wasn't for that. We've signed you up for group in the morning. This is your first night in the hospital, is that correct?"

"Yes."

"And how have you been adjusting so far?"

"Oh, it's been a breeze."

"Great," Shapiro said, either missing or ignoring Charlie's sarcasm. "Well, I was going to ask you to come to my office to talk—"

"And who are you?" Charlie asked.

"Right. I'm Dr. Alan Shapiro."

"No. I know that," Charlie said. He did nothing to hide his hostility. "I mean *who* are you and *why* do you want to speak with me?"

"I'm your psychiatrist." Shapiro rubbed his thumb back and forth against his index finger.

Nervous habit, Charlie thought. *Not a good thing for a psychiatrist.*

"You mean psychiatrist du jour, don't you?"

"I'm sorry . . . I don't . . ."

"It's nothing. When does that door unlock?" Charlie pointed at the door to his sleeping quarters.

Shapiro looked down at his watch. "Ten minutes more. I think it might be a good idea if we touch base, to check and see how you are feeling. Why don't you come down to my office for a minute?"

"No need. I'm feeling fine," Charlie said.

"This can be a tough adjustment. I understand that." Shapiro seemed to completely misjudge Charlie's apprehension. He looked down at his notes. "According to the records I have here, it says you haven't been very forthcoming or open with the staff. You know, it's important that you talk to us, Charlie. We can help. We're here to help you."

"I don't have anything to say to you people. I'm not sick. I don't belong here. This place is going to make me crazy." Charlie waved his arms about to drive his point home.

"I see. Have you had any thoughts of hurting yourself?"

"Before I got here or after?"

"I'm just trying to help, Charlie."

"You want to help me?"

"Yes, I do," Shapiro said.

"Open that goddamn door," Charlie said.

Shapiro took a step back. "There is no need for that type of language, Charlie."

"I'm just making my point, Doc," Charlie said.

Fumbling with a large oval ring that held several dozen different keys, Shapiro unlocked the door to Charlie's room.

"You're only hurting yourself, Charlie. It's important that you begin to open up to us so we can help you to heal faster."

"Funny thing is, Doc, before I came here, I wasn't even sick. Now, you have a good night."

Charlie stepped inside his room and closed the door behind him. The only blessing was that his roommate was locked out as well. That meant a good fifteen minutes of privacy. Charlie's twin-size bed was more like a cot, with fake wood paneling on both ends to mask the cheapness of its construction. In the corner, next to a pine armoire, which held a small dresser, was a small desk with a black vinyl chair. On the adjacent wall hung a rectangular mirror. *You can write your crazy thoughts in your diary while looking at your crazy self in the mirror,* Charlie had thought when he first saw the desk. The bathroom was a white tile masterpiece. A toilet, sink, stall shower with a yellowing shower curtain. Almost all the *inmates* on the floor had a beard, or at minimum a decent amount of growth on their faces. Razor blades, Charlie concluded, were a rare commodity.

His body fell hard onto the thin mattress of the tiny bed. The sheets were stiff and smelled of powerful detergents. The nappy blue blanket itched at his skin. He stared numbly up at the ceiling, his hands interlocked behind his head. His eyes felt heavy. He had no idea what time it was. It could have been eight o'clock in the evening or midnight, for all he knew.

The pressure and stress of his first day at Walderman had been building. Charlie let down his guard, and his eyelids drooped. The door to his room locked only from the outside. It made for a disconcerting sleep, but he couldn't resist—his eyes shut as if willed by another force. And then he slept.

Chapter 29

Charlie dreamt that a shadowy figure snuck up behind him while he was working at his desk at SoluCent and placed a plastic bag over his head. He thrashed about, fighting suffocation. But the nightmare turned real when he awoke in his hospital bed to discover that he couldn't breathe. Something calloused and rough had covered his mouth. It took a moment for his conscious mind to make the connection that it was somebody's hand pressing down hard over his mouth and nose.

Charlie's legs and arms flayed for a moment as he struggled for air. The fingers of his assailant parted, allowing him a small air passage to breathe, but only through his nose. Charlie let out a muffled scream that was no more effective at sounding an alarm than a loud shout into a pillow. Opening his eyes did little to orient him to his attacker. The room lights were off, the door was closed, and the room enveloped in darkness. *What's happening to me? Who?*

Charlie's thoughts were scrambled and disjointed. Adrenaline coursed through his body, but even with that added boost of strength, he was unable to throw his attacker off. Whoever this was, he was remarkably strong. Still able to breathe through his nose, Charlie caught a scent of something strangely familiar to him—the smell of old socks and running clothes. He could see only the shadow of the man's face but knew who it was. On his cheek he felt the daggers from the man's unkempt fingernails.

"The queen wanted me to give you a message," the man said.

Charlie tried to force his attacker's hand from his face, but the pressure tightened. The man pressed the full weight of his body against Charlie's chest, pinning him to the bed.

"I want to tell you something," he whispered in Charlie's ear. "Do you promise not to scream?"

Charlie could give only a muted and unintelligible reply. The man's breath was hot on his face and smelt of a sour, vinegary egg mix, which caused Charlie to cough.

"Do you promise not to scream if I take my hand away?" the man asked again. He lifted his hand an inch off Charlie's mouth to allow him a chance to respond.

"What the fuck!" Charlie yelled.

The man's hand moved back, covering Charlie's mouth and this time pushing even harder against him. Still unable to see him clearly, Charlie knew that their faces were no more than inches apart. Charlie could feel the man's beard against his skin.

"Listen to me," the man's hoarse voice said. "The queen wanted me to tell you that my favorite song should be your favorite song, too. Do you want to guess what song it is?" He pulled his hand away from Charlie's mouth again, presumably to allow Charlie an opportunity to answer.

"No! Get away from me! Get away!" Charlie shouted.

"Fine. I'll go," the man said.

Charlie felt the compression on his chest lessen. He rose from the bed with catlike swiftness. His attacker, perhaps anticipating Charlie's reaction, had moved to the door and turned on the light as soon as Charlie was standing. Charlie failed to cover his eyes in time and was blinded by the sudden change in room light. When his vision returned, Charlie scanned the room but saw no sign of his assailant. His roommate was there. Sound asleep on his bed, undisturbed by the attack, he snored loudly even with the lights on. Charlie walked shakily over to the bathroom, weak-kneed. Something caught his eye. He paused a moment to look at the mirror suspended over the desk. On it, written in crayon, in large block lettering was a message:

YOU'VE GOT A FRIEND. JAMES TAYLOR.

—GEORGE

The sweet melody of James Taylor singing that familiar line played in Charlie's mind. It made him shudder to the core.

Chapter 30

The last time Charlie had attended a group therapy session, it was at the behest of his mother, in support of his brother. The experience had left a single impression—it had made him hate the idea of insanity. Now here he was, attending his own group therapy session, sitting in a circle on a small blue-and-red plastic chair, drinking coffee served in a Styrofoam cup. He was one of a dozen patients participating in the group session, no different from his crazy brother, Joe. The only saving grace was that George, his attacker from the previous night, was not among the patients in this session.

Charlie hadn't reported the incident to any of the floor supervisors. He figured this was something best kept quiet. His plan, from the moment he was committed, was to do his time and get out. The state could only mandate that he stay in lockdown two more days—seventy-two hours total. It would take a court order to keep him locked up a minute longer. The last thing Charlie wanted to do was to suggest the possibility that he still suffered from the paranoid delusions they believed were part of his illness. George could deny the attack ever took place. Then it would be one person's word against another's, and neither had much to offer in the way of credibility. The best offense, Charlie had often suggested to his former Magellan teammates, was sometimes a great defense. Vigilance would be his lifeline for the next forty-eight hours—and that meant not sounding an alarm. Two short days until freedom. The adaptability and cunning needed to survive he had in spades.

Waiting around for group to begin was almost as unbearable as the idea that he was even in a group therapy session in the first place. As with everything he did at Walderman, Charlie tried to keep as low a profile as possible and sat in his chair, eyes forward, hands clasped in his lap. Charlie watched through the corner of his eye as the patient seated next to him rocked back and forth in his chair, and another to his right chewed on the tips of his fingers. When he pulled his fingers out of his mouth, Charlie nearly gagged at how raw and damaged they were.

He thought about taking advantage of the lull preceding the start of group to try and call Joe again. It was bad enough that he'd disappointed Joe by refusing to go with him to his progress meeting tomorrow. Disappearing without a word was inexcusable, and each minute his guilt worsened. Combine Charlie's absence with their mother's coma and Joe might be bordering on hysteria. Since his lockup, he had made only one attempt, after the attack last night. He'd got only the answering machine. The lie he'd left in his message wasn't even scripted. It was inconceivable to think of confessing to Joe where he had spent the hours since going missing. Instead he'd concocted a story about a last-minute job opportunity in California. In his message he'd asked that his brother call him back on his cell phone, even though it had been confiscated, with updates on their mother's condition. He'd added that he planned to return in a couple days, and told Joe to call if he needed anything. He had left clear instructions for Monte's care but wasn't worried about that. Joe and Monte had bonded since they'd moved in. Mrs. Cummings would be the only person with anything to worry about—Joe would be far less vigilant than Charlie about keeping Monte away from her precious Maxine.

Charlie was surprised that his brother didn't pick up, but figured Joe might be working the overnight at his security job. Whatever the reason for his not answering, the good news was that Charlie could be away from his brother guilt free. Joe would have no reason to doubt him, and thanks to the HIPAA, Charlie's medical secrets were safe. The few weeks that he had spent living with Joe was proof enough that he was far more self-reliant than Charlie had given him credit for. If anything, Joe was probably more worried about Charlie not having come home last night than Charlie was worried about Joe being on his own. Charlie would try his brother again after the group session. And, of course, he'd say that he was calling from somewhere in L.A. He wanted to get an update on their mother and Monte, too.

That would be the last call Charlie would make before getting out of Walderman, he promised himself. As much as he despised the idea of group therapy, using the phone in the common area was in some ways a more humiliating experience. There was only one community phone, and that meant a congregation of people, all vying for talk time and eavesdropping on each other's conversations. The lack of privacy was embarrassing and demoralizing.

The man chewing his fingers let out a cry of pain, loud enough to make Charlie jump. *There is never any privacy in this hellhole.* Here a person's darkest moments were on view for all to see. *Nowhere to hide,* he thought. Not in their rooms, when the door opened every fifteen minutes for a room check. Or in the halls, where crazy men talked incessantly to themselves; or in the common area, where others paced back and forth, some rocked in the chairs, some sat stone-faced and cross-legged on the floor. This was a nightmare Charlie had experienced only through the eyes of his brother but had never truly comprehended. If this place, Charlie thought, couldn't make a crazy man sane, it could certainly do the opposite.

Time had no meaning, but he suspected they had been waiting a good ten minutes without a group leader. At the moment Charlie decided to stand and leave, a woman entered the room.

His heart sank. It was Rachel. She greeted the group with a cheery hello. Charlie thought she took extra care not to acknowledge him differently from the others, but the two made brief eye contact. It was enough for him to know that she appreciated and understood the special circumstances. It was helpful, but no less heartbreaking.

"How's everybody today?" Rachel asked the group.

Most of the men spoke simultaneously, some trying to raise their voices above the others.

She laughed. "Apologies for running late, but thank you for the enthusiasm. It's a great way to start today's session. As usual, we're going to go around the room, and each of you will have a chance to tell the others how you're doing. Most of you know me already, but for those who don't, my name is Rachel. I'm director of Neuropsychology and a psychologist here at Walderman. There are some new faces here today, so an extra welcome to you."

This time she held her eyes on Charlie, perhaps intending her gaze to be welcoming. Instead, all Charlie felt was a sharp and hollow pain. The fierceness of the emotion was surprising, but he knew what it was—shame. His only response was to look down at his shoes, to avoid her eyes and his feeling of being judged. His face flushed.

"Charlie," Rachel said, "I usually like to start a group session by introducing some of the newer members to the group. Would you be interested in introducing yourself to the others?"

Charlie hated that she had used his name in such a public forum. He hated even more how patronized and demoralized her presence made him feel. Then he looked up at her and saw the same beauty that had captured him the day they first met. Before all this, the idea of being with her, though unlikely, was at least tenable. Now, with him on a lockdown floor in a mental hospital, it was beyond reach.

Charlie felt twenty pairs of eyes boring into him. His skin prickled. Sweat secreted from his neck ran in a thin trickle over his clavicles and down his shirt. Undeterred, committed to staying disengaged, Charlie kept his eyes fixed on the floor and said nothing.

"Charlie, would you mind starting us off today?" Rachel asked again. "Could you give the group a little update on how you're feeling? Or tell them something about yourself? I'm sure everyone would be interested. It's safe to share here."

Charlie couldn't speak. The paralysis from the chemical restraint was nothing compared to the suffocating anxiety that gripped him now.

A person to his left barked an unintelligible grunt, followed by a very clear expletive. He tried to speak but stuttered his words. "Welcome, Charlie!" the man managed to say after much effort.

Tourette's, Charlie thought. An engineer he knew at SoluCent had the condition. The vocal outburst and the man's involuntary movements were similar. But still, Charlie was frozen and unable to acknowledge the stranger's salutation.

"Welcome, Charlie," many of the others said in unison.

"I'll start. I'll start if he won't speak. Can he speak?" The man raising his hand was the same man who moments before had been eating his fingers.

"Yes, Dennis, you can start," Rachel said. "Although I'm pretty confident that Charlie can speak. Would you like to talk to the group, Charlie? Or would you rather just listen today?"

"I'm not a six-year-old boy," Charlie wanted to shout. Instead he breathed in deeply. *Accept this and get it over with.*

A few short miles away, in Arlington, a man lay dead in a bathtub. It would be only a matter of days before Rudy Gomes's disappearance would become suspicious. After the body was discovered, Charlie knew he'd be thrust into the center of the homicide investigation. At the very least, his firing from SoluCent was enough to make him a person of interest. Any ammunition they could use against him, they would.

Give them nothing, but don't be difficult, Charlie thought. *Answer her as normally as possible.*

Taking another deep breath, Charlie looked up at Rachel, kept his eyes locked on her as he spoke.

"Thank you, Rachel," Charlie said. "But if it's okay with you and the rest of the group, I'd rather just listen today. I'm sure that I can learn a lot by just listening."

Charlie proceeded to make eye contact with each person seated around the room. Many nodded their heads in approval. Some remained expressionless. Rachel gave Charlie a suspicious look but seemed to let it pass.

"Thank you, Charlie," Rachel said. "I appreciate your willingness to participate. Group?" She scanned the circle for consensus.

"Thank you, Charlie," somebody said. The others kept silent.

Inwardly Charlie smiled. Surviving here would mean having to play their game. The more coherent and cooperative he could act, the less reason they would have to hold him in lockdown. Keeping their suspicions about him to a minimum would be a winning strategy. Charlie took in a deep breath. He held it a moment.

"On second thought," Charlie said, "let me tell you why I'm here."

Chapter 31

Rachel concluded the group session an hour to the second after it began. As everyone cleared the area, Rachel caught up with Charlie and grabbed him gently by his arm.

"Hi there," she said.

Charlie felt lost in her emerald green eyes. Nothing in her voice hinted at the absurdity of the strange turn of events that had brought them together. Charlie would have preferred more of a reaction from her. Instead, she was treating him exactly as he expected—like a patient.

"What do you want?" Charlie thought he could see some hurt in her eyes. That wasn't what he'd intended. He didn't blame her, and he certainly didn't want to come across as hostile.

Rachel reached out to him, touching Charlie on the shoulder. "I know this must be very difficult for you, Charlie. I had planned on stopping by today to check and see how you're doing. I've been thinking about you a lot. Have you had a chance to speak with any of the doctors on staff? Was there somebody you particularly liked?"

Each time he tried to look her in the eyes, a deep, sorrowful pit formed in his stomach. His only response was to look away. Her touch was equally painful, a bitter reminder of his circumstances. What he wanted at that moment was impossible for her to give: to open her arms wide and allow him to fall helplessly into her embrace. She stood several feet away, but it was close enough for him to smell the sweet almond oil of her perfume. He took an unconscious step forward, and she perhaps an equally unconscious step back. The three feet separating them might very well have been an ocean.

"I haven't spoken to anybody," Charlie said.

"You really should try to open up to them, Charlie. They can help you."

"Help me what?" he asked. "Help convince me that what I know I saw wasn't there?"

"Perhaps," Rachel said. "Or perhaps something even more. They might be able to help you understand where all this is coming from."

"Where all what is coming from, Rachel? What is this? Right now I have only one true belief, and I have to keep holding on to it with all the strength and conviction I have, or this place *will* make me insane."

"And what is that belief, Charlie? Can you share it with me?"

This time he had no problem making eye contact with her. His passion and conviction returned to him a confidence he thought had been lost forever.

"I believe that Anne Pedersen is real," Charlie began. "I believe that I saw her at Mount Auburn Hospital and that she ran away from me when I chased after her. So tell me, why does that belief qualify me for this?" Charlie gestured to the now empty meeting room. "Rachel, a few weeks ago I was an executive director of a major corporation. Trust me when I tell you that if I believed I needed to be here, it would make this experience a whole lot easier to take."

Rachel started to respond, but something made her pause and think a moment. She looked at Charlie in a different way, he thought. It was with such a deep and honest compassion that for a moment Charlie felt as though he was the only person in the world who truly mattered to her. That was her gift as a psychologist, but he enjoyed believing it could be something more.

"Can I ask you something, Charlie?"

"Yes, of course."

"Normally I wouldn't even offer these questions for you to consider. They should be part of your therapy. But since you seem reluctant to talk to anybody, I feel obliged."

"What's the question?"

"What do you think of the other patients?"

"What do I think? What does that matter?" Charlie asked.

"Call me curious," Rachel said.

"I don't have an opinion." Charlie tried to bluff his way out, but Rachel wasn't fooled.

"I'm not sure that's true," she said. "Do you think the other patients are different from you?"

"No." Again he felt the thinness of his lie and was sure she could as well.

"Do you think that you're better than them?"

"What do you mean, better?"

"Do you think you're incapable of being ill? Of being sick like they are?"

"I guess I don't know."

Charlie turned from Rachel. She continued to talk, but now to his back.

"Anne Pedersen was at Mount Auburn Hospital. Have you ever asked yourself what she was doing there?" she said.

"No."

"Does it make any sense to you, Charlie, that she was there? Why would she suddenly appear—at that hospital, of all places? If she was there, it wasn't a coincidence. We looked for evidence, giving you the benefit of the doubt. But she hadn't checked in for a treatment. There were no visitors registered under that name. It would have had to been you that she came to see. Did you tell anybody but me where you were going?"

Charlie felt his legs weaken. "No," he said.

"Then how did Anne know you were there, Charlie?"

"I don't know."

"Charlie, listen to me. It's important that you listen to me now."

He turned back toward her. His face was ashen; the muscles of his jaw tightened around his clenched teeth.

"The men in here with you are not all off the street, Charlie. Many are professional men. Men with jobs and wives. With children and friends. Their illness is no different than cancer or diabetes or any other ailment that impairs quality of life. It just happens to be more frightening because it's their minds. You have to be willing to embrace all possibilities before you can start to heal, Charlie. You have to be willing to be like everybody else."

"And how do I do that?" Charlie asked.

"You have to let go of your idea of what it means to be mentally ill and allow yourself to be just like the rest of the patients here."

"And just what are the rest of the patients here?" Charlie asked, his eyes narrowing.

"They're people, Charlie. They're all just people."

"Of course they're people," Charlie said.

"You can say it, Charlie, but can you see it? Can you feel it? Can you stand a minute in their shoes and think they could be your shoes as well?"

Charlie thought of George, then of the man eating his fingers and rocking in his chair, of the ward's checkers champion.

"I'm different from them," he said.

"We're all just people, Charlie. All that I'm asking is that you try to see them that way." She reached into her purse and handed Charlie a card.

"What's this?" he asked.

"I want you to talk to somebody, Charlie. If you won't talk to the doctors here, I have a colleague at another facility who might be able to help."

"You're not hearing me, Rachel. I don't need any help. I just need to get out of here."

"We all need help, Charlie. It's sometimes the people who need it the most who can't see that for themselves."

Charlie watched as Rachel walked away. When she was out of sight, he crumpled up the card she had given him and tossed it into a nearby trash can without so much as looking at the name.

Chapter 32

Still too upset about last night's nightmare to write about it, Joe Giles needed to come up with another topic for today's blog post. It was the second time in as many nights that Joe had had the same nightmare. It began with him sitting astride Charlie, slapping at his brother's reddened face. Joe's blows, increasingly fierce, did nothing to deter Charlie from making incessant accusations that Joe had authored the kill list. Then with one frightful smack, Joe's thick hand connected with such force as to rip Charlie's head clear from his body with a sickening sound of muscle tearing and bone cracking.

Charlie's head rolled several feet and came to a rest upon its bloody stump, his maddening eyes glaring back at Joe. Then Charlie's disembodied head started to laugh; then it spoke, insisting Joe was a liar, pausing only for crazed, cackling fits. Joe screamed as a long, fork-tipped tongue uncoiled from deep inside Charlie's bloodied mouth and shot forward. The snaking muscle threaded into Joe's open mouth and slid easily down his throat, until Joe felt intense pressure squeezing his heart. This followed a pulling sensation unlike anything Joe had ever felt before. In the next instant Joe felt something tear inside him, this before seeing a mesmerizing blur explode out from his mouth as Charlie's tongue retracted. Lifting his head to follow the trail of movement, Joe, horrified, watched as his bloody heart, still pumping, danced in midair, suspended above the floor by Charlie's devil tongue, which had wrapped itself around the disinterred organ. Joe woke up screaming.

Perhaps because he hadn't heard from Charlie and was worried about his brother's well-being, he had the nightmare again. Having settled on a topic, Joe suppressed the gruesome images from his nightmare to concentrate on blogging. He had been blogging for several hours when the phone rang. Monte, well exercised after a two-hour walk with Joe, had fallen asleep and was curled into a quiet ball underneath the desk, at Joe's feet. The phone's ring woke him, and he let out a reflexive and sharp bark that startled Joe. The antiquated chimes of the rotary dial bells sounded sickly and haunting in the quiet house, as though a precursor to unwelcome news.

Joe's immediate thought was of his mother. He stood from his wooden desk chair in his bedroom and raced to pick up the phone before the third ring. Monte trotted dutifully behind. Getting to the phone before the chimes of the third ring stopped had much more significance if in fact the call was about her. Joe's superstitions were numerous, and most were garden-variety, widely held beliefs—black cats, walking under ladders, avoiding cracks on the sidewalk. But his superstitions about the phone were uniquely his own.

Joe considered answering the phone on the fourth ring to be a bad omen. For him it was a guarantee that the news on the other end of the line would not be good. It was superstition that kept him from checking the answering machine as well—the three-ring rule still in play, awaiting messages wouldn't be bad news, so long as he didn't check. He couldn't remember a single instance when he had answered the phone on the fourth ring. If he couldn't get to it by the third ring, he usually didn't answer the phone at all. His brother had called his habits stupid, but Joe couldn't remember a time when Charlie had answered the phone on the fourth ring, either. Not once.

"Hello?" Joe was out of breath.

"Joe, it's Charlie."

"Charlie!" Joe shouted with both surprise and delight. "Where have you been?"

At the sound of Charlie's name, Monte started to bark excitedly. Standing on his hind legs, he pawed at Joe's thighs, as though demanding his turn to speak. Joe shushed him and shooed Monte away with his leg.

"I'm out of town on business. Did you get my message?"

"I didn't check," Joe said.

Charlie laughed. "My bad. I forgot you wouldn't have checked the machine."

"I was worried about you," Joe said. "Are you doing okay?"

"I'm fine," Charlie said. "What have you been doing?"

Joe thought a moment. He took careful stock of the last several days. He had practiced his drums both mornings, fed Monte, and taken him for walks. He'd visited his mother at Mount Auburn both days as well. Of course, yesterday was Thursday, and that meant it was chocolate day. Joe always brought chocolate for the nurses on Thursday. Not to mention a truffle that he bought for his favorite nurse, June.

"I've been fine, Charlie. Monte is, too. But I was worried when I didn't hear from you. Is there a chance you'll make it back to town in time to come with me to my progress meeting tomorrow?"

"Sorry, Joe, but I don't think that's going to happen," Charlie said. "I had an unexpected job opportunity come up. I caught the first flight to California. I tried to call you late last night, but you didn't pick up. Were you working?"

Joe thought. After visiting his mother, he had gone to Walderman for an appointment and a prescription refill. Then he'd gone home and watched TV and fallen asleep just after the eleven o'clock news. The funny thing was, he couldn't remember what he'd done between leaving Walderman and going home. It wasn't overly concerning, but he had recently changed his dosage of Risperdal. If anything, it was another reminder of how much he missed his mother and her vigilance in monitoring the side effects of his medication. He'd meant to ask Rachel about the terrible nightmares that kept haunting him at night, but had forgotten. Maybe the lack of sleep was catching up with him. Maybe that was why his memory was fuzzy lately.

"I wasn't working. I never work the overnight on Thursday. Remember we had had pizza together last Thursday? What time did you call?"

There was a pause.

"I can't remember," Charlie said.

"Well, where are you now?" Joe asked.

"I'm . . . I'm still in L.A. I should be back sometime Sunday evening. Are you okay on your own until then? Can you keep taking care of Monte?"

"Charlie, I'm your older brother, remember? I'm fine if you move to California. I'm not an invalid. And I'll gladly adopt your dog. He's been great. A bit eager to visit the Cummingses, though. I guess he's got eyes for Maxine."

Charlie laughed. "You can call it eyes if you like. Anyway, sorry for the short notice on this California trip."

"Not a problem. Send me a tan."

Charlie laughed again. Joe enjoyed hearing his brother laugh. It didn't happen often enough.

"You know, if you're so independent, Joe, can you explain why I'm living with you?"

"Because," Joe said, "that's what Mom wanted."

"Well, maybe she doesn't know how independent you really are."

"Oh, she knows," Joe said. "But you read her will, Charlie. I told her I'd be fine on my own, but she insisted. She's had a rough go of it. Who am I to deny her some peace of mind? Besides, as much as I dislike you, I've sort of gotten used to having you around."

Again there was a long pause. Joe noticed it but didn't know what to make of it.

"It's been better than I thought for me, too, Joe."

"So I'll see you Sunday?"

Joe heard a loudspeaker crackle on Charlie's end of the line. He could make out only some of the words, but those he could understand he found surprising.

"Dr. Alan Shapiro? Carver Seven?" Joe repeated what he thought he'd heard from the loudspeaker's announcement. "Charlie, that's weird. You're in L.A.?"

"Joe, I have to go. . . ."

Charlie sounded rushed, and Joe sensed the change.

"Believe it or not," Joe said, "there is a Dr. Alan Shapiro at Walderman. And a Carver Seven wing in the Mercer building. I should know. I volunteer on Carver Seven once a month to teach basic computer skills. Isn't that a strange coincidence?"

Before Charlie could respond, Joe heard another voice. This time the voice didn't come over a loudspeaker. It sounded to Joe like whoever was talking was standing right next to Charlie.

"The queen has no oven!" Joe heard someone shout through the phone. "You must hang up now and go see the queen."

"Charlie? Charlie, are you there?" Joe said.

The line went dead. Monte trotted back into the room. Barked loudly, seemingly annoyed that Joe had hung up without giving him a chance to speak. He began gnawing on Joe's right shoe. Something about the other man's voice bothered Joe. It was familiar, too, in the same way Shapiro and Carver Seven were familiar. Joe tried to place it but couldn't.

He went back upstairs and sat at his desk, staring at his computer screen. Blogging required the diligent posting of new material, but his current effort was only half done. Joe had never imagined anybody would read his blog and was truly amazed how quickly it had grown in readership. At first readers were interested in Joe's early posts about his musicogenic epilepsy. It endlessly fascinated his readers that a song could put someone into a trancelike state. He had been at first a bit apprehensive to write about it. After all, his condition had nearly got a neighborhood kid killed.

Joe, fifteen at the time, had never been in a fight with the neighborhood bully, two years his senior, before. Surprising he hadn't, considering Joe's frequent and sudden violent outbursts and the bully's hyperactive mouth. If doctors had known Joe was suffering from seizures triggered by music, and had been for two years before that fight, it might never have happened.

Joe had been in one of his trances when the bully made the unfortunate decision to taunt him. Charlie and a few other onlookers had overheard the bully blame Joe for their father leaving. The bully had continued, threatening to hurt Joe's mother with a jackknife he'd pulled from his back pocket. The fight had lasted three punches, but it was enough to send the bully to the hospital for a week. Brain swelling had nearly killed him. Joe had disappeared for several days after, before the police eventually found him.

Readers loved to ask whether all music triggered the symptoms or just that one Miles Davis song. They wanted to know how he kept from having more seizures. Joe answered every question sent to him. The epilepsy itself, he wrote, was the underlying condition, but the seizures could be caused by a number of factors, emotional stress being one of them. The seizures, he explained to his readership, were triggered by the emotional association of jazz music with his father's memory and the specific tonal qualities of his father's favorite song, "So What" by Miles Davis. The two turned out to be a deadly mix for someone with Joe's rare condition. The good news was that once diagnosed, and after exhaustive treatments, he was eventually able to stop taking any epileptic medicine. By far the most popular question posted to his blog was if he had ever heard the Miles Davis tune since completing treatment. He was happy to report that he had not, but made the point that he felt confident that if he did, he could listen without it triggering an episode.

Many also inquired about his ability to drive. Again he was happy to report that he had been seizure-free long enough to get his driver's license. Life had been normal only a few years until Joe got sick again, this time diagnosed with schizophrenia. Several readers asked if the epilepsy was a precursor warning of Joe's later mental disorder. Joe had asked the same, but the question was neither answerable nor relevant. Disease number two had arrived uninvited and was there to stay.

Many of his blog subscribers were schizophrenic like him. They had bonded in the virtual world. It was a way for them to stay connected. It was an outlet to share their unique challenges and at the same time feel no different from anybody else.

To keep his readership engaged, Joe kept a faithful update schedule. A blogger couldn't afford to go stale, not when the competition for readership grew fiercer every day. Mostly he wrote about mental health issues and policy. He did exhaustive research before each post. But tonight he couldn't write a word. He kept waiting for the phone to ring, praying that it would be his brother calling back.

Joe kept repeating the names to himself over and over again. *Shapiro. Carver Seven.*

Then Joe's mouth opened. He bolted up from his desk again, moving as fast as his large, heavyset frame would allow. Grabbing the keys to his car, Joe stepped outside in the cool fall air, started the car, and fired up his InVision system. It was late, but he didn't have a moment to spare. He would use his InVision system to scan for traffic problems and find the quickest route.

"Please select your destination," InVision said.

Joe pushed a single preset selection button.

"Route selected," InVision confirmed. "Scanning for low traffic areas. Now calculating route. One moment, please."

Joe had already pulled out of the driveway. The tires of his thirteen-year-old Camry seared the blacktop with a screech of rubber.

"Turn right in one hundred yards," InVision directed.

Traffic must be light. It's taking me the fastest route there, Joe thought. Turning right, as instructed, Joe began the familiar drive toward what he jokingly referred to as his second home—Walderman Mental Health Hospital.

Chapter 33

Joe couldn't believe his eyes, but there was no denying what he saw. It was his brother; it was Charlie, sitting alone in the common area on the secure floor. The admitting nurse had told him where his brother was being treated. Another patient sat near Charlie, but the two were not speaking. The man had a long beard and wild, stringy hair that fell past his shoulders. His wizened face was etched deep with lines, which showed years of hard living and suggested a certain wisdom and kindness. The face was familiar, perhaps someone Joe recognized from his volunteer work on the floor. But with all the chaos and confusion of the moment, while trying his best to temper the anxiety growing within, Joe simply couldn't focus enough to make the connection. Charlie and Joe held an uncomfortable stare for a moment—each perhaps trying to adjust to the situation and allow time to validate that it was even real. Then Charlie looked away.

Joe approached.

"Charlie, what is going on?" Joe asked.

Charlie didn't answer.

"I thought you said you were in L.A.," Joe said.

"I lied," Charlie said. His voice sounded wounded.

"I don't understand any of this."

The old man with wild hair stood and approached Joe. He extended a hand, and Joe took it without hesitation.

"I'm George," the man said. "George Ferris. Is this your brother?"

Joe's face became illuminated with a jubilant and starstruck enthusiasm. "*The* Dr. Ferris?" Joe asked.

"I suppose. Unless there's another," George said. His words were hurried, and his voice was gravelly, bordering on hoarse. "I've been trying to apologize to your brother for my behavior. I sort of hung up his call for him. He won't accept my apology, and I won't stop giving it until he does."

"I heard a rumor you were here. I was going to come find you and introduce myself. I'm a big fan," said Joe.

George simply nodded. Charlie's jaw dropped open.

"I've been here ten days now," George said. "I'll be here a bit longer. I'm not ready to leave just yet."

"Doctor?" Charlie asked. He looked at George with wary eyes.

"Doctor of computer science, actually," said George.

"Also a writer and brilliant philosopher," Joe added.

"I don't understand," Charlie said. "You've been talking nonsense to me since I got here. You keep saying something about a queen and an oven. You even assaulted me!"

"Yes, well, I'm sorry about that, too," said George. "I don't always have control of my thoughts and actions, Charlie. That's why I'm here, isn't it? My medication and treatment program haven't been working well for a few weeks now. I decided to check myself in for a tune-up, if you will. I truly apologize if I frightened and upset you. I assure you, that wasn't my intention."

"Then what was your intention?" Charlie asked.

"I think I just took an interest in you because you seemed so desperately in need of a friend," George replied. "I really meant the best. Unfortunately, I approached you at moments when I should have kept my distance."

"And attacked me," Charlie added.

"Yes. Regrettable. But after that night in your room and our last run-in, I asked for an increase in my medication. It seems to have helped. I'm better able to organize my thoughts now. Well, at least some of the time." George gave a toothy smile, and Charlie nodded.

"So, Charlie," Joe said. "That's George's story. Why don't you tell me yours?"

Chapter 34

They moved out of the common area and into an adjacent room, one reserved for group meetings and such. They sat on folding chairs arranged in a circle so each could see the other. Charlie stared into George's eyes. The eyes that just the night before had seemed haunting and menacing had softened into something far gentler.

"I was brought here," Charlie said.

"And why were you brought here, Charlie?" George asked.

"Somebody thought I was dangerous," Charlie revealed.

"And are you?" George said.

"No," Charlie said.

"But they locked you up here for a reason, didn't they? You can't get out of here. Somebody decided this was best for you," George said.

"Who? Who thought you were dangerous, Charlie?" Joe asked. "I need to know what's going on."

Joe rose from his seat and began pacing back and forth. Charlie took in a deep breath.

"Joe, you know how I asked you for Rachel's contact information so I could speak with her? And how you and I got into that fight in your practice studio? Well, there are some things you don't know," said Charlie.

"Things I don't know? Like what?" Joe asked.

"Like that I was fired from my job. I didn't resign like I had said," Charlie confessed.

"Fired?" Joe stopped pacing and took a few steps toward Charlie. George stood and put a hand on Joe's shoulder.

"And that's just for starters," Charlie said. "They . . . these doctors I mean, believe I'm delusional."

"Why would they think that?" Joe asked.

"Because I chased after a woman who I believe is real but nobody else has even seen. And also, I had that list. The one we fought about."

"That list . . . ," Joe said but stopped himself, deciding not to say anything more.

"Well, I told Rachel about it. She was concerned that not only was I paranoid but I might be a threat as well. So when I went chasing after this woman, security at the Mount Auburn ER thought I had lost it. They shot me up with Haldol and locked me up in here."

"The Mount Auburn ER?" Joe said, more surprised by that than by Charlie having been administered a chemical restraint. Charlie could see that his brother was becoming disoriented. He noticed Joe's breathing growing heavier and beads of perspiration forming on his brow.

"If I didn't comply, Rachel was going to notify Simon Mackenzie about my list. It would have meant the end of my being able to salvage my reputation and career."

"Are you sick, Charlie? Do you have what I have?" Joe moved away from George and approached his brother. "You're all I have left without Mom. I know that I said that I didn't need you, Charlie. But I lied when I said it. I still need my brother. I do!"

Tears ran down Joe's cheeks. Charlie could tell that his brother was not angry, but frightened. Same as he was. Joe lowered his chin to his chest, but the tears continued to flow. His massive upper body convulsed with sobs, which he tried valiantly to contain.

"I'll always be your brother, Joe," Charlie said.

Charlie didn't think about what happened next. The moment happened before Charlie even knew what he was doing. He opened his arms wide, inviting his brother to come toward him. Joe leaned forward, and Charlie grabbed his brother's broad shoulders, wrapping his arms around him and pulling him close. In response, Joe lifted his arms to embrace Charlie in return. Joe's cries continued until Charlie could no longer contain his own.

"I'm scared, Joe," Charlie said. "I don't want this to be my life. I don't want this at all."

George kept his distance and watched the brothers embrace.

"None of us ask for this, Charlie," George said after a moment. "But it's what we do with what we are given that truly defines us."

Charlie looked up at George as Joe pulled away.

"Tell me, what do I have to do?" Charlie asked.

"If you have the courage to face this head-on, you can find out and treat it. But only if you're willing to be open to all possibilities can you find out," George said. "You have to free yourself from the guilt of what might be. It's not your fault."

"Charlie, you have to listen to him," Joe said. "You have to trust."

Charlie wiped the tears from his eyes and thought a moment.

"Tell me, where do you want to start, Charlie?" George asked. "It's up to you to decide. Your brother and I can help. We understand."

"You're telling me that I have to free myself of guilt before I can move on?" Charlie asked.

"That's what I'm saying," George said.

"Then there is only one place I can start," Charlie said.

"And where is that?" George asked.

"In Arlington. With a dead body."

Chapter 35

It was just after sunset. The red and blue lights from the police car strobes danced about Charlie's face in an uneven frenzy. Before now this sort of police activity and chaos had been the exclusive property of TV shows and movies. They were as much spellbinding to him as they were terrifying. His wrists were bound together by plastic handcuffs, and his hands hung uselessly down the front of his waist.

It had taken several phone calls and a mountain of paperwork to secure Charlie's temporary release. Charlie had agreed to be restrained and under the close supervision of Walderman staff, making approvals easier to obtain. If it weren't for the call to Walderman from Randal Egan, a special agent with the FBI, Charlie doubted anybody would have believed his story, let alone allowed him to leave Walderman under guard. Charlie's one demand, agreed to by the FBI, was that he be allowed on-site when Arlington police retrieved the body, else he wouldn't provide a name or address.

Charlie understood that tipping the police to a dead body's whereabouts was tantamount to implicating himself as the perpetrator of the crime. In discussing his situation with Joe and George, Charlie had conceded that the truth about Gomes would eventually come out. But he had another reason for wanting to see the body again, one that he kept to himself. Soon, Charlie would have the answer he needed.

The commotion, although heightening his anxiety, also had the welcome benefit of distracting him from the constant throbbing pain in his wrists from the handcuffs. All he could do was watch and wait as more police and eventually an ambulance arrived. The lights from the ambulance were flashing, but the siren was hauntingly absent. That was to be expected, given what he had told the police was waiting for them inside the apartment.

Randal had been acting on Charlie's behalf as the go-between with the Arlington police.

"Why do you want to see the body?" Randal had asked.

The two had spent over an hour on the phone, making the arrangements.

"I need to see it for closure," Charlie had said.

Now that he was finally here, Charlie was even more sure of his decision. After all, Gomes's murder was the key link in a long chain of events that had concluded with his involuntary commitment to Walderman. Embracing the possibility that he had committed the crime without memory would be impossible without first seeing the body removed. Charlie needed to witness it for himself and had told Randal as much.

Thankfully, Randal had deep ties and long standing relationships with many local law enforcement officials. Without those connections, the probability of a committed patient witnessing a crime scene would be nil. Luckily for Charlie, the Arlington chief of police and Randal had been to several law enforcement conferences together and over the years had forged a cordial friendship.

As the minutes passed, Charlie grew more anxious. He wanted this part to end quickly so he could mentally ready himself for the next phase of his treatment to begin in earnest. He was closely guarded by two Arlington police officers. His physician escort from Walderman waited in the van that had brought him first to the Arlington police station. Once there, he had been transferred by police cruiser to the crime scene.

His police escorts were as forthcoming with emotion as the Foot Guards of Buckingham Palace and kept a watchful eye over him. Randal had warned Charlie about what to expect, but the reality was far more dramatic than he had imagined. The sheer size of the police force needed to recover a dead body was puzzling. Since it was a recovery mission and not a criminal search, Randal had explained that a warrant wouldn't even be necessary. But Charlie had assumed fewer officers would be involved.

Charlie watched Randal Egan approach from the shadows, with his hands stuffed into his overcoat pockets and his face briefly illuminated by the revolving strobes. Randal flashed the officers guarding Charlie his badge. They moved backward, but with subtle, incomprehensible grunts of disrespect.

"This is all pretty fucked up," Randal said, placing a strong hand on Charlie's shoulder.

"I told you in the bar strange things were happening to me," Charlie said.

"Yeah, but this is a bit more than strange. Now do you want to tell me what's really going on?"

"Am I under arrest?" Charlie asked.

"No."

"Do I have to tell you anything more than I already have?"

"As a friend, yes. As a member of the law enforcement community, you know this isn't my jurisdiction, Giles. Unless it's a federal case. Any reason this would be federal?"

"I'm long past reason," Charlie said.

The two men exchanged an awkward stare, until Charlie broke the tension with a laugh and a smile. It was the first time he had smiled in what felt like years. Randal replied with a laugh of his own, then put his arm around Charlie's shoulders.

"It's going to be okay, buddy," Randal said. "We'll figure this out together."

Charlie felt his friend's concern and had never appreciated the man more. But his brief respite from the intensity of the moment ended when a dark blue Crown Victoria, flashing a single red strobe, turned the corner and sped toward them.

"Who's that?" Charlie whispered to Randal.

"That, my friend, is the Arlington chief of police."

The man who emerged from the police car was strikingly tall. His cheeks were sunken and hollow, as if work, not food, had been his mainstay for years. Every feature on the man was narrow and angular. From the long, thin nose to his fingers drumming restlessly on his legs, to a neck so wiry that his Adam's apple stuck out like a Ping-Pong ball in his throat. There was nothing about the man that suggested comfort. He moved with calm assuredness and projected an aura of complete control. He took no time to adjust to the chaos into which he had entered. His eyes were keen, like those of a hunter, narrowed and searching. He first saw Randal and then set his gaze on Charlie. He held eye contact long enough to make Charlie's pulse quicken. The man seemed capable of sniffing out deception by observation alone. The chief rubbed at the coarse scruffiness of his three-day-old beard and continued his silent stare. Charlie felt certain he had already been judged guilty of something. What that was remained to be seen.

"Charlie, this is Police Chief Sandy Goodkin. Sandy, good to see you again," Randal said, extending a hand.

"Wish I could say the same," Goodkin said. "And you, I suppose, are Mr. Charlie Giles."

"I am." Charlie lifted his cuffed wrists and smiled awkwardly. Goodkin looked at him as if a handshake would be the last thing he wanted.

"Lot of fuss you've caused," Goodkin said. He pulled out a pack of what Charlie thought were Camel cigarettes. Charlie watched as Goodkin put one of the smokes in his mouth, then shoved the whole thing in and began to chew. "I'm quitting," Goodkin explained. "Vera said it was time. These candy cigarettes are a lot cheaper than Nicorette and just as effective, if you ask me. You smoke, Mr. Giles?"

"No," Charlie said. "I don't smoke."

"Well, that's at least one thing you've got going for you. So what's the deal with this circus you've created? Why don't you tell me what's going on in your own words?"

"I'm not here to tell you anything," Charlie said. "I'm here to show you something."

"And why is it you want to be on the scene to play show not tell?"

"It's personal. I need to relive that day. In exchange, I'll give you the body."

"Tell me why you want to relive it," Goodkin said.

"I don't remember anything but seeing a dead body. I want to be back here and face this thing head-on. I want to know if seeing the body again triggers some repressed memory," Charlie explained.

Goodkin's skeptical look prompted Randal to intervene. "Charlie's been going through a lot lately. This was just one of several strange incidents that have been happening to him over the past few weeks for which he has no explanation or memory."

Goodkin nodded his head in a way that suggested he didn't much care but understood. "So did you murder this . . ." Goodkin reached behind him and pulled out a metal folder from the front seat. He then shuffled through the case file papers, scanning them for a name. "Mr. Rudy Gomes?"

Charlie looked Goodkin in the eye but said nothing.

"Well then," Goodkin said to Randal, "this sure is a weird one. No missing persons report filed, either. And by the way, consider any favors that you've earned over the years paid in full."

"Understood," Randal said.

"Since Chatty here seems all out of chat," Goodkin said, "why don't we go inside and have us a look? Shall we?"

Goodkin motioned toward Gomes's apartment, and the three marched side by side across the street. The wind flapped Goodkin's and Egan's overcoats open like capes; the lights from the yellow streetlamps above cast their shadows into superhero-like figures on the march. Police officers milling about parted as they approached. The two Arlington policemen assigned to guard duty kept pace only a few feet behind.

Charlie had been on this street at night only once before, and that was an experience he'd rather soon forget. The jarring sound of shattering glass from Gomes kicking out the window of his BMW was still fresh in his memory.

Goodkin turned to Charlie as they neared the steps to the apartment. "Okay, Mr. Mystery Man," Goodkin said mockingly. "Why don't you talk and I record?" Goodkin held in his hand a small Panasonic digital recorder, a type Charlie had frequently used for recording business meetings.

Charlie was caught off guard at the thought of being recorded. Instinctively he knew any lawyer worth their price would strongly disapprove. But this wasn't about common sense. Charlie shrugged off his apprehension with a slight nod of his head.

Whatever they are going to do to me won't be decided based on a recording, he thought.

His singular mission was to retrace his steps that day. Perhaps some memory of his committing the crime would come back to him. At least that would bring proof of his guilt and provide some closure to this nightmare. Living with doubt, he now believed, was a far worse fate than confronting the truth.

"I came back to this house after my brother, Joe, showed me a note," Charlie began.

"What note?" Goodkin asked.

"You didn't tell me about a note, Charlie," Randal said.

"Doesn't matter now," Charlie said. "The note Joe showed me said, 'One down. Three to go.' It was in my handwriting."

"What does that mean?" Goodkin asked.

"At the time I believed it meant that Rudy Gomes was dead and that the others on this kill list that I found in my brother's house would soon follow," Charlie explained.

"Kill list?" Randal asked.

Charlie nodded. "Apparently I wrote a list, which I titled 'My Kill List.' On it, I put the names of the people who fired me from Solu-Cent. Rudy was one. My boss, Simon Mackenzie, another. And the CEO himself, Leon Yardley, the third."

"Apparently?" Randal asked. "You don't remember writing that list?"

"There's a lot I don't remember these days, Randal," Charlie said.

"But you said there were four names," Goodkin said. "Who's the fourth?"

Charlie shrugged. "I don't know. The note just said that it's a surprise."

They had stopped at the entrance to the apartment. Goodkin kept his focus on Charlie, looking for signs of deceit.

"But you wrote the list," Goodkin said. "So you tell me. Who is the surprise victim?"

"I don't know," Charlie answered. "Like I said, I don't even remember writing the list."

"Where is the list?" Goodkin asked.

Charlie paused. He stared at the door to the apartment. All he wanted to do was to get inside and end this charade once and for all. If he was a monster, as the evidence seemed to indicate, then the author of the list, let alone its whereabouts, was of little consequence.

"I don't know where the list is anymore," Charlie said. He made no attempt to avoid being recorded. "But it doesn't matter, does it?"

he asked. "I wrote it. It was penned in my hand, and Rudy's dead. What else is there?"

"The evidence," Randal said, almost to himself.

"Okay then," Goodkin said. "Let's go have a look at this body."

Goodkin nodded to an officer standing behind him. The officer moved toward the door. Using a set of tools Charlie had never seen before, the entry specialist had the door open in seconds. Goodkin slipped on a set of gloves to protect the crime scene and pushed open the door with his hands.

"Don't touch a thing. Got it?" Goodkin said. "Now, talk to me."

"I came here in the morning," Charlie began.

"Time?"

"Eleven o'clock. Thereabouts," Charlie said. "The door was open."

"How is it locked now?"

At this Charlie paused. "I . . . I don't know," he said.

They entered the hallway. The apartment was dark, until Goodkin turned on a hallway light.

"What next?"

"I first looked into the living room," Charlie said. His mind was racing to retrace his steps from that day.

"Any sign of struggle?" Goodkin asked. "Did you see anything unusual?"

"No. Nothing."

"Then what?" Goodkin prodded.

"Then I walked down the hall toward the bedroom. The layout was familiar to me. It's similar to a lot of the homes in Waltham. Old two-story houses. Like the one I grew up in," Charlie said.

"And?"

"And I stopped at the bathroom door. I heard running water. I opened the door to look inside."

Randal and Goodkin followed close behind as Charlie made his way down the narrow hallway, stopping in front of the bathroom door, halfway to the bedroom at the other end of the hall.

"What next?" Goodkin asked, keeping the recorder close to Charlie.

"I opened the bathroom door. Steam spilled out into the hallway," Charlie answered, covering his eyes with his hands to better visualize every detail. "I went inside the bathroom. It took a moment for the steam to clear. The shower was running. I pulled back the shower curtain, and that's when I saw the body."

Goodkin pushed open the bathroom door and stepped inside. The room was dark, and Goodkin fumbled a moment for the light switch on the inside wall.

Entering the bathroom, the first thing Charlie noticed was what wasn't there. There was no moisture and no smell of decay. He had never turned off the water. It should have been running, same as he had left it.

The shower curtain was pulled across the tub, but he didn't remember pulling it closed before he left. Perhaps he had. The uncertainty was more than a little troubling.

"I don't smell a dead person," Goodkin said in a mocking singsong tone. He ran his hands across the tiled wall and held his fingers close to his face to examine them. "You said the shower was running when you left?"

"It was," Charlie said.

"These walls are pretty dry, Giles. Can you explain?"

"No. I can't." Charlie looked at the shower curtain. A sinking, consuming fear began roiling inside him.

He watched as Goodkin walked over to the tub. Goodkin grabbed hold of the shower curtain and pulled it away with flair. What they saw stunned everyone in the room. Goodkin stared at the tub for several seconds. He rubbed at the stubble of his nascent beard before turning to Charlie.

"Can you explain this?" he asked.

Charlie stared at the tub. His mouth was dry, sweat beading on his brow, his heart thumping in his chest.

"Charlie, what is happening?" Randal asked through clenched teeth.

"I don't . . . I don't know . . . ," Charlie said.

Goodkin dropped down to his knees and put his head in the tub. Charlie could hear him take in a deep breath.

"Well, he's tidy. I'll give him that," Goodkin said.

"This makes no sense," Charlie said. "Rudy was there."

"Well, from what I'm seeing," Goodkin said, "this is a tub. Where is the body?"

"I don't know," Charlie said, with a voice so weak, he might have been talking to himself. "The body was there. His throat was cut open. I saw it with my own eyes."

The three stared at the empty tub for what felt like an eternity.

"No body, Charlie. No crime. Crazy is as crazy does, I guess. Marshall!" Goodkin barked.

A young deputy emerged from the hallway and faced his boss. He stood at attention, ready to receive his orders.

"Try to get in touch with the landlord of this place and explain what we've done to his home without a warrant," Goodkin said.

"And what should I say?" Officer Marshall Winters asked.

"I don't know," Goodkin said. "Some mental patient is having delusions about his tenant. You figure it out." Goodkin turned to Randal. "Randal, I'm going to do the best I can to forget about this incident. But it won't be easy."

Charlie couldn't take his eyes off the empty tub. Not a bloodstain was to be found. Goodkin had called for a black light, but Charlie knew it was pointless. The most sensitive light equipment available would show no signs of Rudy Gomes's death. The tub was empty. There was no body here or anywhere in the apartment.

As the detectives concluded their search of the bathroom, Charlie's knees buckled under the weight of the moment. The room spun and darkened. Charlie fell onto the cold tile bathroom floor. For an instant, right before he passed out, Charlie felt enveloped by a force so foreign and mysterious to him that he could only interpret it as madness.

Chapter 36

Charlie sat just outside the common area, on a scuffed wooden chair splashed with coffee stains, and waited. It was Sunday morning, and Charlie soon would be legally free to leave Walderman and resume his life. Just thirty-six hours ago Charlie had left Gomes's place without seeing Gomes's body. The question on his mind now was if he was really ready to leave.

Charlie's chair was opposite the main entrance, giving him an unobstructed view of the front door. He cursed the lack of any clocks on the walls and decided it couldn't have been more than ten minutes since he'd last asked a nurse the time.

Where was he? Charlie fretted.

Each second that passed fueled the anxiety growing within. From his perch upon the chair, the only thing that helped take his mind off his friend's delay was watching Maliek, the reigning board game champion of Walderman, win game after game of checkers and backgammon. Maliek was young, athletic, and constantly grinning. If only he had his Gibson, Charlie lamented. That would kill the time.

A few patients tried to talk to him, but Charlie repaid their friendliness with silence. Unless it was Randal, bringing with him news of Rudy Gomes's whereabouts, nothing else mattered. As a favor, Randal had promised to dig some into the Gomes mystery using whatever resources were available to him from the FBI. Charlie's only hope now was that Randal would come up with something that might bring credibility to his original story. The other possibility, equally frightening, was the one Chief Sandy Goodkin had already concluded to be true. Charles Giles, software entrepreneur and multimillionaire businessman, was clinically insane.

The entrance door buzzer sounded and startled Charlie. Given the frequency with which the buzzer went off, he should have grown accustomed to the sound of the security door unlocking. But it was always jarring—a shocking reminder of his current situation.

Charlie's hopes dimmed the moment Randal entered the room. The grave expression on Randal's face said it all. He didn't bother to greet Charlie with a perfunctory embrace or even a handshake hello. His head shake was almost imperceptible, but it felt like a punch to Charlie's gut.

"Where can we go to talk?" he asked.

Can this get worse? Charlie thought.

"Follow me," Charlie said.

He led Randal through a door next to the nurses' station and into the large meeting room where days before Charlie had attended his first group therapy session. The chairs were set up in a semicircle for the next session, but that wouldn't be for hours, usually an hour or two after lunch. Randal sat in one of the chairs, his hands folded in his lap. Charlie was far too nervous to sit and opted instead to pace.

"Rudy Gomes resigned from SoluCent three days ago," Randal began.

"Resigned? What do you mean?" Charlie asked.

"I mean he quit. He sent a letter of resignation via e-mail. The day you allegedly say you saw him dead."

"Don't be patronizing, Randal. I don't need that right now. I know what I saw in that apartment. What you're saying doesn't make sense."

"I agree. Especially since his e-mail came hours after you discovered his body in the bathtub."

"But I know Rudy. I know his work ethic and what that job meant to him. He wouldn't just do that. Especially not by e-mail. That wasn't his style."

"Well, according to our computer forensic guys, it was. We traced the e-mail message back to Rudy's home computer. Your IT guy was cooperative as well."

"Lawrence?"

"Yeah," Rudy said. "Lawrence. That sounds familiar."

Charlie thought back to the day he had asked Lawrence for a report on any missing badges in exchange for Red Sox tickets. For a moment he wondered what, if anything, that trace would have unearthed. Perhaps enough to free him—or perhaps, as Randal's expression suggested, nothing.

"How can you be certain it was him?"

"We ran a trace on the IP and had it verified with Verizon. The e-mail came from Randal's apartment. He has a static Internet address, so we're sure of it."

"But that doesn't prove anything," Charlie said. "Anyone could have done that."

"True. But not anyone could buy a ticket to the Bahamas. And stay at a Club Med, and use their credit cards to buy *mojitos* and lingerie."

"What are you saying?"

"I'm saying your man Rudy Gomes is alive and well and vacationing at Club Med."

"But how do you know it's him?"

"We have airport records that show tickets purchased by him and verified by flight security through ID checks. There are credit card receipts for a bunch of mundane purchases, water, newspapers, a cheeseburger at the airport T.G.I. Friday's, all leaving a trail that takes him from Logan Airport to Bimini." Randal looked at the floor in defeat and softly added, "It's time you started to face this, Charlie."

"Face what? I know what I saw, Randal," Charlie said. "I mean, someone could have broken into his apartment, stolen his wallet. The same person who killed him!"

"Don't make me do this, Charlie."

"Do what?"

Randal reached into his blazer pocket and pulled out a small tape recorder, similar to the one Goodkin had shoved in his face the night before.

"What's that for?" Charlie asked.

"I called the Club Med resort where Gomes is registered. I did it because I knew you wouldn't believe me even after giving you this mountain of proof. How well do you know Rudy Gomes?" Randal asked.

"I know him well enough. Why?"

"Would you recognize his voice?"

"I suppose," Charlie said.

Randal pressed PLAY on the recorder. A soft hiss preceded Randal's taped voice.

"This is Special Agent Randal Egan with the FBI, Boston field office. Who am I speaking with?"

"What's this about?"

A chill shot down Charlie's spine. The voice was unmistakable.

"I'm investigating a disappearance of an individual from Arlington, Massachusetts. Do you know a Mr. Rudy Gomes?"

The tape recording was distorted from a chortling laugh.

"Know him? Yeah, I know him," the voice said.

Charlie had now taken a seat and was listening dejectedly to the tape, his face buried in his hands, his body convulsing as he tried to slow his breathing and keep from hyperventilating. The recording continued to play.

"Sir, do you mind my asking how you know Mr. Gomes and if you have seen him lately?"

"Not a problem, Agent Egan," the voice said. "I just look in a mirror and see him. In fact, I'm looking in a mirror right now and seeing him right now."

"How is that?" Randal's recorded voice asked.

"Well, it's simple. I am Rudy Gomes. And trust me when I tell you that I'm not missing. And with all the hot, young tail prancing around this place, half dressed, I'm not missing anything at all."

Chapter 37

Charlie and Rachel were seated in one of three private therapy rooms accessible off the main floor. The shades were drawn. It was midafternoon, and a few slivers of light were all that illuminated the cramped quarters. Charlie kept his eyes closed as instructed. Rachel spoke in a low, soothing tone. She was going through a series of relaxation exercises.

"I want you to feel your hands, Charlie. Clench them tightly into balls. Tense the muscles, don't let go, hold it . . . hold it . . . now relax," she said. She had done the same for his toes, ankles, calves, thighs, hips, and torso and was now working the arms and hands. "Are you relaxing your hands?" she asked. Her voice, barely a whisper, was remarkably calming. The tension escaped from his body, as she had promised it would.

"Yes." He could barely manage even that much of a response as the process continued to work.

"Good. Let's work your neck and your shoulders."

Rachel continued feeding Charlie verbal commands, all part of a prehypnosis routine designed to get him to relax and open his mind to the power of suggestion. Fifteen minutes into the relaxation portion of the session, Charlie could feel his mind wandering freely, his thoughts drifting peacefully away to restful places, which had been more than a bit elusive of late.

"I want you to imagine that you are standing at a door," Rachel said. "The door is large. It is a red door, Charlie. Can you see it?"

"Yes," he said.

"Good. Now I want you to go to the door and try to open it. It should open easily. Can you open it, Charlie?"

In his mind Charlie did as instructed. Picturing the large red door, Charlie added to it a steel handle, which he gripped and pulled, opening it with the ease Rachel had promised.

"Directly in front of you is a staircase. It's dark, but there are some candles that will help you to see each stair. I want you to start climbing the staircase. As you start to climb, you will relax more and more. All your worries and concerns will begin to fade to the back of your mind as you get higher and higher," Rachel said.

With each step, Charlie felt himself relaxing. The idea of hypnosis was not his. Joe had suggested it, and Rachel had volunteered for the job. She had learned the technique as part of her progressive neuropsychological program at Harvard. Joe had used it on several occasions and found its insights remarkable. After Randal's revelation about Gomes's apparent well-being, Charlie felt open to suggestions he'd have discounted before.

Rachel had explained that it might help Charlie unlock potentially damaging thoughts that could be contributing to his delusions. She used the analogy of uncorking a bottle of wine. To get to the sweetness of self-awareness, you first had to remove all blockages. The contradiction between seeing Gomes's dead body and hearing his voice playing through Randal's tape recorder had left Charlie in such a vulnerable state that he would have considered a seaweed wrap if someone had thought it could help.

Rachel had him ascending a staircase that seemed to have no end. He climbed and climbed and climbed until the softness of her voice receded further into his relaxed consciousness. He emerged from the darkness of the stairwell and was standing on a platform, atop an enormously tall tower. Rachel told him that tied to his hands were two balloons, both the same color red as the door. As the balloons lifted higher, so did his hands. His eyes closed, Charlie imagined his hands rising, dragged upward by the gentle pull of the balloons. He was in an early stage of deep hypnosis and was not aware that his hands were in fact playing out the scene in his mind, rising off his lap and eventually over his head.

The balloons continued to pull Charlie skyward, carrying him high above the Boston skyline. He flew over his apartment in Beacon Hill, raced along the Charles River, drifting out toward the suburbs.

"Where are you now, Charlie?" Rachel asked.

"I'm . . . I'm somewhere outside Boston. I can see my mother's house."

"Good. Now, Charlie, I want you to pay close attention to me. I want you to have the balloons take you somewhere. Can you do that for me?"

"Yes. I think so," Charlie said, his voice even and trancelike. "Where?"

"I want you to go to a place that you don't want to go. They can take you any place that you decide. But it must be someplace you don't want to see."

"But where is that?" Charlie asked, his voice weakening with a presleep torpor.

"Your mind is open now, Charlie. Let it stay open. Let yourself feel how good it feels to be free, to have your thoughts unencumbered by fear."

"Yes. But where am I going?" Charlie asked.

"Ask the balloons to bring you someplace where you don't feel this good. Ask them to carry you to someplace else. Can you do that?"

At that instant a gust of wind caught the balloons and Charlie felt himself jerk forward. Rachel actually had to lean forward herself to steady him in his chair, else he might have fallen onto the floor. Within an instant, as if he'd been teleported, Charlie found himself floating high above Rudy Gomes's house.

"Where are you, Charlie?"

"I'm at Rudy's house."

"Good. How does it feel?"

Charlie could see the ground fast approaching. "I'm falling," he said, still in a whisper.

"That's okay, Charlie. Trust everything. You will be fine. Don't have any fear. I want you to leave that place now. Remember the door and the staircase. It took you up high. I want you to forget about Rudy Gomes and his house. It does not exist anymore."

"Yes. The house is gone. There is just a hole in the ground now," Charlie mumbled.

"Good. Are you floating higher?"

"I am. I'm floating higher."

"Great. That's great, Charlie. You're doing so well. Now, I want you to do the same thing again. I want you to go someplace else. The same rules apply. It has to be someplace where you don't feel good. Again, it can be any place at all."

The line between reality and something akin to a living dream had blurred beyond distinction. With Rachel's voice serving as a quiet guide in the background, a gust of wind erupted from the east and pushed Charlie at near sonic speed toward the Pacific coast.

"Do you know where you are, Charlie?" Rachel asked.

Charlie's answer was barely audible. "Yes."

"How does this place make you feel?"

"I don't like it here anymore."

"But you once did?" Rachel asked.

"Yes. I once did."

"Tell me, Charlie, are you looking down at SoluCent? That's the place you once worked."

"No."

Charlie was in a deep hypnotic state and couldn't see Rachel's expression change to one that was both troubled and curious.

"But you say you recognize this place. Can you describe it to me?"

"I don't have to," Charlie said.

"Why is that, Charlie? Is it because you can't describe it?"

"No. It's because you know what it is."

"And what is it, Charlie?"

"I'm back in San Francisco. I'm floating over the Golden Gate Bridge. And I don't like it here anymore."

Chapter 38

Joe Giles walked in erratic circles, looking both at Rachel and Charlie as they discussed the session. "That's the weirdest thing ever. I can't believe it. You were floating?"

"Yes, Joe," Charlie said. "I was floating. But it wasn't real. It was simply another state of consciousness."

"I know what hypnosis is, you jerk. I'm not stupid," said Joe. "What's getting me is that you actually went under!"

"What are you talking about?" Charlie said. "You're the one who suggested hypnosis in the first place."

"Yeah, but I didn't think you'd actually go through with it. Let alone have an experience."

"It wasn't an experience, you jackass. It was a—"

"Different state of consciousness. I know. I know. But still. My brother was hypnotized." Joe rubbed at his temples as though he were embedding the visual in his mind.

"Boys, are you done?" Rachel asked.

"What?" Joe said defensively. "Didn't you grow up with brothers?"

"As a matter of fact, no," she said. "But I did grow up with harried parents, both of whom worked and taught me that time was not to be wasted. And I believe we are dangerously close to breaking that cardinal rule."

Charlie and Joe took their seats and looked at Rachel, who offered only a small conciliatory smile.

"Good," she said. "Now that we've settled that, let's get back to the task at hand. Before the session we agreed that Joe should be present for the analysis. He has the most history with you, and we thought he might be able to help explain some of your experiences while hypnotized."

Rachel glanced over at Joe, who nodded. "Glad I can be of service," he said.

"But it's not necessary," Charlie said. "Although I have no problem if Joe stays for this, I can tell you exactly why I was over the Golden Gate Bridge."

Rachel leaned forward. "And the reason is?"

"I can answer that for him," Joe said. "I never took Charlie for such an emotional person. I mean, to carry this around with him for all these years."

"Carry what?" Rachel asked.

"I mean, is it really possible a bad experience can manifest as psychosis years after the incident?" said Joe.

"Anything is possible where the mind is concerned," Rachel said. "But what happened in San Francisco?"

"Eddie Prescott killed himself," Joe said before Charlie had a chance to answer.

"And who is Eddie Prescott?" asked Rachel.

"Eddie is . . . was . . . my business partner," Charlie began. "We met at MIT. We had the same economics professor and the same dislike for economics. We started cutting class and talking. I learned more in those meetings with Eddie than I think I did all year. He was brilliant. An intellect beyond anyone I'd ever known. He was a mechanical wizard and an idea man. Best of all, for someone as genius as Eddie Prescott was, he had the follow-through. Eddie had more drive than anyone I've ever known. Even me."

"Then what happened?" Rachel asked.

"There was a technology gold rush happening out West, and after MIT we moved and started our company. Eddie's prototypes led to our first big breakthrough and patent. We didn't know that we would end up in the consumer electronics business. But we did know that we were on to something big."

"It got bigger than anyone thought," Joe said. "I still have your *Forbes* interview in my room. Did you know that?"

Charlie blushed at his brother's unfiltered admiration. As distant and unavailable as he had been, it still surprised him that his brother held no grudge.

"And you said Eddie killed himself. Why?" Rachel asked.

"Because I found out that he was stealing money from the company and using it to gamble. It was as simple as that," Charlie explained. "Then he sold some company secrets to a competitor for cash. I fired him and blacklisted Eddie from any big-name tech player in the valley. The only job that Eddie could have gotten within a twenty-mile radius of where he lived was at the mall. Not to mention the stock options Eddie lost out on because he violated the terms of his contract."

"But it was his company. How could you push him out?" Rachel said.

"Because Eddie might have been the brains behind our operation, but I had the smarts. My lawyer was better than his lawyer. And Eddie didn't have a legal leg to stand on. The contract ensured that."

"So what happened after you fired him?" Rachel asked.

Joe couldn't stay quiet for long. "That's the best part. Or the worst," he said. "Depending on whose family you belong to."

"Oh? And how's that?" Rachel asked.

"SoluCent came a-knocking a few months after Eddie got fired," Joe said.

"It was a major payout for the stakeholders. Without any stock in the company, the deal was worthless for Eddie," Charlie added.

"And what did Eddie do?" Rachel replied.

"He threatened me. A bunch. He even broke into my apartment with a gun," Charlie said.

"To kill you?" Rachel asked.

Charlie nodded. "Presumably. But he just stood in the living room, pointing the gun at me and shaking. Then, just as I was about to dive for cover, he turned around and left. It was the last I heard or saw Eddie Prescott until they recovered his body."

"He jumped off the bridge, I'm guessing," Rachel said.

"Yes," Charlie said.

"Verified?" Rachel asked.

"Dental records. But yes, verified by the medical examiner's office. Eddie had no relatives to speak of. I guess he thought of our company as family. And me as a brother." Charlie peered at Joe but turned away when he caught a flash of hurt in Joe's eyes. "I went down to the ME's office to identify the body. It was unrecognizable really, bloated from salt water and decay."

"And do you blame yourself for Eddie's death?" Rachel asked.

"At first I didn't," Charlie said. "But as I got more successful and the company continued to grow, I couldn't help but think that without him, none of that success would have happened."

"How did that make you feel, Charlie?" Rachel asked. She looked over at Joe, her eyes suggesting that if Joe were to leave the room, now would be an appropriate time.

"It's okay," Charlie said. "He can hear this. He should hear this."

Rachel nodded. "Okay, Charlie. But I'd like for you to share whatever you feel comfortable sharing."

Charlie took in a deep breath before he spoke. "I felt a bit like a fraud, I suppose," he said. "I mean, Eddie was brilliant. He had the most amazing mind for technology that I've ever had the privilege of knowing. I took Eddie's idea and ran with it. Without Eddie there would have been no business. The technology that InVision is based on would never have been brought to market, and who knows where that would have left me."

Joe shook his head at that. "But it was you who made the company happen, Charlie. Not Eddie," he said. Rachel shot Joe a disapproving look.

Joe threw his hands high above his head. "What? What? It's true."

"Thank you, Joe. I appreciate that," Charlie said.

"Joe, if you can't be a listener right now, you're going to have to sit outside. It's important that Charlie continue to share in an uninhibited way," Rachel said.

"Okay. Okay. You're the boss. I'm just saying Charlie might be shortchanging his significance here," Joe said.

"Charlie, do you feel that way?"

"Well, I know my talents. But I also know my limitations. Without Eddie I might have been a vice president of a software company, but

I can't say for sure that I'd have orchestrated a multimillion-dollar acquisition. In the end, it was Eddie's doing, even though he didn't actually do it."

"And have you felt guilty about your success ever since?" Rachel asked.

"I tried not to think about it. I wanted the sale. I wanted it more than anything. It meant . . . it meant . . ." Charlie's voice trailed off.

"Meant what, Charlie?" Rachel said.

Charlie gritted his teeth. Saying the words was more uncomfortable than thinking the thoughts. "I grew up in a family that was less than perfect," Charlie said. "My father left us when we were boys and needed him most. He had his issues. And I hate to admit it, but I was angry at Joe. At his sickness and what it did to me and to our mother." Charlie looked at Joe, half-expecting to see his brother in tears.

"You think that's news to me, Charlie?" Joe said. "You've been angry since the day I was diagnosed. And I've watched you run and run to try and distance yourself from us . . . from yourself. But in the end you came back home, and now you're facing the same demons you thought you'd outrun. Being rich doesn't mean you've beaten your past. It just means you have money. But the tree still comes from the same roots. Always has and always will."

Charlie tried to keep stone-faced, but the words stung. "I thought that the success and money would prove that I had won," he said. "Maybe Joe's right. Nothing can ever change your past."

"That's true. But people can change. And so can you, Charlie. It sounds to me like Eddie's death had a much more profound impact on you than you first thought," Rachel said.

"Perhaps," Charlie said.

"The good news is that you are in control of you. Admitting that you have vulnerabilities and seeking help is the first step in taking control and changing your life."

"How do I do that?"

"You've been here for seventy-two hours now. You know as well as I do that we legally can't keep you here any longer. You can walk out those doors right now, Charlie. But the rest is up to you."

"What do I need to do?"

"Again, I can't tell you what to do or give you any professional advice, but as a friend I can say that I think you should continue therapy. I want you to see a professional. To work through this guilt and to make decisions with a psychiatrist to come up with a diagnosis and figure out what medications might be available to help you confront some of the delusions you've been experiencing."

"I know it feels like you've lost, Charlie," Joe said. "But sometimes seeking help is the strongest and most brave thing a person can do. It says a lot more about you than the size of your bank account."

"So that's it? I just walk out the door and try to put my life back together?" Charlie asked.

Rachel nodded. "That's it. The law says if we determine you're not a threat to others, which I know your doctors have, there is no reason to hold you longer. But you need to trust the people who love you. There is help out there. You need to be willing and ready to embrace it." Rachel looked down at her watch. "I have an appointment, Charlie. I need to go. Will you please call me and tell me what you've decided? I really do care, and I hope that you'll continue seeking treatment."

Charlie stood and shook Rachel's hand. Her skin felt velvety against his. How long had it been since he'd felt such attraction to a woman? The barrier that would keep them apart was almost as disheartening as the journey that awaited him. Still, in her kind and inviting eyes he saw hope. Once this was past, he would find another woman like Rachel. It wouldn't be easy, but it was something he knew he wanted.

"Thank you, Rachel. Thank you for everything."

"Joe knows where you can collect your things," Rachel said. "You'll need to see the head nurse and doctor on duty for formal discharge. Please take care of yourself, Charlie. It's all that matters right now."

"I will," Charlie said. Then he put an arm around his brother.

"Ready to go, bro?" Joe said.

"Ready as I'll ever be," Charlie said.

Before the brothers could leave, Dr. Alan Shapiro, who days earlier had attempted to bar Charlie's entry into his sleeping quarters, burst into the therapy room. He was breathless and seemed agitated.

"Rachel, can I speak with you?" he said.

"Alan, I'm on my way to see a patient. Can it wait?" said Rachel.

"No, it can't. It concerns him." Dr. Shapiro pointed to Charlie.

"Charlie's done with us, Alan. He's leaving now," Rachel replied.

"Not if I have anything to say about it," Shapiro said.

Rachel frowned. "Alan, what are you talking about?"

"The cleaning people found this in Charlie's room. We matched it to the handwriting on his admittance forms. It's definitely his penmanship," Shapiro said.

Shapiro handed Rachel a folded piece of yellow, lined legal paper. She opened it carefully and read the note. Charlie watched as her skin whitened and her eyes widened.

"Charlie, I'm so sorry," she said. "I wish I had seen this before I spoke about you leaving us."

"What's that note?" Charlie cried.

"Charlie, we can't let you leave now," Shapiro said. "This note represents a direct threat."

"Give me that note!" Charlie shouted.

Rachel put it in her pocket. "I can't do that. It's evidence now, and I can't risk you destroying it. Alan, why don't you get security down here?"

"Already here," Shapiro said.

Two men, one of whom Charlie recognized as the guard who had kept watch over him during his admittance interview, entered the room.

"Charlie, this note makes a direct threat to harm people you worked with," Rachel announced.

"Which people?" Charlie asked. "What are you talking about?"

Rachel pulled out the piece of paper and read from it. "When I'm out of here, I'm going to finish the job. One down, three to go. Mac and Yardley die next. The last is still my surprise. I can't wait for the killing to begin again."

Charlie stared at Rachel. "I didn't write that . . . I didn't . . ."

"I'm sorry, Charlie. But we can't just let you leave. Now, you have a right to demand a court appointment to seek an overturn of this decision," Rachel explained. "Right now this note represents a direct threat to named individuals. To let you walk out of here would be irresponsible of us. Ethically and legally. "

"I didn't write that!" Charlie's face reddened as he turned to Joe. "Tell them! Tell them, Joe."

Joe took a step backward. "I'm sorry, Charlie. I don't know what to say. They're the doctors. And doctors know best."

Chapter 39

Charlie lay in his bed, staring up at the ceiling. His request for a judge's ruling to overturn his involuntary commitment had been filed and, last he heard, delayed. Before the mandatory lights out, Rachel had stopped by to check in on him and to share the disappointing news. Charlie had been surprised to learn that the judge's chambers were located right on the Walderman campus. Rachel had explained that many of the larger mental health facilities had such a setup to reduce the burden on an already overextended court system.

Unfortunately, the judge dedicated to Walderman's caseload was attending a conference in Phoenix. Her substitute was booked solid with other cases. Charlie's hearing was scheduled, but it would have to wait, perhaps as long as forty-eight hours. Efforts to find an alternate judge were made for special circumstances, but only for cases that concerned less volatile patients. Charlie had been labeled a high-risk, potentially violent patient by his doctors. That assessment had sealed his fate. He wasn't going anywhere soon. Joe would be his lifeline to the outside world. He had promised to take good care of Monte, do his best to keep him from "visiting" Maxine, and provide regular updates about their mother's condition. Joe's support did help to ease his frustration and stress, but only a little.

Charlie's roommate, the narcoleptic, had been released yesterday. For a brief period Charlie had enjoyed the privilege of solitude. He was moments from drifting off to sleep when, without a knock, Dr. Alan Shapiro barged in. Apparently, the common civility of a knock on the door didn't extend to patients.

Shapiro escorted a man, a boy really, into Charlie's quarters. The boy was tall, scary thin, with dyed jet-black hair, lathered with gel to make it stand up in short, tight spikes at the top of his head. He wore a black sleeveless T-shirt with a skull design and ripped, faded jeans, tucked inside a pair of scuffed black leather boots laced up to the ankles with bright yellow laces. His arms, dangling by his sides like two thin branches of a tree, had the muscular definition of his wrists. To Charlie he looked no more than twenty. His eyes were wide with fear. Charlie assumed the boy's demeanor was similar to the stunned expression on his own face when he'd first seen his new sleeping accommodations. Sadly now, this sterile room was as familiar to him as his Beacon Hill apartment. Perhaps even more so.

Shapiro showed a smile so fake, Charlie wanted to punch it off his smug face. That it was Shapiro who'd gotten in the way of Charlie's freedom didn't do much to endear the doctor to him, anyway. Charlie could tell that Shapiro enjoyed the control and took twisted pleasure in having brought Charlie down.

"Maxim, this is Charlie. Charlie, I'd like you to meet your new roommate, Maxim."

Charlie lifted himself off the bed and walked over to greet Maxim. "Do you go by Max?" Charlie asked.

Maxim said nothing. He stared at the wall in front of him.

"He's not talking right now. Perhaps, Charlie, you and he could talk for a bit. Get to know each other."

"Perhaps," Charlie said. "And perhaps you can get out now."

Shapiro seemed aware of the hostility. He stepped backward toward the door. "Charlie can show you around the room. There are clothes for you to sleep in. They're clean. We do laundry daily."

Maxim looked away from the wall and stared back at Shapiro. His shoulders were hunched forward as though he were deflating before Charlie's eyes.

"Well then. You two get to know each other, and good night. We're here if you need us for anything," Shapiro said.

"I think you've done enough already," Charlie said.

Shapiro didn't bother with a response.

"Well then," Charlie said to Maxim. "What are you in for?"

Maxim went over to the vacant bed and sat down. He looked up at Charlie with big, sad eyes but said nothing. This boy seemed lost beyond help. In a way, Charlie thought he looked like the skull on his shirt, with just a thin layer of skin for cover. *Is this how sad and lost I seem to Rachel?* he wondered. The thought sickened him.

"I'm guessing that you're not much of a talker," Charlie said. "Well, that's just fine with me. I'm not much of a talker, either. There isn't much to show you. Bed, desk, bathroom. If you want pajamas to sleep in, they're in that drawer there," he continued, pointing to the third drawer down.

Maxim didn't bother nodding. Instead, he lifted his legs up onto the bed, putting himself in a supine position, and kept staring in front of him, this time up at the ceiling. At that moment the boy reminded Charlie even more of himself. There was no need to ask if Maxim minded the lights going out. Given the boy's confused state, Charlie didn't think he would even notice the change.

Even with the room seeped in darkness, it was not surprising that Charlie couldn't sleep. He was sure Maxim was awake as well. The absurdity of two strangers staring blankly up at the ceiling, each lost in their own mental maze, brought a thin smile to Charlie's lips. In the dark Charlie watched the spots dance about his eyes as they adjusted to the sudden blackness. To combat the boredom and insomnia, Charlie had invented a game. He timed how long it took for his eyes to make out the edges of the ceiling tiles and then how many tiles he could count. He'd been playing this game since the first night of his commitment. It had taken nearly ten minutes by his estimation to count eight tiles in the dark of the room the first night he played. Practice had helped to get that time down to three minutes and almost twenty tiles simply through focus and concentration. It was a small victory over his mind, in a battle he now felt he was losing.

From the darkness, just as he counted his eighteenth ceiling tile, Charlie heard a voice.

"Charlie, listen to me."

Charlie sat bolt upright in his bed. "What did you say?" he asked in the direction of Maxim. In the dark of the room Charlie couldn't see if Maxim had even moved. Perhaps he was talking in his sleep. Charlie got out of bed and turned on the light. There was something about what he'd heard that was disturbingly familiar.

Maxim blinked his eyes as he adjusted to the light.

"What did you say?" Charlie asked.

Maxim didn't respond. He just shook his head.

"I guess you were just talking in your sleep," Charlie said.

He went back to his bed. This time he kept the lights on and his eyes fixed on the ceiling.

The voice came again, almost the moment he lay down. *"Charlie, you killed me."*

The voice sounded no different than a stereo recording in Charlie's ears. He turned to Maxim. "Stop fucking with me," Charlie shouted at him and jumped out of bed.

This time Maxim reacted. He lifted his knees against his chest and curled himself into a tight ball on the bed.

Charlie sat back down on his bed and stared across the room at Maxim. "I'm watching you. I'll watch you all night if I have to," he said.

"You killed me, Charlie," the voice called out again.

Charlie had kept vigilant watch over Maxim. The boy's jaw hadn't moved at all. His mouth had stayed closed the entire time. But the voice was as loud and clear as if the person was seated on the edge of his bed.

"Are you some sort of ventriloquist?" Charlie scowled.

Maxim turned to Charlie, his thin, weak frame and sunken eyes suggesting both innocence and confusion. "I'm not talking to you," Maxim said.

Those were the first words Charlie had heard him speak. His voice was high-pitched and weak. It sounded nothing like the voice he'd heard. *Could he be a master of both ventriloquism and imitation?* Charlie thought. It was doubtful.

"Do you want to know the secret of your mind?"

Charlie's heart sped up. That voice. He knew it now. How could he have ever forgotten?

"Everything can be explained. But you must get out, Charlie. Leave here now and everything can be explained."

"Stop it! Stop it! You're dead!" Charlie shouted to the ceiling.

"Yes," the voice said, *"I am dead."*

"He answered me," Charlie said to himself. "I'm not just hearing this."

"I'm dead, Charlie. You killed me. And the only hope you have of saving your life is to trust me. You must leave this place."

Charlie shook his head in a futile attempt to get the voice to stop. "You're not real," he muttered. "I know what is real. You can't be real."

"*All can be explained. You must believe me,*" the voice of Eddie Prescott hissed. "*Leave this place now so I can help you.*"

"I can't leave!" Charlie cried out to the air. "I'm locked up here."

"*I can help you explain everything—Rudy Gomes, the kill list, Anne Pedersen. Everything has an answer, and nothing is as it seems. Leave here tomorrow. And trust that you will be guided.*"

"Who are you talking to, man?" Maxim asked. "You're really freaking me out."

"You can't hear that? Tell me you can't hear that voice," Charlie said.

Maxim bolted from his bed, ripped open the room door and tumbled into the dimly lit hallway. "Hey!" he cried. "Get me outta here! This guy's a freak!"

"But you're dead." Charlie sobbed into his hands. "You're dead, Eddie. You can't talk."

"*Yes.*" Eddie's voice echoed in Charlie's mind. "*I'm dead, and the only hope you have to survive.*"

Dr. Shapiro barged into the room, followed by two imposing orderlies. Maxim stood in the hallway, safeguarded behind Shapiro and his entourage, and didn't follow when they stepped inside. Charlie lay on his bed, curled in a fetal position.

"Charlie. Charlie!" Dr. Shapiro said. "This is Dr. Alan Shapiro. Can you hear me?"

Charlie leapt to his feet at the sound of Shapiro's voice. He began pacing in frantic, erratic circles around his bed. Shapiro moved to calm and restrain him. The orderlies gripped Charlie by the shoulders. It took the full strength of both men to muscle him back down onto the bed.

Once Charlie was seated, Shapiro jammed a needle through the thin fabric of Charlie's pajamas, breaking the skin of his thigh. Charlie barely flinched.

"I need you to calm down, Charlie," Shapiro said. "It's important that you regain control. Can you do that for me, Charlie?"

Charlie looked up at Shapiro, his eyes wild with confusion and fear.

"You have to get out of here if you want to survive, Charlie," Eddie said. *"They're trying to kill you."*

"Did you hear that? Did you?" Charlie pleaded.

"No, Charlie," Shapiro said. "There is nobody talking to you. The only voice you should hear right now is my own."

"Oh, but he's wrong, Charlie. There is someone talking to you," Eddie hissed. *"And I'm the only friend you have left."*

As the chemical surged through Charlie's body, a smile broke out across his face. Somehow, someway, Eddie Prescott had found him. Before this descent into madness, ghosts and phantoms had held no sway with him. But Charlie was certain of one thing. Eddie Prescott's ghostly voice was as real as their days together. Eddie spoke as clearly as if he were sitting on the bed next to him. Except that nobody else could hear the conversation. It was meant for Charlie alone. How Eddie Prescott had broken through the other side was of little consequence now. Charlie preferred getting answers over questioning the impossible. Eddie's words were a call to action. Charlie couldn't wait any longer to act.

Chapter 40

The drugs had worn off. Charlie awoke with a splitting headache, his mouth parched and sticky with sleep and his stomach roiling with sickness. Flashes of the night before sent waves of confusion through him. Charlie wasn't the type to believe in spirits or in the afterlife. If something didn't have a logical explanation, Charlie assumed it to be some sort of hoax or misunderstanding.

Now his foundation was shaken to the core. The dead had contacted him.

As he lay on the bed, his mind raced to come up with a logical explanation. Perhaps it was the hypnosis. Something Rachel did opened up a part of my mind, he thought. Hypnosis was the only thing that made sense, but he struggled to accept that Eddie's voice was merely a figment of his imagination. He had heard Eddie Prescott speak, and each word had ripped away his belief in logic and rational thought.

"Wake up, Charlie. It's a big day today. It's leaving day," Eddie hissed in his ear.

"Shut up!" Charlie shouted skyward. "Leave me alone."

"Get your bags packed . . . ," Eddie hissed again. *"Your life depends on it. . . ."*

Charlie's roommate had been relocated during the night. Charlie was alone in his quarters, but that didn't matter. Even if Maxim had been in the room, he wouldn't be able to hear Eddie Prescott's voice. That privilege was Charlie's alone. Why Eddie was trying to help him, Charlie didn't know. What he did know was that Eddie was a wake-up call. For too long now, Charlie had played the part of a victim. Charlie wasn't accustomed to playing by other people's rules. He was the one who made the rules. Now all of that was about to change—thanks in large part to his dead partner's prodding.

Dressing quickly, Charlie left his room. His legs ached from the narcotic and carried him with the sure-footedness of a seasick mariner. The common area was mostly deserted. Breakfast was still in progress.

Good, he thought. *That makes finding him easier.*

Charlie headed toward the stairwell, where he would be greeted, then escorted, by a duty nurse down to the basement-level cafeteria. There he was certain he'd find George Ferris eating his morning eggs. And with George's help, freedom would be mere hours away.

Charlie entered the cafeteria and took no more than a few seconds to spot George seated alone at a corner table. He was careful to avoid being seen by any of the on-duty psychiatrists—not wanting to answer for last night's incident. They would come and find him soon enough, he reasoned.

George hadn't shaved or combed his hair. In fact, he hadn't made any noticeable attempts to civilize his appearance, despite claims that his medication changes had substantially improved his reasoning. Charlie surmised it was part of a mad professor mystique that George was cultivating.

Taking an empty seat at George's table, Charlie watched as the man scooped up a mouthful of egg onto his plastic fork and then shoveled it indiscriminately into his mouth. The utensils provided by Walderman were rounded and dull. Everything accessible to patients was plastic and carefully manufactured to ensure they couldn't use them against the staff, or themselves.

"You look spry and refreshed," George said after he finished chewing.

"I'm guessing you're being a bit sarcastic," Charlie said.

"Just a bit."

"Well, you're not much of a sight for sore eyes yourself, George," Charlie said.

George laughed. "I may be wild-looking, but at least I'm happy. You, on the other hand, seem troubled this morning. I can see it in your eyes."

Charlie took a deep breath. Shame passed through him over how he had first judged George. Now the person he had once reviled proved more insightful than himself and might be the one to help set him free. If what Eddie Prescott had said was true and Charlie's life was in danger, it would be fitting that George be the one to help save him.

Charlie wasted no time. "I need your help, George," Charlie said, leaning in close, nearly whispering the words.

"My help? With what?"

"I need to get out of here."

George laughed. A few patients eating nearby turned and took notice. Charlie shook his head and held his finger up to his lips.

"No need for secrecy, my friend. Why don't you just leave?" George asked. "Your time here is up."

"It's not that simple anymore," Charlie said. "Apparently they found a note in my handwriting, threatening to kill my former bosses. I demanded a court ruling on my commitment, but the judge is unavailable. I'm involuntarily committed until I can get that hearing."

"Well, that's not a problem," George said, talking while chewing, offering Charlie an unpleasantly unobstructed view of the contents of his mouth. "You should get a hearing in the next day or two. It's pretty uncommon to keep someone locked up who hasn't committed a crime."

"I don't have a day or two," Charlie said.

"Why?"

"I don't know," Charlie replied. "I just know that somebody contacted me and told me that I needed to get out of here. Today. He said that everything would be explained once I did, and that my life was in danger if I stayed."

George twirled the long hair of his beard. "And who told you this?" he asked.

"You'd think I'm crazy if I told you," Charlie said.

George laughed and covered his mouth to keep food from spilling out. "Well now, that's a new one," he said.

"Are you mocking me?" Charlie asked.

"No. I'm merely highlighting the irony of your situation," George said. "Fear of being judged crazy by a crazy person in a mental hospital. It's really precious, if you think about it. So tell me, who gave you this warning?"

Charlie's mind churned through his options. If anyone would understand and believe him, it would be George.

"My dead business partner. Okay?" Charlie tried, unconvincingly, to mask the absurdity of the statement. "He started talking to me last night. I'd just finished hypnotherapy. The session was related to Eddie. Perhaps something about the hypnosis made it possible for him to contact me."

"From the grave?" George asked.

Charlie stared into George's eyes, searching them for any sign of doubt and condemnation. "I guess. I don't know. He's the one who gave me the warning. And yes, he died years ago."

George didn't even flinch at the audacity of the story. "And let me guess," he said. "You're the only one who heard him."

"That's right," Charlie said.

"And what do you make of this, Charlie?" George asked.

"It sounds crazy, I know. But trust me, George, this is different."

"Why?" George asked, his eyes suggesting that he already knew the answer. "Because it happened to you?"

"No," Charlie said. "Because it happened. I heard it. Eddie told me that I'm not crazy. There is an explanation for everything that's been happening, and he wants to help me figure it out."

"And what about other people who hear voices?" George asked. "Are they equally sane?"

"It's different. I can't explain it. It was as real as this conversation is now. He's trying to help me."

"You don't think that a deep hypnosis could have unlocked something you've been suppressing for years? As a result, to combat the guilt or shame, or whatever you suppressed, you've manifested the voice of Eddie yourself."

"It wasn't like a voice in my head, George," Charlie said. "It was no different than you and I talking now. I didn't make it up."

George rested his elbows on the table, clasping his hands together and using his thumbs to support the weight of his chin.

"Have you ever read Joseph Heller?" George asked.

Charlie laughed a bit, having likened the book to his situation on several occasions already. "Sure. Back in high school. *Catch-Twenty-two*."

"Think about it. A crazy person locked in a mental hospital hears voices. If the voices are real, then he's not crazy. It's miraculous even. If he says that he hears voices nobody else can hear, then he belongs in the mental hospital. Now tell me, Charlie, what's a person to do with that?" George took his elbows off the table and went back to eating.

"I am out of options, George. This is the first opportunity since everything bad started happening to me that I can actually do something about. If I don't listen to what I heard, if I don't act on it, I may be passing up the only chance I have to save myself. I'm not ready to go down without a fight. So what's it going to be? Will you help me or not?"

George sat upright. He set his fork down on his half-eaten plate of food and looked into Charlie's eyes.

"Well?" Charlie asked again.

"Of course I'll help," George said. "After all, that's what friends are for."

Chapter 41

The common area was the usual buzz of activity. Patients played board games. Some watched the televisions mounted high on the walls, while others paced up and down the halls. Some talked to themselves, and several sat in chairs, waiting for visitors. Charlie kept his usual low profile, even though today would be anything but usual. He hadn't heard from Eddie since leaving his room, but that didn't much matter. He knew what had to be done, and with George's help it would happen.

The last person Charlie wanted or expected to see that morning was Rachel. She tapped him on the shoulder. Charlie spun around, startling her.

"Hey!" she said. "A little jumpy today?"

Charlie could hear his blood pounding in his ears. He needed to be alone. Rachel had the capacity to ruin everything.

"I'm sorry," Charlie said. "Perhaps a little, after the other night, I mean."

Rachel's eyes sparkled with concern. "Yes. I know. I heard about that. Dr. Shapiro mentioned the incident in our morning staff meeting. I'm so sorry, Charlie."

For a moment Charlie let himself become lost in Rachel's interest. Then, quick as he'd succumbed, he iced up. He needed to get her out of the way.

"What do you want, Rachel?" Charlie's eyes narrowed. He allowed himself to become aggressive, hostile even.

Rachel took a step backward. "I just wanted to update you on the situation with the judge," she said. "I think we can get you a hearing the day after tomorrow. But I have to say, last night's incident didn't help your cause much."

Charlie nodded. "I'm sure the staff is even warier of me now," he said. "It must have been a dream. Perhaps it was something triggered by the hypnosis." Offering a logical explanation and accepting responsibility for the incident might be enough to get her to move along and leave him alone.

"You have counseling scheduled for today?" Rachel asked.

"Yes. In the afternoon, I think. But I'm done with group."

"I do hope that will change," Rachel said.

Charlie was aware of her style now, though her compassion seemed boundless. The worse his situation deteriorated, the more determined Rachel seemed to help. Perhaps, Charlie thought, the same could be said of his attraction to her. The more unbalanced his life became, the more appealing she seemed. He brushed those thoughts aside.

"Listen, Charlie," Rachel said. "It's not common practice, but I'd be happy to talk to you as a friend if you need. Sometimes that can be the best therapy of all."

"Thanks, Rachel," Charlie said. "I'll think about it. Now, if you'll excuse me . . ."

Out of the corner of his eye, Charlie kept careful watch over George. Without the benefit of clocks to synchronize their plan, the two had agreed to use hand signals to communicate. Per the plan, George was engaged in a game of checkers against Maliek. When the game was over and George gave Charlie the sign, everything would start to happen. Fast.

"Charlie, there is something else I want to talk to you about," Rachel said. "Something about Joe."

"I don't care about Joe right now, Rachel. And I don't care much about you, either. I want you to go away from me and leave me alone."

"But, Charlie . . . ," Rachel said.

"What part of 'go away' don't you get?" Charlie asked. "Leave me alone, now." He kept his voice low.

The harshness took Rachel by surprise. She stepped back. "Please, Charlie," Rachel said. "Don't be like that."

Charlie couldn't let up now. "Don't you get it, Rachel?" he asked. "I don't want you to talk to me. I don't want you to be near me, and I don't want a friend. I want you to go away."

The hurt in Rachel's eyes stung Charlie more than he had expected. She backed away but did not avert her gaze.

"You need help, Charlie," she said. "You need to trust us."

"What I need is for you to disappear, Rachel." Charlie spat out the words through clenched teeth. "You did this to me. You're the reason I'm here. I never want to see you again. Is that clear enough for you? Get away from me!"

Charlie couldn't believe the harshness of his own words. Still, they rang true. If he had never contacted Rachel in the first place, he might never have been locked up in this hellhole.

Rachel covered her mouth. Charlie thought he saw tears well up in her eyes. Without another word, she turned and raced down the hallway. He watched as she exited through the floor's security doors and then disappeared down the stairwell.

The timing couldn't have been better, even though he felt sick about what he had said. The moment she was gone, George finished the game of checkers. He locked his fingers together, stretching his arms and his interlocked hands high above his head.

This was the signal Charlie was waiting for. The show was about to begin. Charlie took the cue and moved closer to the security doors that sealed off the floor's only entrance and exit.

With his hands still locked together above his head, George screamed, "You're a cheater! A cheater!"

With that, George thrust his balled hands downward, smashing them hard onto the gaming table. Checker pieces clattered onto the floor, sent in every direction by the force of the impact. Maliek stood up and retreated.

From his vantage point, Charlie could still see the action unfolding, but he stayed close enough to the doors to ensure that the plan worked as designed. Charlie couldn't believe how well George was playing it up. It was an Oscar-worthy performance, only lacking a film crew to capture the beauty of it.

"I didn't cheat!" Maliek said. "I won the game fair and square."

"You're a cheater!" George yelled again. Following their choreography to perfection, George flipped over the gaming table, which sounded a deafening crash as it eventually settled to a stop on the floor.

Nurses rushed to the unfolding drama but kept their distance. George picked up a chair and pushed it threateningly at them, in the way a lion tamer would to keep a predator at bay. They hadn't discussed that particular move during their planning, but the improvisation added a level of authenticity to George's outburst.

Following protocol, Charlie watched the day nurse in charge pick up the phone at the nurses' station, presumably to dial security. Charlie kept his position against the wall. He was standing to the right of the security doors. Once they opened, he'd have only seconds to react.

"George, put the chair down," one of the nurses said. "Listen to me, George. You need to put it down."

"Get away from me! Get away!" George shouted.

Orderlies and several nurses had formed a semicircle around George and closed in. Charlie's heart raced. Although his eyes were fixated on George, his ears were attuned to the doors. He was waiting for the buzzer, a sound that would allow security to enter and him to leave.

A nurse had come over to the doors with her card key in hand. She kept peering out the small window of one of the thick ward floor doors, ready to press the buzzer the moment security arrived. She pressed the open button at the same instant security rang the bell. The doors buzzed loudly in Charlie's ears and then were thrust open. Two sizable armed men burst into the room and darted off in George's direction.

The nurse took no notice of Charlie. Her focus, as with every staffer on the floor, was on George. The doors started to close. They were on a hinge and closed slowly enough for Charlie to use his foot as a doorstop.

Propping one of the doors open, Charlie wasted no time in making his exit. If the doors didn't close within a certain amount of time, a buzzer would sound an alarm. Removing his foot from underneath the door, Charlie slipped his body through the shrinking crack between the door and the doorjamb. At last, he was outside the floor walls without an escort. Charlie's footsteps echoed loudly in the stairwell as he bounded down the concrete steps, two at a time.

At the bottom landing, he pushed open the unlocked fire exit door. He emerged into the sunlight and breathed the fresh air for the first time in days. With adrenaline still coursing through him, Charlie somehow managed to keep his pace unhurried. He kept his eyes focused forward, careful to not look around and perhaps rouse suspicions. Charlie breathed in the coolness of the fall day. His skin prickled with excitement.

Never looking back, Charlie headed east, away from the main campus, down a grassy knoll toward busy Belmont Street. He walked with calm, unhurried steps. It was just like a free man would walk.

Chapter 42

Charlie had only one thought on his mind: how much time before they discovered him missing? He didn't need a degree in psychiatry or a law enforcement background to speculate that his escape would raise alarms. As far as Walderman was concerned, Charlie was a potentially violent and dangerous escaped mental patient. The police would be looking for him soon enough.

Worse, he didn't know what he should do now that he was out. Eddie Prescott had spoken to him from the grave. He was the one who had set these events in motion. Charlie was certain of that. But Eddie had offered warnings only. The moves Charlie made now would have to be his alone. Free from Walderman and presumably away from the danger Eddie had warned him about, Charlie felt adrift. It surprised him how quickly he had adapted to the routine of institutionalized life. Freedom took far more effort.

Fortunately, nothing about his appearance would draw attention. His clothes and shoes were his own. At least Walderman didn't further cement the stigma of commitment by forcing patients to wear hospital clothes or a uniform. But with the police looking for him, he needed a better disguise—a hat and sunglasses, at least. That would take money. Money was something he didn't have, not to mention a watch, a cell phone, or ID of any sort. Going home for those items would be ill-advised. They would track him there. The same held true for contacting Joe. If he wanted to maintain his freedom, it was imperative that he stay away from his former life.

Charlie strolled down Belmont Avenue. He kept an even pace, certain that he still had hours before anyone would notice him missing. He had a scheduled therapy session later in the afternoon. When he didn't show for that, the alarms would sound.

His thoughts drifted back to Eddie Prescott's voice. Eddie's words remained ingrained in his memory, as though he were reading them written down.

"I will be your guide," Eddie had said. *"Everything can be explained. Nothing is as it seems."*

Charlie burst into laughter. His circumstances were so surreal, laughing felt as justified as crying.

He looked around, grateful that he had not drawn attention to himself. Twenty minutes of walking and Charlie had come to Fresh Pond Circle in Cambridge. The area was a major oasis for the outlier city dwellers of Cambridge. Paths for bikers, walkers, and runners crisscrossed the 150-acre tract of land surrounding the city public water supply. He was near Alewife Station on the Red Line. The subway could take him deep into the heart of Boston or away from the city, into other suburban towns accessible by bus.

The Fresh Pond area always drew an eclectic crowd, and today was no exception. Charlie was grateful for the increase in pedestrian traffic. It would help keep him concealed.

He fell into step with the shoppers walking in and out of stores in the Fresh Pond Mall. Charlie took notice of a group of young people—some teenagers, some older—loitering outside the Staples near the Fresh Pond Mall cinema. Most were dressed in black, tattered clothes, their bodies adorned with pierced jewelry and tattoos. One boy, sitting idle on the curb, caught Charlie's attention. At first he didn't believe it possible. Curiosity getting the better of him, Charlie slipped behind a group of women shoppers with their small children in tow to get closer to the youths without being spotted.

The boy sitting on the curb was Maxim, his bunk mate from the night before. Maxim sat with his shoulders hunched forward, his head hung low, and his eyes cast downward. He wore the same skull T-shirt that he'd had on when they were first introduced. His jewelry returned, Maxim glistened in the sunlight like a chain-mailed gothic warrior.

Most of Maxim's companions were thin like him. They swarmed about the empty parking lot on their skateboards and BMX bikes. The skaters would hit the curb, flipping their boards, and almost without fail miss the landing. Maxim looked up and Charlie jumped. He darted into the Whole Foods Market, praying that Maxim hadn't noticed him. To blend in with the crowd, he wandered the aisles, carrying a basket and placing a few items inside. As far as store security was concerned Charlie was just another shopper out on a busy afternoon.

A few minutes wandering the aisles was all it took for Charlie to decide he needed to move on. He figured he'd walk into Boston from here. His best chance of staying free was to stay hidden. And the best place for that was in the city. Belmont police would probably take the lead on his recapture. But coordinating with Boston police would add some confusion and delay to the process. Charlie was certain he'd be safer in Boston than anywhere else. At least then he'd have time to plan his next move. Or maybe Eddie Prescott would return and tell him where to go next.

Charlie was in the bread aisle, returning one of the items he had placed in his basket, when Eddie spoke to him.

"You have to get to the Seacoast Motel. The answers are there," Eddie whispered.

Charlie whirled around. Six people were in the aisle. A plus-size black woman with a cart crammed with enough food to feed a family of twelve stood across from two elderly women who were examining the ingredients of some baking product. On the same side of the aisle as Charlie but some twenty feet away was an elderly man who walked with a cane. He wore a dark blue baseball cap. A shock of white hair spilled out from underneath it. Across from him was a mother, shopping with her two-year-old wedged safely in the shopping cart seat.

Charlie was looking directly at the old man when Eddie spoke again.

"The Seacoast Motel in Revere. All the answers are there. Room two-twenty-four. Go there and everything will become clear."

The old man and the woman didn't react to Eddie's voice at all.

They can't hear him, Charlie thought. *I'm the only one who can.*

Charlie looked over at the black woman, who was still filling her cart with food.

"You are running out of time," Eddie warned.

The black woman didn't flinch. The older women kept examining different ingredients, unfazed. Eddie was speaking to him alone, guiding the way.

Charlie couldn't help but laugh. Unlike Eddie's voice, his laugh was heard by both the black woman and the elderly shoppers. They turned and looked at Charlie. He held up a box of crackers.

"Can you believe these prices?" he said.

"Best quality, but they sure make you pay for it," the black woman agreed.

"They sure do," Charlie said.

"The Seacoast Motel in Revere. Room two-twenty-four. Go now . . . ," Eddie hissed.

Charlie had nowhere else to go. Nothing was left to hold him back. He had no home, no job, no family to turn to. The police would be looking for him, and ghosts were talking to him. He put the crackers back and carried his basket toward the exit.

Eddie had spoken, and Charlie was ready to obey. The only thing he needed now was money. And if there was one thing Charles Giles was good at, it was getting cash.

Chapter 43

Stepping outside the Whole Foods Market, Charlie scanned the parking lot for Maxim. It didn't take long for him to spot the same gang of Goths, clustered together in a circle at the far end of the mall parking lot. As Charlie approached, he could see that they had gathered around a fellow Goth, a thin, muscular boy who was demonstrating his talent for gravity-defying stunts on a BMX bike. Sitting on the curb, smoking a cigarette and seemingly disinterested in the exhibition taken place, was Maxim. His lanky frame, jet-black hair, ripped jeans, and thin arms adorned with spiked bracelets, made him a perfect fit for this crowd.

As Charlie approached, Maxim turned, saw him, and then stood. The expression on Maxim's face was an awkward combination of fear and surprise.

"Dude . . . what the . . . dude," he said, pointing to Charlie. The encounter had understandably caught the boy off guard. It was not surprising that Charlie's sudden appearance, like a mirage shimmering from desert sands, had left him speechless. His friends now took notice. The agitation in Maxim's voice was enough to turn their attention away from the stunt rider and toward Charlie.

"Who is that?" a woman said to Maxim. She had a shock of short pink hair, perhaps a dozen piercings in her nose and ears, as well as a snaking barbed-wire tattoo that ran up the length of her neck.

The fact that Maxim could identify Charlie to the authorities didn't concern him much. This crew didn't seem the type to embrace any sort of police involvement.

"I don't know," Maxim said. "I've never seen him before."

Spotting the opening to make his attack, Charlie's eyes sparkled.

He didn't tell them where he spent the night, Charlie thought. *That's good.*

"Well, he's coming to talk to you," she said.

Maxim took a step forward. "Don't worry. I'll take care of it," he said. Maxim stood up and gave Charlie the most menacing look he could muster. "Back away, freak, or you'll regret it," he said.

Charlie stopped about five feet away. "Take it easy, buddy," he said. "It seems that I've locked my keys in the car. I can get them without calling a tow or the police, but I could use an extra set of hands."

"Well, I'm not it. So bug off, prick," Maxim said.

"My mistake," Charlie said. "I misjudged. I took you for the honest, helpful type. So tell me, do any of them know?" Charlie kept smiling.

The pink-haired woman was joined by another boy, perhaps Maxim's age, but even thinner. A few of the other Goths had inched closer to get a better look at the scene unfolding. Before Walderman, Charlie would have dismissed them all as wastes—no-good punks high on drugs and going nowhere fast. His time in Walderman had changed all that. George had changed that thinking forever. *Who knows what lies underneath the surface?* Charlie thought. A Goth dressed in black, tattooed, and adorned with spikes could be a brilliant mathematician, while the businessman who drove the nice car, was clean shaven, and wore a suit might murder his family.

Maxim's eyes narrowed. "Dude, do you need me to show you the way out?" He stood and took a few steps forward. His words sounded forced, as if he was acting the part of the angry young man.

Charlie knew better. He saw fear, not anger, in Maxim's eyes. Fear that Charlie might share his secret with his friends.

"Look, I just needed some help, that's all. No worries if you don't want to help out," Charlie said.

"And why should he help you?" the pink-haired woman asked. "What's in it for him?"

Charlie smiled. "I don't know." He shrugged. "I guess he just seemed the type to pitch in. Perhaps I misjudged."

"Well, trust me. He's not that type," she said.

"Oh, really?" Charlie asked. "Why doesn't he answer for himself?" His smile broadened.

"Because I know him, that's why," she said. "He doesn't have to talk, you jerk-off."

The bait had been taken. It was time to end the hunt. "Is that so? Well, maybe you don't know everything there is to know about him. Is that possible?" Charlie watched Maxim's eyes widen and knew that the subtext was not lost on him.

Stepping forward, Maxim got between the pink-haired woman and Charlie.

"It's all right, Louisa," Maxim said. "I'll help this guy. I've been reading about karma lately. If anyone could use some, it's me."

Louisa shook her bright pink head in disbelief. "You're right," she said to Charlie. "I guess I don't know everything about him."

Maxim confronted Charlie as soon as the two were a safe distance away. "Dude, what the fuck are you doing here? Are you nuts?" he asked and then laughed. "Oh, forget about that. You are nuts."

"And what about you? Where did you spend last night? A Holiday Inn?"

"I'm out because I didn't need to be there," Maxim said. "I had one bad showdown at home, and my mom called nine-one-one on me. I was a bit out of control, so they sedated me good and took me to lockup. Lucky for me, I got to be roommates with a real wacko. I told my dad about it, and he had me out of there in an hour. But you really shouldn't be on the street right now, should you?"

"Perhaps."

"And let me guess. You need my help."

"You're getting warmer."

"I don't have any money, dude. You're barking up the wrong tree."

"Actually, I was wondering if you wanted to make some money," Charlie said.

As they walked down rows of cars, Charlie kept an eye out for a vehicle that wasn't locked. He stopped by a blue '96 Buick Century. Either the owner was forgetful or the power door lock actuator was broken. Either way, the car doors were unlocked.

Charlie stood by the driver's side door, pretending to fiddle with the window. They were still close enough to Maxim's crew for them to become suspicious.

Maxim, more intrigued than angry, went along. "I could use the money. What do I have to do?"

"How old are you?"

Maxim took a step back. "Dude! I've seen guys like you on TV. I ain't into that shit."

Charlie shook his head. "No. Are you old enough to drink?"

"Not legally," Maxim said with a devilish grin.

Charlie had suspected this was the case. He had put Maxim at around nineteen or twenty. He could cruise Harvard Square until he found another partner for this crime, someone who had a bogus ID, but then he would risk exposing himself to a lot more people than he wanted. Maxim would do just fine.

"But you drink?"

"Yeah."

"Fake ID?"

"Who doesn't?"

"Then that's all you need. Five hundred dollars sound good to you?"

Maxim's eyes narrowed. "Dude, you swear you're not some sort of freak sex fiend? Because I don't do that shit."

Charlie laughed aloud. "Sorry, Maxim," he said. "You're not my type. No. This is strictly about money. But I can't promise you it's entirely on the level. If you want the cash, I can get it for you. Interested?"

"Yeah. I'm interested," Maxim said.

With that Charlie pulled open the door to the Buick. He looked over at the Goths. At least Louisa had taken notice. Charlie shook Maxim's hand.

"There is an Internet café on Prospect Street. Do you know it?" Charlie asked.

Maxim nodded.

"Meet me there in an hour."

Maxim nodded again. "Dude, can I ask you something?"

"Sure," Charlie said. "What is it?"

"Are you still . . . still . . . hearing voices and shit?"

Eddie Prescott's words flooded Charlie's thoughts, sending shivers of fear through his body.

"No, man. That was just the drugs they gave me. You know how that place is. I'm good. And I'm going to help you get that cash. Deal?"

They shook hands again as Charlie closed the car door.

"They're going to wonder why you didn't drive away."

"Just tell them I had other errands to run. Make up something."

"I can do that," Maxim said.

Charlie turned to leave. He got a few steps away and stopped, turning back toward Maxim.

"Oh, and Maxim? Don't get cute. This is between us. I'm not held to the same confidentiality standards as Walderman. Got it?"

"Don't worry. I got it."

It was a fifteen-minute walk to the Internet café on Prospect. Charlie stepped inside. A girl, perhaps still in high school, was working behind the counter. She smiled at him. The place had a few people working on computers and a couple others drinking coffee.

"Welcome to Cyber Café," the girl said. "Can I get something for you?"

"Not right now. Thank you. I'm just going to work on the computer for a minute."

"Great!" she said. "Let me know if I can get you anything to eat or drink."

"I will," Charlie said, holding back a smile.

Deviousness, if not the mother, was at least a cousin of invention. Charlie had never desired the prestige super hackers sought and few achieved, but he understood the appeal and knew his fair share of "experts" who regularly plied the craft. His motivation now was desperation and not glory. For the first time in his life, Charlie was about to steal. And he wasn't the least bit scared about transforming the coffee shop into a bank. The only thing that bothered him about it was that he was actually enjoying the rush.

Chapter 44

Eddie Prescott hadn't spoken to him since leaving the market. In a way, Charlie missed hearing his voice. With Eddie talking to him from the grave, Charlie was a man on a mission. It was impossible for his logical mind to justify what he was doing and why, but he was willing to suspend his disbelief for something far more powerful than skepticism. Hope. Charlie kept Eddie's voice alive by obsessing on his dead partner's mantra.

The Seacoast Motel in Revere. All the answers are there.

What awaited him at that motel, he could only speculate. Perhaps it would explain what he had seen in the bathroom of Rudy Gomes's apartment. Or who Anne Pedersen was, and why she'd followed him to the hospital. Maybe he'd learn the origin of the kill list, and why the voice of his dead partner filled his head. All that he knew was that he was a man on the run from the police and willing to do almost anything to stop running. Even if that meant stealing.

Internet cafés were a dying breed, but enough people without laptops, willing to pay a per minute usage fee, kept a few still in business. There was a total of four computers in the café. That was the right number. More, and it might take him much longer to get what he needed. Two of the four computers at the café were already in use. Charlie took a seat at one of two available terminals. The chair reminded Charlie of the mangy fixtures that masqueraded as furniture at Walderman. The thought of that place made him shiver.

Charlie clicked the Internet Explorer icon, and the café's home page loaded. The home page was exactly what he'd expected: a simple Web form with a series of fields for customers to fill out: name, address, credit card number and expiration date, and Card Verification Value Code, the three- or four-digit code on the back of every credit card.

Charlie knew his credit card number as well as the CVV from memory, but he wasn't about to use them here. If the police were smart, they would flag his accounts.

Charlie feigned entering the information into the log-on screen. The computer station he'd selected faced the café's service counter. Only people using the bathroom would be able to get a good look at what he was doing. He could keep an eye out for that and could hide his activity if needed.

Step one in his plan was to build a duplicate Web form—identical to the form the café required customers to complete for Internet access. He was thankful they hadn't converted to free Wi-Fi yet. Charlie saved the graphics in a folder on the C drive on the computer. He then opened a notepad document and started to code.

Thirty minutes later Charlie had re-created the Web form, only he wasn't going through a Web server to display the Web page. The page, in fact, was local to the computer, and the Web form would be programmed to capture any information customers entered into the fields and to output that data to another file on the same computer. Any user, familiar or not with this particular Internet café, would have a difficult time detecting that the form they were entering their most personal information into was actually a forgery.

He made the credit card information fields encrypted for added authenticity. That way when a user typed in those boxes, they would see asterisks in place of numbers. Those sorts of simple security measures were an industry standard now. When a user saw that type of encryption on a site, they understood it meant that their information was protected. Of course, that couldn't be further from the truth.

Next, Charlie wrote a simple program in less time than it had taken him to create the forged Web page. There were only fifteen lines of code in his program. If he were a more practiced software engineer, he could probably have done it in five. But his chops had rusted long ago. It was hard enough to dig through his mental archives and remember the basics.

His program was a relatively simple one: take the values that a user entered into the text boxes on his dummy log-on page, and then write that data to a text file stored in a hidden location that Charlie had specified on the café's computer.

Charlie's dummy home page was not connected to the Internet. That meant it couldn't process any credit card information. To keep suspicion of his handiwork to a minimum, Charlie added to his program a simple browser redirect. Right after a user clicked the submit button on his forged log-on page, Charlie's program would not only write the data to a text file, but it would also redirect the user to the real log-on page. That way users would think their information didn't process and they'd simply enter it again, but this time on the form that would grant them access to the Internet at three dollars per hour.

It took only a simple modification to the Web browser's preferences to make it load Charlie's forged form instead of the real Cyber Café log-on page. A technologically savvy ownership would have security in place to prevent customers from changing configuration settings. But most of these mom-and-pop cafés had no idea of their vulnerabilities to hackers.

When it was done and tested, Charlie got up and exited the café. It was the cyber equivalent of lobster fishing. Set the trap; the store itself was the bait. An unsuspecting user would walk into the café. They would open the Web browser, needing to check an e-mail or whatever. They would get Charlie's dummy log-on page, looking just like the real deal. They'd pull out their wallet, enter in their credit card information, and click SUBMIT. The page would reload. They'd see the log-on page again. All the security information fields would be blank. Perhaps they would sigh aloud, blaming a faulty Internet connection, suspecting nothing. They'd enter their credit card information again, and voilà, they'd be on the Internet, surfing away and paying by the hour. Meanwhile, their precious credit card information would now exist in a text file on that computer's hard drive—a file that Charlie could retrieve at any time.

Maxim showed up outside the café as scheduled.

"Are you ready to do this?" Charlie asked.

"I need the cash. At least so I can get away from my old lady, who got me locked up in that hellhole in the first place."

Charlie hesitated. Everything depended on this. If they failed, he might as well go back to Walderman and forget about the truth. Regardless, he could forget about his life.

"Listen carefully, then," Charlie said. "You walk into the café. Smile at the counter person. Sit at the computer closest to the bathroom. Do you have anything to write with?"

Maxim nodded. "I have a notebook. I write poetry sometimes."

"Poetry?"

"Yeah. Want to hear some?"

Charlie smiled. "I don't think I'm really in the mood for a poem."

Charlie finished with his instructions, and Maxim nodded his head, comprehending every one. Ten minutes later he walked out of the café and up Prospect Street to where Charlie was waiting.

"Somebody used the computer?" Charlie asked.

Maxim nodded.

"Did you delete all the files?"

"I did," Maxim said.

"And the home page?"

"I set it back to the regular log-on page as the default, just like you said."

"Most important, the card?"

Maxim handed him a piece of paper with all the information sniffed from his program. Charlie felt in his pockets for a quarter and blushed. He had forgotten for a moment that he was broke and didn't even have a quarter for a call.

Maxim reached into his pockets and dug out a quarter. "You sure this is going to work, man?"

"Yes."

"What if I get caught?"

"Your ID is bogus." Charlie didn't mention the security cameras that would capture Maxim's picture as he took the money. "If for some reason you do get caught, all you have to say is that you were scammed. You were trying to help out a guy who needed some cash.

You got the money for him. You gave him all of it, except for a hundred bucks, which you kept as a thank-you."

"But you said you'd give me five hundred."

Charlie shook his head. "Anything under two-fifty is a misdemeanor if we get caught. You get five but say you took no more than a hundred. Got it?"

Charlie used the word *we,* knowing full well that Maxim was the most at risk. It would be easier for the police to get to him. But it would be impossible for them to get to Charlie. He had no address. He was already on the run. Maxim hadn't put that together yet. Probably he was too caught up in getting the fast cash and escaping from a difficult home life for a while. Charlie felt terrible taking advantage of the kid but didn't see another way. The Seacoast Motel and getting to Revere from Boston took money. Maxim would survive.

Charlie walked over to a pay phone and dialed the number for Western Union, using a business card he'd taken from one of the outlets near the Fresh Pond Mall. He gave them the name and number from the stolen credit card.

"The money is going to a Jeffrey Carmichael," Charlie said, holding up Maxim's bogus ID for reference. Then he paused. "Yes, he has ID. Thirty minutes. Thank you."

Charlie hung up the phone. The two walked in silence to the Western Union. Thirty minutes later Maxim emerged from the store with two thousand dollars in cash. At Charlie's suggestion, he'd bought a baseball hat and sunglasses on the way to the store, and he took them off as he stepped outside. He handed Charlie fifteen hundred dollars and pocketed the rest. Charlie gave him a twenty for the outfit.

"Will I get caught?" Maxim asked again.

Charlie shook his head. "I doubt it. Cameras won't tell them much. If you get on the news for the scam, will your friends rat you out?"

"My friends are loyal, dude, no matter what," Maxim said.

Charlie thought of Eddie. He thought of how furious he had been at Eddie's deception and how committed it had made him to destroying Eddie's career. He had shown Eddie no forgiveness. No loyalty. And yet somehow, Eddie was reaching out to him—even from the grave, Eddie Prescott was trying to be his friend.

Shaking Maxim's hand, Charlie said, "You take care of yourself."

"Thanks. I will." Maxim turned and headed back toward his crew, still hanging out in the mall parking lot.

Charlie made his way to the Red Line at Alewife Station. Soon he'd be in Revere, at the Seacoast Motel, where the answers to all his questions were waiting.

Chapter 45

Charlie had to accept Maxim's word that the boy had no plans for future use of the stolen credit card information. Such abuse, Charlie assured him, would undoubtedly come to the attention of the authorities. If that were to happen, Maxim's role in the theft would be exposed.

Charlie tore up the stolen credit card information and tossed the confetti-sized pieces into an overflowing trash barrel. He took some comfort in knowing that the cardholder would not incur a personal loss from the theft; the credit card company's theft protection plan would cover the loss.

Yet, as incomprehensible to him as it was, a mountain of evidence suggested that this wasn't Charlie's first criminal act. It was torturous to have no memory of his other transgressions. He would pay back the money he'd stolen—provided the memory of this particular crime didn't recede into the blackness of his subconscious.

Before Maxim had left, he'd used part of Charlie's share of the take to buy Charlie a large Red Sox T-shirt, a gray-and-blue sport Windbreaker, a plain blue baseball hat without any identifying logo, and sunglasses. Cocooned within a fresh change of clothes, Charlie felt more comfortable exposing himself to the impressive array of security cameras that kept watchful eyes over the city's many streets and stores.

Charlie and Maxim had shaken hands and parted ways. Nothing in their good-bye had suggested they would ever see each other again. *Transaction complete, the job done, have a nice life.*

He marched down Alewife Brook Parkway, his old clothes

bunched tightly inside a plastic Olympia Sports shopping bag. Purchasing a single token, Charlie boarded the Red Line and set off for Revere Beach. He would need to transfer at Park Street, where he could take the Green Line to Government Center. He'd transfer again to the Blue Line and take that train all the way to the Wonderland Station, across from the Wonderland dog track in Revere. Once in Revere, he figured he'd find a gas station and get directions to the Seacoast Motel. Although he assumed, as the name implied, that it would be located on or at least near the water, he had no map or address to go by.

Charlie shook his head at the thought. *A ghost guided me out of a mental hospital, and I'm irritated that he didn't give me the exact address,* he thought. *I truly have gone mad.*

During the forty-five-minute ride, the absence of Eddie's voice brought with it contradictory emotions. Eddie's voice gave Charlie renewed purpose and meaning but also confused him. Reflecting on Eddie's words felt like the fuzzy outline of a distant memory. It opened up possibilities that Charlie preferred not to embrace.

What if I'm simply delusional?

As the train barreled along and the passengers changed at each stop, Charlie managed to suppress those thoughts. Eddie's voice had come to him as clear as any voice he'd heard before. It was impossible for something that real to have been imagined. He didn't know whether others who claimed similar experiences were equally convinced about the voices they heard in their heads. He knew only of his own experience.

Charlie exited at Wonderland, mindful to keep his hat and glasses on at all times. Without access to the Internet, he couldn't know whether his escape had been publicized. Until he knew the extent to which people would be looking for him, everyone posed a risk.

Charlie hadn't been to Revere in years but remembered that the waterfront area had little to offer in terms of seaside attractions. It was mostly housing developments that ran the length of the shore. Several of the buildings were high-rise condos, some for the rich, some for the poor, and a bunch for the retired.

The most popular Revere attraction by far, aside from the dog track, was Kelly's Roast Beef. Kelly's was a restaurant, a shack really, that stood directly across from the ocean. A staple of Revere Beach,

Kelly's was best known for serving heaping portions of prime-cut roast beef and fries in a comforting seaside setting.

A yellow flyer taped to one of the station stanchions at Wonderland advertised a weekend special at the Seacoast Motel. The Seacoast Motel was located on the same small strip of beach as Kelly's Roast Beef. The motel, with an Ocean Avenue address, was just across from Revere Beach Boulevard and a short walk from Butler Circle and Wonderland Greyhound Park, where he had exited the train. It was a relief to not have to stop and ask for directions.

Revere Beach was no more three miles from Logan Airport. The few people—mostly elderly, but some younger—who strolled peacefully along the cool sandy beach seemed undisturbed by the approach and departure of the large jet airplanes passing overhead. Charlie couldn't ignore the roar of the engines as easily. Perhaps his nerves were still frayed from the escape.

When he finally arrived at the Seacoast Motel, Charlie found its appearance as unpleasant as the noise above. The motel suffered from neglect and stood out like a relic of a bygone era. It was reminiscent of the mom-and-pop businesses that had once provided much of the region's character but were now rapidly being replaced by the larger chains. As further proof, a newly constructed Comfort Inn loomed high above the Seacoast Motel on an adjacent lot and seemed to foretell the motel's bleak future. It wouldn't be long before this decaying relic was acquired and torn down.

The differing styles of motel architecture were in stark contrast to each other. Whereas the Comfort Inn went eight stories high and seemed replete with all the modern amenities, the Seacoast Motel was a single-level structure fronted by blue wooden doors adorned with gold-plated room numbers, which were visible from the street. The outside walls of the Seacoast Motel were spotted with large swaths of peeling white paint. The few black shutters still in place hung in varying degrees of looseness and framed room windows that blocked out the sun with thick floral curtains.

How this decaying excuse for a building was connected to him was a question he prayed would soon be answered. Charlie stood outside the motel and stared at it for several minutes. He wondered if Eddie might speak to him again. All was silent. After five long minutes Charlie walked to the motel office.

Room two-twenty-four, Charlie thought. *What waits for me be-hind that door?*

Charlie stood alone inside the wood-paneled office of the Sea-coast Motel. Having grown accustomed to the cold sterility of Wal-derman and now enjoying the gift of freedom, Charlie took in his surroundings with a keener awareness and appreciation. Nothing special about the office caught his attention. A wood-paneled counter, just a shade lighter than the paneling on the walls, separated the waiting area from the back office. Aside from a couple of bridge chairs for seating and a table displaying yesterday's *Herald* along with a few ancient magazines, the office was empty. Behind the counter were pigeon holes that held room keys. Atop a bedroom dresser next to the pigeon holes was a fax machine. A photocopier rested on the floor, adjacent to the dresser. Nothing here offered any clue as to why this motel was where Eddie wanted him to go. On the counter Charlie saw the bell, with a few spots of rust on it. He hit it twice, each time barely making a sound.

"Coming! I'm coming!" a voice called out from the back. Charlie heard the flush of a toilet and watched as a door, concealed to seem like part of the paneled wall, swung open.

The man who emerged from the bathroom was in no better shape than the motel. Portly, reeking of cigar smoke, he wore a green-and-black plaid shirt, which he proceeded to tuck inside his grimy chino pants. His belly stood out a heart attack's distance from the buckle of his belt. What he had left for hair had been slicked with oil and loosely covered the top of his head in tight gray-and-black clumps. The sea and salt air, rejuvenating for many, had weathered his face leathery, leaving it pockmarked and full of crevices that mimicked erosion.

"Yeah? What can I do for you?" His voice was hoarse, perhaps from cigar smoke. He spoke with a low, guttural growl. His thick Boston accent, distinguished by its proclivity to drop consonants, made it difficult to tell whether he was pleased to receive a new customer or not.

"I need a room," Charlie said.

"Okay. ID?"

"Well, that's a bit of a problem. You see, I don't have one," Charlie explained.

The man leaned forward, resting his full weight on the counter. "How long you gonna be here?"

Eddie hadn't provided any details on that. How long was he here? No more than a few days, he supposed. No matter what Eddie had in store, Charlie couldn't risk staying in one place for too long.

"Two nights to start," Charlie said. He pulled out the sizable wad of cash so that the man could see that he was good for the money. If the guy was as desperate as he looked, he'd figure Charlie might be worth even more than a two-night stay. Charlie noted there were far more pigeon holes with keys than without.

"So you're paying cash? Up front?" The man's eyes narrowed.

"Yeah, cash," Charlie said.

"Okay. Fill this out."

He pushed a clipboard toward Charlie. Clipped to the board was a card to fill in personal information, such as address and phone number.

"Is there really a need for this if I pay you up front?" Charlie asked.

The man eyed him again.

Charlie set a few hundred dollars down on the counter. "Plus deposit," Charlie added.

"Well, I guess not," the man said. Reaching behind him, he fished out a key from the nearest pigeon hole. "Room two-sixteen," he said. "It's in the back."

"Actually," Charlie said, "I was wondering if I could get room two-twenty-four. I saw it on my way in, and I liked the view."

The man grunted and turned. He looked at the pigeon holes and stopped. "Two-twenty-four?" he asked, with his back still turned to Charlie.

"Yes, if it's available."

The man pulled out an envelope from inside the cubby marked 224. He opened it and took out what Charlie thought to be a driver's license or a laminated ID of sorts.

"What's your name?" the man asked, his eyes narrowing on Charlie.

"Craig Devlin," Charlie said. Without thinking, he had selected the name of one of his favorite professors from MIT.

"Yeah? Craig Devlin, eh? Then tell me, who is this?"

The man slapped down the ID on the counter. Charlie's breathing grew shallower, and he shook his head, as though the motion would change what he couldn't believe he was seeing. On the counter the man had placed Charlie's driver's license. The picture was facing up.

"Room two-twenty-four is paid in full. It has been rented through next month and was paid for in cash, too. I got this in the mail just a few days ago. The instructions were to rent it to the guy in the ID. I'm not a specialist or anything, but you look a lot like him, amigo," the man said. His twisted grin suggested that he enjoyed the mystery of the situation almost as much as the money he was making off the room.

"Could I see that note?" Charlie stammered.

The man fished it out of the envelope. The handwriting was unmistakably his own. Charlie's blood turned ice cold as he read the undated, handwritten note.

To whom it may concern:

I will be arriving at this motel, requesting room 224. I will not have ID. Do not ask me any questions. In exchange, I will rent the room for two months at your standard rate, although I expect that my stay will be much shorter. Please return to me my ID and give me the keys to room 224 upon my arrival.

"It's impossible," Charlie muttered. "I don't understand."

"I don't, either," the man said. "But I do understand one thing, and that's money. I've kept in business this long by keeping quiet. You're the guy in the ID. You've paid for the room. It's yours."

He slid the ID across the counter. Charlie picked it up and appraised it, quickly convinced of its authenticity. He couldn't figure out how they had his ID. If anything, it should still be in his wallet at Walderman. The man next pushed the key to room 224 across the counter. Charlie picked it up and held it loosely in his hand, as though it were diseased.

"I'll take it," Charlie said and pocketed the key.

Charlie stepped outside the office and inhaled the cool ocean air. Then he walked toward room 224.

Chapter 46

The room was standard-issue motel. In the center stood a queen bed covered with an orange polyester bedspread. Directly across from it, resting on a nondescript bureau, was a nineteen-inch color TV. The TV had a built-in VCR but no DVD player. Charlie figured the Seacoast Motel didn't provide much in the way of on-demand entertainment.

It was fitting, then, that as a substitute the motel offered a "bring your own video" service. He noticed that the bathroom lights, at the other end of the room, were on. He found that a bit odd since he was the only one who should be in the room, unless a cleaning person had left them on accidentally. The motel owner didn't seem the sort to waste electricity.

He had no idea how long the room had been vacant. Although he had meant to ask, it didn't surprise him to have forgotten. He was still in shock from discovering he had a connection to this motel that seemed to predate his being committed. Charlie made a mental note to check back in with the owner and try to figure out exactly when the letter with his ID had arrived. It might help him construct a time line of events.

Charlie hovered in the center of the room, pondering what seemed to be an endless supply of questions. *When did I send him that note and money? I've never even heard of this place before. Why here?*

Nearly as startling as his having rented a room without any recollection of doing so was the realization that this was the first room he'd been in in nearly a week that locked from the inside. Moreover, it smelled more like other people than it did disinfectant, and had a color scheme that actually deviated from shades of white.

"Good-bye, Walderman," Charlie said aloud.

Taking off his Windbreaker, Charlie realized his shirt felt damp with sweat. Given all that he'd been through, that wasn't entirely surprising. He wondered if there was a clothing store nearby or at the very least a Laundromat. A clean change of clothes and a shower would do him a world of good.

He looked at the time on the digital clock next to the bed and realized that he could catch the evening news. As long as his escape wasn't broadcast, he felt a certain safety. At the least the motel would make a good hideout for a short while.

Praying that local and national events would steal the spotlight from his escapades, Charlie turned on the television. He sat on the edge of the bed, gritting through a tightness forming in his chest. Fifteen minutes later he breathed a loud sigh of relief. There had been a shooting in Dorchester. Three-alarm fire at a home in Beverly. All occupants were rescued, including the cat. Police were still trying to make an arrest in a string of car break-ins in Newton. But there was nothing, not even a tease for the eleven o'clock news, about a former software executive turned escaped mental patient, considered dangerous and out prowling the streets. He was certain the police had been alerted to his escape, but suspected Walderman Hospital had earned enough political capital over the years to keep the security breach quiet. *Quiet at least for the moment,* Charlie reminded himself. Time was a luxury he didn't have.

Spent with exhaustion, Charlie buried his head in his hands. He took some pleasure from evading capture, but for what purpose? The note waiting for him at the motel was a dagger thrust into his heart. The idea of Eddie Prescott guiding him from beyond the grave felt foolish and, even worse, sad. What other answer could there be, save for his complete and total madness?

The only thing that kept him from walking outside and surrendering to the authorities was a sudden and overpowering feeling of exhaustion. His eyelids grew heavy as his muscles gave way to relaxation. The sensation he felt was not unlike his earlier experience during the hypnosis session with Rachel. Images flashed through his mind with a hazy recollection. The faces of his former Magellan teammates from SoluCent were interspersed with images of his mother and Joe. He felt sick to his stomach, but rather than attempt the fifteen-foot trek to the bathroom, Charlie managed to fight back the urge to vomit. Even if he couldn't resist the urge, Charlie doubted he'd have the strength to even make it there. His legs felt too heavy to move.

He thought again of his mother. He hadn't even checked in on her condition. For all he knew, she could be out of her coma, although that was doubtful. Every update they had ever gotten was the same—no change. But he still hadn't ruled out that improvement was a possibility. Unlike how he felt about his own future, Charlie still held out hope for hers.

Although he was free, he was essentially locked up again. It was just a different prison: one of his own making, which kept getting smaller and smaller. First he was a prisoner of this motel room, and now he felt a prisoner of the bed. He was too weak and exhausted even to stand.

His head began to buzz, then tingle. It wasn't an alarming sensation; it felt calming. Exhaustion had won out. Charlie's thoughts drifted between his desire for sleep and a desperate need for answers.

Perhaps I could sleep a minute. I'll figure things out later. I don't remember sending money to this motel. I'm so lost. Just close my eyes . . .

The tingling in his head retreated a moment, only to swell up again. With closed eyes, Charlie watched as the faces of Rachel, Randal, Sandy Goodkin, and Joe spun around in his imagination in a wild, frenzied dance. George's laugh echoed from somewhere deep in the recesses of his mind. There was a moment when Charlie felt himself falling, but the sensation was blessedly brief. He had only a vague awareness that he was lying on the bed. His legs felt as if they had melted into the mattress, and his feet were glued to the floor. The tingling in his head stopped at last.

"I'll close my eyes for just a minute," Charlie muttered. "Then I'll figure it out. I'll figure everything out. . . ."

His voice trailed off. Faces of people in his life ceased haunting his thoughts. They were replaced by the blackest infinity he had ever faced. The only feeling now was the familiar disconnect of body from brain, signaling the onset of sleep. As that feeling took him deeper into a blessed slumber, it brought along the one thing that had been most elusive in Charlie's life of late. It brought him a moment of peace.

Charlie awoke with a start. His back ached, and his legs were still draped over the foot of the bed. He went to stand, but his feet were numb and prickling; his muscles had fallen asleep from having stayed in the same awkward position for too long. Eventually he forced himself to his feet and shook his head vigorously from side to side to clear the fog. A film of mucus covered his eyes and blurred his vision. He rubbed it away so that he could see. His shirt, damp before, was now soaked through with sweat. He walked over to the bathroom on wobbly legs and ran cold water from the sink over his face. The person who greeted him in the bathroom mirror had become even more of a stranger than the last time he looked at his reflection. His skin was a ghastly gray. The grit of his beard extended well down his neck. His hair had grown, too, and was long past its normal cropped length. Worry lines, similar to his mother's crow's-feet, were visible on the sides of his eyes. Nothing about the man in the mirror reminded Charlie of the person he once had been.

As he took off his drenched shirt, he noticed that his hands were caked with dried blood. Pulling the shirt over his head and draping it on the shower curtain rod to dry, Charlie rinsed the blood off his hands. He searched them for a wound.

He had no memory of having cut himself. He supposed it was possible that he had scratched his hand in fitful dreams. *Hard enough to draw blood, but not wake me?* It seemed unlikely.

With the blood removed from his hands, Charlie searched again for the source. He didn't find even a trace of a scratch, let alone an open cut.

As his shirt began to dry, Charlie noticed first a spot, then several spots that were darker than the rest of the fabric. Pulling the shirt down, Charlie examined the dark areas more closely. He held the shirt up to his face and pressed the fabric to his nose. The smell, like rusted iron mixed with sweet marigolds, was unmistakably blood.

How did I cut myself? Charlie wondered. And how did I heal so quickly?

Charlie left the bathroom and went to retrieve his other shirt, still crumpled inside the plastic Olympia Sports bag. It should have been on the chair nearest the room entrance, where he had left it. He looked on the chair and under it, but the plastic bag wasn't where it should be. Perhaps, in his exhaustion he had placed it in the room closet and forgot. Not an unlikely scenario, given how forgetful he'd become.

For a moment the blood on his hands and shirt faded into the back of his thoughts. He opened the closet door and flicked on the closet light on the inside left wall. He was certain he'd find the empty plastic bag crumpled on the floor inside and the clothing within neatly folded and tucked on a shelf.

The moment the light came on, Charlie screamed. He sank to his knees and buried his face in his hands.

The plastic bag was, as he expected, crumpled on the floor. But the closet was filled with clothes. There were shirts, pants, sweaters, all draped on hangers in a tight row on the chrome rod. On the shelf above were more shirts and pants. All the clothes were neatly folded, just the way he would have done it. And all the clothes were his.

Chapter 47

Charlie stayed on his knees until five minutes had passed. Shakily, he rose to his feet, bracing himself against the doorjamb before backing out of the closet. The first thing that caught his attention was the smell of blood. It was more pronounced now than when he'd first noticed blood on his hands and shirt in the bathroom. There was another foul odor that penetrated his senses as well. This one was a rank and disturbingly unfamiliar scent. He could equate it only with rot and decay. His right hand caressed his left; he was still hopeful that he'd feel a gash or scratch that could explain the blood he'd found earlier. It was a pointless gesture. The smell of blood in the air was far too intense to have come from anything less than a serious cut.

He sank down onto the bed. The morning light that managed to seep into the room through the drawn shades did little to brighten the drab interior. A quick glance at the digital clock on the nightstand told him it was almost 6:20 a.m. The last time he had noticed the time was more than twelve hours earlier.

What happened to me during that time? Charlie shuddered to think.

Sitting on the bed, with his feet set on the floor, elbows resting on his knees, and head cradled atop his knuckles, he felt like a sad imitation of Rodin's *The Thinker.* He glanced at the small color television on the bureau at the foot of the bed, then gasped aloud. A piece of paper, recognizable as the Seacoast Motel stationery and most likely having come from a pad of the stationery on the room desk, was taped to the TV monitor.

The mattress springs creaked as Charlie rose from the bed. He kept his gaze transfixed on the television and reached for the paper. With trembling hands, he pulled the note free. To steady his shaking, he had to hold the paper with both hands. As with the other notes, this one was undeniably in his penmanship.

The only thing left for him to do was to laugh. He fell hard to the floor, both knees crashing painfully onto the thin floor carpeting. All these events, it now appeared, were meant to lead him to this final moment. His fate had been scribed in four simple words penned in his hand, written on the plain white stationery belonging to the Seacoast Motel. The note read simply:

Look under the bed.

Chapter 48

Charlie shifted his body position from kneeling to prone on the floor. Without hesitation, he lifted away the bedspread and peered into the darkness underneath the bed. The stench of blood and rot was much stronger under the bed than anywhere else in the room. It made him gag, and he had to cover his mouth to keep from vomiting. The silhouette of a shoe-box-sized object was easily discernible, even in the dim room lighting.

With his chest pressed hard into the floor, Charlie reached with both hands and pulled the box toward him. The box was slick to the touch, and the palms of his hands felt wet. The box slid out easily. In the light, he could tell that the box was seeping with blood. It left in its wake a dark trail and an even wider stain around its resting place under the bed.

There was a manila envelope, similar to the one containing the kill list, taped to the top of the box. Charlie left the box covered on the floor and stood up. He stared down at it for several moments. He closed his eyes and prayed that when he opened them, the nightmare would have simply passed. He would wake up on the bed, having just had the most terrible of dreams.

Once certain that wasn't the case, Charlie took a deep breath and held it. Reaching down, he lifted the top of the box off and dropped it to the floor.

The first thing that caught his eye was a glint of gold. It was gold from a ring that Charlie had seen too many times to count. The owner of the ring had made certain to show it off every chance he could. It featured a shield encasing three raised engravings of books.

Together the letters on the books spelled out the word *veritas,* Latin for "truth." Below the shield was the school's name in raised gold lettering. *Harvard.* The ring was still lodged firmly on the finger of a bloodied hand, crudely severed at the wrist and stuffed inside the box.

Another hand was in the box as well. Although both hands were badly mutilated from having been sawed off, the skin of the ringed hand was clearly that of an older man. The skin of the other hand, though of a similar deadened pallor, was certainly that of a much younger man. His breathing became uneven and his heart raced, as though he had overdosed on caffeine.

Even in his cloud of confusion, Charlie knew one thing about the contents of the box. The hand with the ring belonged to Leon Yardley. The other, he assumed, was Simon Mackenzie's, his former boss at SoluCent.

Sitting on the nappy, shallow carpet of the motel room floor, Charlie stared at the box across from him. His focus shifted to the top of the box, a foot away and within reach. The manila envelope was still attached.

He felt almost no need to open the envelope. This was a pattern he had become accustomed to. A note would be inside. He would be its author. It would identify Yardley and Mackenzie as the victims. The kill list would be complete, save for one significant exception. There would be a fourth victim. The surprise.

The last victim's name, Charlie was certain, would be revealed. *Do I know that because my subconscious is reminding me that I am the author?* he wondered. Charlie stayed quiet in his seated position on the floor and tried to recollect the night before. The last thing he remembered was sitting on the bed, glancing at the digital clock and noting that the time was nearly 6:00 p.m. He had watched the news, and the next thing he recalled was waking up, still in his clothes, some twelve hours later. He woke up in basically the same position in which he had fallen asleep—lying with his back on the bed and his feet still on the floor. There was blood on his shirt and hands. He knew whose blood it was. There were body parts under the bed.

"What did I do?" he cried. "What monster have I become?"

Charlie paced the room. He kicked the box with the mangled hands back under the bed but left the top of the box where it was.

His thoughts spiraled in every direction. He needed something to help him focus and think. He tried convincing himself that this was a delusion. He slapped his right cheek hard with his open palm and then his left. The blows stung but did not shake away any visions. The box top was still on the floor where he had dropped it. The blood on the top's sides was unmistakable.

My God, this is for real.

If this wasn't a delusion, then these men, men he knew well and liked, were both dead. Their murders should be on the news. Charlie's name would be at the top of the list of suspects. The owner of the Seacoast Motel would know just where to find him. Room 224.

Chapter 49

Charlie's remaining time depended largely on the Seacoast Motel owner's interest in the morning news. If the murders were the lead story, as he suspected they would be, it was only a matter of time before the owner called the police.

Charlie turned on Channel 5 and stood in front of the television. It was the start of the 6:30 morning edition, and the graphic accompanying the story said it all: BREAKING NEWS—MURDER IN CONCORD. Charlie turned up the volume, keenly interested in the details reported by the anchor.

"Breaking news out of Concord this morning. Police are investigating the brutal murder of SoluCent CEO Leon Yardley. He was discovered early this morning by his wife, at around 5:00 a.m. It's unclear at this time if she was held captive during the assault, although we have heard some reports suggesting she might have been drugged. Details are still coming in, and we will provide updates on this tragic story as they become available. Meanwhile, police are asking for your help. They are interested in locating Charlie Giles, a former employee of SoluCent, wanted for questioning in connection to the murder. Police are describing Mr. Giles only as a person of interest at this time."

Charlie's picture replaced the "breaking news" graphic. He assumed the news desk had pulled that photo off Google; he recognized the picture as one taken by a PR firm nearly two years ago, after the acquisition. The man in the photograph was a phantom from Charlie's past. He was strong, full of fight, and looked like a winner.

"Channel Five's investigative team has uncovered some interesting, but still unsubstantiated reports that Mr. Giles was involuntarily committed to Walderman Mental Health Hospital in Belmont and that he recently escaped from a secure floor, pending a judge's ruling on the status of his commitment. We want to emphasize that Mr. Giles has not to our knowledge been charged with any crimes. However, if you do know his whereabouts, you are asked to contact the Concord police immediately. He may be armed and dangerous, so police are also urging caution should you happen to come into contact with him."

The next stories recapped much of the news he had watched the previous night. There was no mention of Simon Mackenzie, although Charlie had no doubt the man was dead. It was only a matter of time before his body was discovered. As he thought of Mac's corpse waiting to be found, he thought, too, of Rudy Gomes.

Was his murder imagined? he wondered. If not, what happened to the body? And who was the man on the tape Randal played for me?

The more he thought, the less he understood. The truths that remained painfully obvious were the putrid smell of death in the room and the manila envelope still unopened and taped to the box top. Charlie extracted the envelope from the top, half-expecting to hear sirens blaring and the door exploding inward as police burst in. The envelope was sealed same as the envelope that contained the kill list he found under the sofa. Charlie carefully peeled away the tape, his meticulous nature unwavering even when tested beyond limits. He saw only one item in the envelope. He pulled it out and held a photograph in front of him.

The photograph, of Charlie with his brother and mother, was the same one he had framed and put in his mother's hospital room. The same one he had scanned and hung on the refrigerator door. Charlie and Joe stood like bookends with their mother between them. A ballpoint pen had scratched out Charlie's face and made large, irregular circles around his mother's head. Through tearing eyes Charlie read the words scratched into the back of the photograph, written in his penmanship.

Surprise no more. Good-bye, Mother.

Chapter 50

Charlie threw the photograph and envelope to the floor, asking himself one unanswerable question.

Why her?

Clearly, a deeply disturbed and divided man lurked inside him. The names on the kill list were the names of those he blamed for his downfall. Could it be that his mother represented some deep-seated anger over his lost childhood? Was this twisted retribution perhaps for the attention she'd given to Joe and not to him?

Finding the truth would require a conversation with a part of his mind that was unavailable to him. Nothing about the Charlie present in the room wanted any harm to befall his mother, any more than he had wanted the murders of Yardley, Mackenzie, and Rudy Gomes. But the evidence against him was overwhelming.

To follow through with that gruesome promise seemed impossible, given the manhunt to find him. Yet that notion brought little comfort. His private Mr. Hyde seemed capable of following through with any plan, even under the most challenging circumstances. Charlie picked up the photograph. He tucked it in his pants pocket. His mother's fate, so long as he lived and roamed free, was in a peril far greater than a coma.

Charlie heard the siren wail of a police cruiser's or fire engine's approach. He raced to the window, peeling back the curtain to see if the sirens were headed in his direction. One police car, then another, sped past the motel on Ocean Avenue. They were heading west toward the Wonderland train station. Then something else caught his eye. Parked out front of his motel room was a BMW. It was without doubt his car's make and model.

Charlie hesitated before opening the motel room door. He half-expected a hail of bullets to greet him. When he realized that might just be the greatest gift of all, he threw open the door and stepped outside into the cool fall morning air. Frost from the night before encased the BMW's windows. As a gesture of brotherly affection, Joe had repaired the broken window after retrieving the car from the tow yard. Without opening the BMW and looking inside, it would be impossible to conclude if the car was his own.

He looked around and noticed nothing unusual or alarming. The parking lot was mostly empty, as it had been the night before. No other motel guests milled about. Ocean Avenue was just beginning to fill with morning commuters.

Charlie wondered what day it was, and sighed. The day of the week, like his life, felt irrelevant.

He approached the driver's side door and peered into the window. The car was equipped with the latest model InVision system. Charlie tried the door and found it unlocked. The interior was devoid of any papers, coffee cups, pens, or loose change. It was exactly how he kept his car. He didn't bother to check the glove compartment. He already knew. This was his car. The key was still in the ignition.

Sitting in the driver's seat, Charlie envisioned a scenario that held the horrifying possibility of being both plausible and true. In some sort of psychotic split, he speculated, he might have taken a cab or train back to his childhood home in Waltham. There he could have slipped inside the house, using a key hidden under a rock in the backyard. Once inside, he could have taken his car key hanging on a hook by the front door and driven to Concord or to Lincoln, where he knew Mackenzie lived. Then he would have driven back to the Seacoast Motel, parked the car in front of his room, and fallen asleep on the bed. At some point, he took the photograph from the frame in the living room, inscribed the death threat to his own mother on the back, and taped it on top of the box filled with body parts, which he slid under the bed. Lastly, a note taped to the TV would remind him to look in the morning.

Though he had no conscious memory of having done any of that, the timing would have worked. All the notes, from the very first Post-it note he found on the inside flap of his BlackBerry case, were perhaps his own personal silent alarm—a plea to stop before it was too late.

Unlike all the mysteries haunting him, the route driven by his car was verifiable. InVision would have a record of his travels. It was a product feature he himself had championed ánd consumers seemed to like. In a number of instances, clients had used the trip-log feature to verify infidelity and other unscrupulous behaviors. At no point when he planned the work for the current model did he ever imagine it would do the same for him.

With a turn of the key, the car came to life.

"Hello, Charlie. I hope you're having a great day," InVision announced in its programmatically cheery default greeting.

With a couple of keystrokes, Charlie retrieved the trip log. It showed, as he had already suspected, a thirteen-mile drive from Waltham to Concord. The next trip was an eight-mile drive to Lincoln, Massachusetts, that ended near Flint's Pond. The trip to Concord occurred at 2:20 a.m. this morning. The trip to Lincoln started at 4:00 a.m., with the last trip logged from Lincoln to Revere. Most of that drive took place along Route 2, and it was finished just after 5:30 in the morning. Simon, Charlie knew, ran at an obscenely early hour every morning. It was part of his type A, take-no-prisoners personality.

Mackenzie's body, Charlie believed—without any conscious recollection—would be discovered in the woods surrounding Flint's Pond. His wife had probably already reported him missing. The time line, according to InVision, had given Charlie plenty of opportunity to write the notes and put the box under the bed.

Charlie scanned the interior of the car for any evidence of blood. Nothing was noticeable. He popped the trunk with a pull of a lever under the dashboard casing and exited the car. He didn't need to open the trunk to detect a smell coming from inside that was not unlike the smell from underneath the motel room bed. Once the trunk was opened, he peered inside it and staggered back a few steps at the sight of the bloodied hacksaw inside. There was blood all over the trunk's carpeting, too, but at least no other body parts were visible.

The only other item in the trunk brought him a feeling of relief. There was a way out of the nightmare, and he now knew it. His mother's life would be spared. Joe's life, too, in a way, for her death would shorten his brother's life substantially. He couldn't face a lifetime in prison. He was certain of that. Especially having to live each day without any memory of the crimes for which he'd be convicted. There was, however, a simple way out. And he was looking right at it. Charlie reached down and pulled out his father's .38 Special. He must have taken it from the house when he went there to get the keys to his BMW. The chamber was loaded.

There wasn't any note to guide him on what to do next. Eddie Prescott didn't speak to him. But now none of that was necessary. Only one course of action made any sense.

With the gun in hand, Charlie climbed back into the front seat of his BMW. He felt comforted by the gun's steely weight and coolness. It was the first time since he was a kid that he had touched the gun, at least the first time he remembered. His mother had kept it in a shoe box in the attic. It was a memento from her former life, but she wasn't one to let go of much. The house, with its old furniture and appliances, was testament to that.

Charlie hoisted the gun to his head. His finger trembled on the trigger.

How much pain will I feel? he wondered. *How much pain have I caused?*

With the gun pressed against his temple, Charlie closed his eyes and prayed that the end wouldn't hurt as much as he imagined.

Chapter 51

Bill Evans, the great jazz pianist, once recorded a cover of the Johnny Mandel and Mike Altman classic, "Suicide Is Painless." The song became famous as the theme for both the movie and TV series *M*A*S*H*. Toward the end Charlie's father seemed to favor the eerie Evans rendition, perhaps expressing his darkest thoughts without words. It seemed fitting for Charlie to remember that song at this moment. He had even learned to play the tune note perfect on guitar, but his father had been unimpressed. He had never been one to gush, but toward the end he'd been void of all emotion. Perhaps his father had followed through with his secret wish. Perhaps they would meet soon.

That his life would come to an end in the parking lot of a decrepit motel in Revere was as stunning and disappointing to him as the horrific crimes he had committed without memory. In newspaper articles about his life reporters would portray the events as they saw fit. It would be a sad and tragic tale that would feed an insatiable public's hungry appetite for sensational stories. It would catch fire the way a match could vaporize a tank of gasoline. His legacy, all that he'd worked so hard to achieve, would not only be wasted, but he would forever be associated with some of history's most notorious psychopaths. For a man who had risen to the top, not because he'd let other people dictate outcomes for him, but because he'd controlled everything around him, this end was hardly a fitting one. The thought of the press having a field day at his expense, tearing apart his life and what little legacy he had, was nearly as revolting as the act of suicide itself.

Charlie set the gun down on the seat beside him. He was going to die. Given the risk to his mother's safety and his own unwillingness to live his days behind bars, no other alternative was acceptable.

But his unyielding need for control would not allow him to disappear from earth without at least some say in how he would be portrayed in the press. Charlie reached into the glove compartment to retrieve the pen and paper he kept inside for recording his BMW's maintenance history. Extracting the notebook from the glove compartment, Charlie set it down next to the gun and opened the notebook flap.

He would write a short explanation of events. It wouldn't be a confession, as he had no memory to confess. It would be, as best as he could offer, an explanation and an apology. Rather than admit or deny guilt, an expression of remorse would at least leave the impression of a sorrowful man and not just a wretched, unspeakable evil.

Charlie noticed the yellow Post-it note stuck to the inside flap of the notebook. It caught his attention. It was the first note that he had written to himself. The one he'd found attached to the inside flap of his BlackBerry. The words were as cryptic and prophetic now as they had been then.

If not yourself, then who can you believe?

The words blurred as tears welled in his eyes. He reached into his pocket and pulled out the folded picture of his family. He unfolded it and looked down at his mother's head circled in pen. He and Joe stood on either side of her like dutiful guardian sons. A wave of hopelessness swept through him. The idea of leaving an explanatory note behind now seemed ridiculous.

What difference does it make how the public sees me? he thought. *I am a monster. What good could come from leaving a note behind?*

Charlie set the photograph down on his left leg, turning it over so that the photographic visages of his mother and Joe wouldn't bear witness to his death. The Post-it note he tacked to his right leg. The messages written rested on his legs like signposts of his confusion. He hoisted the gun again to his head. This time he pressed the barrel of the gun harder to his temple until he felt the steel end boring painfully into the bone of his skull. His head dropped and his eyes closed. His finger began to tense, and he drew the trigger toward the pistol grip.

"I won't die with my eyes closed," Charlie said aloud.

He was looking down at his lap when he opened his eyes. He saw the two notes, the one written on the back of the photograph, the other penned on the yellow Post-it note. The words on the back of the photograph seemed fitting last words to see before he died.

Surprise no more. Good-bye, Mother.

He read the yellow Post-it note again, as well, believing for a moment that he could remember having written those words down.

If not yourself, then who can you believe?

He stared at the two notes side by side, one on each leg. Then he held his breath.

Something about them is wrong, he thought.

He set the gun down again and picked up the notes to examine them more closely. As he did, a stunning similarity became evident. As individual writing samples, they were both unmistakably his penmanship. But they also had something else much more significant in common. On each of the notes, the letter *u* had a slight bulge at the letter's counter, the unenclosed part of the *u*. It looked to Charlie as if the pen had made two or three passes at that part of the letter, leaving behind thicker and darker lines, which weren't present on any other letters. More disturbing was the exact similarity of the markings on the letter *u* in the two different notes. It wasn't just a close similarity; the bulge and thickness of the line beneath the counter of the *u* in each note were identical. That sort of precision similarity had only one possible explanation. Whatever it was that wrote these notes, it wasn't human.

Leaving the gun on the seat, Charlie jumped out of the car and raced back into the motel room. He picked up the note that had been taped to the TV from the top of the bureau, where he had left it, and dashed back out of the room. Stepping back into the car, Charlie held up the three notes in his hands to compare them.

Surprise no more. Good-bye, Mother.

If not yourself, then who can you believe?

Look under the bed.

The markings beneath the counter of the *u* in each note had the exact same thickness and bulge. All three were identical typographical mistakes. And the only thing capable of making the same exact typographical mistake, without variation, countless numbers of times was a computer.

Still, he had to be sure. And for that, there was only one place he could check. Turning the car on again, the InVision system, as designed, hummed back to life.

"Hello, Charlie," InVision cooed again. "I hope you're having a great day."

"Call," Charlie said.

"Please confirm," InVision said. "Did you say 'Call'?"

"Yes."

"Who would you like to call?" InVision asked.

"Dr. Rachel Evans," Charlie said.

Chapter 52

Rachel Evans had had a hell of a day yesterday, and this one wasn't shaping up to be much better. She had spent seven exhausting hours with the Walderman top brass, reviewing security procedures in the aftermath of Charlie's escape.

Then, against her better judgment, she'd taken a call from Joe Giles on her private line. He wouldn't say why over the phone, but he'd begged her to meet him in her office as soon as possible. She had planned to go to the office early, anyway, to check for new developments in Charlie's case. She'd agreed to meet Joe at 7:30 a.m., which didn't leave much time to get dressed and ready.

Joe's frantic tone had been more than troubling. She worried about behavioral regression. Given all that she had invested in his treatment and the fact that Joe's progress was partly responsible for her meteoric rise within Walderman, his well-being was particularly important to her.

Even though she was running late, she couldn't resist her morning habit of checking e-mail and her favorite news sites before leaving for work. It was then she learned of the all-out manhunt for Charlie. It was the lead story on both Boston.com and the *Herald*, as well as two other local news sites she'd bookmarked.

Rachel gasped when she read the grisly emerging details of Leon Yardley's murder in his Concord home. The story named Charlie as a "person of interest." The political favor Walderman had cashed in with the Belmont police to keep the escape out of the public eye had been a tragic case of poor judgment, she concluded. She had warned her superiors about the dangers of politicizing patient care. That ar-

gument held little sway with the facility directors, who constantly bat-
tled public opinion and fears of safety to keep the grants, licensing,
and tax conditions working in their favor. Without those, Walderman's future would be jeopardized and the care of patients threatened. Creating public alarm every time a borderline patient might
pose a public threat would create an air of mistrust between the
community and the care center.

The perception of security was paramount to the institution's survival. Only patients classified as an immediate threat to public safety
justified a press release and news conference. Otherwise, good relations with the police typically kept such incidents under the radar of
public awareness. An escapee would certainly threaten facility fund-
ing. Also a certainty, Shapiro would be one of the first to go if the
money dried up. He was the one who had convinced Walderman's
board that Charlie would merely continue to fantasize about killing,
and had doubted such fantasies would manifest into actual violence.
They had put hospital interests ahead of public safety, and it would
cost them a lot more than the loss of public confidence.

Rachel finished reading an updated report on WBZ-TV's local
news Web site. Charlie wasn't named a suspect on that report, either,
just a person of interest. But his escape from Walderman was clearly
and accurately documented in the piece. She wondered where they
had got their information.

Joe was waiting outside her office when she arrived and seemed
in a frantic state. He wore a blue T-shirt, ripped slightly at the bottom, a navy blue Windbreaker, and jeans spotted with dark brown
stains of varying sizes. His eyes darted about the room, as if he were
afraid he might be assaulted, and he continually rubbed his hands
together. Rachel observed that he would interlock his fingers, crack
his knuckles, and start rubbing his hands together again, as though
he were massaging hand cream into the skin. His hair was a tangled,
bushy mess. When he wasn't rubbing his hands together, Joe ran his
fingers though his hair and pulled at the roots.

"Sit down, Joe," Rachel said. "Please sit."

"I can't. I can't!" Joe cried.

Rachel assumed he had already heard the news about his brother
and that was why he needed to see her. A guiding principle of her
profession was that the patient had to provide all the answers, not

the therapist. That philosophy held true even when the answers were obvious.

"Joe, please tell me what is going on."

"The nightmares are getting worse," Joe said. "They're even more violent and real. I'm worried I'm regressing. I don't want to go back to where I was." Joe paused a moment. "I won't," he added.

Rachel was stunned. He hadn't read or seen the news this morning. Charlie's plight might push him over the edge. Even so, concealing the truth, as Charlie's situation tragically reinforced, was not how she operated.

"Joe, please sit down," Rachel said.

Joe hesitated. "Do we need to do a full review of my medications?" he asked. "When Mom wakes up, she'll be heartbroken if I lose my job. I can't get angry again. I just can't."

"Listen to me," Rachel said. "We have something more immediate to discuss."

"What?" Joe asked.

Before Rachel could answer, her cell phone rang. She looked down at the number and gasped.

"What?" Joe asked.

"Oh my God," Rachel breathed.

"What is it?" Joe asked again.

Rachel picked up the cell phone. Flipping it open, she answered the call. "Charlie? Charlie, it's Rachel. Where are you?"

"Rachel! Rachel! Thank God you answered. You have to help me."

Charlie didn't sound scared. He sounded almost euphoric. That was even more disturbing, she thought.

"Why is Charlie calling you?" Joe asked. "Where is he?"

Joe knew about Charlie's escape, but Rachel was certain he had no idea of the real trouble Charlie was in.

"Charlie, you must turn yourself in to the police. Where are you? Please tell me," Rachel said.

"Is my brother with you? I thought I heard his voice," Charlie said.

"Yes. He's in my office."

"I'll call you back on your office line. Put me on speaker. I want Joe to hear this as well."

Chapter 53

Charlie had InVision call Rachel again. This time he dialed the office line. Rachel picked up on the first ring.

"Charlie, the police are looking for you. You have to turn yourself in." Rachel issued her demand before Charlie had a chance to say a word.

"Rachel, am I on speaker?"

"No. Your brother is in a highly agitated state. His nightmares are getting worse, and he's worried he's regressing and that his anger management issues might be resurfacing."

"I don't care about that," Charlie said. "I want Joe to hear this. He's seen the notes I've left. He might remember something."

Joe had been the next call he was going to make. He might need his brother's help if what he believed proved true.

"What are you talking about? What do your notes have to do with this?" Rachel said. "Charlie, you're wanted for murder."

"Just put me on speaker!" Charlie shouted. He hadn't meant to raise his voice, but his adrenaline had taken over.

Moments later he heard something click and then his brother's voice on the other end of the line.

"Charlie? Where are you? You can't just leave without telling people," Joe scolded. "What is Rachel talking about? Why did she say you're wanted for murder?"

"Just listen, both of you," Charlie said. "Rachel, I need you to grab the note Dr. Shapiro found in my room."

"Charlie, I can't—"

Charlie cut her off. "Get it now, dammit! It's a matter of life and death."

Rachel went to her files. She didn't have the original copy. Dr. Shapiro had that. But she had made a photocopy for her own records.

"I have the note," she said, sitting back at her desk. "Now tell me where you are."

"Look at the note," Charlie said. "Are there any words in that note containing the letter *u*?" Charlie was already reaching for his pen and paper.

"Yes," Rachel said.

Charlie scratched out the words *Look under the bed* on his notebook and compared that to the note he'd found taped to the TV in the motel room. The lettering in the two notes was identical, with one exception. The letter *u* was different. The *u* in the word *under* that he had just written in the notebook didn't have the bulge or extra thickness as the other notes did. He wrote the sentence three more times, even trying to replicate the distinct marking, but without success.

"Charlie, are you there?" Rachel called out through the car's speakers. "Talk to me!"

"I'm here. Do you have a camera on your cell phone?"

"Yes," Rachel said.

"Good. Take a picture of the note and send it to this number. Are you ready?"

"Yes," she said.

Charlie gave Rachel the phone number, repeating the sequence twice.

Moments latter the InVision screen changed, informing him that a new message had arrived. Charlie switched views and downloaded the picture taken from Rachel's cell phone, storing it in InVision's vast hard drive. InVision allowed customers not only to store digital photos but also to download them wirelessly from cell phones and even send them wirelessly to printers and other devices. The marketing pitch used in the current advertisements featured a family out on a picnic, downloading pictures from a camera's full flash drive to make room for new pictures of family fun to send to Grandma, who was a thousand miles away. The announcer said, "Now your camera goes wherever you drive. Welcome to InVision." When Charlie had approved those ads, he'd never imagined using the picture-sharing feature in this way. InVision, which had launched his career, now could be used to help save his life.

The quality of the photograph from Rachel's camera wasn't perfect. Still, it was good enough to show him what he needed to see. Charlie used the touch screen buttons to zoom in on the word *surprise*. It was the last word in the sentence "The last is still my surprise."

He took the note from the motel TV and the note written on the back of the photograph and held them up to the screen on the InVision system to compare. The letter *u* in all three notes was in fact identical. No matter how he'd tried, he couldn't replicate that script exactly, even though all three notes had allegedly come from his hand.

"Charlie, talk to me," Rachel said. "Tell me what's going on."

"I didn't write these notes," Charlie said.

"What are you talking about?" she asked.

"The markings on the letter *u* in each note, they're identical."

"What does that mean?"

"It means that they're too identical. I can't replicate the penmanship, and believe me, I've tried. The only thing I know that can be that precise is a machine."

"You're saying those are machine-written notes?"

"That's exactly what I'm saying," Charlie said. "A pen driven by a computer program with a custom-built font library based on my handwriting could do just that."

"I've never heard of that before," Rachel said.

"It exists. And it's a technology used more widely than you might realize. I just read about an author who used something similar to sign fans' books at a virtual book signing. She was in California. They were in New York. Her pen transferred her signature. A computer on the other end picked up the signal, and a pen re-created the lines exactly as she had written them."

"Charlie, that's an interesting theory, but not really relevant right now. You are wanted by the police for murder."

Charlie heard Joe cry out in the background, "What do you mean, murder?"

"You have to believe me, Rachel. I didn't write these notes. Why should I believe I killed anybody?"

"Because delusions can be more compelling than reality, Charlie," Rachel said. "You're a sick man, and you need help. Where are you? You have to turn yourself in."

Charlie ignored her. "Joe, can you get to your car?"

"Yes," Joe said. "Why did Rachel say you're wanted for murder?"

"Forget about that right now," said Charlie. "Do you know how to use the tracking feature on your InVision system? My car is programmed into yours. All you have to do is select TRACKING from the menu and then select my car. Can you do that?"

"Yes," Joe said.

"I need you to go to your car now. Turn that feature on. I'll call you and give you directions about what to do next," Charlie instructed.

"Okay, Charlie. I'll wait for you in my car," Joe said.

"Joe," Rachel said. "You can't help him. That's a crime. You could be charged with obstruction of justice or worse. Your brother is sick and delusional. There is no reason for you to believe him or to help him."

"Yes, there is," Joe said. "He's my family."

Charlie smiled. Nobody was more loyal or forgiving than Joe. When this was over, he promised himself he'd repay his brother's loyalty and kindness. A wave of relief washed through him. It was an awakening he could liken only to a feeling of rebirth. He was convinced, without a doubt, that he hadn't written the notes. He knew it with a deep, unwavering conviction. A machine had done it. And that meant everything else was up for grabs. From the mysterious Anne Pedersen to the body parts rotting under the bed in his motel room, something evil was at work, but that no longer meant that he was the source. Charlie was determined not to stop until he figured out what it was and why it was happening to him.

"Joe, you're the best," Charlie shouted. "I need you to move now. Get to your car. Start the tracking process. You got it?"

"Got it, bro," Joe said.

"No. You can't do that, Joe. That's aiding and abetting a criminal. It's a serious crime," Rachel protested.

"You can't stop me," Joe said to Rachel. Charlie had forgotten that Joe possessed an iron will similar to his own.

"Joe, this is too dangerous a situation. Charlie, you have to turn yourself in," Rachel said.

"Sorry, Rachel," Charlie said. "The only way to get to me is to go with Joe. If you want me, you should go with him."

It was a gamble bringing Rachel into this, but the old adage applied to this situation as well as to his business dealings: "Keep your friends close and your enemies closer." He didn't know which side of the coin Rachel was on, but at least she and Joe were together. Her levelheaded thinking would help to keep Joe calm and focused. That would work in his favor.

"Besides," Charlie continued, "if you let Joe go now and something happened to him, could you ever forgive yourself? Joe, I'll call you shortly." He hung up without giving Rachel a chance to respond.

Charlie sat in his BMW for several minutes, poring over the notes. It was, he decided, a rebirth. He had been moments away from death. He needed time to contemplate what it meant to be alive. The idea that his mind might still be his own gave him a sense of euphoric freedom. But two questions remained: who was behind those notes and why?

His euphoria ebbed and quickly turned to fear. From behind he heard the blaring of sirens. He looked in his rearview mirror, and his eyes widened. Four police cruisers, lights on and sirens screeching, sped into the parking lot of the Seacoast Motel.

Chapter 54

Charlie gripped the steering wheel with white-knuckling force. His instinct for self-preservation in full command, he turned the ignition and fired the engine. The evidence against him was almost laughable. Inside the motel room, police investigators would discover body parts from men he had threatened to kill. Not to mention that upon his arrest, a bloody hacksaw and a gun would be recovered from his car. A jury would need but a fraction of the evidence to send him away for life. Moments ago he had been prepared to die for these crimes. Now he was prepared to run. His only hope for redemption depended on his ability to escape.

The wheels of his BMW screamed in reverse. A cloud of toxic smoke spewed skyward from his tires as they melted away against the asphalt. Charlie spun the steering wheel hard left, then shifted the car out of first, jamming it into second gear. He straightened the wheels at the same instant, gunning the accelerator. Taking quick inventory of his surroundings, Charlie also searched his memory for any possible escape routes.

Revere's narrow, congested streets limited his options. He had seen the surrounding area only briefly during his walk from the Wonderland MBTA station to the Seacoast Motel. There was, he remembered, another station stop between Wonderland and the motel. Revere Beach Station, he thought it was called. It was at most a quarter-mile walk from Wonderland to the Revere Beach MBTA station, which meant about a mile's drive from the motel.

Outrunning the police in a car, even if that car was a BMW, he knew had a low, if not infinitesimal probability for success. He had seen enough high-speed chases on the TV news to know that most ended in the capture or the death of the pursued. The police presence coming after him now would escalate like wildfire the moment he ran. If he could make it to an MBTA station, perhaps he would have a chance. *Perhaps.*

The problem with getting to the Revere Beach Station was that it required him to travel almost a mile, driving the wrong way, heading north on Ocean Avenue. The traffic traveling the adjacent road, Revere Beach Boulevard, was heading in the right direction. But to get onto Revere Beach Boulevard meant having to jump the concrete median strip that separated the two main ocean drives. A quick glance ahead told him that the median was far too high for the BMW to traverse successfully.

An equally dismal prospect would be to go with the flow of traffic, south on Ocean Avenue, until he got to the nearest turnaround. A statistic his friend Randal Egan had once quoted during a discussion about Randal's law enforcement career came to mind: most chases that ended in escape didn't last longer than two miles. If the turnaround was even a half mile down the road, it would mean capture.

The same instinct that made him fire up his car now pushed his foot harder against the accelerator. The Beamer lunged over the parking lot curb and screamed across a patch of grass that separated the motel parking lot from the sidewalk. Debris was kicked up by the back tires as they spun across the narrow patch of green. The car shot cannonball-like over the cracked sidewalk running adjacent to Ocean Avenue. A couple was approaching arm in arm and jumped sideways to avoid what would have been a fatal hit. Ocean Avenue was wide enough to permit curbside car parking. It made beach strolling easier and essentially eliminated the need for unsightly parking lots. Thankfully, none of the parked cars blocked his exit.

The BMW came down hard onto Ocean Avenue. The car's low suspension was entirely unforgiving. The car skidded out into the middle of the road and came to stop parallel to the oncoming traffic closing in fast. It had stalled.

Charlie looked left and saw the fast approach of oncoming traffic. He turned the ignition again, depressed the clutch, and pressed hard on the accelerator. The car lurched forward, screaming toward the median between the two main boulevards fast enough to leave a pit in Charlie's stomach. The cars traveling south on Ocean Avenue were easily going forty miles per hour and had little time to react to a BMW surging parallel to the flow of traffic across the three-lane road. No more than fifty feet from Charlie's car, the driver of a red sedan slammed on the brakes and fishtailed, too surprised by the sudden appearance of the BMW to have even blasted his horn.

The cruisers elected to take the parking lot exit, rather than follow Charlie's improvised route over the grassy strip. If they wanted to give chase, they'd have to either take the risk of driving the wrong way or make for the turnaround south on Ocean. Their need to protect public safety was what he was counting on. A smile crept across his lips as he saw them turn right and drive in the opposite direction. Precious seconds perhaps, but that might make all the difference.

The oncoming traffic parted for Charlie's BMW as if jerked to the side by some magnetic force. As he passed one car, Charlie grimaced at the sickening crunch of metal, which blended with the shrieking sounds of police sirens from behind. Allowing himself only a quick glance in his rearview mirror, Charlie noticed that one of the cars he had narrowly missed was now turned completely around. Another had jumped the median and crashed sideways into one of the many trees planted along the strip. Up ahead he could see the turnoff onto Shirley Avenue. It was no more than five hundred yards away.

Car horns blasted him. Most of the cars in his direct path pulled to the right and came to a safe stop alongside the cars parked curbside. A car that was already too far left to get out of his way made a reactive choice to hit the median rather than risk a head-on collision with Charlie. Through the rearview mirror, he could see that the distance between his BMW and the police cars had narrowed considerably. Driving with the flow of traffic, not against it, allowed them the necessary speed to catch up and keep pursuit. Still, they were separated by an impassable median.

Charlie slammed on his horn and pressed the gas with as much force as he could generate. He had to extract every bit of juice from the machine that he could. He drove headlong down the middle of the road, praying he gave drivers in both the left and right lanes equal chance to react and avoid a collision.

As he neared Shirley Avenue, Charlie drifted the BMW into the far left lane. The police were only a few hundred yards behind him now.

He spun the wheel clockwise and at the same time downshifted from fourth gear to first. Charlie hit the brakes and shifted his body weight against the driver's side door as the car listed right. The screech of tires was deafening; the air was now heavy with smoke from burnt rubber. For a moment both driver's side wheels hung suspended in midair. The BMW then crashed down onto the road, leaving behind a spiderweb crack in the front windshield. Charlie's seat belt locked him in tight.

Keeping one hand on the horn, Charlie shifted into second, then third as he fishtailed the car onto Shirley Avenue. To his right, Charlie saw the MBTA logo of Revere Beach Station as he drove the car onto the sidewalk. Simultaneously, he pressed the call button on the InVision touch screen dashboard with his free hand.

"Call Joe!" he shouted loudly.

"Command not recognized," InVision responded.

"Call Joe!" he shouted again.

"Command not recognized," InVision said again.

Charlie couldn't concentrate on both his driving and the call. He had taken his eyes off the sidewalk for no more than a second. When he looked up again, he was only a few feet from a concrete support beam that was part of the Revere Beach Station's entranceway. Risking a glance at the dashboard, Charlie realized, with some alarm, that he was traveling almost thirty miles per hour. Next he heard the screech of his tires as he applied his brakes. He swung the wheel counterclockwise to avoid a front impact. It was the best option available given the lack of reaction time. Charlie's head snapped left with enough force to crack the driver's side window with his skull. What followed was a horrific crunch of metal on concrete, accented with the sound of shattering glass. The middle of the car wrapped around the concrete support beam like a steel ribbon. Having taken the brunt of the impact, the passenger-side air bag deployed with a thunderous burst of air.

The first sound Charlie heard as his consciousness slowly returned was police sirens. Unbuckling his seat belt, Charlie opened the driver's side door, which wasn't damaged in the crash. He looked behind and saw the cruisers making their turn onto Shirley Avenue. He had only seconds left to escape. He felt no pain, only the rush of adrenaline. Barreling through the entrance doorway, he sped past an elderly station attendant. Then he slid onto his belly and underneath the turnstile's plastic doors.

The way the station was laid out, the station attendant wouldn't be able to tell the police if he had gone inbound or outbound. Charlie wasn't certain which way he'd go, either. Then he heard a buzz that he knew signaled a soon-to-be departing train. It was coming from the outbound direction. Charlie took the subway stairs two at a time, falling more than running down the fifty-some-odd steps to the bottom. He reached the train just as the doors were closing. Without hesitating, he shot his arm forward between the black rubber stoppers on the sides of the doors. The safety catch clicked, and the doors automatically reopened. Charlie slipped inside the empty train and looked out the grimy subway car window to see if anyone had followed him down the outbound stairwell. As the train pulled away, the only sight he saw was the lights from Revere Beach Station dimming in the distance.

Chapter 55

"Wonderland. Last stop on the train. All passengers please exit at this time."

The hollow, nearly unintelligible voice of the PA announcer reverberated joylessly throughout the empty subway car. Charlie was already at the car window, peering out at the station platform as it came into view. He half-expected to see the platform swarming with police. Then again, the time it took for him to travel between Revere Beach Station and Wonderland was less than three minutes. It was doubtful the police would have had enough time to mobilize a force. *Doubtful,* he thought, *but not out of the question.*

He exhaled as the train slowed to a stop. In the reflection of the train's window, Charlie took stock of his injuries. With the adrenaline from the chase wearing off, his body had time to ache and throb. Surprisingly, there was no blood or open wounds, only aches and pains, which were certain to become more intense as time went on.

The platform on the outbound side was blessedly deserted. The inbound platform was crammed with morning commuters. Wonderland, unlike most MBTA stations, was an outdoor station. The platform area was easily accessible from a twenty-five-foot concrete ramp that rose at an almost imperceptible incline to the tracks five feet above ground level. The front of the station was a vast parking lot, already filled to near capacity with commuter cars. This station in particular was a haven for commuters who enjoyed the easy access to Boston, as well as for the dog race lovers, who flocked to Wonderland Greyhound Park after which the station was named.

Charlie scanned the parking lot, watchful for any signs of a police presence. Cars were still entering the lot, searching for the few remaining spaces. He needed to get to a phone but couldn't risk the exposure. Descending the concrete ramp to the parking lot, Charlie continued his vigilant lookout for the police. Their arrival, he knew, was imminent. But Charlie's appearance played in his favor. Because he wasn't visibly injured, he shouldn't raise suspicions with the commuters. He stood in front of the entrance to the inbound platform and approached a man buying a copy of the *Herald* from a metal dispenser. The man was heavyset, dressed in jeans and a beige polo shirt. His mouth was accented by a thick black mustache that matched the wave and body of his hair. Charlie spotted a cell phone clipped to his waist.

"Pardon me, sir," Charlie said.

The man, bent over, took out the paper, and then rose to look at Charlie. At first he seemed annoyed, perhaps thinking Charlie was another panhandler. Then he softened.

"Yes?" he asked.

"I seem to have left my cell phone at home. I was wondering if I could make a quick call to tell my associate where to meet me in Boston."

The man hesitated just a moment. Then he reached down and pulled the phone off his belt. "Sure thing," he said. "I guess I can spare a minute or two," he added with a chuckle.

Charlie thanked him and dialed his brother. Joe picked up on the first ring.

"Hello?" Joe asked. Charlie guessed that the unfamiliar phone number had confused him.

"Joe, it's Charlie," he said. Charlie kept the phone pressed tight to his ear so the man whose phone he'd borrowed wouldn't hear Joe screaming on the other end.

"Charlie! Charlie!" Joe shouted. "Where are you? We trailed your car to Revere but lost the signal a few moments ago. We've been driving around looking for you. The police are swarming all over the place. What's going on?"

"Right. Sure, I'll wait here," Charlie said.

"What? What are you talking about?" Joe screamed into the phone.

Rachel added, "Charlie, you have to turn yourself in. Now!"

"Not a problem. Why don't I just wait for you at Wonderland? Sure, that's easier," said Charlie. "I may still be reading that report. Although that policy is really too far right in my opinion. Too far right and away from the mainstream for me."

"I don't know what you're talking about," Joe said.

"Make sure you get my attention, because I'll be deep in thought. Three beeps and wait. See you at Wonderland." Charlie hung up the phone and handed it back to the man. "Thanks," he said.

The man smiled, arching his mustache, which looked like a bushy caterpillar crawling across his lip.

"Anytime," he said. "Anytime."

Chapter 56

Charlie kept an even pace as he moved away from the platform and, more importantly, from the commuters. There was nothing worse than feeling exposed and vulnerable. The good news, as much as good news was possible, was that the police had not yet secured the station area. The respite wouldn't last much longer.

The call he had made to Joe was necessary, but it was also costly. He had lost valuable time, not to mention creating a witness for the police. If the police questioned the right man, somebody would have no problem placing Charlie at Wonderland.

From behind, Charlie heard the rumbling of the inbound train as it made its arrival. The air-pressured doors opened with a swoosh, which was followed by the dance between those entering and those exiting the train. It was another bit of luck. The only person who could positively ID Charlie would be gone in moments.

The parking lot offered little in terms of good hiding places. It was a vast expanse of asphalt with row upon row of cars, trucks, and SUVs. There were several stores nearby, many in adjacent lots, but those would have security cameras, not to mention more potential witnesses. If luck continued his way, he wouldn't need to hide for long. That, of course, depended on Joe having understood their brief phone conversation.

The inbound train to Boston had yet to depart. That only added to Charlie's mounting anxiety. Although the station platform was now deserted, he still worried about raising people's suspicions. As far as he was concerned, the fewer people around, the better. Commuters continued arriving, but there weren't enough people for him to get lost in a crowd.

Charlie picked up his pace, moving to the far right corner of the parking lot. It was a safe distance away from the main road. He also wanted to create as much distance between the commuters and himself as possible.

The corner of the parking lot had the advantage of giving him additional cover. It was a good hundred yards from the platform and maybe 150 yards from the main road. Nearly fifty cars were parked along the fence that secured the parking lot from the train tracks. Next, Charlie scoured the ground for something he could use to break into one of the cars. It didn't take long to find the perfect object lying beside the chain-link fence: half of a red brick, a remnant of some past construction project.

Cupping the brick in his hand, Charlie headed to the last car in the row directly in front of the chain-link fence. The vehicle had a rear vent window, as he had hoped. The smaller window would be easier to break without attracting so much attention. He checked and made certain the driver's side door of the silver Chevy Lumina was locked before breaking the window; there was no reason to risk unnecessary attention.

Charlie played out how it would look to the police when they started patrolling the station for him. Unless they got out of their cars, they wouldn't see the broken window, since it was on the driver's side of the last car in the row. There was no reason to believe they would search every car on the lot. He wasn't even sure they had the legal authority to do so. He didn't look suspicious, either. Anybody who saw him standing beside the car wouldn't give it a second thought. Just another commuter on his way to work. This type of observation and situational analysis had made him a rising star at SoluCent; they were probably the same skills needed by a top cop, he thought with some amusement.

Charlie waited for the train to leave the station. Hoisting the brick waist high, he thrust it forward with a quick jabbing motion. The rear ventilation window shattered on impact. The sound of breaking glass was louder than Charlie had wanted. But it was partially drowned out by the departing train and the sound of police sirens roaring in the distance.

Charlie checked to see if anybody had noticed him, and felt safe to continue. He reached his hand inside the car and unlocked the driver's side rear door. The sound of sirens grew louder. They were coming for him.

Charlie slid into the backseat of the Chevy Lumina and closed the door behind him. He kept his body low to the floor and out of view. The car, he now realized, was not the cleanest in the world. Not by a mile. And whoever owned the vehicle wasn't much of a brand loyalist. The backseat was littered with fast-food wrappers, McDonald's and Burger King mostly, with some Wendy's and Dunkin' Donuts thrown in for good measure.

The air inside was heavy and stale, as if the broken window was the first taste of fresh air the interior had ever experienced. It had the unpleasant stench of stale cigarette smoke. There was enough smoke residue and buildup on the windows that it was actually difficult to see outside. Disgusting as it was, Charlie hoped it would be equally difficult for anybody to see in, should the police start a car-by-car search of the parking lot.

The other overpowering olfactory experience was the smell of dirty laundry. Dirty clothes were strewn about the backseat: sweatshirts, pants, and crumpled dress shirts mostly.

Not only was this person unclean, Charlie thought, but it seemed he was actually living out of his car. The clothes behind the driver's, seat covered in glass fragments, sparkled in the sunlight. Laws of probability demanded that some of the glass had also fallen to the floor, and some was surely visible on the ground outside the car. Charlie again hoped it wasn't enough to attract the attention of the police.

Despite his preference for a cleaner hideout, he knew this was the safest place for him. How long he could remain hidden was a matter of life and death.

Charlie pressed his body to the floor, trying to ignore the sour smell of ketchup and mustard soaked into the countless fast-food wrappers discarded there. Reaching above, he pulled the clothes from the backseat atop him in an attempt to further camouflage his location. Then he waited.

The sirens in the distance continued to screech like banshees. Charlie's body stiffened, and he tried to flatten himself even more, although he was as hidden as he could be. More sirens. Had they sent a SWAT team after him? It took all his willpower to resist the urge to pick his head up and have a look. He had to rely on what he heard to give him some sort of visual of the scene unfolding.

Car tires screeched to a stop. Was it next to the station platform entrance or closer to him? It was difficult to tell. He heard the slamming of doors, the crackling static and unintelligible commands from police scanners and radios. Then he heard a sound that made it nearly impossible to breathe. It was the sound of footsteps.

Chapter 57

Rachel stared in disbelief out Joe's Camry window, watching an armada of police scream past. Everything had happened so fast. Now she worried that everything was also spiraling out of control. This was serious. They had information about the whereabouts of a suspected murderer and they were intentionally keeping it from the police. If she hadn't already broken the law, she was at the very least bending it to the breaking point.

At the time, going with Joe had seemed not only the right thing to do but the only option she had. If she followed Joe, not only could she look after Joe's well-being during what understandably was a high-stress situation, dangerous for a man with his condition, but also he would lead her to Charlie. *But for what?* Not only was Charlie delusional, but he was also a criminal and most likely extremely dangerous. Then again, was there some other reason she had opted to go with Joe and track Charlie with this InVision GPS thing? Perhaps there was, she thought. Reaching into her purse, which was more like a miniaturized duffel bag, she fished out the note Alan Shapiro had found in Charlie's room at Walderman. She looked it over, recalling the phone conversation between them less than an hour ago. The note was as haunting as it had been the first time she'd read it.

When I'm out of here, I'm going to finish the job. One down, three to go. Mac and Yardley die next. The last is still my surprise. I can't wait for the killing to begin again.

She looked most carefully at the word *surprise*. The *u* did in fact have distinct markings and characteristics. It was, as Charlie had said, different from the other letters. But she had nothing against which to compare it.

Her clinical mind couldn't equate murder with the man she had grown to know and in many ways admire. On more than one occasion she had thought if the situation between them had been different, she could actually see herself with a man like Charlie. Determined, intelligent, not to mention strikingly handsome.

At Walderman, Charlie had shown her his more vulnerable and available side. It was a part of him she believed he kept hidden, not only from his closest relations, but from himself as well. His harsh words their last day together had stung and left her unsettled. But she understood now why he had been so cruel: he'd been preparing to escape, and her presence must have jeopardized those plans. She felt almost relieved to realize it wasn't personal. What bothered her so? She believed in her heart that Charlie was a sick man. That wasn't really even a question. But was he a killer? She was a woman accustomed to black and white, turning the sick into the healed. Shades of gray she found most unsettling.

"Charlie didn't kill anyone," Joe said. "I know it in my soul."

His words took Rachel by surprise. It was as if Joe had been reading her thoughts. She folded her arms across her lap. "It's not for us to decide," she said. "We're breaking the law here."

"So why did you come?" Joe asked.

"Because I wanted to make sure you didn't get hurt, or worse," she said.

"Is that all?" Joe asked.

More police drove past. They had seen the wreck outside the Revere Beach Station from a distance. Neither bothered to confirm it was Charlie's BMW. The police presence alone suggested this was much more than a routine traffic accident. It had taken them only twenty minutes to drive from Belmont to Revere, thanks to the reverse commute traffic. The last location the InVision GPS had provided for Charlie's car before his signal went dark was right outside this station. With all the police swarming about, Joe didn't dare step outside his car.

"Charlie has been threatening to kill SoluCent employees for weeks now," Rachel said. "He escaped from our facility, and since that time at least one high-ranking employee of his company has died. Do you want to have others on your conscience?"

"I want the truth," Joe said. "I want my family back. My mother is still in a coma, and my brother will be shot on sight if I don't help him."

"You can't control everything, Joe," Rachel said. "Life doesn't work that way."

"I'm going to get my brother," Joe said. "I can control that. If you're not going to help me, then you have to get out of the car, Rachel. It's not negotiable."

Rachel paused. Technically she hadn't yet broken the law. If she did find Charlie, she could find some way to turn him in. If she didn't go, Joe's life could be in danger. He wouldn't stop until he found and rescued his brother. She knew that. Would Charlie even turn on his own brother? A Cain and Abel tragedy. Knowing Joe, he would stand by his brother, even if it meant him getting killed. He was stubborn that way. Once his mind was made up, it was made up.

"Charlie told us where we could find him. He's at Wonderland," Joe added. "He's somewhere where he can hide. And I'm going there now. Are you coming with me?"

Rachel unfolded her arms. She looked into Joe's worried eyes. She thought of Charlie. She felt awash with uncertainty. After a moment that seemed almost eternal, she spoke in a low voice.

"Drive," she said.

Chapter 58

It was impossible for him to lie any lower on the floor of the Chevy Lumina, but Charlie tried. Garbled voices crackling from police radios and scanners broke the silence of an otherwise noiseless part of the parking lot. He had crawled inside the car from the driver's side passenger door. As a result, Charlie's head was closest to the voices outside. He couldn't believe how near the police were to him. They were close enough for him to hear their radio conversation without having to strain.

"Unit Seven, Unit Seven, requesting a ten-twenty," said a staticky voice.

"Unit Seven, we're on-site at Wonderland. Over."

"Roger, Unit Seven. What's your nine-five-two?"

"Situation unchanged. Over. Suspect remains at large."

"Ten-four, Unit Seven. Over."

"Over and out."

Charlie felt the weight of the vehicle shift left and noticed the light inside the car unexpectedly turn darker. It wasn't at all like shadows cast from a passing car or even a cloud. The patrolling officers were directly outside of the Lumina's passenger-side door. If they simply turned and looked down, the wide, fear-filled eyes of Charlie would be there to greet them. One of the officers had apparently leaned up against the car and caused it to shift on its axles. It was his girth that partially obscured the morning light, which prior had filled much of the interior. From inside the car their voices sounded muffled but were also easily understood. It was no different than a conversation overheard from behind closed doors.

"Fuck this, Gary," one of the officers said. He had a low baritone voice that suggested an innate meanness.

"Yeah. This asshole could be anywhere." Gary had a thick Boston accent, much more pronounced than his partner's.

"Anywhere," Gary's partner agreed.

"So do we check every car?"

Charlie heard the sound of knuckles banging loudly against the windshield just above his head. The officer had knocked on the glass for emphasis. For a moment it felt as if Charlie's heart had stopped beating. It was a feeling more terrifying than holding a loaded gun to his temple.

"Look around," the baritone voice said. "There must be two hundred cars in this lot. Not to mention at least fifty stores within a ten-minute walk."

"And are we sure the guy went outbound?" Gary asked.

"We're not sure of shit," his partner said. "Train logs show two trains arrived at Revere Beach Station at the same time this asshole booked it down the stairwell. We must have every cop in the city and then some out looking for him. The staties and SWAT are coming in, too. You better believe that."

"Fucking guy," Gary said.

"Yeah. Great way to start the day."

Charlie hadn't realized he had been holding his breath until the officers moved away from the Lumina. The interior filled again with sunlight. That wasn't necessarily a good thing, either. It meant it might be easier to spot his body sprawled out on the floor in the back of the car. Hopefully grimy windows from what the stench suggested was a voluminous number of cigarettes would help conceal him. He listened as their footsteps faded.

Then he heard the sound of a car approaching. Tire wheels crunching against loose stone and asphalt. The car came to a stop not far from where Charlie was hiding. Next, Charlie heard three short beeps. *Three car beeps,* Charlie thought. *Joe!*

Not chancing a look, Charlie listened to confirm his hopes.

"Hey there," he heard his brother's voice call out.

It's him, Charlie thought. *Thank God for Joe. Thank God.*

Charlie tried to gauge how much Joe had taken from their conversation. If he understood everything, he would know where Charlie was hiding. It seemed a good possibility. Joe knew Charlie was at Wonderland. He also knew the signal. Three beeps. Smartly, Joe had used it to get the attention of the police. For what, Charlie wasn't sure. What he did know was that it didn't draw their attention to the Lumina, and that was a good thing. There was no way Joe could know which car he was hiding in, but he could take a guess as to his general vicinity. Charlie had given him that much to work with.

"What do you need?" Charlie heard one of the two police officers ask. They were too far away for him to tell which it was. Whoever spoke didn't seem too enthusiastic about having a morning chat with Joe.

"What's going on?" Joe asked. "There's a lot of activity here."

"We're looking for someone," a different voice said. Charlie recognized that voice as the more Boston of the two. The man named Gary.

"Is he dangerous?" Joe asked.

"Yes. Why?" said Gary

They now sounded suspicious.

Joe, don't do anything stupid, Charlie thought.

"Well, I did see something . . . It's probably nothing, though. . . ." Joe let his voice trail off.

The tenor of Gary's voice changed. He sounded interested. "Oh? What did you see?"

"A man," Joe began. "Maybe thirty-five, definitely under forty. White guy. Thin. Short hair. He looked a bit cut up, now that I think about it. Like he'd been in an accident or something. Anyway, I thought that I saw him breaking into a car back there. That's why I drove over. It's probably not the guy you're looking for, though," he added.

"White guy, you said?" Gary's partner asked.

Joe nodded. "Yeah, white. It was funny because he looked more like a businessman, you know? Commuter type more than a criminal. That's what really threw me off. I didn't see if he had actually broken into the car. But now that I know you're looking for somebody, I kinda think he was acting suspicious."

"Which car?" Gary asked.

Charlie didn't hear anything for a moment. He assumed it was because Joe was scanning the lot. Charlie couldn't believe how calm and in control Joe was acting. If he didn't know what was going on, Charlie would have easily believed Joe had in fact just witnessed a crime. It was almost comical that what Joe was really doing was preparing to commit one.

"Well, I can't be sure now," Charlie heard Joe say. "It was definitely on the other side of the lot. Closer to the road. I guess I could walk over with you and take a look, if that would help."

"That would be good," Gary's partner said.

"But you'll need to stay at least fifty feet away from the car once you identify it," Gary added. "Do you understand?"

"Sure. I understand," Joe said. "Jackie, do you mind driving over to meet me? I'll walk these officers over to where we thought we saw that guy."

"Sure. Not a problem. Anything to help."

Charlie's pulse jumped a beat. That voice, of the woman Joe had called Jackie, it was Rachel's. Charlie listened as Joe's voice faded as the officers followed him. Charlie could tell they were continuing to question him, but out of earshot.

A minute passed. He hadn't heard Rachel start the car. Charlie finally dared to lift his head. When he did, he saw Rachel exiting Joe's Camry. Then she walked around the front of the vehicle and sat down in the driver's seat.

Charlie saw that Joe and the police were a good hundred yards away. Other officers had joined in the search as well. Joe was pointing in a direction that was exactly opposite to Charlie's physical location.

"Genius," Charlie muttered. "Simply genius."

Like a snake, without raising his body more than an inch off the floor, Charlie shifted position until his head was at the driver's side passenger door and his feet were where his head had been before. Then, with extreme caution, he lifted the door handle and slowly pushed open the Chevy Lumina's passenger door, slipping outside undetected and onto the ground. He closed the door silently with his foot. Some shards of shattered glass rubbed against his arms, face, and chest. The shatterproof glass was irritating, but at least it didn't break the skin.

Lying flat on his stomach like some Army Special Forces guy in the midst of a dangerous mission, Charlie crawled along the pavement toward the front of the Camry. Joe had parked the car in front of the car next to the Lumina. Joe's car would have to turn around or back out to exit the lot. The driver's side door to the Camry was open. The Camry was in as good a location as he could have hoped.

Charlie saw that Rachel was just about to close the Camry door. He made a *pssst* sound with his mouth, and Rachel looked in the direction of the noise. She spotted Charlie's head extended past the hood of the Lumina. He used the side of the Lumina to conceal most of his body. Her eyes widened with an expression that seemed to suggest both relief and anger. She made a move to get out of the car, but Charlie held up his hand.

Rising to his knees, he extended his body a bit farther out in front of the Lumina's hood and pantomimed the motion of opening a door. Rachel nodded and, without exiting the car, stretched her long arms and torso, reached behind and pulled on the driver's side rear door handle. When he saw the door open a crack, Charlie motioned with his head in the direction of Joe and the police. Rachel looked behind her. Turning back toward Charlie, she made urgent motions for him to make his move.

Charlie crawled on his hands and knees the twenty feet to Joe's car. He kept his eyes fixed on the ground and resisted the powerful urge to stand and sprint toward the car. Once alongside the Camry, Charlie pulled the rear driver's side door open with the tips of his fingers. Again using snakelike movements, he slithered his body inside the car and sank low to the backseat floor. There were blankets in the backseat of Joe's car. They had been there for years. Charlie pulled them down and used them to cover as much of his body as he could.

"I should turn you in to the police," Rachel growled at him.

Charlie kept the blankets over his head. "But you won't?" Charlie asked.

"Not yet," Rachel said.

"Why?" Charlie asked.

"I want you to prove to me that you didn't kill that man. I want to see those notes myself. You have them?"

"I do," Charlie said.

Rachel reached behind her and pulled the passenger door shut. She started the car and ran it in reverse.

The car stopped a short distance later. Charlie listened to her step outside. He was still buried underneath the blankets in the backseat. He kept his body as still as the dead.

"Well, I'm sorry I couldn't be of more help," Charlie could hear Joe say. "I could have sworn it was that Grand Am."

"Don't mention it," someone said. It sounded like a cop but was not a voice Charlie recognized.

"Yeah. Thanks for keeping an eye out."

That was Gary, Charlie thought.

"Well, these days, with terrorism and all, vigilance is all of our responsibility," Joe said with pride.

"That's right. If you do see anything suspicious, please let the police know right away. We're going to get this guy soon enough," Gary said.

"I hope you do," Joe said. Charlie imagined the smile on his brother's face.

Joe and Rachel got back into the Camry. Joe took the driver's seat. Charlie felt the seat press against his legs as his brother adjusted it back to its usual position.

"Well, Jackie," Joe said. "How did you do?"

"I did well," Rachel said. She reached behind and with her left hand tapped on the blankets covering Charlie's body. Her touch made Charlie flinch, and the blankets moved just a bit. Joe said nothing. From underneath the blankets Charlie listened as the engine roared to life. Joe backed the car up a few feet. Then he put it into drive. Within minutes they were going well over twenty miles an hour. It wasn't until they were traveling at highway speed that Charlie dared to lift his head.

Chapter 59

Charlie didn't say a word. He kept the blankets over him. The only voice speaking was the InVision system, directing Joe toward the MassPike and away from Boston. They were taking Route 16 and heading toward Route 1A.

"Prepare to enter highway in ninety yards," InVision directed.

The car pulled up to a toll booth. Charlie held his breath. Were his feet completely covered? Joe barely stopped the car. Charlie heard the sound of a machine spitting out a turnpike ticket and breathed again. All he wanted was to get distance between himself and Revere. Only then could he think clearly.

"How far?" Joe asked.

From underneath the blankets Charlie's muffled voice said, "At least get us past Framingham. Then we'll talk."

"To Framingham we go," Joe said.

Charlie couldn't believe the man driving, who had just saved his life, was his brother. Joe, the person Charlie blamed for much of his youthful frustration, was far more of a man than Charlie had ever believed possible. It was then he realized how little he knew his brother. Aside from the descriptive labels that he could ascribe to him—schizophrenic, classic rock music fan, novice drummer, security guard—he had never really invested much time in getting to know him as a person. He had thought of him as a brother but never as a friend. And yet Joe didn't think twice about risking his life to save Charlie's.

His mother had always seen the goodness in Joe, the compassion and loyalty that best defined him. Those were his brother's traits that

Charlie had never seen. But they had always been there, just waiting for Charlie to reach out and discover them on his own. Their mother had never once wavered in her love for Joe. No matter who he became, he'd remained forever her son, whom she loved dearly. She'd never believed the disease had robbed Joe of his spirit and soul. But that was what made mothers different: they had the power to see deep into the soul. What would she think if she looked inside his? It was an answer he didn't really want to know, certain she'd be disappointed with the man he'd become. Charlie said a silent prayer for her recovery. God had never factored much into his life before. If he survived this ordeal, he decided, agnosticism might be a choice worth revisiting.

"Is it safe?" Charlie asked from the floor of the backseat.

"Safe," Joe said.

Charlie pulled off the blankets and worked himself up into the middle of the backseat. He put his arms around the front seats and gently touched both Joe's and Rachel's shoulders with his hands.

"Thank you," he breathed. "Thank you."

"Don't thank anyone yet," Rachel said. "We're not out of this. Not by a long shot." She avoided eye contact, and he could detect in the tone of her voice more than a hint of regret. Perhaps the adrenaline of the moment had worn off. Perhaps she had a chance to question her actions more objectively. It was clear Charlie had a long way to go before he was a free man in her eyes.

"I understand," said Charlie. "But what you did back there for me is something I will never forget."

"You're my brother, Charlie. You'd do the same for me," Joe said.

Charlie squeezed Joe's broad shoulder with his left hand. They drove west without speaking for a while. Rachel finally broke the silence.

"I want to see those notes," Rachel said. "I can't drive with you any farther until I see this for myself."

"Take this exit," Charlie said, pointing right.

Joe pulled off the MassPike and into a large service area just past Exit 7W in Framingham. Given the volume of cars pulling in and out of the parking lot, the service area offered terrific cover. It had all the trappings of what made a Mass Turnpike service center the ultimate pit stop: McDonald's, Honey Dew Donuts, and a bunch of other fast-food restaurants, all inside a large shopping complex. They parked the Camry near a picnic bench and got out.

Charlie sat on the opposite side of the picnic table from Rachel. The disappointment in her eyes overpowered the fear she should have been feeling, given her involvement with a fugitive. Charlie wanted her to believe in his innocence. He wanted her to believe the way he believed.

Joe, however, needed no convincing. He operated on something much more persuasive. Instinct.

"Show me the notes," Rachel said.

Charlie fished in his front pants pocket and pulled out two notes. The first was the Post-it note he had found in his BlackBerry holder. The other was the one on the Seacoast Motel stationery. From his other pocket he took out the photograph.

"Joe," Charlie said, "this photograph is very upsetting. I just want you to know that I didn't do this. I know that you'll believe me. But I have to show this to Rachel."

Charlie slid the notes across the picnic table. Rachel picked them up and put a hand to her mouth when she turned the photograph over and read the writing on the back. Joe saw the photograph and pulled it from her hand.

"Joe . . . ," Charlie said.

Joe read the back of the photograph and gave Charlie a ferocious and terrifying stare. "You wouldn't hurt her."

It wasn't a question.

"I would never hurt our mother," Charlie said. "I would kill myself before I'd do that. In fact I almost did. I was in my car at the Seacoast Motel. Don't ask me how my car got there. I have no idea. Anyway, I had a gun, loaded, ready to pull the trigger. These notes stopped me."

Rachel continued to read the notes. Then she reached into her purse and pulled out a pen and piece of paper. She put them in front of Charlie.

"Write," she said.

"What do you want me to write?" Charlie asked.

"Write the note we found at Walderman," she said.

Charlie did as instructed and showed it to Rachel. She studied it with the intensity and focus he found so attractive.

If only . . .

He let the idea pass before it hollowed him out even more.

"Amazing," Rachel said. "I don't know what to make of it."

"There is only one possible answer," Charlie said. "These notes are machine made. They're computer-generated."

Joe looked at them and nodded. "The *u* is the only letter that looks different. But each *u* looks exactly the same in each note. Only one different is the note Charlie just wrote. It doesn't have the darker extra lines at the base of the letter."

"Because I didn't write these notes," Charlie said. "The only note that I know I wrote is this one." He held up the note he had just written.

"I don't understand," Rachel said. Her voice was hard to hear over the trucks and cars roaring past. "I agree, Charlie, this doesn't look right. These letters look exactly the same. Now that I'm looking at them together, they look too similar."

"Sort of like type?" Charlie asked.

Rachel thought a moment. She nodded. "Yes," she said. "Like type."

"But how is that possible?" Joe asked.

"If somebody were smart enough and made a font library out of my handwriting, they could write any note that they wanted. It would be indiscernible from my penmanship," Charlie explained. "Except that this program had a bug with the letter *u*. Perhaps it was a glitch in the software the author didn't notice. It's really only evident when compared to other samples."

"And now that you mention it, Rachel," Joe said, "these notes are almost too similar. Real handwriting would always have some variation in it, don't you think?"

"I'm not a handwriting expert," Rachel said. "But I've been around them enough. Psychiatrists use it all the time, same as the police, when we build psychological profiles. I have examined samples from different cases and patients. But I agree with Joe. Penmanship is never this perfect."

Charlie felt a wave of relief wash over him. He no longer saw doubt in Rachel's eyes. Doubt had been replaced with confusion. Still, it was progress.

"But there's so much more that doesn't make sense," Rachel said. "At least one person is dead. They have the body. And the incident with Anne Pedersen, how do you explain the paranoia? It's symptomatic of somebody with schizophrenic or paranoid delusional thinking. That came from you, Charlie, not these notes."

"It came from experiences I had," Charlie said. "But I agree I can't explain any of it."

"So where do we go from here?" Joe asked.

"If it wasn't me who wrote these notes," Charlie said, "we start by figuring out who did."

Chapter 60

They continued their westward drive along the Pike, away from Boston. Charlie sat in the front passenger seat, while Joe drove and Rachel had a seat in the back. Rachel had the notes, the ones they now believed were machine produced, fanned out on the seat beside her. She was deep in thought, tapping into her limited experience with handwriting analysis to see if anything else might be learned from them. Joe had fished out a baseball cap from the Camry's trunk for Charlie and had also given him an extra pair of sunglasses he kept in the glove compartment. With the added cover, Charlie felt it was safe to sit up front. Even so, he never looked at passing motorists and kept a keen eye out for the police.

They listened to 1030 WBZ news radio for updates on the investigation. The Yardley murder and Charlie's unknown whereabouts were, of course, the lead story. Urging listeners to contact police with any information on Charlie's whereabouts, the report dominated most of the five minutes of news coverage before the station went to commercial. Charlie turned off the radio using a touch screen button on the InVision control display.

Rachel sighed from the backseat. "I can't do anything with these," she said. "What are you going to do, Charlie? Run forever? You'll get caught."

"I'll make a new identity. I'm a computer guy. I can do that easily," said Charlie.

"But you might also be sick," Rachel said. "We haven't figured out everything yet. For all I know, you wrote the software used to write these notes."

Charlie lowered his sunglasses and gave Rachel his best "you don't really believe that, do you?" look.

"Well, all I'm saying is we have no plan," Rachel pointed out. "And I'm not sure I can support just letting you run. If we're wrong, things could get much worse. More people could get hurt."

"What are you suggesting, Rachel?" Charlie asked. He kept his eyes focused forward.

Joe stayed silent.

"I'm suggesting that you turn yourself in to the police. Let's get them to look at this. We need more help to piece this together."

"There are other things I haven't told you," Charlie said.

Rachel leaned forward so her body extended into the front seat area. "Like what?" she asked.

"Like, I found body parts in my motel room. Two hands. And they weren't from the same person."

"Jesus," Rachel whispered.

"Not to mention my car was parked outside the motel," Charlie added. "Our father's gun and a bloody hacksaw were in the trunk. The police probably have already recovered the body parts, and they have the car, because I crashed it."

"Charlie, that does it. You have to turn yourself in," Rachel insisted. "I'm sorry, but I'm going to call the police."

"Rachel, please," Charlie said, but not forcibly. In a way, the idea of turning himself in felt like a relief. Once in custody, he could get Randal to help. Whoever or whatever was responsible for framing him, Charlie didn't have the time or freedom to figure it out. "They'll charge me with murder."

"You'll plead not guilty. You'll get a lawyer, and then we'll work together to try to get to the truth." Rachel paused. "No matter what that truth might be."

Charlie took in a deep breath. He held it a moment before exhaling. What choice was there? He could run. The question was, for how long? "The longer this goes on, the worse it is for you and Joe," he said. He sounded like a man resolved to his fate.

"Good. Good." Rachel nodded.

"There's a state police station a few miles down the road," Charlie said. "We can go there. I'll explain everything. We just need to make sure we have a consistent story that absolves you both of any accountability. Sound good?"

"Yes," Rachel said.

"Joe, what do you think?" Charlie asked.

Joe didn't answer. Instead, an unexpected sound filled the car. The sound wasn't strange because it was unfamiliar. No, it was very familiar. It was music, jazz music. But the idea of Joe listening to jazz music after all these years, given the effect it had on his brain, was as incongruous as the sound of seagull cries in a Midwestern city.

The music continued to spill out of the InVision speakers. Charlie checked and confirmed that the radio was turned off. Yet the music continued to play, even growing louder. Charlie saw that the CD player was empty, too. Where was this music coming from? Charlie wondered. Then came a bright flash of white light, not unlike the powerful strobes underneath an airplane's wings. The light pulsed in regular intervals and seemed to emanate from the large quartz InVision display screen.

Charlie could identify the song. Its melodic theme was unmistakable. The blue notes defined its unique melody, which was expertly played on the trumpet by one of the all-time jazz greats. Behind the melody, he could hear the syncopated rhythms that gave this particular tune its infectious and unforgettable groove.

This had been their father's favorite song. It was this song that had inspired their father's passion for jazz in the first place. The notes of this song were in many ways an extension of their father's heart. Joe and Charlie had listened to this very song while they read the note he had left for them on the kitchen table. It was the song that Joe's doctors eventually concluded had both a tonal uniqueness and emotional context capable of triggering powerful seizures in Joe's brain. Musicogenic epilepsy. Joe never had another seizure after he stopped listening to that song. The song playing was the Miles Davis classic "So What."

Charlie knew the symptoms well. Joe's past episodes had been forever implanted in his memory. He was afraid Joe had regressed and had had a seizure the night they fought over the kill list. Now he was certain Joe was having one. The patient first lost track of time as they entered into a trancelike state. They could respond to verbal commands but most often were not aware of their actions, as if they were sleepwalking. They might hallucinate as well, the result of extreme neurological changes in the front temporal lobe.

"What's going on?" Rachel asked from the backseat.

"I don't know," Charlie said. "Joe?"

Again, Joe didn't respond. But a hollow, mechanical voice answered in his place. It was a terrifyingly familiar voice at that. It was the emotionless, computer-programmed voice of InVision. But it was saying something Charlie had never even contemplated possible, an action it was certainly never programmed to perform.

"Joe," InVision said, "Charlie and Rachel are not your friends. They are going to kill your mother."

Joe nodded.

InVision continued to speak. "You must trust me. I know what is going to happen. It's up to you to stop them."

"Joe, what is going on?" Charlie shouted.

InVision answered for him. "Joe, prepare to exit highway in three hundred yards. Then prepare to kill them."

Chapter 61

Joe took Exit 7A, as InVision instructed. He had no idea where he was. He was driving but knew nothing more. How had he come to be in a car, or his intended destination, he couldn't recall. His feet worked the gas and brake expertly. That was good. He didn't want to get into an accident. He wasn't sure that he even had his driver's license. Mother wouldn't want him to get in trouble about that.

Joe looked to his right and saw a man seated next to him. The man looked familiar. Joe processed the man's face. He squinted to help sharpen his focus. Then it came to him. It was not because he recognized the man. He actually didn't. But the voice of his friend told him who he was. *Yes, of course,* Joe thought with a smile. *How could I forget?* The man was his brother. This was Charlie.

He glanced in the rearview mirror. A woman was sitting in the back. She, too, looked familiar. Same as with Charlie, he couldn't recall her name. Her name was Rachel, he suddenly remembered. She was his doctor.

Joe came to the end of the ramp and turned right. He followed the flow of traffic. His brother and Rachel were shouting at him. They were talking too fast for him to understand. Their voices were loud. His ears rang as if he were hearing the loud crash of pots and pans dropping to the floor from a good height.

Then they went silent, though their mouths continued moving. They looked at him as though they were in a Buster Keaton film. The image made Joe laugh aloud. When he laughed, they looked afraid. That made him laugh even louder.

But what was he doing, and where was he going?

Something was wrong, but what?

If only . . . if only . . . if only his friend would talk to him.

Then, as if a mind reader, his friend spoke. Unlike with Charlie and Rachel, Joe could hear his friend's words clearly. They were like focused sonic beams directed into his eardrums. There wasn't a word he couldn't understand. Yet what his friend said made little sense.

His brother and his doctor were going to kill his mother? How could that be?

"I don't believe you," Joe told his friend.

His friend didn't give up that easily. "The doctor has drugs. Your brother has motive. He didn't want to live with you anymore. With your mother dead, he could leave you all alone. He and Rachel will run away together. They will leave you all alone, Joe. That is, unless you stop them. Will you stop them, Joe?"

There was nothing erratic about Joe's driving. He drove with the flow of traffic. Out of the corner of his eye, Joe caught a glimpse of Charlie leaning forward and reaching for the InVision system. Joe couldn't allow that to happen. That was where his friend lived. If Charlie shut off InVision, he would shut his friend off, too.

What would happen then? he wondered. *To his mother?*

Joe couldn't let that happen. He wouldn't. He needed more answers. There was no reason for him not to believe what his friend had said. These two were evil. And they had to be stopped.

Joe made an arching motion with his arm. With his hand held flat, palm facing down, he cut his arm through the air like a knife. The side of his hand connected with the soft flesh of Charlie's throat. He saw his brother's head snap backward. He seemed unconscious, but the seat belt kept Charlie's body upright, while his head slumped forward until his chin rested against his chest.

"Yes! Yes! You will save your mother, Joe! Yes!" his friend said.

The doctor. Her name again . . . What was her name?

Joe tried, but he couldn't remember her name. Just when he thought it was coming to him, a flash of light made him lose his thought again. It didn't matter. She was evil, too. No different than his brother. Her mouth was open wide, and it looked to Joe as if she was screaming. If she was, he couldn't hear any noise coming from her. For all he knew, she could just be singing loudly. An opera star, like the ones he had watched with his mother on PBS. He thought again of his poor mother. He could remember the hospital where she lay.

Did the voice just remind him of that? He wasn't sure if his friend had just spoken to him. Everything was so confused. How long had he been driving? Where was he going? It didn't matter. His mother mattered most of all. She didn't deserve to die. He would never allow them to kill her.

The woman started to reach for the door. He wondered if she could survive the impact of leaping out of the moving car. He didn't care about that. But he wanted to know what she was going to do to his mother. If she got out of the car, he might never know. Joe pressed the automatic door lock and then the window lock. He made certain the woman couldn't unlock the door from the backseat. She was his prisoner.

"Let's see you hurt Mom now," he said.

Then he turned off the main road and drove a quarter mile down another street. Why did he turn? Then he remembered. His friend, the voice, had told him to turn. It was guiding him.

"Turn right on Drum Hill Road," InVision directed.

Joe turned right.

"Follow road to the end," InVision said.

Joe drove to the end of the road. He pulled the car to a stop at the far side of a small cul-de-sac. He looked around. The road was deserted. There were only a few houses on it. There were no people on the sidewalks or out on their lawns. It didn't matter if people were walking about. What he was doing was right. Anyone who asked would understand. He was saving his mother.

Charlie remained still, slumped over in his seat. The woman continued screaming or singing, whatever. Reaching for her, he felt nothing as she swung her fists wildly at him, landing blow after blow. In fact she had cut the skin of his arm with her nails, but he didn't notice until he looked down and saw blood. No matter. The cuts didn't hurt at all.

Joe asked his friend what he should do with them. He wasn't sure his friend could even hear him. He was glad he could.

"Put them in the trunk," InVision said.

Chapter 62

Charlie came to in total darkness. His memories were a jumbled collection of disjointed images. He could recall some of what had transpired, but they were isolated experiences and all out of sequence. The sensation of darkness was not yet terrifying. It was merely unnerving. There was no reason at that moment to feel fear. Charlie roused with a logy awakening, like a bear emerging from deep winter hibernation. It was that slow reconnection of his nerves to his brain that helped suppress the panic he should have been feeling.

Charlie felt off balance and knew that he was lying down. He just didn't know where. He tried to lift himself up. His head cracked hard against something metallic. A bolt of pain followed. It was a staggering blow that left him dazed. In its wake, the blow produced a stinging ache that pulsed in powerful waves and seemed to linger forever. Worse, the echo made by the impact didn't travel far. Wherever he was, Charlie thought, the space was frighteningly small.

Both for good and for bad, the pain of smashing his head accelerated the return of his memory. His thoughts, though still scattered, were at least now in sequence.

Joe, he first recalled. Joe was driving. The InVision system. Music. No, jazz music came from it. I heard a voice. There were lights. Blinding strobes. The voice issued commands. It was a warning about me. No, it was about us. . . .

As quickly as those thoughts came, they began to trail off. Panic started to set in. He knew where he was now. Charlie's ears perked up and caught the sound of wheels revolving fast along the ground.

He could feel a steady side-to-side rocking that suggested movement at a significant velocity.

Then something brushed against his leg. Whatever it was, it wasn't inanimate. The object touched him again, this time purposefully. It suggested a certain sense of urgency, as if it were pleading for him to do something.

My God, Charlie thought. *It's Rachel.*

Charlie's hands were not bound. He could move them, but not much, given the cramped quarters inside the Camry's trunk. Rachel must be pressed up against him. In the total darkness it was hard to tell, but his eyes were starting to adjust to the little light there was. He could now make out the silhouette of her body. They were lying sideways in the Camry's trunk. She was closest to the backseat. Her feet were at his head.

"Rachel? Rachel? Can you hear me?" Charlie asked.

He heard only a muffled cry.

Had Joe gagged her? he wondered.

"Are you hurt? Can you press into my body one time if you're okay, twice if you're injured?" Charlie asked.

Rachel pushed against him with her legs and torso. She did it once, not more.

"Thank God," Charlie said. "I'm going to get us out of here. Hang in there, Rachel. I'll get us out of this."

Again he felt her body press into his. He knew this meant that she believed him. He also knew that the consequence of failure would be death.

"Joe! Joe, it's Charlie," he called out. "Can you hear me?"

Charlie concentrated. At first he heard nothing. Then he heard music. It was the distinct first few notes of Miles Davis's horn announcing the melody to follow. *The song must be on loop,* Charlie thought. The first blue notes from Miles's trumpet wailed from the car speakers. The steady roll of the snare drum and the rhythmic accents from the piano set the trumpet off, then blanketed it. The lonesome wail of Miles's trumpet faded and was replaced with the desperate, almost frenetic melody from a saxophone—Coltrane's sax. The song "So What," as it had years ago, had put Joe under its spell again.

So what if my brother kills me? Charlie thought. *So what if I die in the trunk of a car?*

Charlie called to his brother again. This time he didn't hold back.

"Joe! You listen to me now!" Charlie slammed his hand against the metal roof of the trunk. He felt Rachel jump. "Joe? Are you listening to me?"

Whenever Joe had a seizure, his trancelike state allowed for certain people, those he trusted, it seemed, to command him. He would follow their instructions to the letter. Stand up. Sit down. Come to dinner. But while he was seizing, Joe had no memory of any action he did. Charlie had witnessed the phenomenon himself on many occasions, but nobody had realized it was even happening until after Joe's diagnosis. They had explained away Joe's robotic behavior as him being lost in thought.

Charlie recalled something about Joe's fight with the bully. The prefight crowd circled around the combatants had caught the attention of their mother. She had raced outside to stop them but had arrived too late. If she hadn't commanded Joe to stop fighting, it was doubtful he would have. Charlie prayed he wielded the same authority she once did.

As Charlie shouted at Joe, the music only grew louder.

Is Joe turning up the volume to drown me out? Charlie wondered. *Or is somebody else doing it?*

In the dark Charlie felt Rachel's fingers scratching against the side of his leg. She was gagged, Charlie thought, but perhaps her hands weren't bound. Then he felt her fingers reaching in the dark for his hand. When she found it, she parted his fingers and slipped her hand into his. She squeezed his hand, and he did the same. Then he felt her thumb caress the side of his hand. In that moment he believed he could feel her fear.

With his free hand, Charlie again banged loudly on the inside top of the trunk. He was desperate to get Joe's attention. Maybe even the attention of a pedestrian or another motorist, he hoped.

"Joe, you have to let us out of here right now," Charlie said. "We are both in very serious trouble. You don't want to hurt us, Joe. We are not the enemy."

Joe didn't respond. InVision did.

"Continue straight along Worchester Street. Then bear right onto Route one-ten, Sterling Street."

Charlie tried to guess their location using what little information he had. It was no use. The streets and route were unfamiliar to him. They could be anywhere. He had no idea how long they'd been in the trunk.

"Joe!" Charlie shouted. "Don't listen to what that thing is saying. Stop the car right now!"

The car did not stop. Instead, Charlie felt it accelerate.

"Continue building speed," InVision commanded. "Then continue straight on Sterling Street in one hundred yards."

"For God's sake, Joe, you have to stop this car now!" Charlie cried out.

Rachel in turn clutched his hand even tighter.

"Please, Joe . . . Please stop. . . ." Charlie's voice this time was barely a whisper.

The song "So What" had finished and began to play again. The commands from InVision boomed out from the speakers loud enough to rise above the blaring music. Charlie assumed the strobe lights continued to pulse in their steady intervals. Between the music and strobe lights, InVision was keeping his brother's seizure in full effect.

But who was controlling InVision? Charlie wondered.

"Prepare to enter bridge in two hundred yards," InVision said. "Continue to accelerate. Increase speed to seventy miles per hour."

Why go so fast? Charlie wondered.

He felt the car lurch forward. The kick of acceleration pushed him tighter against Rachel.

"Prepare to cross the bridge over the reservoir," InVision said.

Reservoir? Charlie's heart began to race wildly. He gripped Rachel's hand, and she sensed his growing fear.

"Joe, stop! Stop the car!" he yelled.

"Prepare to drive the car off the bridge and into the reservoir in fifty yards," the voice of InVision said calmly.

Charlie heard Rachel expel a gasp, muted by the gag still covering her mouth.

"Please, Joe! Please!" Charlie cried aloud.

"Prepare to drive off the bridge in ten yards," said InVision.

"No!" Charlie shouted.

"Turn the car hard right. Keep accelerating. Turn now!" InVision commanded.

For a moment there was silence. No music. No commands issued from InVision. The car turned and then continued straight. Charlie's body shifted forward as the Camry accelerated. The force of him pressing against Rachel must have been crushing. Instinct must have made Joe apply the brakes. From underneath he heard the screeching sound of tires, followed by the acrid smell of burnt rubber as it filled the trunk.

Next, there came a loud crash. It sounded to Charlie like metal on metal, followed by the twinkling chime of glass shattering. The force of the impact pushed Charlie violently forward. Rachel's body absorbed the brunt of the blow. She cushioned his impact, but she paid the price. She let out a soft, muffled cry; he had hurt her.

For a moment Charlie felt weightless. Then his face slammed against the top of the trunk. Blood flowed freely from his nose and rolled in two warm streams across each cheek. At that instant the car listed forward and Charlie's body pressed even harder against Rachel's. He could hear air expelling from her lungs, the weight of his body magnified tenfold by the velocity of the free-falling car.

He felt a sickening drop in his stomach. It felt like a roller coaster's first dip. The last sound he heard before he was once again knocked unconscious was a great big splash.

Chapter 63

The car seemed to float on the surface of the water. Charlie's blackout lasted no more than a few seconds. For the moment, at least, they were horizontal. He was no longer crushing Rachel with the weight of his body. That reprieve, he knew, wouldn't last long. The weight of the engine would drag the front of the Camry forward. It would sink the car from front to back. As it did, Charlie would once again be pinned against her. Neither of them would have much use of their limbs, making escape an impossibility.

As dreadful as the cramped, dark quarters were, it was nothing compared to the sucking sound of water, displaced by metal, rushing inside the car and beginning to fill the trunk. A strange calmness came over Charlie as he listened to water cascading into the car through vents and window seals. He thought about death. Would it be, he wondered, as dark as this trunk, but without any fear and pain? He had never given much thought to how he would die. Ironic that twice in one day it was all he thought about. Hours ago he had held a gun to his head, ready to pull the trigger.

Compared to drowning, shooting himself would have been a walk in the park. The pain from a single gunshot would probably have been too much for his mind even to have registered. But this death would be agonizingly slow. It would constrict his breath until it tricked his mind into thinking he could actually breathe water. It would be merciless.

The car shifted position, just as Charlie knew it would.

"Joe," he heard himself say.

Water began seeping into the trunk through the wheel casings. It soaked his back and legs with a numbing cold. The sensation was jar-ring, but more than that, it was illuminating. It awoke something that was asleep inside him. Adrenaline began pumping through his veins. Its power heightened his senses. The sound of water was richer in his ears. The shape of Rachel's body became more distinguishable in the darkness.

This was alertness unlike anything he had ever known. It was as though the world moved in slow motion, while his thoughts contin-ued lightning fast. A singular, overpowering urge coursed through him like a current of high-voltage electricity. And it brought with it a voice from somewhere deep inside him. The voice was begging him to live. Joe drove an older model Camry, so there was no glow-in-the-dark trunk release that could free them.

"Rachel, listen to me," Charlie said. "I need you to feel around. See if there is anything we could use to pry open this trunk. Can you do that?"

It was hard to be heard over the sloshing of water. The rear of the car lifted skyward as water weighed down the front. The water that had soaked the inside of the trunk was pulled forward by gravity and sloshed against the backseat, which walled off the trunk from the car's cabin. The backsplash sprayed icy water into Charlie's face. *Joe may already be submerged,* Charlie thought. He was probably al-ready dead. Then the car listed left. It came back to center, only to angle right soon after. The Camry rocked from side to side as the water sought equilibrium.

The car again came back to center. All four wheels were level and below the water's surface. Then, without warning, it tilted right again. The sudden movement took Charlie by surprise. He cracked his head against the inside wall of the trunk. His left hand instinc-tively reached for his head in response to the pain. It wasn't easy given the limited space in which they had to move. His arm was pinned up against Rachel's leg. He lifted his shoulder toward his ear to pull that arm free. Then he rested his hand against his chest and slowly brought it across his body to touch the lump on his head. He hadn't realized until that moment that blood flow to his arm had been cut off. His hand tingled, his muscles reacting to a lack of oxy-gen in his blood. Charlie moved his hand away from his head and lowered it by Rachel's feet. Stretching his fingers as far as he could, he slid them into the gap in the backseat and gripped tightly for leverage. Then he felt something. His fingers probed until at last they gripped what he believed to be a lever.

"Rachel!" Charlie shouted. "I think I've found a release. We can lower the backseat and then slide out."

Rachel grunted and pressed her body against his. She was communicating with him. Charlie pulled at the lever and felt it give.

"Rachel," he said, "slide your body onto mine. Use your feet to push against the seat. Can you do that?"

This time she didn't bother to respond. Charlie felt her body weight shifting. Her head moved toward his feet; her legs toward the backseat, nearest his head. Her movement at first was deliberate but soon became more frantic and forced as she tried to work herself into position. It took almost a half a minute, but she was eventually able to push the seat forward with her feet.

"Amazing! You're wonderful, Rachel."

The water level in the backseat wasn't high enough yet to prevent the seat from going down. If it was, it would have probably filled the trunk and killed them. But it didn't mean the water level wasn't rising.

"You have to slide out, Rachel. Can you do that?"

Again her body contorted and shifted as she made her move. The Camry pitched left. The angle change helped her pass through the opening. She already had her ankles out of the trunk and into the backseat. The shift helped to push the rest of her body through. Rachel's head was still inside the trunk and rested on Charlie's chest.

With his free hand, Charlie felt for the gag that covered her mouth. It was a bandanna. Joe had tied it too tight for her to have untied the knot herself, given her limited mobility. Charlie loosened the knot with his right hand and pushed the bandanna away from her mouth. Rachel exhaled loudly and then gasped for air.

"Hurry," Charlie said. "We don't have much time."

"Then you better follow me," Rachel said.

Chapter 64

Rachel managed to snake her body through the small aperture of the reclined trunk pass-through. Her wool pants were soaked through to the skin. Her legs and feet began to get numb from the cold. Water seeped inside the car through a small crack in the passenger-side window at an alarming rate.

The view through the front windshield into the world outside made her wish, just for a moment, that she could return to the dark ignorance of the Camry's trunk. The Camry itself was suspended at a thirty-five-, maybe forty-degree slant, with the front of the car pointing downward into the blackest water Rachel had ever seen. The view through the windshield reminded her of an Amazon exhibit she'd seen during a Walderman outing to the Franklin Park Zoo. The glass enclosure of the exhibit provided visitors with a simultaneous viewing of the tropical forest floor and life beneath the Amazon River water.

The waterline bisecting the front windshield of the Camry had a similar effect. It offered Rachel a glimpse of both the morning sunlight and the dim, murky waters that masked an unknown depth.

"I think I can get out the back door," Rachel shouted. She turned her head so that Charlie could hear. He was still inside the trunk. "I think the car is elevated enough."

Joe, if he was still conscious, didn't even flinch at the sound of her voice. She could see him sitting in the driver's seat. His seat belt was still fastened. Even though he'd been aggressive with her, she felt as though it wasn't really Joe who had assaulted her, as if his mind were not his own. She hadn't gone into that trunk easily by any means.

She had punched and kicked him repeatedly. They'd been vicious blows, forceful enough, she believed, to have done some damage. She would have screamed for help had his first move not been to gag her. It was as if Joe had been completely detached from the man who'd attacked her. He had been a moving statue. He seemed that way now. Joe kept completely still, and his head stayed focused forward. Only the gentle rise and fall of his shoulders from his heavy breathing indicated any sign of life.

Rachel gripped the door handle and pushed hard. It wouldn't budge. Part of the door, she now observed, was well below the waterline. Pressure from the volume of water pushing against it would make her effort no different than trying to open a door that was flush against a concrete wall.

"There's nothing I can do!" Rachel shouted. "The door won't open."

"Hang on," Charlie cried out. "There's more room for me to maneuver back here. I'll find you something to break the window."

Because it was weighted down by water, the front of the car lifted the rear of the Camry even higher in the air. It pushed Rachel higher as well. She had to brace herself against the front seat with her arms and knees to keep from falling forward.

"Joe," Rachel called to him. "Can you hear me, Joe?" She put her hand on Joe's shoulder. He didn't move at her touch. Not the slightest reaction.

"I think I've found something," she heard Charlie call out.

"Joe's not responding to me," Rachel said.

"He's having a seizure. I'll get to Joe. You just get that window open!" Charlie shouted back.

The water level was already up to Joe's chest. The water had begun seeping quicker into the backseat through small gaps in the rear door frames as well as the window seals. Icy water pooled on the floor by Rachel's feet. It stood now at ankle level. It bit into her skin until the nerves froze with cold. Half of the rear window was well below the waterline. She hadn't noticed it had progressed that far down.

Were they sinking even faster? she wondered.

Breaking the window would spill water inside the car with the force of a class-five rapid.

"Reach for my hand," Charlie called out.

Rachel reached behind her into the black opening of the Camry's trunk. She waited a moment until she felt something press into her palm. It was the wooden handle of a hammer. She pulled her hand out and hoisted the hammer to eye level.

"When I break the window, the car is going to sink fast," she said.

"I'm in position to move quickly," Charlie said. "You get out. Swim to shore. I'll get Joe. Do it, Rachel. Before the car sinks any lower."

As if on cue, the back of the Camry rose a foot higher. Not expecting the sudden shift, Rachel fell forward, banging her shoulder into the front seat. She let out a cry.

"Rachel!" Charlie's voice echoed from behind. "Are you okay?"

"I'm fine. I'm ready to break the window!" she called back.

"Do it now!"

Rachel crashed the hammer into the window and shattered the glass with a single strike. Water cascaded into the car. The counterweight of the inflow of water forced the rear of the Camry down toward the water's surface. Rachel struggled to see through the spray and splash of the icy water, which mercilessly pummeled her face. She opened her mouth to scream, only to have her throat fill with the brackish water. Blinded, she reached in front of her, praying to stumble upon the opening she had made.

It was like pushing against a fire hose. The only sound she could hear was the roar of water. Then something sharp punctured the skin of her palms. She never thought she'd be so happy to slice her hand. As if jolted by a powerful electrical shock, she recoiled from the pain. The pain was worth every nerve she had sliced. It meant she had found the way out.

Ignore the pain, she told herself. *Ignore it.*

Rachel pulled herself forward. She found strength she didn't know she possessed. Blocking out the pain in her hands, ignoring the stinging cold of the water on her face and in her mouth, Rachel gave one final push.

Within seconds she was completely submerged. Her body froze as it adjusted to her new, unconstrained surroundings. Then she began the frantic climb back to the surface. Her instinct to climb was the most powerful urge she had ever experienced. She had no thought of Charlie.

When she broke the surface, she regretted not calling out to him. It wouldn't have mattered, she figured. There was no possible way he could have heard her over the water.

Rachel began treading water. The Camry hadn't completely submerged, but it was sinking now at an alarming rate. Only a few feet away, she worried about the force of the sinking car pulling her under with it. Taking her eyes off the Camry for only a moment, she looked up to the bridge overpass from which they had fallen. The fall must have been fifteen or twenty feet, she calculated. The metal guardrail that ran the span of the bridge looked as if it had been pried open by giant metal shears. Where the Camry had driven through, the guardrail was twisted into knots like a steel pretzel.

This road may not be heavily traveled, she thought. No onlookers appeared, and she heard no rescue sirens. Rachel looked back at the Camry as it made a sudden dip forward. Then the car began listing violently onto its left side. She swam away with several strong backstrokes, never once taking her eyes off the car.

Again she treaded water. Adrenaline helped her stay warm. Her body adjusted to the water, for the air temperature felt far more intimidating. Her eyes, unblinking, kept watch over the Camry for any sign of life. Seconds passed, perhaps as many as thirty, before she decided to swim back to the car.

As she neared, a sucking sound hollowed out the morning silence. The vehicle bucked from front to back. Water continued to pour into the broken window. She could see that the car was now almost full. Then like an animal sucking in its final breath, the car made one last tilt upward from the front. Seconds later it was gone.

Chapter 65

Her legs began to tire, but only when she was certain she could no longer tread water did Rachel begin the short swim to the shoreline. There she found a rocky, dirt-covered bank directly below the reservoir overpass. Using her last bit of strength, Rachel crawled out of the water on her hands and knees and collapsed in a heap onto the hard dirt shore. Her body trembled with cold, and she worried about going into shock.

Rachel clutched her knees to her chest for warmth. As she continued to shake, she kept scanning the water for any sign of life. The absolute stillness of the surface made it impossible to believe that a car had been resting atop it moments before.

"Charlie . . . Joe . . . ," she muttered. Then she stood up with a newfound determination. "Charlie! Joe!" she called out louder. "Help! Help us!"

Rachel began inching herself back into the water. A chilling wind made the idea of submerging herself again almost bearable. She had waded out as far as to knee depth when something caught her eye. She looked toward where the Camry had been, and then she smiled.

"Bubbles," she said. Then she shouted, "Bubbles!"

Charlie Giles burst through the water surface. His head and neck craned skyward for breath. "Help! Help me, Rachel!" he called out.

In an instant he was under again. Rachel didn't hesitate. She dove in after him. Using a strong freestyle stroke, which she'd honed in a Cambridge YMCA competitive swimming program, she reached Charlie before he could utter a third cry for help. Rachel expected him to grapple with her in a desperate bid to save his life.

"I'm holding Joe!" he shouted. "He's too heavy. I need your help pulling him to shore."

Rachel reached down, fumbled a moment, until she found and gripped Joe's shirt. Unable to stand, they kicked frantically until they were able to get to shallower water.

"Pull! Pull!" Charlie shouted as he hoisted Joe's inert frame out of the water.

Charlie went to perform CPR, but Rachel stopped him. "No!" she said. "We have to get the water out. Flip him over. We'll give him the Heimlich maneuver."

Rachel's training in CPR and emergency response took over. *Airway, breathing, circulation,* she reminded herself.

"We'll get his airway clear. Then we'll be able to get air into the lungs," she said.

With Joe lying on his back, Rachel turned his face to his right side, allowing the water to drain from his mouth. Then kneeling astride Joe's hips, she began to press on his upper abdomen with a quick upward thrust. Joe didn't respond. His coloring began to change to a horrifying blue.

"Rachel!" Charlie said. "We're losing him!"

"No, we're not," Rachel said through gritted teeth.

She pushed on Joe's abdomen until he coughed once, then twice. Joe's body twitched and thrashed on the reservoir bank as he fought to push air into his lungs. The color of his skin returned to a far less alarming white. Joe rolled over to his side. He managed to get onto his knees. He vomited out a stomach-churning mixture of food and stale water, then collapsed face-first into the wet shoreline mud.

"Thank God," Rachel said. "Thank God."

Charlie walked toward his brother and knelt down beside him. "You scared us. You really fucking scared us." Charlie's breathing was hard. He sat down on the ground cross-legged and massaged Joe's massive shoulders with his hands. Charlie looked at Rachel and smiled. "You're amazing," he said. "Do you know that?"

Rachel brushed aside strands of wet hair that framed her face. Charlie stood. Reaching down, he helped Rachel to her feet. Their faces were inches apart. Both of them were breathing heavily from their exertion. Joe moaned and rolled onto his back. His chest was rising and falling in a steady rhythm. Charlie moved closer to Rachel. She put a hand gently on his cheek.

"Thank you," Charlie whispered.

Rachel expected Charlie to move even closer to her. Kiss her even. She would not resist if he did. She would embrace him with passion. It would be an affirmation of life. But Charlie turned away. He stared out at the still water of the vast reservoir and began to walk to the shoreline.

"Charlie?" Rachel asked.

Joe tried to stand, but he was too weak to move. He lay on his stomach. In the quiet of the morning they could hear him cry.

"My brother is not a monster," Charlie said to her. He stood ankle-deep in the water. "But somebody is, and I'm not going to rest until I know who."

Without another word, Charlie dove into the frigid water and disappeared into its inky blackness. Rachel waited, puzzled, on the shoreline and prayed for him to surface. She checked Joe's pulse. It felt strong. She kept vigilant watch for any signs of Charlie.

What was he doing? she wondered.

A minute passed. Then two. Rachel began to walk, then run, into the water. She got no farther than knee-deep when Charlie broke through the surface. He gasped loudly and began an awkward swim toward shore.

Was he holding on to something? Rachel wondered. Charlie used only one arm as he swam. Ten feet from the shoreline he could stand. Water cascaded down his shirt and pants. His breathing was shallow and erratic. Rachel could now see what it was he had dove down for. Charlie held the object in his hand like a fisherman hoisting a prized trophy fish for a photograph. It was the Camry's InVision system.

Chapter 66

Charlie slumped down on the dirt bank. He was shaking, shivering with cold. Hypothermia remained a risk, but with the sun shining and the air temperature unseasonably warm, the chances of developing the condition were slim. Still, the light breeze, which on most days he would not have even noticed, felt like needles puncturing his skin. Charlie held the InVision system by its handle. He was grateful that he had installed the newer model into Joe's Camry. The inaugural product line didn't allow for complete system removal—the brains, as the engineers called it. After a few bigger resellers had reported an increase in customer complaints regarding break-ins and theft, the Magellan Team had led a project to devise a portable unit that could be extracted from a vehicle and stowed safely away.

Rachel walked over to Charlie and put an arm around his shoulder. She rubbed his back, and it did help to warm him. Joe had managed to get himself into a seated position. He still seemed too disoriented and out of sorts to stand.

"Why did you go back under?" Rachel asked.

"My brother tried to kill us," Charlie said. "But that wasn't my brother."

"I'm not sure I'm following," Rachel said.

"You know about Joe's condition."

"He's schizophrenic, yes, but that doesn't mean he's prone to violence. You know that."

Charlie shook his head to correct her. "No," he said. "I mean yes, he has schizophrenia, but years ago he was diagnosed and treated for epilepsy."

Rachel paused a moment. Her expression changed from doubt to confirmation as she mentally traversed Joe's case file. "That's right," she said. "We stopped his medication almost eight years ago."

"Because his seizures were not common. In fact, they could be predictably triggered."

Joe stood shakily. Stumbling, he approached. "They were triggered by music," he said. "It was jazz music."

"More than jazz music," Charlie added. "It was that song. Our father's favorite song. 'So What.'"

"I don't understand," Rachel said. "Why would Joe play that song if it causes him to have a seizure?"

"He wouldn't," Charlie said. "When I play guitar, I play jazz. But Joe used to love jazz almost as much as me. In fact, I stopped listening to the music and playing guitar almost as soon as we learned what it could do to him. He nearly killed a boy during a fight while he had a seizure and then fled for three days after. When the police caught up with him, he had no memory of where he'd been or what he'd done. All he could tell them was that he was home, listening to his father's favorite record. Next thing he knew, he was awake up in the woods."

"Mom knew that something was wrong with me," Joe added. "But she didn't know what it was. She would tell me things. She would tell me to stand up, sit down, anything really, and I would do it. Only I had no idea what I was doing. It really upset her."

"That was the seizure," said Charlie. "And once he stopped listening to that song, the seizures stopped as well. His doctors eventually diagnosed him as having musicogenic epilepsy."

"I blogged about it," Joe said.

"Somebody knew about Joe's condition. Maybe they read it on his blog. I don't know," Charlie said. "But they knew enough to trigger a seizure. And enough to use the voice command capability of InVision to control him."

Rachel sat down on the ground, her skin whitening from both cold and shocked disbelief. "Who would do that?" she asked.

"Who would forge notes in my handwriting?" Charlie asked in return. "It's somebody who has a terrible grudge against me and possibly my brother. Maybe someone I worked with at SoluCent. I've cut down a few trees on my way to the top of the mountain."

"And the voices? Eddie's voice? The dead bodies?" asked Rachel.

Charlie looked down. "I can't explain everything," he said. "But I can tell you that those bodies are real. People have died."

"Who killed them?" Rachel asked. Without meaning to, she glanced at Joe.

"No . . . no . . . ," Joe said, shaking his head violently from side to side. "I wouldn't do that! I couldn't."

Charlie put a firm hand on his brother's shoulder. "Joe, you almost killed us," he said. "No matter what we find out, it's not on you. You are the victim here."

Joe turned his head so he wouldn't have to look at Charlie. Charlie took his brother's chin and turned Joe's head until their eyes locked.

"Joe, listen to me. I will never abandon you. I will never let anything bad happen to you. You're my brother. You're the only brother I have." Charlie paused. He looked as though he wanted to say more, but couldn't.

"I get what you're saying, Charlie. But tell me what you're doing with the InVision system," Rachel said.

"Whoever knew about Joe's condition also knew how to control him. But to control him, the person would have to communicate with InVision. The GPS signals are Wi-Fi transmission. That is done via a standard wireless protocol. It wouldn't be easy for somebody to hijack that signal. But we support IP communication as well."

"IP as in Internet protocol?" Rachel asked.

Charlied nodded. "Exactly. It's what's used to send and receive Web pages over the Internet. It's just a communication mechanism for one machine to connect with another."

"And you're saying that somebody might have used an IP to control InVision?" said Rachel.

"Somebody who knows technology could have figured out how to use cellular transmission and static IP to hack the system," Charlie explained. "With access to the operating system, they could override the Wi-Fi signal and substitute their own voice commands and play whatever media, be it music, light, or any sound they wanted."

"You're suggesting that somebody sabotaged Joe's InVision system?" Rachel said.

"That's exactly what I'm suggesting," Charlie said, holding up the InVision brains for added effect.

"But who?" Joe asked. He was unable to hide the desperation in his voice.

"That's what I'm going to find out," said Charlie. "You see, the OS has a built-in registry. The registry is used to store information about the system, much of it used to boot up the device, but it also maintains customer preferences, date and time setting, and that sort of thing. Anybody who hacked into the device would have had to write their IP address to the registry to maintain two-way communication. If I can get to that IP address, I can get to a physical address as well."

"How are you going to do that?" Rachel asked.

"The best InVision hacker I know lives twenty miles outside Boston. His name is Arthur Bean. We get to him and we get the IP address." Charlie paused. "Either that, or he's the guy who rigged it."

Chapter 67

The three walked under the bridge and trudged up a steep bank to the roadside. They watched from the cover of the underbrush as a few cars drove past the mangled guardrail. They heard no sirens, but that didn't mean at least one of the passing motorists hadn't called the police.

Charlie had no idea how far from Revere they had traveled, and Joe couldn't remember anything before coming to on the reservoir shore. If they were stopped and questioned by the police, it wouldn't take long for them to ID Charlie. A wanted homicide suspect on the run was high-priority bulletin material for every police station from Boston to Springfield. They would have to keep to the woods if they wanted to remain hidden.

Joe did most of the clearing, using his girth and raw strength to rip down branches and obstacles that inhibited their passage. Rachel kept watch, making sure the main road stayed in sight. Though they were all cold, none as yet were suffering from hypothermia. Even so, getting lost in the woods held the prospect of becoming a wrong turn from which they couldn't recover.

Charlie stayed silent and lost in thought. His mind raced to pick a prime suspect for the InVision sabotage. He recalled names of employees from California whom he had fired prior to the acquisition. Were any so angry they could have done something so deadly? Nobody he could think of seemed to fit the profile of a killer.

No, Charlie thought. *This person is special. They have to know the OS. It is an amazing feat of technical sabotage.*

Arthur Bean, the quality assurance engineer whose dismissal from SoluCent he had instigated, came to mind. He had the skills. The hack he'd posted broadcasting the minor security flaw to management proved that. *But what about the motive?* Charlie wondered. Did his dismissal warrant such a violent response? And why bring Joe into it? Something wasn't adding up. There was more to this, other pieces of the puzzle that just weren't fitting together.

Who was Anne Pedersen? Was she involved? What did he see in Rudy Gomes's apartment? How did it explain Randal's tape recording of Gomes's voice? These questions dominated Charlie's thoughts as the three continued their silent march through the woods. And the question that stood out above all others was why?

Rachel broke the silence. She was pointing northeast, about a hundred yards from the edge of the woods. "That looks like a gas station," she said.

Charlie saw the outer edges of a white building. He defogged his glasses and was able to make out what appeared to be rusted oil drums leaning up against a low chain-link fence some one hundred yards away.

"Rachel, I can't risk being identified. You go alone. Joe and I will wait here."

"And what is it that you want me to do?" she asked, hands on her hips. "I'm soaking wet. I have no ID, no cash, and no idea what we're doing."

Charlie just smiled. He reached into his pants pocket and fished out a large, wet wad of cash. It was the remainder of the money he and Maxim had stolen. He didn't know how much was there but figured it was enough to buy them a break.

"The guy's name is Arthur Bean," he said. "I need to get his address. You should be able to do that with a quick call to information. He lives in Waltham."

"How do you know that?" Rachel asked.

"Because I had to sign a formal letter of reprimand from HR after he leaked secrets about InVision. He used an unorthodox approach to convincing us to beef up InVision security," Charlie explained. "I remember that he lived in Waltham, because Joe and my mother lived there as well. That letter might have very well cost him his job."

"He tried to help you guys out, and you personally slammed him?" she asked.

"Yeah," Charlie said. "Ain't I a peach?"

"Okay, so I get Bean's address. What then?" said Rachel.

"Get us a ride to his house. No questions asked," Charlie replied.

Rachel stretched out her arm, palm to the sky. Charlie stuffed the soaking wet wad of cash in the palm of her hand.

Chapter 68

Rachel leapt over the chain-link fence separating the building's grounds from the woods' edge with a hurdler's grace. She walked to the front of the building, mindful that her wet clothes were enough to raise suspicions. The front lot was littered with cars, all in varying stages of being disassembled, presumably for parts.

The place was Wilson's Automotive Repair, at least according to the sign hanging crooked above the large garage bay doors. Where the paint hadn't faded, large rust stains made certain most of the sign was illegible. The unkempt grounds around Wilson's Automotive Repair and the paint-chipped building exterior suggested that whoever the owner was, he relied heavily on his car repair skills and not aesthetics to lure potential customers into the shop. What little grass there was had been overrun by weeds and adorned with discarded car parts or crumpled soda cans.

The repair shop featured two large bays, each with its own hydraulic lift. Both bays were empty. If Wilson was working, she couldn't tell. Both of the bay doors were open, and Rachel could hear music. She entered through the right repair bay, careful not to step in several small pools of oil and fluids congealing on the cement floor.

"Hello," she called out. "Anybody here?"

From a small office at the back of the shop she heard the soft shuffle of footsteps. A man emerged. He wore a greasy Red Sox cap and a black T-shirt with the word *taxes* in the center of a thick red circle with a slash running through it. He had on a pair of denim jeans covered by several wide, dark stains. His face was wrinkled and hard, but she took him to be more wise than angry. The white of his beard helped to soften some of his hardness. *Santa's grease monkey*.

"Yeah?" he called out, rubbing dirt and grime from his hands onto his jeans.

"I need your help," Rachel said.

He made it a point to look around the shop and shook his head. "Gonna be at least a week before I could get to it," he said. "We're booked solid."

She looked around the empty bays and outside at the lot full of junked cars. The words *we* and *booked solid* almost made her laugh; still she managed the needed restraint.

"I have a different request," Rachel said.

"Oh?"

"I was wondering if I could use your phone."

"Sure," he said. "Phone's in the office."

He pointed behind him. As she neared, he could see that her clothes and hair were soaked. He made it a point to look outside, in case he had missed that it was raining. When he saw the sun shining, his eyes narrowed.

"What's going on here?" he asked. "You in some kind of trouble?"

"What if I said yes?" Rachel said.

The man laughed. It was a warm laugh, one that evoked countless nights of whiskey, cards, and raw jokes. "I'd say why didn't you go to the police?"

He wasn't flirting. There was, however, something playful about him. She liked him even more.

"I can't go to the police," was all she said.

He cocked a knowing grin. "Oh, you can't, can you?" he said. "Well, I know a thing or two about that. Think they're on your side, and next thing you know, they're shutting you down because of some fucking permit that's run out. Assholes."

"So you get it?" Rachel asked. She was playing into the antiestablishment philosophy advertised on his T-shirt.

"Yeah, I get it. Nearly shut this place. Didn't care none that Dorothy wouldn't have been able to afford her medication. I'd have had to go to Canada to get it, and who knows what quality I'd be getting? Assholes."

"Right," Rachel said, smiling more. "I have something for you, but it comes with favor number two."

He cocked his head sideways and gave her a shifty, skeptical look. "Favor number two?"

"It would buy a lot of medicine," Rachel said. She pulled the wad of wet cash from her pocket.

Wilson's eyes widened. "What's the favor?" he asked.

"I need a ride. You got a pickup?"

Wilson nodded.

"Two friends are coming. They both go in the back, under a tarp. Drive us to Waltham. I'll use your phone to get the address. No questions asked."

Wilson took the cash and began to count. "That's a lot of money for a short ride," he said. Then he paused and let loose another crooked smile. "But I do have trouble turning down a tax-free job."

Chapter 69

Charlie's spirits brightened. A white pickup truck had pulled parallel to the road, then had backed up until its tailgate nearly abutted the chain-link fence. A man got out of the driver's side and walked back toward the rear of the truck. He lowered the tailgate and climbed back into the cab. Charlie heard police sirens wail. He held up a hand to Joe, who seemed ready to make a dash for the fence. He wanted to wait for the first batch of sirens to pass before they made their move.

From their crouched position, concealed from view by brush and trees, the brothers watched as first one, then three more police cruisers screamed past. A fire truck, ambulance, and several civilian cars followed, each with strobe lights attached. Charlie assumed those were the volunteer firefighters' cars. There was no doubt they were heading to the bridge. Somebody had seen the smashed guardrail, but probably not the crash. When it was safe, Charlie signaled and the brothers took off running.

Charlie helped Joe step over the fence. They climbed into the truck bed and slipped under a blue plastic tarp. There was only dim, bluish-hued light underneath the tarp, and the air within grew increasingly stale. Charlie grabbed a corner of the tarp and pulled it back a bit. From outside they heard footsteps.

"Charlie, we're getting a ride," Rachel said. "I have the address. Dave here is kind enough to take us. We need to bungee the tarp to keep it from blowing off during the drive. Put these blankets over you to fight off the cold."

Charlie caught only a glimpse of Rachel when she uncovered the tarp to hand them the blankets. Her eyes felt more warming than the sun.

"Thank you," Charlie whispered to her.

She smiled down at him but said nothing. They were once again plunged into the dark bluish light under the tarp. But at least they were warmer. The truck bed vibrated from the churn of the motor. The wheels crunched the gravel and stone underneath. Seconds later they were heading in the opposite direction of the bridge, west on some main road. The brothers pulled their legs tightly to their chests to shield them from the cold. Thankfully Rachel had had the foresight to give them the blankets. If not, they'd both be icicles by the time they got to Bean's apartment.

They rode in silence until Joe spoke.

"I'm so sorry," Joe said.

"Joe, it wasn't you, got that?" Charlie said. "Somebody knew enough to use you. That's all."

"But I killed people," Joe said. "I did it."

Charlie shifted position so that he could see his brother's face. The truck had picked up speed. They were on the highway now. Charlie had to shout to be heard.

"Do you remember anything?" Charlie asked. "Rudy Gomes? Do you remember ever meeting him? Hurting him?"

Joe shook his head. "Nothing," he said. "I don't remember a thing. All I can remember are these horrible nightmares I've been having lately. I killed two men in the one I had last night."

"That doesn't prove anything," Charlie said.

"I'm scared, Charlie."

"Whatever happens," Charlie called out, "you're my brother. I will fight for you. We both know the truth. I won't let anything happen to you."

"You know something?" Joe shouted back. "For the first time since we were kids, I actually believe you."

Chapter 70

Rachel, Charlie, and Joe stood outside Arthur Bean's apartment in Waltham. Charlie never saw the face of the man who had driven them there. Rachel had waved good-bye and said something to the driver. He'd left with a single toot of his horn, turned the truck right onto Main Street, and driven out of sight.

Charlie knew the neighborhood well. It couldn't be more than a few miles from where Joe lived with their mother. Where they all lived, he reminded himself. Arthur Bean lived on Pleasant Street, only a short walk to a robust downtown with plenty of shopping, restaurants, and a well-respected art house cinema.

Charlie didn't know much about Bean but thought he was married. Rachel made a move toward the apartment entrance. She stopped at the steps.

"My watch died when it got wet," she said, looking down at her wrist. "But it has to be after ten. What makes you think he'll be home?"

Charlie laughed. "Bean's like a lot of coders I know. Even if he got a new job, that guy keeps vampire hours. The only way he's not home is if he's on vacation."

"Let's hope for you that he kept his new gig local," Rachel said.

Together they climbed the short flight of stairs and rang the bell to the second-floor apartment. Then they waited.

Charlie heard footsteps and he saw through a window on the door Arthur Bean run down the stairs to the small foyer. Bean was a short, stocky man with a flat nose, deep-set eyes, and a wide face bordered by a bushy dark beard. Between the beard and his thick arms and legs, Charlie couldn't help but think of the dwarf from the film trilogy *The Lord of the Rings*. He held a steaming mug of coffee, which dropped and shattered on the wooden floor once he saw who was greeting him.

"Holy Jesus," he said. "Charlie, everybody is looking for . . . I mean, everybody," he stammered. He managed another "Holy Jesus" before backing away.

Charlie didn't hesitate. He stepped inside the small foyer as Bean backed himself up the stairs leading to his second-floor apartment.

"Arthur, I need your help," Charlie said.

Bean continued his retreat. "You need more than my help," he said.

"I know what the police reports are saying," Charlie said. "But it's not as it seems. This is Dr. Rachel Evans." Charlie motioned toward her. "She's with Walderman Hospital in Belmont. And this is my brother, Joe."

"Yeah?" Bean asked. "Great to meet you all. Now, if you don't mind, I have to call the cops."

"Arthur," Rachel said in her best psychologist tone. "Somebody is using InVision to control Charlie's brother. They've hacked into it and used sound and music to trigger epileptic seizures."

Bean interrupted his retreat a moment and crossed his arms. He was a third of the way up the stairs. "Hacked into InVision," he breathed. "I told you that OS was a sieve."

"I know you did, Arthur. I know. But now I need your help," said Charlie.

"You're wanted for murder, Charlie," Bean said. "I can't help you."

"Look," Charlie said, holding up the waterlogged InVision system he had extracted from Joe's Camry. "I need to get at the system registry. Somebody hacked it, and I'm hoping there is still an artifact of the IP used. Just give me ten minutes of your time. Take a look at the OS. If you don't see anything that looks like a hack to you, I'll dial the cops myself."

Rachel and Joe looked at Charlie with alarm. Bean uncrossed his arms. Charlie took his blank expression as him calculating his next move.

"Look, Arthur," Charlie said. "I know that I treated you unfairly. I was wrong. But there is nothing I can do to take it back. If I could, I would. But I promise you, what we're saying is true. And you're the only person who can keep my brother and me from spending the rest of our lives in prison for something we didn't do. Ten minutes, that's all I'm asking."

"You guys are soaked," Bean said.

"The InVision system triggered my seizure," Joe said. "Then it commanded me to drive my car off a bridge and into a lake. I would have killed my brother and Rachel. Arthur, please help us. We have to know what is going on."

"I knew that thing was a traveling security hole," Bean said.

"Will you help us?" Rachel asked.

"Ten minutes," Bean said. "If I don't find anything, I'm calling the cops. Give me five minutes to set up a Webcam. If you guys try anything stupid, all I have to do is hit SEND and I'll have the police here faster than you can say nine-one-one."

Chapter 71

"Holy shit," Bean whispered.

"What is it?" Charlie asked, leaning over Bean's shoulder to get a better look.

Arthur Bean's crowded office looked like a science experiment gone haywire. Dozens of computers were strewn about the tiny room, which had once been the back porch. He had converted it into his personal lab. At least half of the computers were open, revealing a multitude of wires and circuit boards.

Bean had put the waterlogged InVision system onto his desk and plugged it into his desktop computer through a standard USB connection. Arthur Bean was able to access the system's computer code and the OS using a graphical user interface tool designed for coders and instrumental in debugging applications. He was scanning through endless lines of complex computer code with the efficiency of a speed reader.

"Unbelievable," Bean said.

"What? What's unbelievable?" Charlie asked, peering closer at the nineteen-inch flat-panel computer monitor.

"This is no hack job," Bean said.

"What do you mean?" Charlie asked.

Joe and Rachel remained seated on a sofa at the far end of the makeshift lab. Their ears perked up. They both leaned in closer to get a better listen.

"I mean, whoever modified the application knew a lot more about the internal workings than just a regular hack."

"So you agree the code's been compromised?" Charlie asked.

"Agree? The freaking thing has been rewritten," said Bean.

"By whom?" Charlie asked, more to himself than to Bean.

"Well, that's the best part. So you're right about the protocol used to control this InVision system. It's not the Wi-Fi. It's definitely the IP. But what's great is that there's a lot of work put into masking any trace of the IP."

"What's great about that?" Charlie asked. "Without an IP, I won't be able to trace the source."

"Well, let's just say, if your clothes weren't soaking wet, we might be out of luck."

Charlie looked blankly at Bean. "I don't understand," he said.

"Whoever did this had to write the IP to the OS registry. Otherwise the ports communicating from wherever this person was located back to the InVision system would have been closed. The application is coded to erase the IP once a session ends. It's like deleting an e-mail or a voice mail, but in such a way that it could never be retrieved, because it's written at the lowest level of the operating system. When it's gone, it's gone forever."

"But what does that have to do with our wet clothes?" Charlie asked.

Bean looked up at Charlie from his perch upon his high-tech Herman Miller chair with a wide, almost devious smile.

"Because when this thing hit the water, the OS fried. That little cleaner application never got a chance to clean."

Charlie slapped Bean on the shoulder. "Did I ever tell you that I should have promoted you to the Magellan Team?" he asked.

"No. I don't think that was mentioned during my exit interview," Bean said.

"Look, Arthur," Charlie said, "I'll never forget this. I'll make it up to you. I promise."

"Yeah, well, we're not out of the woods yet," Bean said. "I still need to get the IP."

Bean worked for several minutes before calling Charlie back over to his desk. "Got it," he said.

Using a Web browser, Bean plugged the IP address into a WHOIS database that listed the owner of all registered IP addresses. "An IP is really no different than your home address," he told Rachel and Joe.

"If this guy uses a static IP, we'll be able to give you the town, street, and apartment that it is registered to."

"And if not?" Charlie asked.

Bean didn't answer. He hit SEND and frowned at the search results. "Well, that's a problem," he said.

"What? What?" Charlie asked.

"This is a Verizon IP. I'd need to get into the Verizon database to pull up the physical address."

"Is that hard?" Charlie asked.

"Hard?" Bean said with a laugh. "Try almost impossible. Unless you know somebody who works for Verizon."

"Your hacker club?" Charlie asked.

Bean nodded. "I have contacts all over the world. It's what we do for fun. Some people like to go to the movies. We like to find weaknesses in computer systems."

"And someone in your hacker posse works for Verizon?" said Charlie.

"You name a major company and I can find you a hacker on the inside," Bean said.

"Arthur," Charlie said, "I need that address."

Bean thought a moment. He looked at Rachel and Joe, who sat quietly and helplessly on his sofa.

"He really has this . . ." Bean tried to recall the term.

"Musicogenic epilepsy," Rachel answered. "And yes, he really does."

"And somebody was controlling him?" Bean asked.

Rachel and Joe nodded in unison.

"So you're saying that you're being framed," Bean said to Charlie.

"There is no other explanation," Charlie said.

Bean nodded. "Okay, then let me see what I can do."

Rachel and Joe stood up and walked toward Arthur and stood behind Charlie.

"There's one more thing, Arthur," Charlie said.

"Yeah? What's that?" Bean asked.

"When you get the address," Charlie said, "I'm going to need to borrow your car."

Chapter 72

Arthur Bean didn't require much convincing. At least, he didn't require as much as Charlie had anticipated. After all, if things went poorly, then Bean could be charged with aiding and abetting a murder suspect. Perhaps it was the thrill of the mystery, or the power he enjoyed having over Charlie. Whatever his motivation, the only demand he made before handing over the car keys was that one of the three stay behind. It was, as he put it, a little collateral to ensure he'd get his car back. He also insisted that Charlie take one of his cell phones. It had a built-in GPS, so he could track their location. If the car went anywhere other than to the South Boston address, Bean made it clear that he wouldn't hesitate to call the police. Charlie programmed Bean's home number on the cell phone speed dial.

"Why don't you just go to the police?" Bean asked.

Charlie had already thought that one through. "There is more evidence against me than I can even imagine," he said. "The police aren't going to be quick to believe me, and even if they did, I'm the only person I trust to make sure all the evidence I need to exonerate myself is collected. I'm not burdened with search warrant responsibility," he added.

Nobody disagreed with his logic. Rachel volunteered to stay behind, acknowledging that Joe's physical size and strength might be an asset in what could be an extremely dangerous situation.

"We'll track you via GPS," Rachel said. "If things go bad, call and we'll get the police to the address ASAP."

Charlie thanked her. They embraced briefly. "I can't thank you enough," he whispered in her ear.

She pulled him closer. "Just get what you need and get out," she whispered back. "I'm looking forward to the dinner date you haven't asked me out on yet."

Their eyes locked briefly. They held their embrace long enough for Joe to do a quick double take. Charlie held up a hand to keep his brother from saying something that didn't need to be said. Moments later Charlie and Joe were in Arthur Bean's Ford Taurus, heading east toward Boston.

Bean's source at Verizon found the static IP registered to an address on K Street in South Boston. Charlie knew the area well enough to know it was near Summer Street, but that was about it. The GPS would get them there without needing to stop for directions. Arthur also had a FAST LANE tag, which meant they could avoid risking detection by one of the MassPike toll collectors. So long as they drove at the speed limit and didn't get into an accident, they felt confident they could make it into the city without being spotted.

A bigger concern was what awaited them on K Street. Charlie hoped that whoever was behind this thought they were dead. Then they wouldn't be in such a rush to close up shop and make their getaway.

But who? Charlie wondered. Who had the skills to compromise the InVision OS with such insider knowledge? Who knew enough about the available security holes that enabled the sabotage? Not to mention Joe's condition and his own history with Eddie Prescott?

Charlie's mind raced through the Magellan Team members. The name Harry Wessner jumped to the top of the list. It wasn't the first time Charlie had considered Harry a suspect. Still, he couldn't fathom what Harry had to gain from his demise. Then again, Harry had access to a lot of tech talent at SoluCent. Money? How would Charlie's death help Harry Wessner financially? Charlie believed Harry could have pulled it off. But the unanswerable question remained why.

It wasn't until they were driving down K Street, along the wide, trash-strewn boulevard, flanked by tall, seemingly abandoned warehouses and factories, that he forgot all about the questions. He started to focus his energy on the most important thing of all. Getting the answers.

Chapter 73

They turned off Summer Street onto East First Street and drove until they crossed over to K Street. The address was on the corner of East First and K. As Charlie drove past K Street, he craned his neck to see if he could make out any of the street addresses on the massive brick-and-stone warehouses. He couldn't and decided to pull over on East First and parallel park the Taurus behind a green Jeep Cherokee.

The brothers walked in silence toward the intersection. The streets were eerily quiet, nearly void of pedestrians, and with hardly any traffic to speak of. This wasn't a bustling part of town. Factories that had once been the epicenter of Boston's long-ago manufacturing heart were now shuttered or enduring the painfully slow conversion process into condominiums. The area was mostly vacant, a concrete sea of construction sites, replete with trucks and heavy equipment resting aside large piles of rubble from crumbling buildings. It was the perfect place to hide.

They came to the address and there found a steel door, held partially ajar by a crushed plastic milk container. A rat, only slightly smaller than a Chihuahua, scurried over the chipped and deteriorating concrete landing and slithered its seemingly boneless body into an impossibly tiny crack at the base of the foundation. Charlie jumped and Joe steadied him.

"That's a rat," Joe said. "If that's got you spooked, we're in big trouble. You okay, brother?"

Charlie blushed and then laughed at himself. "Yeah. Yeah. I'm fine. You sure you want to do this?" he asked.

"We're family," Joe said. "So yeah, I don't only want to do this. I have to. Besides, as much as I don't like people using you, I don't like the idea of them using me, either."

The address was now only an outline of rust from where the numbers once were, but it was still legible.

"Thirteen thirty-three K Street," Charlie said. "This is it."

They pushed open the door and entered into a dark, dank-smelling hallway that reeked of trash and neglect. Stairs led up into total blackness. A building permit on yellow card stock was taped to the inside wall. The building had been sold recently and authorized for construction. Charlie knew it was a long shot that a name on the construction permit would be somebody he'd know, but he checked, anyway.

"What is it?" Joe asked.

Charlie held his hand to his lips to quiet him. "No talking," he whispered.

He gestured up the dark stairs. Joe nodded and fell into step behind his brother. They climbed to the first landing. Charlie went over to a large sliding steel door. There was a bolt lock on the outside of the door. He motioned with his head to continue climbing higher.

Harry Wessner, Charlie thought again. *Would he get my job?* He hadn't been promoted in several years. Harry had known Eddie Prescott. So many questions without answers. His pace quickened as he climbed the stairs to the third landing. The door on the third landing, same as the one below it, was a sliding steel door. It, too, was locked from the outside.

The top landing, however, was different. The door here was a steel door, but on hinges, not rollers. Charlie didn't see any locks on this door. He motioned with his head for Joe to take a position on the left side of the door. Joe pressed himself flat against the wall. Charlie gripped the door handle and he pulled. The door opened with a soft creak. Charlie peered inside. The space in front of him was too dark to see clearly. Charlie stepped into the room and pressed himself against the wall closest to the door. He hoped it was enough to conceal him. Joe followed Charlie inside and stood in the center of the entrance. A yellowish glow from the stairwell illuminated his figure.

"Joe," Charlie whispered.

Joe didn't answer.

"Joe, take cover," Charlie whispered again.

"Forget that," Joe said.

Joe walked ahead. This time Charlie fell into step behind him. They came to a closed steel-and-glass door. The room behind the door was shrouded in darkness. Charlie could see shapes through the mesh glass of the door's window. They looked like large metal bookshelves. The door wasn't locked. They stepped inside. Joe felt along the inside brick wall until he found a light switch. Light from a bank of fluorescent bulbs flickered overhead.

Charlie stood in the center of the room. His mouth fell agape. If Arthur Bean's laboratory was a computer scientist's fantasy, this room was a veritable bacchanal. Racks of computers, five rows in total, ran the full width of the twenty-foot-wide room. The ceiling was almost twelve feet high, and Charlie noticed that the floor was raised. The air in the room was cool from a powerful air-conditioning unit that pumped cold air under the raised floor and kept the computers from overheating.

This wasn't just a hobbyist at work, Charlie concluded. It was a professional network operations center. What it was used for, he had no idea. He was certain of one thing: whatever its purpose, it wasn't good.

"What is this place?" Joe asked.

"Evil," Charlie said. "This is the heart of evil."

Charlie pointed, and the brothers crossed the room to the door on the opposite side. It wasn't locked, either. Whoever owned this equipment was here, Charlie thought. And they weren't expecting any company.

The room into which they passed was smaller than the computer lab, with tables of monitors and network hubs that connected them to the computers in the lab. The room was softly lit from the glow of monitor screen savers.

On one of the tables closest to him, Charlie took notice of a machine unlike any he'd ever seen. It was networked through a USB hub into a computer underneath the table. The machine was like a miniature crane. A metal boom was nailed into a wood platform. A pendulum was attached to the top of the boom. Anchored to the end of the pendulum was a pen, and below the pen, a piece of paper.

Charlie grabbed the paper and realized it was a photograph. He turned the photograph over and bit his lip. It was a picture of him, Joe, and their mother. The one he'd found in his motel room.

Charlie moved the mouse until the monitor flicked on. A Word document was open, and Charlie read a familiar and deeply troubling text: *Surprise no more. Good-bye, Mother.*

It took Charlie only a few seconds to find the command to print from the machine. Whoever wrote this software had made the command an extension of the Microsoft Word file menu. It was just like a normal print command, only this one read: PRINT HANDWRITING. The machine sputtered to life with the whirling sound of gears churning. The pen scratched out the words from the computer screen onto the back of the photograph. It was a perfect re-creation of Charlie's handwriting with one notable exception—the letter *u*.

Chapter 74

"Well, that proves one theory," Charlie said. He handed Joe the photograph. Joe took the photograph and shook his head.

Staying in position, Charlie looked around the rest of the room. Something on a chair in the far corner of the room, nearest the street side of the building, caught his attention. At first it looked like an ordinary baseball cap.

He looked closer. There was something underneath it that he couldn't identify. As he neared, he wondered if the cap was resting on some sort of furry rag. Then something about the baseball cap itself triggered a memory—of the grocery store after he had escaped from Walderman. He had been in Whole Foods when Eddie Prescott spoke to him. Charlie tried to remember the other people in that aisle with him that day: a black woman, two elderly ladies, and an elderly man. The man had had white hair, a dark blue baseball cap, and a cane.

Charlie reached down and picked up the cap. Sewed into the inside lining of the baseball cap was a white wig. He held the cap and noticed a black patch that was almost the same color as the cap itself and had been sewn into the front.

Charlie pried off the patch, and out fell a small, flat black disc. Charlie picked up the disc and held it to his eye. He'd never seen anything like it.

"What's that?" Joe asked.

"I have no idea," Charlie said. "I remember seeing an old man wearing this hat in Whole Foods. But I have no idea what this is."

"I do."

The voice came from behind Joe. Charlie shuddered at the sound. *That voice,* Charlie thought. *It can't be.*

Joe whirled around. He took a step forward, then started to back away. Joe continued walking slowly backward toward Charlie.

"Keep going," said the man. "Keep going."

Joe stood beside his brother.

In one hand the man clutched a cane; in the other he held a gun. Charlie didn't know the make and model. It didn't matter. He knew the most important thing: it was loaded.

"Eddie," Charlie said.

"Hi ya, Charlie," Eddie Prescott said. "So tell me, did you enjoy your little trip on the crazy train? I know I did."

Eddie Prescott still wore his wavy brown hair down to his shoulders. It had always made him look younger than his years. It was an homage to the carefree '70s, he would say.

Eddie seemed weak and bone-thin. Not surprising that he walked with a cane. But a gun had a way of giving someone added muscle. He was wearing an olive green army jacket, the jacket Charlie had seen on the lone man sitting in the waiting room at Mount Auburn Hospital.

Eddie kept the gun perfectly level. He stood fifteen feet away from the brothers. Joe took a step toward him, but Eddie pointed his gun at Joe's head.

"Now, now, Joseph," Eddie said. "Let's not die just yet."

"But you died, Eddie," Charlie said. "The ME identified your remains."

"The ME identified remains," Eddie said. "But dental records are a somewhat unreliable way to name the deceased. All that I had to do was switch the name that came up in the ME's database search to my own. It didn't matter that my records and the records they had from some corpse in the morgue were nothing alike. All that mattered was a name on the form, and my little hack did nothing more than put my name on a coroner's report. And voilà, Eddie Prescott—who, yes, did jump from the Golden Gate Bridge but who survived—became Eddie Prescott, the dead jumper."

"Why?" Charlie asked. "Why fake your death? Why not just take it as a second chance at life?"

"Well," Eddie said, "I guess you could say I was really disappointed with myself. You see, I should have shot you, Charlie. I was really, really mad that I didn't. I mean, let's face it, you screwed me."

"You did that to yourself," Charlie said.

"Oh, really? I didn't cut me out of the business, Charlie. You did that. I stood in your living room, this gun pointed at your chest to get my revenge. But I was too weak to pull the trigger. So what did I do instead? I gave up, Charlie. I gave up living, and I jumped off the bridge. What was the point? I was nothing but a failure. "

"You were never broke, Eddie," Charlie said. "You had more than enough money to get by. You could have started over if you'd wanted to. You were a gambling addict. You didn't have to steal our money for your bets. You could have used your inheritance."

"And shame my parents even more? I don't think so," Eddie said. "Besides, I found a much better use for that money than I ever dreamed." Eddie used the gun to gesture at the room and all the computer equipment. "I see you found my little hat," he said, motioning with the gun to the cap in Charlie's hand. "That was my favorite part. You really thought you were hearing voices from beyond the grave." Eddie laughed as he said it. "Funny, I never thought you could be so easily fooled."

"What is this?" Charlie said, holding up the flat black disc.

"We can thank a local company for that." Eddie grinned. "That, my friend, is what the inventors call the Audio Spotlight. It creates a narrow beam of sound. Just like light from a flashlight, but it's sound beams instead. Point it at somebody and they'll hear stereo sound in their ears while the person standing next to them will hear nada. I put one on that cap there, concealed under cloth because cloth doesn't inhibit sound waves. I paid one of the cleaners at Walderman to install another disc, plus a microphone, in the ceiling tiles of your hospital room. Did you like that room, Charlie? Really, such a treat that you wound up there. I honestly had no idea that would happen when I started this."

"You crazy, fucking bastard," Charlie spat. He made a move toward Eddie.

Eddie raised the gun and pointed it at Charlie's head. "Trust me. I'm not going to be a coward about it this time."

"Why?" Charlie asked. "What was this all about?"

Eddie laughed. "Well, it's about you, isn't it?" he said. "It's about you. Just like it's always been. I decided after I survived that jump that my life had a higher calling. I couldn't figure out what it was. And then one day, really by happenstance, my higher calling became clear. Him actually." Eddie motioned with the gun toward Joe.

"Eddie, I haven't talked to you in years," Joe said.

"Oh, but there you're wrong," Eddie said. "You talk to people all the time. You just don't know it. You blog, Joe. I was searching the Internet, and there it was. Your blog. And that blog not only gave me a great idea. It gave me purpose."

Chapter 75

Eddie didn't bother to elaborate. He motioned with his gun for Charlie and Joe to exit back the way they came. They passed through the computer lab and climbed the stairs in the main stairwell. Once at the top, they opened the door that led out onto the roof.

"Walk single file," Eddie said. "If one of you so much as takes a single step out of line, I will shoot to kill. Worst case, the other gets me, but one of you dies no matter what. So walk."

The outside air had turned chilly. The wind was strong, blowing dust and sand into their faces.

"What are we doing up here, Eddie?" Charlie asked. "Why don't you end this now?"

"That's exactly what we're doing," Eddie said. "We're ending this now."

"I still don't understand how Joe's blog factors into this," Charlie said.

"Because," Eddie said, "it gave me the idea for how to kill you." He pointed his gun back at Charlie. "You see, Giles, just shooting you didn't seem an appropriate ending for you given how you'd humiliated me. You took away everything I had and everything I'd worked for. I survived that fall for a reason. Very few people do. It's mostly the lucky ones who somehow manage to land in a seated position. They have the best chance. So when I got myself to the shore, I knew that I was meant to complete what I had started."

"What does that have to do with me and Joe?" Charlie asked.

The brothers were pinned up against the stairwell housing. Eddie kept his gun leveled at them. His back was to the street side of the building.

"I faked my death to give me time to think," said Eddie. "But I wasn't coming up with anything. No death I could fathom would serve you right. And then I read Joe's blog—about his seizures and the music that put him into a trance. I realized that I had built a product that could be used to control another person. And then the idea hit me. What if I could get you, Charlie Giles, self-important asshole, to put a bullet in your own head?"

"You sick bastard," Charlie said.

"The irony was inspiring. I wasn't going to die by my own hand. You were going to die by yours. But I knew that wouldn't be easy. You would have to think you were a true monster to take your own life. I mean, a real savage that you never knew was lurking inside you. Look at me," Eddie said, lifting his cane slightly off the ground. "The fall made me a cripple. I couldn't do the dirty work to frame you. I could have used hit men, but that would have left a trail, because hit men have memories. Joe, at least according to his blog, would have none."

"You hijacked his InVision system?" Charlie said.

"Yes. I did. But I needed more anxiety in his life to make sure the seizures were triggered. It seemed that emotional stress was a key ingredient . . . so I poisoned your mother. And to think, I used toxin from a Brazilian caterpillar to do it."

"You did what?" Charlie shouted.

"*Sim, senhor*," Eddie answered in perfect Portuguese. "I took a little trip to Brazil and paid some locals a hefty fee to help me track down the lovely and deadly *Lonomia obliqua* caterpillar. Then I extracted a plentiful supply of venom. It's an impressively potent anticoagulant venom, really toxic stuff. I was careful to apply just the right amount to her lipstick so it wouldn't kill but would cause kidney failure and, if I got lucky, a massive stroke. But I got even luckier."

Charlie now understood why his mother was also hemorrhaging and needed the IV platelets and vitamin K drips. The poison could have made a small bruise potentially lethal.

"What do you mean, you got luckier?" Charlie asked. By now he was shaking with rage.

"Well, it was pure luck that she had a living will," Eddie said. "To make my plan work, I needed Joe to be anxious. Lengthy hospitalization was what I was after. What I didn't know was that you'd end up living with the schizophrenic brother you so despised."

"Don't say that about Joe," Charlie said. "You know nothing about our family. Fuck you, Eddie."

"No, Charlie." Eddie laughed. "Fuck *you*."

A blinding flash erupted from the barrel of the gun. Charlie turned just in time to see Joe crumple to the ground.

Chapter 76

Charlie lunged toward Eddie. The barrel flashed again. The time between the flash and a blinding explosion of pain was instantaneous. Charlie fell hard onto the roof, his knee a pulpy mush of blood, tendon, shattered bone, and muscle. His scream was loud enough to echo off of the distant buildings.

"Now, Charlie," Eddie said as he knelt down beside him. "You didn't need to do that, did you? I was enjoying our little chat."

Charlie heard his brother groan.

"He's not dead, Charlie," Eddie whispered in his ear. "But he's not about to run a marathon, either."

"Who did my brother kill for you?" Charlie asked, gritting his teeth through the pain.

"All of them but your mother, of course. You were supposed to kill yourself before we got to that. You might think I'm a monster, but even monsters have their limits."

"But Rudy Gomes? His body?"

"I added that last-minute detail after you got committed. I was just going to leave him rotting in the tub, but you got the bright idea to bring the police into it. Figured I could use it to my advantage and make you look even nuttier. Do you know that I was watching you in the hospital from a hidden camera? Same guy I paid to plant the Audio Spotlight wired a camera and mic for me. So I knew all about your little body retrieval operation. Cleaning that place of blood wasn't hard. He bled only in the bathtub. I bet the look on your face was priceless when you didn't see him there."

"But I heard Rudy's voice," Charlie said, gasping for breath. He tried to push himself away from Eddie, but the pain was too intense to move but an inch.

"Digital re-creation," Eddie said. "It was a good thing I hid a listening device and microphone outside Gomes's living room after you lost your job, Charlie. I wanted to make sure I knew what Gomes, Yardley, and Mac were up to. I had no idea how handy his recordings would become. My little bug is quite the wonder, you know. Too bad, Giles. After the SoluCent deal we could have started an electronics surveillance company with what I built. Anyway, this little bug of mine was powerful enough to hear through walls. Didn't need much, but got enough snippets of his conversations to sample his voice.

"I then used a digital simulator, one that masked my voice and made mine sound like his. Simple really. Stealing his identity was easy, too, since he was careless about how he discarded his trash. I quit his job for him, bought me a ticket to the Bahamas so that your FBI friend could track me there. I left that afternoon, right after he called. Dreadful place, really. I'm not much for the sun, but you already knew that."

"The body?"

"Oh, Rudy's in the basement of your brother's house, rotting as we speak. Joe moved him there. He did a lot of that work for me. Slipped notes under the sofa, too. But I was the one who hijacked your computer and wrote you that little message in Word to go look under there for the kill list. Did you like that? The kill list, I mean. Clever, huh? You really thought you were a killer, didn't you, Charlie?"

Joe had managed to roll onto his back. His groans rose above the steady cry of the wind like those of a mournful, wounded animal. Charlie bit down hard on the inside of his cheek to distract him from the pain, then shifted himself to a sitting position and slid backward on his rear until his back rested against the wall of the stairwell.

As he moved backward, Charlie slid one hand into his front pants pocket. The cell phone Arthur Bean had given him was on. Charlie was glad to have programmed a speed dial to his house. All he had to do was hit the number one and SEND, and it would make the call. Rachel would know what to do next. He didn't make his movements obvious. In minutes he'd know he'd hit the right keys, if he heard police sirens.

Panting from the exertion, he asked, "Who was Anne Pedersen?" Charlie had to keep Eddie talking if he wanted to live.

"An actress," Eddie said. "A drug-addicted one at that. As long as I gave her money for drugs, she played what she thought was a practical joke. Getting her a fake badge was easy. That was almost as easy as it was for me to put a wireless router by your office. That way I could have you surfing porn and sending out inappropriate e-mails at all hours of the day without you even knowing it.

"But I needed a real inexplicable experience to set things in motion. So I created Anne. I did just enough research about the company to get what I needed to know about the internal politics. It's really amazing what your colleagues will say to someone who's buying them drinks. Nancy Lord, your assistant, she's really got her fingers on the pulse of the organization, Charlie. You really ought to do something to keep her."

"So you made me believe I was delusional."

"You got yourself committed, Charlie. That wasn't me."

"You wrote the kill list. All those notes."

"And I paid for your little motel room and moved your clothes there myself. I even used computers to make a duplicate of your ID. That was what I mailed to the motel."

"And the hands?"

"Well, the good thing about selecting that motel, and I checked, believe you me, is that nobody ever passes by at night. I covered the door handle to your motel room with liquid Fentanyl. Five patches secreted enough sedative to be absorbed through your skin and put you to sleep. You couldn't hear me enter your room, and you didn't feel it when I injected you with Nembutal to keep you knocked out. I returned hours later and put the hands under the bed. Joe did the heavy lifting, but I took care of the sawing myself. I drove your car to Revere. All you needed to do, Charlie, was put a bullet in your head. I even brought you your father's gun. Now, was it that hard to do?"

Charlie grunted in disgust and spat blood onto the black tar rooftop. Joe had managed to roll himself over onto his stomach. He was groaning less but was talking softly to comfort himself. Charlie could see a large, horrific bloodstain expanding on the back of Joe's shirt where the bullet had passed clean through.

"As genius as you are, Eddie, it was a bug that did you in," Charlie said.

"A bug, yes." Eddie grimaced. "I listened to your conversation in Joe's car. Very clever of you to notice, Charlie. I'm not sure how I missed that, but I assure you our QA department will pay dearly." Eddie then started to laugh.

"And you put us into the water, Eddie, but that gave us the chance to find you."

"Yes," Eddie said, rubbing his hand on his chin. "I couldn't figure out how you got here. Then I guessed my IP address hadn't been erased from the registry. Another odd circumstance," he said. "But regardless, let's finish what we started, shall we? Stand up."

Eddie pointed the gun at Charlie's temple.

"I can't stand," Charlie said.

"Stand, or I'll put a bullet through your brother's brain."

Charlie used the stairwell housing to hoist himself up. He balanced his entire weight on one leg and used the wall behind him for support.

"Now, here's the new deal," Eddie said. "Get yourself over to the edge of the building and jump. If you don't, I'll shoot you both. If you do, I'll let Joe live. Even call an ambulance for him."

"Go to hell, Eddie."

"I'm counting, starting now. I won't pass fifteen. You get extra time on account of you're crippled like me."

Charlie hobbled on one leg toward the edge of the building. Joe's groans returned. Even if Charlie did jump, he had no reason to believe for a second that Eddie would honor his word. Still, Charlie needed time to think, and the only way he was going to get time was to do as Eddie said and make the walk to the building's ledge. His foot and leg tingled as if being tapped by thousands of tiny pinpricks, and he figured it was symptomatic of massive blood loss. It would be a miracle to survive this, let alone save his leg from amputation.

It was a fifty-foot jump to the ground. Charlie peered over the edge. He turned back around to face Eddie. He caught a glimpse of Joe in his peripheral vision. Did Joe just smile at me? Charlie wondered. He couldn't be sure. What he did know was that he had to keep Eddie distracted. Charlie watched with widening eyes as Joe, still bleeding and lying on his stomach, inched himself closer to Eddie.

"You can still end this, Eddie," Charlie said. "You don't have to go through with it."

"Turn around and jump, Charlie," Eddie said. "Say good-bye to Joe, and finish what I started. Take your life the same way you took mine. Otherwise, watch him die before I shoot you."

Eddie pointed the gun at Joe's head. He cocked the hammer. At that instant Joe grunted loudly and, using his leg, swept Eddie's foot from underneath him. Letting out a wild cry, Eddie Prescott fell backward. The gun fired harmlessly into the air. When Eddie connected hard with the rooftop, the gun was jarred free.

Both brothers wasted no time closing in. Joe only had to roll himself on top of Eddie to pin him down. Charlie used his one good leg to hop over to them. He picked up the gun.

"Get up," Charlie shouted to Eddie. "Get up!"

"I can't stand," Eddie said. "I need my cane."

"Joe, can you get off him?" said Charlie.

Joe rolled to the side and stood shakily. Blood continued to flow from him. Still, he managed to walk over to where Eddie's cane had fallen and bent over to pick it up.

"Give him his cane," Charlie said.

Eddie Prescott used the cane to stand. He pushed away wisps of his long, wavy hair from his face. From the distance sirens could be heard fast approaching.

"They're coming for you, Eddie," Charlie said. "Life in jail, my friend. That's what you amounted to. Life in jail."

Eddie said nothing.

"I'm going to help you, Eddie," Charlie said.

"Charlie, what are you doing?" Joe asked.

"Joe, keep pressure on your wound and stay out of this," Charlie said. The bleeding from Charlie's gunshot wound had abetted some. Still, he felt light-headed. He didn't know how much time he had before losing consciousness.

"You can't help me," Eddie said. "Don't you remember? You already killed me once."

"No, Eddie, you did that to yourself. So here's my deal. Why don't you finish what you started?"

"What do you mean?" Eddie asked.

"Walk to the edge and jump," Charlie said. "I'm giving you a chance, Eddie. Back at MIT we were more than friends. I thought of you like a brother. We had ideas that would change the world, and you know what? We did it. Together. Without you, Eddie, I never would have been as successful as I am. I know that now, and I knew that then. But you betrayed me and us. I couldn't let that go. I had to do what was right."

"Because the only person you love is yourself," Eddie said.

Charlie looked over at Joe. Joe's hand was bloody from where he'd been pressing his wound.

"That's not true," Charlie said. "That's why I'm offering you this chance. Finish what you started, Eddie. Life in jail. Is that how you want to honor your parents' memory? Is that your legacy? Finish what you started. I'm giving you this out because we were once like brothers."

Eddie Prescott walked backward toward the edge of the building. The wail of the sirens was louder now. It sounded to Charlie like an armada approaching.

"You know what, Charlie?" Eddie asked.

"What?"

"If I'm alive, people will think of me when they remember these crimes. But if I'm gone, you'll be the only memory of what actually happened here. These murders will in the public's eye be more your doing than mine. You'll be alive to represent them. Funny, huh? But with me dead, we're linked forever. Good-bye, Charlie."

With that Eddie turned. And he jumped.

Epilogue

The last time Charlie had been in Chaps Sports Bar in Kenmore Square, he was meeting his friend Randal. He was meeting Randal again, although this time under much different circumstances.

Randal was hunkered over his little slice of the bar, clutching a freshly poured Guinness stout. He spied Charlie and waved.

The crutches would be with Charlie another few weeks at most, his doctors predicted. Having grown tired of his other walking buddies, Monte was perhaps even more disappointed than Charlie about his temporary handicap. Even with the weeks that he'd been on them, he still hadn't mastered the extra agility and strength the crutches required. It was even harder with his prized Gibson ES-175 slung over his shoulder, making his entrance into Chaps even more graceless than usual and drawing the attention of the other patrons. He wondered when his face would no longer be associated with one of the most spectacular and sensational crimes in the area's history. Three men from SoluCent had been murdered, and even though Charlie had been cleared of the crimes, his name would forever be linked to them. In a way, Eddie's prophecy was proving true.

Joe's case was more complex than Charlie's. DNA had linked his brother to three murders. It would be up to the testimony of countless experts to win his exoneration.

Charlie had posted his brother's million-dollar bond and secured him a topflight team of attorneys. They'd told him that Rachel's first-hand account of the events, plus the evidence the FBI's cybercrime unit had taken from Eddie's warehouse apartment, should be enough to win Joe's freedom.

Charlie waved to Randal. By now he was aware he would be watched by the curious. He had yet to find a way to ignore the unwanted attention. He wondered when their stares would stop and their whispers would end. It couldn't happen soon enough.

"Bartender," Randal called out as Charlie hoisted himself onto the stool beside his friend. "A Guinness and a whiskey. Jack straight?" Randal asked Charlie.

Charlie nodded. "You look good," he said.

The bartender poured two whiskeys. Charlie downed his and dropped his shot glass for another. The bartender poured and mumbled something under his breath.

"You got a problem?" Randal scowled.

"No, man. No problem." The bartender moved to the other side of the bar.

"I'm used to it," Charlie said, brushing the moment aside with a wave of his hand.

"Well, I'm not."

"It'll pass," Charlie assured him. "People are still a bit freaked out about what happened. When your picture is splashed all over the news and your name is linked to such an infamous crime, people tend to gawk, even at the innocent."

Randal shook his head in disgust. "So, when are you going to tell me what really happened on that roof?"

"The guy jumped. End of story."

"Yeah," Randal said. "He jumped. And Rachel?"

"We're . . . dating," Charlie said.

"Dating?"

"Well, neither of us wants an artificial closeness. Traumatic events can do that. So we're taking it slow. Seeing where it goes."

"I see. And what about your mom?"

"They're calling it the miracle awakening. She came out of the coma after I got Joe out of Bridgewater. The miracle seekers are saying she stayed in a coma until the worst had passed. God gave her a blessed out so that she didn't have to bear witness. Crazy, huh?"

"I've heard crazier. Like random jumpers," Randal said. "That's good news about your mom. Miracle or not."

"Joe's been at her bedside ever since I posted his bond," Charlie said.

"I can't believe the D.A. is taking him to trial," Randal said.

"Joe is as innocent as I am. It was Eddie who killed those men."

Randal nodded. "Let's focus on getting the jury to agree as well. So what's with the ax?" Randal asked, pointing to Charlie's guitar, propped up against an empty bar stool.

"Oh, I got a gig tonight," Charlie said.

"Live? I thought you didn't play live," Randal said.

"I don't," Charlie replied. "But this drummer I know just loves my playing. Says that I'm masterful with the solo. Can you believe that? Me a soloist? It's a rock gig, not jazz, but still, it's hard to turn down a gig when somebody is that complimentary."

"Yeah? Where's the gig?"

"Well, it's sort of a benefit concert for Walderman Hospital. Rachel's going."

"And Joe?"

"Joe?" Charlie smiled. "Well, actually Joe's the drummer."

Their drinks arrived. Randal hoisted his for a toast.

"To the drummer, then," Randal said. "For somehow managing to get you out of your shell and onto the stage. You're a great player. You should be heard."

"Joe heard me. To Joe," Charlie said as he lifted his drink.

Acknowledgments

Years ago, I wrote a short story and my father-in-law, Stephen, asked if he could read it aloud. Hearing somebody else read my words gave me an "ah-ha" moment. "That sounds like a real story," I said to him. "I think I'm going to become a fiction writer." I was a dot-commer at the time, living in New York City, and the bubble that kept me employed had just popped. I told my wife the good news. "Great," she said. And from that moment on she supported my every effort and never stopped believing in me. My love and gratitude are beyond measure.

I have many others to thank for their patience, encouragement, critiques, and expertise. I want to thank my mom for reading and re-reading these words. Her thoughtful feedback was an incalculable help. I want to thank my father, who encouraged me to coauthor a short story with him, and introduced me to a wonderful community of thriller writers. Thanks to him I no longer look out an office window and wish that I were working at something else.

A debt is owed to my Uncle David, whose Infiniti G3 inspired me to invent InVision. Without his expertise in neurology this story would never have been. I am equally grateful to Susan Parks and Dr. Joel Solomon. Their insights into mental health treatments and facilities gave me the confidence to tell Joe's story.

Clair "Answer Girl" Lamb helped me shape the story and best-selling author, Joe Finder has been part friend and part mentor to me, and always a power of example of how to do it right. Priscilla Gilman put a sun's worth of energy into this project and was a big reason I finished the book. My in-laws, Marjorie and Stephen, played a significant part in encouraging my creativity. Richard, Matthew, Ethan, and Luke, offered sound advice along the way. My friends, Phillip Redman and Peter Karlson, provided invaluable technical support.

A special thanks goes out to my agent, Meg Ruley, from the Jane Rotrosen Agency, for saying those four incredible words that every author begs to hear: "I liked your book." To Peggy, who said, "I could," despite those who said, "I could not." And to Jane, who has done so much for my family over the years that she's become family to us. The enthusiasm shown to me by the publishing team at Kensington, especially that of John, Laurie, Walter, and Steven, is matched only by my enthusiasm for them.

And lastly, I want to acknowledge my children, Benjamin and Sophie, who remind me daily that life's simple joys are the sweetest joys of all.